Praise for Carolyn
Regency Brides: A Promise of Hope

"Fans of Christian Regency romances by Sarah Ladd, Sarah Eden, and Michelle Griep will adore Carolyn Miller's books!"

DAWN CRANDALL, award-winning author of
The Everstone Chronicles

"Perfect for fans of Heyer, Austen, Klassen, Ladd, and Hunter, Carolyn Miller's series is witty, romantic, and heartwarming, with a gentle dose of faith-boldness too. Layered characters and attention to historical detail make each book a great read!"

READING IS MY SUPERPOWER, blog,
readingismysuperpower.org

"This delightful story has just the right blend of family drama, faith, romance, and redemption. Separated by a heartbreaking misunderstanding in the past, Catherine and Jon's journey will keep you turning pages and longing for them to learn the truth. Readers who are looking for an English historical romance reminiscent of Jane Austen and Georgette Heyer will be delighted with *Winning Miss Winthrop*!"

CARRIE TURANSKY, award-winning author of
Across the Blue and *Shine Like the Dawn*

"*Winning Miss Winthrop* is a touching, charming tale of love won and lost and won again. Carolyn Miller writes with skill and grace that brings the Regency period to vivid life."

JULIANNA DEERING, author of the Drew Farthering Mysteries

"Carolyn Miller doesn't disappoint with yet another engaging Regency novel that leaves you wanting more. . . . With impeccable accuracy, witty dialogue, and seamless integration of Christian faith, Carolyn weaves a classic tale that is sure to become a permanent addition to your collection."

AMBER MILLER STOCKTON, best-selling author of
Liberty's Promise

MISS SERENA'S
SECRET

REGENCY BRIDES

A Promise *of* Hope

MISS SERENA'S
SECRET

CAROLYN MILLER

Kregel
Publications

ISBN 978-0-8254-4534-7

Printed in the United States of America
18 19 20 21 22 23 24 25 26 27 / 5 4 3 2 1

For my daughters, Caitlin & Asher

Keep fanning the flames of creativity
and see God's extraordinary purpose in your lives.
I love you!

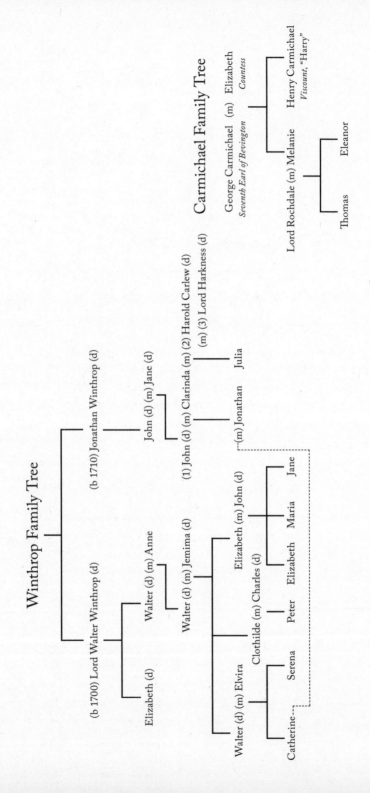

🎴 Chapter One

Bath, Somerset
June 1817

WARM SUMMER SUN lit the scene before her: a golden-yellow oak table boasting a squat blue vase with an arrangement of ferns and pink roses. The tension forever lining Serena Winthrop's heart eased a fraction, as if in obedience to the florist's intention. Perhaps this lesson might prove less discomfiting than the last. She dipped her brush into the china palette, dabbed it on the thick vellum, then leaned back. Tilted her head. Wrinkled her nose. No. The precise blue of the receptacle still evaded her. Egyptian blue? No. Prussian? Definitely not. Perhaps more like . . .

A smile slanted her lips as she wiped her brush over the cake of pigment then added a few drops of water to the mixing tile. The colors swirled together, into an exact blend to precisely capture the slight glassy sheen of the vase. She leaned forward and smeared it on in tiny movements. There. Perfection!

"Ah, Miss Serena."

Her shoulders tensed again.

"I believe you are holding that brush incorrectly. Allow me to help you. Oh, and Miss Hatherleigh." The voice grew flat. "You are here, too."

Serena peeked across at the Honorable Caroline Hatherleigh, daughter of the Viscount Aynsley, whose pretty yet bored expression had miraculously transformed into something approximating calf love as she openly gazed at their art master. Caroline did not seem to notice that he never looked back.

Her stomach tightened as Mr. Goode drew near. Art lessons, her favorite times at Miss Haverstock's Seminary for Young Ladies, had proved to be her escape from the wicked whispers of the world. When she sketched, or better, when she painted, she seemed to enter a different place, a place of possibility and freedom, yet a place she could control. Creativity seemed to ignite something within her, something so all-consuming that she could paint for hours without noticing she had missed deportment lessons, or a meal, or an engagement with a friend.

Initially, having such a handsome art master had not exactly hindered her enthusiasm, especially as he'd been quick to praise her efforts, even going so far as to declare to Miss Haverstock that Serena was a budding genius. That thought had warmed her, as had the principal's request for a watercolor for the school's foyer. Of course she had obliged, thrilled at the compliment, less thrilled by the envy the other girls had displayed. But she had striven to forget them, content to focus her energies on her next challenge. A portrait. A portrait of the art master.

She'd been working on determining the exact color of his eyes—a hazel, requiring a dab of yellow ochre mixed with Vandyke brown—when she had looked up at him one day in class. She'd noticed he liked to help her more than the other girls, and so she had avoided looking at him for too long, not wanting to draw unnecessary attention. But he did have an interesting face, with a smile other girls said made their hearts skip, so she'd been studying his features to capture something of his essence. Only she had not realized just what she had captured. Not until that look that lasted too long.

Somehow in that too-long perusal, his face had subtly altered from that of a slightly too-handsome art master to the features of a man whose eyes and lips told of an interest far deeper than that of her other teachers. Never mind that the other teachers were all females, and at least a hundred years older than he; she had seen that look before. Nausea rippled through her stomach.

"Serena," his voice now purred in her ear, his hand brushing hers. She jerked away. "Now, now. No need to be skittish. I want you to hold it"—he caressed her fingers, causing her skin to goose-pimple, as he twisted the squirrel-tipped brush slightly—"just so."

"Sir, I—"

"Yes, I know it's a little difficult to get used to a new technique." He moved closer, his arm stretching along hers so she could feel his body heat seeping through the thin muslin of her sleeve. "But you have such talent. You could be even better if you trust my direction."

She'd sooner trust a ferret with a baby bird. She angled her head away, but he moved behind her so all she could see was his dark coat sleeve. He continued to hold her hand prisoner. His breath tickled her ear, setting her hair's tiny curls to quiver against her nape.

Suddenly she wished for a fichu to cover up her neckline. Whilst not immoderately low, the round-necked bodice still revealed far too much skin for her liking—especially when he stood above her, looking down, and she could tell from his breathing the view was to his liking.

Again, she tried to remove her hand from his grasp; again, he held on more firmly.

"Please let me go," she said, just loud enough for him to hear, but not Caroline. The Aynsley girls had never been known for their discretion, and after the scandal surrounding her sister earlier this year, Serena had no wish to invite more speculation about the Winthrop family.

"I would . . . if I could." He uttered a tiny chuckle that suggested he was enjoying this game. "I am sorry, but it seems as though fair Diana has stolen all reason away."

"Diana?"

"Pardon me. Serena."

His words left her with the now-familiar uncertainty, shifting her emotions like the sea might toss a sailboat, his words sometimes innocent, sometimes not. But apart from a too-long hand-holding—even now his hand guided hers in the long, fluid movements the watercolors required—he had not done anything obviously wrong.

"Mr. Goode?" called Caroline. "Would you please come and look at my painting? I fear the shape of the urn is a little out of proportion."

"Of course. I will be with you in just a moment."

His other hand snaked around Serena's body, touching her waist. She froze. "Sir—"

"Shh. Everything will be all right, you'll see. Trust me."

She shook her head, moving vainly to twist her body away. "I will speak to Miss Haverstock. She will—"

"Do nothing," he finished in a silky voice. "Just like last time. Remember?"

Something cold gripped her chest, pooling bile in her mouth. A previous complaint to the headmistress about Mr. Goode's overt attention had fallen on ears seemingly as beguiled as the other young ladies. Helpless, his actions concealed from the room's other occupant, she tried not to flinch as he stroked her waist.

"You want to become a better artist, do you not?"

She swallowed. "Y-yes."

"Then let me help you."

"I do not like your way of helping," she muttered.

He laughed again. "Alas, we do not always get what we want."

"Mr. Goode?" Caroline's voice sounded petulant. "Have you finished with Serena yet?"

"Not by any means," he murmured for her ears only, before finally releasing her and moving to the other side of the room.

Serena heaved out a shaky breath. Forced her attention back to the still life. Forced her whirling senses to concentrate, to narrow down, to fixate on the swirl of light gilding the vase's rounded base. Gradually her galloping pulse reduced to something more of a canter as the methodical practice continued and she worked to overcome the soiled feeling in her soul.

Dip brush into water, then dab the cake of pigment. Apply to paper. Clean brush. Repeat.

The composition was nearly complete when she grew aware of his presence again. Her neck tingled, raising the hairs, as if every particle of her being was conscious of his perusal.

"I will miss you when you leave," he said, in a louder voice than before.

She glanced behind her. Caroline had gone. Her heart began a rapid tattoo.

"I do hope your dear mama will be agreeable to private tutorials."

Serena tried to ignore him, to concentrate on the canvas, but trying to ignore him for the past few months had resulted in this situation. If only she had not looked into his eyes! Mr. Goode might have been the most handsome man the seminary had ever employed, but there was something oily and unclean about him. If only the other girls knew, they would not envy his attentions to Serena one jot.

He was as far removed from the upright bearing and nature of her sister's new husband as could be imagined. Jonathan Carlew Winthrop was everything decent and kind, his generosity as remarked upon as his wealth. It did not matter that he had come from a background less titled than hers, or that some people sneered at his connections in trade; the man he was now embodied everything she hoped to find one day for herself. Mr. Goode was the opposite of all that.

"Miss Serena? You are very quiet. Perhaps you would prefer to finish this later."

"I'd prefer to complete it now."

"Really? You would not prefer to do other things now?" A finger traced down her cheek.

She could not move, frozen, mouselike, before a cat. What could she do? If she spoke to Miss Haverstock again, she would not be believed. But if she did not, how far would his attentions go? Mama would dismiss her claims as fanciful. Papa was gone. Catherine and her new brother-in-law were still away on the Continent on an extended honeymoon. Who could she turn to? Who could protect her?

She had no one. Nothing.

A tear tracked down her cheek as his fingers went lower, under her chin, down her throat. Her heart pounded frantically against the cage of her ribs as a silent scream ballooned inside. *Lord, help me!*

Grosvenor Square, London

A kaleidoscope of noise and color filled the ballroom, mirrors and diamonds flashing, conversation thrumming under the tinkle of laughter.

Viscount Henry Carmichael smoothed his neckcloth and moved to the young brunette beside the pillar, standing with her mother, a rather formidable-looking creature of heavy dark brows and down-turned mouth. "Good evening, fair ladies."

"Ah, Lord Carmichael. How lovely to see you again." The elder held out her hand and received the peck he bestowed there.

"And you, madam." Though Harry had forgotten her name. Never mind. He was always rather impressed with how far he could sustain conversation without using names. "I wonder, does your sister dance?"

"My sister?" Her frown smoothed as the young lady smothered a giggle. "I suppose you mean dear Eliza here."

"I suppose I do," he said with an easy smile.

"Naughty man."

He bowed his head to acquiesce and turned to the brunette. "Tell me, Miss Eliza, do you dance, or do you prefer to stand by pillars and show them up by your beauty?"

Another giggle. "I like to dance, sir."

"Shall I see if I can find a partner for you?"

"Oh, but—"

"Come." He held out his hand, her crestfallen face lighting once more. "I do not see anyone worthy enough for you to dance with."

"Save yourself?" she suggested.

"Oh, I'm not terribly worthy." He led her into the set that was just forming.

"But you are a viscount."

Her innocent comment soured the champagne lining his stomach. He forced his smile to remain fixed as they completed the maneuvers.

She was not the first young lady, nor would she be the last, to focus on his title and someday ascension to the earldom. He had known it all his life, had seen the wheedling and cajolery given to members of his family as people he once thought friends had tried to use him for their own purposes. And while he liked to help, he did not like the feeling of being manipulated, nor friendships that seemed based on undercurrents he was yet to ascertain.

He twirled Miss Eliza to the end of the row, his thoughts whirling in time to the music. Perhaps that was why he enjoyed Jon Carlew's—no, he grinned, the new Lord Winthrop's—company so much. Since meeting early in their Oxford days, the man's principled honesty had appealed as much as his refusal to engage in the social-climbing practices common among Harry's friends, Jon's merchant background less important than his proving to be one of the few people Harry knew he could trust. Which meant the newly married baron was one of the few friends who knew Harry's deepest secret.

"Lord Carmichael?"

He almost stumbled, suddenly conscious the music had drawn to a close and his partner was gazing up at him anxiously. "Shall we find your dear *mater*?"

After escorting her back to her mother—and pillar—Harry ambled off to the card room. He had done the pretty, done what was expected and asked a wallflower to dance, and now he could spend time doing what he preferred. As he moved beneath the glittering chandelier, a hand accosted him. "Dear boy."

"Lady Harkness!" He bowed to the redheaded woman draped in green and flashing emeralds. "The night has suddenly improved."

"Tell me, have you heard from Jon?"

"I'm afraid not. Which leads me to suspect he is enjoying his new bride very much."

She laughed. "And so he should. They have waited long enough, don't you agree?"

He nodded, as a thin spear of envy prodded within. Once he had wondered about pursuing Miss Catherine Winthrop, before realizing her heart had long been secured by his best friend. But to find another like her, someone whose patience and sweetness meant she truly deserved a man of Jon's caliber, why, that would be nigh impossible.

"Have you seen Hawkesbury? He's here somewhere, with that pretty wife of his. I do like her. She's quite a refreshing thing." The green eyes danced around the room. "Especially when one meets so many bores."

"Something of which you can never be accused, madam." He bowed. "If your son deigns to call, I shall send him your regards."

"And when Jon contacts me, I'll be sure to let him know you'd like to visit Winthrop again."

He laughed. "You know me well. Good evening, madam."

And with a final bow, he escaped his best friend's mother and strode to the card room. Now to play—

"Lord Carmichael?"

He turned, his impatience dissipating as he recognized the copper-blonde lady before him. "Lady Hawkesbury." He executed a bow. "A complete pleasure."

Her smile seemed tinged with amusement at his antics, which made his grin all the more genuine. "I wonder, have you seen that husband of mine? He was here moments ago, offering to procure me some water, but I rather suspect he got waylaid by one of those parliamentarians who share a rather less liberal view of the world."

"Shall I send out a search party?"

"If you would." She fanned herself.

"And I shall find you some water, also. Come." He led her to a vacant space on a settee. "I shall return directly."

"I shall await you." Her sweet, ingenuous smile filled her face. "Thank you."

He threaded through the crowd, found a footman, and secured a tall glass of iced water. Delivering it to the countess, he realized she was another like the new Lady Winthrop, a woman of character and passion. His father had given him to understand that many of Hawkesbury's schemes to help the underprivileged had originated with his wife, the daughter of a clergyman. Father had even sounded impressed, urging Harry to foster that connection. "For I believe that man will hold office one day."

A brief search found the earl himself—as his wife had suspected—holding court in the blue salon, half a dozen men crowding in, asking questions, spouting opinions. Harry stood on the fringes, waiting until sufficient pause could allow him to catch the earl's attention, working to tamp down his frustration. Why he was here as a messenger when he'd much rather be winning at cards—

"Carmichael! How are you? Come and tell us"—the earl gestured him nearer—"what are your thoughts on the Corn Laws? Do you not agree they do the working man a grave injustice?"

Harry glanced at the men standing nearby, some of whom he knew, all of whom knew his father, and knew that his father, while widely considered a somewhat benevolent earl, would also be opposed to anything that reduced his personal income. "I do not have a ready opinion, I'm afraid," he hedged.

"Ah." Hawkesbury's face, voice, conveyed disappointment. "I trust time will change that?"

"Time has a way of changing most things."

"True."

"If I might interrupt your political musings, your wife is asking after you, my lord."

"Then I must take my leave of you, gentlemen." Hawkesbury inclined his head. "Until next time." He clapped Harry on the shoulder as they exited. "Thank you, Carmichael. I trust Lavinia is well?"

"Of course."

"Good." Hawkesbury glanced at Harry. "Tell me, what do you see for yourself in the future?"

The memory of desires from long ago stirred faintly, lifting then falling like the scent of rain on the wind. "I would hope to marry, run the estate as my father and grandfather have done."

"Good ambitions, those. But in that far-off, distant day when you assume the title, do you see yourself joining the parliamentary debates or merely leaving that to others?"

"I . . . I had not thought of it."

The earl's eyes glinted. "Neither did I until a few years ago. But life moved drastically and then I found myself in a situation where I had little desire to be, and even less understanding of what to do. Might I encourage you to think ahead? It is never too early to make decisions that help mold you into the man you are destined to be."

The words ate into Harry's contentment, and he forced himself to murmur something inconsequential. He didn't want to think ahead. Life was for living, for enjoying oneself. It was far too soon for thoughts of settling down.

The lights and noise suddenly faded as his earlier musings rose to the fore. Perhaps it was not simple luck that Jon and Lord Hawkesbury had gained wives of such charm and integrity. They had proved themselves men worthy of such ladies.

He made his bows to the earl and countess, and finally made good his escape to the card room, where he was soon engaged in a game of whist that quickly intensified into a high-stakes game of hazard. Harry had to work to maintain his well-known air of insouciance even as the earl's words continued to challenge, a seam of discontent in his soul.

What kind of man did he wish to be? Honest, like Carlew. Sincere and assured, like Hawkesbury. Someone others could trust and could rely on for more than just a prettily turned compliment. His spirits dipped.

Could he ever become such a man?

❧ Chapter Two

Bath
July

THE MISS HAVERSTOCK Select Seminary for Young Ladies was, by all accounts, an excellent institution for the education of young ladies of good breeding and excellent resources. Such select young ladies held all the accomplishments—their French and Italian as proficient as their manners were polished, their dispositions honed to that mild meekness society deemed appropriate in a young lady about to enter the marriage mart.

The rigid strictures employed at the seminary were thus very effective for daughters of lesser peers and higher gentry, training them to become effective companions and helpmeets for the sons of lesser peers and higher gentry in later life. Indeed, to mamas of prospective sons, being a "selectee" (as the girls referred to themselves) was almost as high cachet as the news she was worth twenty thousand. "Oh, one of Haverstock's!" was the comfortable assurance. "She's sure to be a good gel," with the implication that she was sure to bring an additional degree of civility and polish to the family. Such was the distinction of attending Haverstock's, the waiting list extended to dozens of families, all anxious to see their "gel" attend with the decided aim of becoming ever more eligible and hence more marriageable.

Except, thought Serena, as she listened to Miss Haverstock's closing address, even before the indecent attentions of Mr. Evil-not-Goode,

Serena knew herself to be scarcely eligible, let alone marriageable anymore.

She glanced sidelong at her sister, who held hands with Jon as though still on their honeymoon, careless of the wide-eyed looks of Mama and other matrons. Catherine was lucky, having found someone who could take her away from Mama's disapprobation, even if the dower cottage was less than a mile away from Winthrop Manor. Not that Serena wished to be married. She had no use for any man—her hands clenched—would *never* have any use for any man, because, apart from Jon, all men were scoundrels and had evil designs—

"Dearest," Catherine whispered, "forget him." She reached across and gently squeezed Serena's hand.

Serena forced herself to relax, to breathe. This would be the last time she need be here, then they could put the whole sorry mess behind them.

Catherine's recent unexpected visit had proved the catalyst, whereupon Serena's refusal to even talk about her artwork surprised her sister so much she had quickly worried the answer from her. Her horror at Serena's predicament had resulted in her telling Jon, much to Serena's embarrassment. But her deep-voiced brother-in-law had quickly turned her shame into renewed respect through his effecting Mr. Goode's immediate dismissal, and Miss Haverstock's tremulous apologies. The only reason Serena had remained was for the chance to be with her friends for the final fortnight of lessons—and the fact Jon had been so successful at hushing things over. So efficiently had the deed been done that the girls had woken on the Monday to learn that Art Studies was being replaced by German language lessons, effective immediately. There had been some speculation, and though some had wondered aloud why the headmistress had not looked Serena in the eye since, nobody ever asked Serena directly. Yes, it was a relief for Serena to finally be leaving.

But she would *never* pick up a paintbrush again.

A hollow, cold feeling swept through her. She schooled her features to indifference, listened to the rest of the speech without interest, and then went through the motions of afternoon tea—eating, drinking, introductions—the chief lesson Haverstock's seemed to have taught being the social importance of maintaining polite fiction. Thus, she pretended interest in Caroline's talk of her London come out next April, an event society deemed necessary for daughters of the aristocracy, but one Serena could scarcely think of with anything less than loathing.

"Serena, are you ready to leave?"

"Yes, Mama." Relief filled her, and she curtsied her farewell to Lady Aynsley and her daughters.

Within the hour, they were in the Winthrop coach on their return home, the fast team Jon preferred lending an element of dash and style to their usual transport. Mama was dozing beside her, whilst on the seat opposite Catherine slept as Jon looked over reports.

He peered across the top of some papers, smiled. "Are you quite comfortable?"

"Thank you, yes."

"Is there anything you require?" He motioned to the basket on the floor. "Food, a pillow?"

"I ate sufficiently earlier, and the coach is very smooth."

"I apologize for not being particularly sociable, but these reports—"

"You are a man of business. I understand. I am content with my own thoughts." She forced a smile to cover her lie, relieved when he merely eyed her thoughtfully and nodded.

But she was not content. She gazed out the window; the country-side blurred. What would she do now? What *could* she do now? Her education had finished. How would she fill her days? Catherine had always seemed satisfied to live quietly at home, happy with her sewing or the occasional horse-riding expedition. But Serena loathed such things. The only talent she'd ever known was now gone. The loss of her art felt like another death in her family, only Papa's death last year was something others understood, could express sympathy for. Nobody seemed to realize how it felt to be unable to create—worse, to have lost the will to *want* to create. Inside she felt numb, half dead. The dreams she'd once believed had proved but vain imaginings now she was forced to live in the cold harsh light of day.

So she had nothing. Nothing to look forward to. Nothing to aspire to. No man would wish her as his bride. She had no money of her own, although she suspected Jon's magnanimity might lend itself to some form of dowry. And if a man were so foolishly inclined as to make her his choice, he would quickly learn the error of his ways. She shuddered. To grow an old maid was her only alternative, caring for Mama . . .

Serena glanced at Mama, softly snoring beside her, the lines of discontent marking her face more relaxed in repose. A twinge of pity crossed her heart. Poor Mama. The past year had not been easy, with Papa's sudden death and all the changes that ensued. Of course, Mama had not made things any easier, with her strident opposition to Jonathan and his family, although she seemed well pleased with the connection now. Serena's attention moved to her sister, smiling in her sleep. Catherine deserved to be happy, deserved such a good man as Jon. Even now he was conscious of her, gently readjusting a light blanket around her shoulders to keep her warm. He was so considerate, such a good, *good* man . . .

Unlike Papa.

A queasy feeling filled her stomach. She tried to force away disloyal thoughts but they resurfaced anyway. After her initial shock and grief at her father's death had come the revelations of his vices, which had caused no end of gossip in Bath. His gambling had decimated their income, reducing her dowry to virtually nil, forcing Mama and Catherine to live a near-penury existence for several months, and forcing Serena to reevaluate everything she had thought she'd known about the father she once adored. How could he be so selfish, how could he pretend to care about them when his actions destroyed their world? How could their trust in him be so misplaced?

Really, apart from Jon, what man could be trusted? They were liars, cheats, and scoundrels, who stole money—and worse.

Her hands clenched. No. Of all that she had learned in recent years, only two things signified.

She would never meet a man's gaze again.

And if, by some miracle, a gentleman wished to overlook the stain of her past and seek to court her, she might be able to overcome the revulsion their nearness elicited, but . . .

She would *never* have anything to do with someone who gambled.

⁓

Whites Gentlemen's Club, London
One week later

Satisfied with his afternoon winnings, Harry had just been served his plate of braised salmon when Jonathan Carlew entered the dining room. *Lord Winthrop*, he corrected himself as he waved Jon over. The habit was too ingrained, his friend would never be anything but Carlew to him; good thing Jon seemed to understand.

Pleasantries properly exchanged, his friend was soon settled and awaiting his own meal, eyeing Harry with a half smile.

"I gather you've been visiting Old Bond Street again?"

Harry touched the fading bruise on his cheek. "Jackson was not quite the gentleman on this occasion."

"I've never understood the attraction of the boxing ring."

"And I've never understood why you don't. It is an excellent form of exercise."

"Says the man with Corinthian aspirations."

"Aspirations, indeed. I have always maintained that it does not hurt to take care of oneself, whether it be by maintenance of one's health through exercise or one's form by way of fresh and elegant apparel."

"Hmm." Jon nodded as a soup bowl was placed before him. "Another new coat?"

"You like this?" Harry fingered the collar. "But of course you do. One of Weston's better attempts. I could put in a word for you."

"Thank you, no. I'm content with my attire."

"Very sober-sides businessman. I trust the meeting went well today?"

"Well enough," Jon said. "Some of the board are wondering about branching into tobacco, but I'm not convinced."

Harry nodded, spearing another piece of fish. The salmon melted in his mouth, creamy and delicious. "And how is sweet Catherine?"

"Sweet. And beautiful. And *very* happy to be married to me," Jon added with a self-satisfied smirk.

"I don't want to imagine."

"No, please don't. But you've put me in mind of something. Knowing you are forever angling for an invitation to stay at Winthrop—"

"Now that is a harsh statement. I never angle. I ask directly."

"A quality I've always admired."

"As you ought," Harry murmured, forking in another piece of velvety fish.

"Catherine said she would be very happy for you to visit, for as long as necessary, at your convenience."

"I knew her as a sensible woman."

"Sensible as well as tenderhearted. She has a thing for strays."

"I'm hardly a stray. I simply enjoy other people's company more than my own."

"Why is that, I wonder?" The blue-gray gaze, so quick to turn serious, eyed him thoughtfully. Harry maintained a smiling demeanor, but the words rankled.

Truth be told, time alone meant too much time for personal recriminations. Other people's expectations, his own expectations (to which he fell far short), and regrets chewed into any pleasure he might derive from walking around the estate or going riding by himself. It was far easier to preserve his reputation as an amusing fribble or a capable sportsman than be taken less than seriously for aspiring to be more. Heaven knew how many times those attempts at his heart's aspirations had been scorned.

"You *are* welcome, Carmichael."

The words, softly spoken, bored into the recesses of his heart, revealing as they did something of the generous steadiness of character Carlew had always shown him. He cleared his throat. Sipped his wine.

"You are sure Catherine won't mind?" He tilted the glass. "I know your wife is a remarkably good woman—has to be to put up with you—but an unexpected visitor might not be quite to her liking."

Carlew grinned. "Catherine is remarkably good, and what I find even more remarkable is that she seems to find your company agreeable."

"I don't know why you'd find that so odd. I *am* extremely personable, and witty, and I suppose most women would find me a more interesting companion than a dull dog such as yourself, old man."

"You do remember I am only one day older than you?"

"I aim to never forget."

"Hmm." Jon eyed him with that serious blue stare that portended Harry's certain discomfort. "There is one thing of which you should probably be aware."

"You have convinced dear sweet Catherine of the delights of eating curries and other subcontinent delicacies? No? Or is it that you plan another voyage overseas, to Sydney Town perhaps, and you wish for my support for such a scheme?"

Carlew ignored him, continuing in his deep voice. "My mother- and sister-in-law visit quite often, and if you remember back to the wedding . . ."

Oh, yes, he remembered. The cool-eyed blonde whose tranquil countenance might live up to her name but belied her biting tongue. His lips pushed to one side. Miss Serena Winthrop had made no bones about her dislike of him and men of his ilk, and her comments at the wedding breakfast were even more pointed than on their previous two encounters. What was it she had said? Something about him being little more than a bag of moonshine?

He pushed aside the sting. "Ah, yes. The fair Miss Winthrop. I'm sure she is dying to renew my acquaintance."

"That's the thing. I would appreciate it if you did not go out of your way to . . . charm her."

"Good heavens! I'm hardly likely to snatch at a schoolroom miss!"

A strange look crossed Carlew's features. "She has finished school, but is a little . . ."

"Shrewish? Yes, I must agree. A sad quality in one so young, but—"

"It is not that."

"What then? She's turned blue, is a tad too educated?"

"You could say so," Carlew muttered.

"What?" Harry's mood dipped as he recognized the weight shading his friend's eyes. "Old man?"

He shook his head. "I cannot fail—Julia . . ."

"You do not want her to follow Julia's path."

"No."

The word was spoken in a voice textured with pain and frustration. Harry nodded, focusing on the plate before him as he allowed Jon a moment to regain his composure. While he could understand something of the grief his friend carried about his sister's disappearance, it was nothing compared to Jon living daily with the blunt force of failure. Sometimes he'd wondered how his family would have coped should Melanie have eloped. For Carlew to have maintained such dignity in the face of yet another scandal embroiling his family was nothing short of miraculous. But perhaps that was his secret. Unlike Harry, Carlew lived like he believed miracles could still happen today.

"Are you planning on studying your salmon remains all day?"

Harry lifted his gaze, met the mockery in his friend's eyes, prompting his own ready spirits to push to the fore. "I have come to the conclusion—"

"Of your lunch?"

"That this salmon has had a hard life."

"And a harder death. Do you always mangle your fish like that, or was it simply for my benefit?"

"I was unaware you were so sensitive to my fish-carving skills."

"Or lack thereof."

"Clearly your wife would do better to teach you to overlook such matters, rather than do whatever it is she is doing."

Carlew's smile grew knowing. "I quite enjoy what she is doing . . ."

"Enough! Is it not enough to know I shall be forced to endure the lovebirds a-twittering without being reminded as to the benefits?"

"You could get married yourself, you know."

"So my dear father reminds me nearly daily. Which is why I'll be so glad to visit you and be relieved of the burden of any such notion. Leg-shackled? Me?"

"You will fall for a young miss one day, and I will enjoy your discomfort."

Harry shook his head. "You forget I must marry to oblige my family. I cannot indulge the whims of the heart."

"Love, real love, is not a romantical whim. It is a choice—"

"You make it sound so appealing."

"A choice I gladly make every day, because I love Catherine, and wish to place her feelings and considerations ahead of my own."

"Truly commendable, old man, but not something available for all. However, I can assure you of one thing."

"Yes?"

"You need never worry about the fair Serena and my intentions."

"Promise?"

"I will only ever be as a brother to her, of that you have my word."

And he chose to ignore the faint mocking glint in the blue-gray eyes. Carlew doubt his word?

Well, this time he *would* keep it!

❧ Chapter Three

Winthrop Manor
August

"Mama, I have no wish to go to London next year."

"Of course you do, my dear," said Mama, glancing around at the room's other occupants.

Serena bit her tongue, aware of the heavy speculation from the other guests.

Catherine, ever the peacemaker, said gently, "I am not overly fond of London myself. It always seems so dirty."

"I agree," said Lavinia, Countess of Hawkesbury. "I have always preferred this little patch of Gloucestershire."

"But surely, dear Countess, you would agree that for a girl to make her mark upon the world requires spending time in Town." Mama's smiling countenance took on a brittle quality. "When one has the chance to engage in parties, and concerts, and dinners galore, one has the opportunity to circulate with the best people."

"I would think that depends on what mark one wishes to make upon the world," the countess replied before sipping her tea, her gray eyes smiling at Serena.

Serena smiled back. Lavinia Hawkesbury might have been married to a peer for nearly four years but she remained as irrepressible as ever.

"Serena!"

Her mother's sharp voice drew her attention. "Yes, Mama?"

"This is a serious matter. I do not want you wasting your life hiding away in the back hills of beyond. How do you think you are to find a husband?"

"I found my husband when I was hiding away here," Lavinia said, taking another sip.

"As did I," Catherine agreed.

"But you *first* met Jon in London," Mama said triumphantly.

Catherine lifted a shoulder, exchanging a glance with the room's other occupant.

Lady Harkness, the flame-haired, flamboyant mother of Jon, had been uncharacteristically silent through the exchange. Her green eyes now gazed thoughtfully on Serena. "May I ask why you do not wish to go to London?"

"Clarinda, it does not matter what Serena wishes—"

"Forgive me, but I think it does."

"But all your friends are going to be presented," Mama said, refocusing on Serena. "Caroline will be there. You could enjoy shopping, concerts, dancing, meeting nice gentlemen, catching up on nice gossip—"

"No!"

At Serena's outburst, Mama sat back, her face closing in affront.

"One has to wonder if gossip is ever truly nice," Lavinia asked the room.

Through the French doors the gardens beckoned. Serena placed her teacup on the small table beside her and pushed to her feet. "Please excuse me."

She caught a glimpse of Catherine's worried face as she exited the room, her feet steering to the passageway that led to the back garden. A few minutes later, she was sitting in the secret grove she had frequented as a child.

Serena closed her eyes, listening to the birdsong, the chatter of sparrows, and the loud, long notes of a faraway mistle thrush. The clean scent of pine drifted to her, and she breathed in more deeply, slowly. Her eyes opened. From this position, high up on the hill, the rambling manor house rested quietly amongst trees planted generations ago. On sunny days like today, she could catch the merest glimpse of the silvery Severn as it wound its way from Gloucester. A landscape she had tried to capture many times, in pencils, charcoal, oils.

The tension ebbed away.

Thank God for the comfort of a garden, for vistas of beauty, for the peace they instilled.

Thank God Catherine had married Jon, and he was so amenable to their frequent visits. She would not survive living with Mama in the dower house without the means to escape. As good as the improvements were that Jon had instituted, they could never make up for the lack of space, the lack of view, the feeling she was boxed in. Trapped.

If only she could stay here at Winthrop Manor forever.

There came a crackling of branches as they were moved aside. "I thought you might be here," her sister said, moving to perch on the other wrought iron chair.

"Mama . . ." Serena shrugged helplessly.

"I know."

For a moment they sat quietly, the familiarity of the unspoken adding further ease.

Far off, the bird's melodious song continued, lifting her spirits. Was it letting its mate know its whereabouts? Marking its territory? Or simply sharing her enjoyment in respite from the earlier storm? "Shouldn't you be attending to your guests?"

"No," Catherine said mildly. "They are family, save for Lavinia, and I don't really think she requires my attentions, do you?"

Serena smiled, well able to picture the scene. The two older matrons politely jostling for the role of hostess, while the higher-ranked young mother ignored their pretensions.

"Dearest, tell me what has got you so wound up."

"Mama can be so . . ." She swallowed, fighting against bitterness.

"I understand."

"I wish *she* could understand."

"Mama wants you to be happy."

"Perhaps." While Serena wanted to believe it was so, a cynical streak couldn't help but remember the times Mama's decisions seemed to chiefly benefit herself. Was it dishonoring to one's parents to think such things?

"What is it about London that concerns you most?"

A myriad of answers flashed to mind: strangers, crowds, men.

"Since . . ." She could not speak it. Bile soured her mouth, halting further speech.

"Since the incident?" Catherine prompted gently.

"Yes. Since then, I have felt—I have realized there are so many things that can hurt me, things I never knew before."

Her sister reached across and held her hand.

"I don't want to go to London. I want to be here, where I'm . . ."

"Safe."

"Yes!" She blinked away the burn. "Elsewhere has so much unknown."

"We cannot always control our circumstances."

"But I don't feel ready to go someplace where I'll be forced to dance with men I don't know, to have them look at me like"—she swallowed again—"like *he* did."

"Not all men will, dearest. You know Jon regards you as a sister, and the earl is only ever kind, is he not?"

"Yes."

"Is there someone else whose attentions have made you wary?"

A face flashed into mind. A handsome, laughing man, whose manners always seemed too smooth. She shook her head, as if she could shake away the image.

"My dear, I do not want you to carry this fear forever."

"I do not want to carry it, either."

"But if you avoid all new experiences, are you not reinforcing the fears within?"

"Perhaps, but—"

"I know Mama can be trying, but I do believe she honestly thinks a season in London will be for your best. Just think, you could see the art at the Royal Academy exhibition." Serena's heart thudded. Now *that* thought had some merit. "And a visit would provide distraction from remembering less . . . pleasant things."

She managed a ghost of a smile. "Does Jon appreciate your gift for understatement?"

Catherine's lips curved. "He appreciates many things, but I don't know if that is one."

"I just feel like I need some time before I have a season, and am forced to think about . . . marriage."

"And that is very understandable." Her sister nodded thoughtfully. "I suppose there is no reason why it should be next season."

"No." Hope lit her heart. If Catherine—and naturally Jon—were willing to support a postponement of her come out . . .

"It does mean you will live very quietly for a good part of the year." Her spirits sank. "At the cottage."

Catherine's brow wrinkled. "Perhaps Mama could be encouraged to take an extended visit to Aunt Drusilla again."

"Or visit the aunts at Avebury."

"Then you could live here with us." Her sister's smile flashed. "That would be wonderful, especially when Jon is away on business."

"I would not be in your way when he is at home?"

"It is large enough for you to know when to be elsewhere." Serena's cheeks heated as her sister laughed. "Dearest, one day you will meet a man with whom you will want to share everything. Don't let fear build a wall that will keep hope out. Now"—she rose to her feet—"I will talk with Jon as soon as he finishes his discussion with Lord Hawkesbury."

"Oh, thank you, Catherine!"

"Don't thank me yet. We've still got to persuade Mama as to the benefits of such a scheme."

"Of course." *Please, Lord, let Mama agree.*

Catherine's head tilted, her dark eyes serious. "Would you still feel safe if you traveled with us? Sometimes we're invited to stay with Jon's friends and associates, which can feel daunting. But if you are with us, then it might prove an effective way of getting to know some of the people you will be introduced to during your presentation season. This might prove less overwhelming."

"I suppose so."

"Good." Her sister moved a few feet away then turned. "That reminds me. I probably should have told you we are expecting another guest tonight."

"Who?"

A sudden foreboding chilled her. *Dear God, please let it not be—*

"Lord Carmichael."

Hard-won ease drained away as the sun dipped behind a cloud.

"Ah, Lord Carmichael. What a pleasure."

"Lady Harkness, as always, the pleasure is mine." Harry bowed, skimming her knuckles with his lips before straightening to address the next lady. "And my dear Countess. Your presence here is also a delight."

"I'm so glad you think so," Lady Hawkesbury said, a twinkle in her eyes. "I would hate to think my presence displeasing."

"That could never be the case."

"Oh, you'd be surprised," she murmured.

"One would be a slowtop to not appreciate such grace, such beauty—"

"Are you quite finished flattering my wife, Carmichael?"

"Indeed, I am." Harry grinned, offering the earl a bow before glancing back at the countess. "For the moment, anyway."

"I'm glad to hear it," she said with a laugh.

Harry moved to the next personage, seated on the couch with an expression partway between bemusement and high dignity. "And Lady Winthrop. Good evening."

She inclined her head. "Lord Carmichael. I trust you have been made welcome."

"Your daughter does you credit, my lady, and has employed a veritable army to see to my needs."

He turned to the young lady seated on the far settee, her expression as cool as ever. He opened his mouth to speak—

"Do you require an army to assist you, sir?"

He blinked. "I beg your—"

"Serena!" hissed her mother.

The young blonde's chin lifted. "Are all viscounts as delicate as you?"

His host laughed, and Harry dragged his gaze from the unconventional miss to Carlew as he said, "Not all, Serena, but Carmichael here is a special case."

"I am special, it is true," Harry agreed humbly, to a titter of laughter. From all except the cool blonde with the stormy sea-blue eyes.

Dinner that night was delicious, his host's budget as generous as the cook's abilities. White soup for the entrée, followed by a haunch of venison, lobster, goose, quail, French beans, peas, asparagus, and an assortment of pastries. Candlelight flickered, conversation simmered, the tinkle and scrape of silver on porcelain, it was a meal of friends—save for the silent girl opposite.

Harry swallowed another piece of lobster—really, quite delectable—and eyed the serene Miss Winthrop. Yes, he remembered Jon's warning to not engage her in frivolous flirtations, and to be honest, he had no desire to do so, certain as he was that she would give him another set down. But he *did* want to see her smile.

His neighbor, the Countess of Hawkesbury, murmured a request for the quail, and Harry obliged, serving her from the platter nearby.

"Thank you, sir."

"You are most welcome. Lady Hawkesbury, my sources tell me you have lived in this area for some time."

"Your sources are correct," she replied. "I have lived here all my life apart from our stints at Hawkesbury House and the town house."

"You do not prefer such places?"

"Hawkesbury House is a little too grand for Nicholas and myself and our baby, although we do visit from time to time"—her voice lowered—"as much as to remind ourselves of its existence as to remind his mother of ours."

He chuckled. "I understand. It can be hard for one generation to make room for the next. The only way my grandmother survived my parents' assumption to the title was through her insistence that the dower house be modified to replicate Welmsley Hall. Of course, it does not have quite the same prospect, but I think she is resigned to it now."

"She sounds quite formidable."

"She is the sweetest lady imaginable," Jon said, from his position at the end of the table. "I still remember her kindnesses when I visited Harry during Oxford days."

"You should visit us there again sometime, Jon," Harry said, sipping his wine. "Bring your lovely wife, of course."

"That sounds an excellent plan."

"Especially now that the season is done." He glanced over. A shadow crossed the ever-composed face. In a voice he hoped sounded devoid of all tease, he said, "Miss Winthrop, do you look forward to making your presentation next year?"

Her eyes touched his then glanced away, her mouth one tight line, as her mother trilled, "Of course she does, Lord Carmichael. One can only hope the Queen will remain well and have no need to delay the drawing rooms like this year. Serena is looking forward to it immensely."

He caught a flicker in the blue eyes, the slight curling of her lip. Somehow he did not think the young lady agreed. "I'm sure you will find London pleasurable," he said politely.

Beside him, the countess cleared her throat. "We were talking of that earlier, weren't we, Serena? I'm afraid, Lord Carmichael, that Miss Winthrop and I are agreed that we much prefer the delights of country living to the noise and smells of the city."

He glanced between them, conscious of some strange tension around the table that Lady Hawkesbury's words seemed to have dispelled. "Then I'm sure you would enjoy my part of the world. We may not have such pretty hills as the Cotswolds in our back garden, but our peaks and valleys are considered to be amongst the finest in England." A rush of longing for his home surged through his chest. "Many artists visit my part of Derbyshire because of its vast beauty."

"You make it sound very lovely, my lord." The countess leaned forward. "Tell me, Serena, how goes your art?" She glanced up at him. "Serena has a wonderful gift, you know. Drawing, painting, why, she can take a subject's likeness in just a few minutes."

He nodded, glancing across to see the young artist's suddenly stricken look, her expression twisting the corners of his heart. As Lady Hawkesbury quickly turned the subject, he turned to Jon, noting the knit brow and slight shake of his head. His heart pulled a little more.

Clearly Miss Serena was not as tranquil as her countenance had led him to believe.

ℜ Chapter Four

THE WALLS WERE closing in. Freshly painted, decorated without too much of Mama's rococo aesthetic, and with a fire crackling in the hearth, the drawing room of the dower house was certainly much nicer than before, but it could never compare to the grand reception rooms of Winthrop Manor. Here, the squared windows might look sweet from outside, but there was no view, and the light that *was* permitted often shrouded by curtains—and definitely no good for drawing.

Shards of regret splintered her heart. She shook her head, trying to ignore the pain.

"What was that?" Mama asked from the opposite sofa. "Do you not agree?"

What had Mama been speaking of? "I . . . er . . ."

"Oh, I don't know what was the use of spending all that money at Haverstock's if the best conversation you can manage is none!"

Serena narrowed her eyes a fraction, kept the words she *could* say firmly locked away.

"Now don't look at me like so. You know such looks always give me a chill. What ails you? I never see you pick up a paintbrush these days. What was the point of all those private lessons?"

Nausea wrestled with guilt. Mama didn't know. Catherine and Jon had counseled it was better that way, worn down as Mama had become from the scandals of the past year; no one wanted to add further weight to her worries or to add Mama's fretting to Serena's concerns. Serena's own disgrace was best hushed over, at least for the present, something she had heartily endorsed. She never wanted to think on those days again.

"I do not know what has got into you. If you only knew what we'd been forced to endure while you were away having the time of your life."

Serena stifled a sigh as her mother began another dissertation on the folly of gossip, in particular the propensity *certain members* of the wider neighborhood had for such things, which was code for Lady Milton, whose fraying friendship with Mama had finally snapped this year. Serena knew only too well what Mama and Catherine had endured, Mama having spoken of it often enough. In contrast, her sister was too focused on her current happiness to want to spend much time dwelling on the past.

Her heart thumped. Perhaps the words from her morning Bible reading were correct, and the apostle Paul's exhortation to forget the past and reach forth unto the future helped heal a soul. At least it seemed to have worked for Catherine.

"Mama, how did Catherine spend her time here?"

Her mother frowned. "Are you saying you're bored?"

Yes. "No." Not exactly. "I am just not finding a great deal to occupy my time—"

"Well you would if you took up your paint box again!"

"I find I have little inclination for art these days," she said carefully. "And you know my sewing skills are limited at best."

"A fact which practice could only improve."

Serena held up her sad mess of embroidery.

"Hmm. Perhaps you should do something else and stop wasting all our thread." Mama sighed. "I've never understood how you have patience for your daubs but not for anything else."

She swallowed an indignant reply to manage a mild-sounding, "It *is* a mystery."

"Well, I suppose seeing you've no talent for needlework or music or anything of the gentler arts . . ." The two lines between Mama's brows plunged deeper. "You could see if Mrs. Jones needs assistance in the kitchen."

Serena stared at her. Was Mama serious?

"Now there's no need to look at me like that! You know those looks of yours always give me the shivers."

"I think I might go for a walk," Serena said, pushing to her feet. "I find it a little stuffy in here."

Her mother drew herself up as if readying for argument, so she forced a quick smile and escaped, closing the door on further censure. Grabbing her wide-brimmed bonnet and shawl, she hurried out the front door, out the front gate, walking quickly down the lane before her mother could call after her.

The morning light held a brightness she could not fail to appreciate. The thick hedge that hid most of the cottage looked almost pretty, the emerald hues of the leaves glowing in the sunshine. Her steps soon found her to the crossroads; she turned left, hugging the estate border which led to the Foley farm.

In the yard stood a young woman, her stomach large, holding the hand of an unsteady toddler.

As she neared, the woman placed a hand to shade her eyes, before her mouth dropped open. "Never tell me—is that you, Miss Serena?"

Her lips curved. "Do you wish me to tell you or not, Miss—?"

"Lizzie. 'Member? From up at the Manor? 'Course, I served your sister more than you."

She blinked. "Lizzie?" Catherine's former maid.

"'Cept I'm a missus now." She showed her plain gold band proudly. The tiny girl yanked her arm back. "Stop it, Mary! I'm talking to the young lady here." She tilted her head at the toddler. "This here's my first. She's a mite fractious these days. Paining from her teeth."

Serena nodded, lowering to the child's eye level. "Have your teeth been hurting?"

The little girl studied her, her big blue eyes serious, before she ducked behind her mother's skirts.

Serena straightened. "She is very pretty."

"Aye, that she is, miss. And pretty noisy too, sometimes, but I guess that's children." Lizzie sighed and rubbed her middle.

"How long to go?"

"A couple of months. I'll be right glad when it's over, I tell you. Sometimes the pain's so bad I think it must be almost ready."

As if in sympathy Serena's own stomach tightened, the bands of pressure signaling another episode would eventuate in a few days. She fought the wince, fought the emotion clogging her throat, her heart. Her monthly pains held no promise she would ever bear a child.

"So, you've returned after that fancy school."

"Yes."

The wide face brightened. "Please, Miss Serena. I remember you being that quick with a pencil. Could you not draw little Mary here? We don't have nothing to pay you with—"

"I could never accept payment!"

"Then you will?" The large eyes widened. "We have some lovely Devonshire Quarrendens ready fer eating. I remember you saying they were yer favorite apples."

"No! That is, I . . . I couldn't. I don't draw anymore, you see."

"Oh." The face drooped.

"I'm sorry."

Regret stirred her heart as she managed a farewell and turned away, but to explain why she no longer did what she once loved was too hard, still felt too raw.

At the crossroads her steps halted. Should she return to the cottage for more of Mama's disappointed discontent, or undergo further exploration to see what other changes had ensued at Winthrop?

Adventure it was.

She climbed over a stile and walked through a field. Jon wouldn't mind her trespassing. Late summer scents begged for appreciation, the hedgerows were already reddening, wild blackberries had darkened to ripeness, the sloes held their purple-blue waxy bloom. The heaviness from earlier eased as she drank in the beauty of fields she had always known.

The back of her neck was growing damp by the time she had

climbed the slope of the long field—aptly named. She picked up her skirts, shaking out the two inches of dust coating the hem, then peered more closely. Was that a tear?

The far-off whinny of a horse drew her gaze up sharply. Mama would say Serena was not fit to be seen, but Winthrop Manor was only hosting family at the moment. Oh—her chest grew tight—and Lord Carmichael. Not that she cared for his good opinion. He might be a viscount, but he also appeared too sure of himself, and with that dark hair and muddy green eyes he was too handsome. And she could not trust handsome men.

She climbed through the repaired wooden railings of the top fence, another of Jon's improvements, and resumed her walk, chewing her bottom lip. The viscount should be someone who remained nothing to her, someone who left her heart closed and cold. But ever since meeting him in Bath in March for Catherine's birthday he'd stirred heated antipathy. Why did she dislike him so? Was it his carefree manners, his sense of ease with everyone, the way he walked into a room and seemed to expect everyone to lavish him with attention? Perhaps it was the way he talked—was he serious about nothing?

Granted, last night he had not tried to flatter her. In fact—remorse shafted her chest—he had overlooked her rudeness, which said something about his good nature. He'd even tried to engage her in conversation, but his choice of topics had failed dismally. Thank goodness for Lavinia's quickness in changing the subject. The countess was sensitive in that way, although Serena was surprised Lavinia could stand his nonsensical charm; she'd always been strong-minded about such things. Perhaps time changed people.

Another whinny, followed by the clank and clatter of wheels and hooves, soon brought the familiar sight of Catherine and her gig into view. Serena waved, as Catherine slowed her beloved Ginger to a halt. "Good morning!"

"Good morning. You're just the person I was coming to see." Catherine motioned her closer. "Jon and Harry are riding behind and I wanted to ask you this before they arrived. Now, are you sure about coming to stay with us?"

After her morning of dreariness? "Absolutely."

"And travel with us, despite your . . . affliction?"

She bit her lip. "I had almost forgotten."

"That is a good thing, is it not? May I ask how long since the last major episode?"

"Not since . . ." She swallowed bile as the memory flashed into mind. The night following the assault. Writhing in her bed, clutching her midsection as her vision blurred and the pains billowed within. Coupled with her soul shame, it was a time she had no wish to remember. "Perhaps I should not—"

"Nonsense. One cannot hide forever for fear of what may arise. Should your pains recur, I will do everything I can to help you, and shield you from speculation."

The back of her eyes heated. "You are a good sister."

"I am, aren't I?" Catherine laughed. "So, is that confirmation? You will travel with us?"

"Yes, please."

"Come. Let's go beard the dragon in her den."

"The dragon?"

"Mama."

※

This patch of Gloucestershire might be pretty, especially in the late afternoon light, but he couldn't help but feel it also a trifle dull. Harry's gaze dropped from the window as he quashed the feeling as disloyal. Perhaps Jon did not mind the rural monotony. Certainly, his business dealings in London would supply enough drama for him to prefer such rustication, and Jon's stories from his time in India suggested he need not seek out fresh adventures. So perhaps Jon enjoyed the quiet life, but, as Harry's father had pointed out too many times, Harry could not.

Thankfully, Jon's preference for mellow ways did not extend so far as to preclude a billiards table. With a flick of his wrist, the cue struck the white ball, which in turn gently thumped the red into a pocket. As he lined up the next shot, the door opened, admitting his host.

"Found you."

"I was not aware we were playing hide-and-seek." He sunk the next ball, and the next, flashing a grin at his friend. "Looks like I haven't completely lost my touch."

"Your skill invites the question of exactly how much time you devote to such pursuits."

"Not nearly enough, old man. Not nearly enough. Beware such questions, else you begin to sound rather like my old man, and that would never do. I should be forced to drop your acquaintance immediately."

Carlew laughed. "It is funny you should say that, just as I have hopes of renewing his."

Harry straightened. "So you'll come?"

"As soon as your parents are agreeable."

"Wonderful! I'm sure your dear wife will enjoy the scenery immensely."

"There is just one thing."

"I sense equivocation."

"Serena will need to accompany us."

He stared. "Why?" Started. "Forgive me, that sounds rude. But I was not aware the young lady had any desire to be near me."

Carlew's expression turned wry. "You'll pardon the obvious, as she appears to be one of the few young ladies who do *not* desire deeper acquaintanceship with you—"

"No. Truly?"

"—but I suspect it stems less from a desire to go and more from a desire not to stay."

"Ah. So you're saying she is prepared to overlook my many gross insufficiencies in order to escape the dearth of good company she finds here." Harry shrugged. "Very well."

"I have appreciated the lack of attention you have shown her."

"At the risk of being thought impolite, she has not made that task terribly hard, much as I usually do enjoy being brought to task for my every crime."

"I'm sure she does not mean such things."

"At least such disapproval suggests she will get on well with my parents." He quashed the timeworn regrets and sunk another red ball. "So, old man, are you ready to play and be defeated?"

His host laughed and removed his coat, enabling Harry some sweet distraction from the disappointment sure to be his when he finally returned home to Derbyshire.

THE NEXT THREE days Harry strove to hide his increasing boredom, surrounded as he was by a welter of domesticities, mainly centering on the upcoming departure of Catherine's mother, off to visit relatives in Dorset. This morning he'd stumbled downstairs to breakfast, an occasion he generally missed if he could. Today, however, the persistent twitter of a sparrow directly outside his window had rendered pleasant dreams impossible, thus he had found himself witness to Carlew's receiving of an invitation to Hampton Hall for a dinner hosted by the Earl and Countess of Hawkesbury.

"It seems the earl's been surprised by a visit from an old friend and would be much obliged for our attendance at such short notice." Carlew looked to his wife, seated at the foot of the table. "Shall we accept?"

"We have no other engagement."

"What say you, Harry? I suspect you would appreciate a chance to socialize beyond these four walls."

A twinge of remorse crossed his heart. Had he not hidden his flagging enthusiasm sufficiently well? But there were only so many rides and games of billiards a man could cope with, after all. He inclined his head to his hostess. "Madam, I'm afraid I must inform you that your husband is a mischief-maker. I have enjoyed my time here immensely."

She smiled and said something soothing, and for a moment he was struck by her similarity to her sister. While they were not alike in temperament or coloring, there was still something about the thin nose and elegant poise that revealed their aristocratic lineage. Doubtless if Miss Serena were here, she'd say something far more impolite to his avowal of contentment. His lips twitched. He could almost see her upraised brow and hear a disbelieving, "Have you?"

He became aware of Carlew's and Catherine's amused looks. "What? I have! I don't know why you would think otherwise."

"So you have not been missing the pleasures of London?"

"What, dancing with society's young misses without a word to say? I think not. Though I do confess to missing the fun of a good gossip and a few hands of whist at Pall Mall."

Catherine bit her lip and looked down.

Harry looked a question at Carlew, who shook his head and returned his attention to his wife.

"We shall attend then, my dear?"

"Oh, yes." She stood, compelling them to rise also. "Please excuse me while I inform Cook we shall be dining out tonight."

"Of course."

Once she had left the room and they were reseated, Harry raised his brows at Carlew. "Did I say something amiss?"

Carlew sipped his coffee, eyed him over the rim of his cup. "The previous Lord Winthrop . . ."

"Catherine's father."

"Was a gambler. As he lost nearly all the family fortune, it would be wise not to mention your penchant for deep play, as it will not be received well by Catherine or her mother."

Harry nodded, his thoughts tumbling. He'd be willing to bet the Bevington silver another person would take grave offense at the pastime he indulged in to keep the demons at bay.

Miss Serena Winthrop.

❧ Chapter Five

Within a minute of arriving at Hampton Hall, Serena knew she and Catherine should not have come. The reason: Sophia Thornton *née* Milton, whose selfish disdain for others and gossipy mother had made Catherine's life a misery earlier this year. One glance at her sister's face was enough to raise her own personal hackles and determine tonight would be as enjoyable and unremarkable for Catherine as Serena could possibly make it.

Their entrance into the yellow drawing room was met first by an apologetic earl and countess before further introductions were interrupted by a high squeal.

"Dearest Catherine!" Serena watched as her sister was engulfed in a pink satin embrace. "Oh, it's been simply ages."

"Yes."

"Still as chatty as ever, I see." Sophia glanced up at Jon. "And this must be your husband. Well, you *are* handsome, aren't you? But so tall!" She laughed and cupped a hand around her mouth. "Hello, up there!"

"Good evening."

Serena almost applauded Jon, every inch the gentleman, right down to the slight expression of contempt she'd never seen him wear before.

"Sophia," the Countess of Hawkesbury said desperately, "this is Lord Winthrop, and his friend, the Viscount Carmichael."

Serena watched the viscount's face as pink-swathed Sophia fluttered her attentions. His expression ranged from surprised disdain to something even less holy. She bit back a smile, pleased at his ability to see through Sophy's shallow pretensions.

"And sweet Serena. How are you?"

Before she could answer, Sophy had butterflied off to drag over a tall blond man.

"Captain Thornton!" Catherine held out her hand. "It is good to see you. It has been several years now, but you don't seem a day older."

"Apart from some gray hairs, you mean?" He smiled a genuine-looking smile that recalled memories of Catherine's whispered conversations from years ago about the earl and his best friend. He turned to Jon and the viscount, offering bows and murmured conversation, as Sophia pulled Catherine toward the chairs. "You must tell me all your news!" she effused, and then proceeded to share all her news.

Lavinia moved to her side, offering Serena a look of apology followed by a sigh. "I am sorry. I know Sophy and her family will never be true friends with yours. But I could not disappoint Nicholas; he has not seen Thornton in an age. And I thought if she saw Catherine here she would not feel it necessary to impose a visit upon your Mama."

Serena shuddered. "That would not be a good idea."

"So although tonight might prove challenging, I thought between us all, we might be able to protect Catherine from Sophy's excesses. You, me, Lord Winthrop, Lord Carmichael."

"The viscount?"

"Oh, yes." Lavinia nodded. "I believe him to possess depths far greater than his charm."

"You do?"

The dinner gong sounded, precluding Lavinia's reply.

Over dinner, Serena was able to gain a closer look at the man who'd chosen to marry the foolish Sophy, as she was seated between him and Jon. The viscount sat opposite, between Sophy and Catherine, so she was able to see something of his manner also.

Thornton was an affable man, his conversation pleasant, his knowledge of her time in Bath so limited she was able to provide an edited version which did not stray too far from the truth. On the other side of her, Jon's deep rumbling conversation with Lavinia also provided assurance the evening might proceed more favorably than she'd feared. And, to her considerable surprise, a large part of the credit would have to go to the viscount.

She couldn't help but appreciate the efforts he went to in ensuring Sophia talked only of herself. At times Serena imagined she caught a twinkle in his eye, a dimple lurking in his cheek, that suggested he enjoyed exposing folly. She even saw him once raise his napkin to his lips and smother a yawn as Sophia continued talking about her children. Serena had been forced to bite back more than one smile.

"You seem to find Carmichael's antics amusing," Jon said discreetly.

"Do I?"

"There is no need to act surprised. One of the reasons I enjoy his company is because of his social nous that sees beyond the polished veneer to the person below. He can be quite a shrewd judge of character when he chooses."

"Really?"

"I know you find his manners a little over the top at times, but can you imagine this meal without his social aplomb?"

Serena glanced around the table at the little conversations. Catherine was chatting animatedly to the earl and Thornton, Sophia was monopolizing the viscount and Lavinia's attention. She exhaled. If the viscount were not here, no doubt Sophia's domineering manner would be causing offense to the more polite guests at the table.

"He's soaking up her attention," she acknowledged. And at the cost of enjoying conversation with people whose company he might enjoy. "Like a sponge."

Jon chuckled.

Sophia ceased from her conversation to glance their direction and smile. "What secrets has dear little Serena been whispering to make you laugh, sir?"

Serena froze, and Jon murmured something noncommittal. How dare she insinuate something untoward between them? How dare she imply Serena was too young to be here!

"Oh, but I insist on knowing!" Sophy gave a tinkly laugh. "Now I think on it, my mother mentioned something about you, Serena. Now, what was it?"

Her gaze narrowed. "Your mother doubtless says many things."

There was a moment of stunned silence, followed by the clearing of throats and smothered laughter, as Sophy closed her mouth, her own eyes tapering.

As Lord Hawkesbury immediately drew Thornton and Catherine back into conversation, the viscount, after a swift glance at Serena, turned to his dinner companion. "Tell me, dear Mrs. Thornton, how long can the neighborhood expect the pleasure of your company?"

"I—that is, we have not fully determined our plans."

"Such a shame." He picked up his wineglass, eyeing Jon and Serena as he said, "I myself am traveling home very soon, and plan on kidnapping Jon and Catherine and Miss Serena here for the journey north."

"Kidnapping?" Sophia said, wide-eyed.

"Well, 'tis more of an invitation really."

"Oh." Her brow smoothed. "And what part of England do you come from, Lord Carmichael?"

"The Peak District in Derbyshire," he said, taking another sip of wine.

"Derbyshire? Oh, I *love* Derbyshire," she gushed.

"Really? What part have you visited?"

"Oh. I haven't actually visited. Not yet anyway," she added, with a coquettish smile. Clearly angling for an invitation, Serena thought in disgust.

"Well, when you do, make sure you take time to visit a mine."

"A what?"

"A mine. Our part of the country is filled with them: lead, copper, calcite, fluorspar. Mrs. Thornton, did you know we call fluorspar 'Blue John'?" She shook her head. "From the French *Bleu et Jaune*, which describes the color of the bandings. In fact, if you consider Miss Serena over there, I believe her eyes hold something of the variable nature of fluorspar, or fluropha, as some say. Sometimes a stormy green, sometimes almost purple in color, and sometimes what we see now, the perfect shade of mid-blue."

Serena felt a frown form between her brows. Was he serious, or was this performance for her benefit as well as Sophy's?

Sophy's forehead creased again. "I confess I have never really noticed Serena's eye color before—"

"That does not surprise me, madam," he said.

"I'm rather surprised at *your* noticing, sir."

"Ah, but what I care to notice in this world is both varied *and* diverse."

Serena smothered a laugh, watching the confused expression on Sophy's face as the smooth baritone continued.

"May I say, dear madam, you seem someone with great capacity for surprise."

"I am?"

"Carmichael . . ." Jon said in an undertone.

The viscount looked across, grinned briefly, before his attention returned to his seatmate. "But back to fluorspar. I wonder, can you guess what color the bandings be?"

"Er—"

"Blue, that's right!" He grinned across the table at Thornton and said in a louder voice, "May I congratulate you, sir, on attaining such a remarkable wife?"

As Thornton responded with something appropriate, Serena found herself doing something she had promised herself she would never do.

And she held the viscount's gaze whilst giving him her biggest smile.

When the ladies had passed through to the drawing room after dinner, the earl went through the motions of offering port. When first Jon and then Harry declined, good manners meant poor Thornton had no option but to refuse, even though he seemed the man who most needed a drink. He would have to, being married to such a silly widgeon. Harry shook his head, following his host as they hurried to the drawing room. Hurried, because Hawkesbury no doubt suspected the damage that lady might do after Serena's little outburst.

He swallowed a smile. That cool look with which she seemed to favor the silly Sophia Thornton was an expression of which a duchess might be proud. Certainly his grandmother would enjoy meeting someone less simpering miss than ice queen. But whether that was enough to stop the venomous talk from a very silly woman . . .

The door opened. He could tell at one glance they were too late. Catherine looked as though she might cry, Lady Hawkesbury and Serena both wore frustrated expressions, whilst the less-than-sweet Sophia looked smug.

"Ah, ladies." He strode forward, screening Catherine as her husband comforted her. "We were desolate without your company. Can I hope that we were missed, too?"

"You were," Serena muttered, as the countess murmured something about Lady Milton's gossip, but his attention remained on the younger girl, even now shooting a dark look at Sophy.

Had she meant the ladies missed the tempering nature of the men, or was it something more particular, and Miss Serena missed him? His heart constricted again, just as it had done earlier when she'd beamed a smile at him.

In that earlier moment, he'd lost the train of his thought, conscious only of her fair loveliness, enhanced by the dining table's flickering candlelight. Somehow in that brief space of time she had subtly metamorphosed from someone akin to the younger sister he'd never had into someone quite different, someone quite enchanting, for whom he could never hold a mere brotherly regard. It had taken Mrs. Thornton's touch on his sleeve to bring him back to himself and drag his gaze away—only to encounter Carlew's slight frown. He had tried to communicate reassurance, but doubted his success, and still hoped to find time later tonight to repledge his commitment to treating Catherine's sister in strictly a neighborly way.

He glanced over to see Catherine more composed, though Carlew's frown remained. In a softer voice he said, "Your sister seems calmer now."

"That woman!" Serena's small hands clenched. "She, she—"

"Softly now," he cautioned. "Don't let her win again."

"Again?"

"Her poison has already touched your sister. Do not give her the satisfaction of seeing you disconcerted also."

Her gaze met his, locked and held. A tapping started in his chest. Fluorspar, indeed. Her eyes were more like sapphires, filled with the most entrancing light . . .

She blinked, breaking the connection, and forced her lips upward. "Better?"

"More grimace than grin, but you'll do."

He smiled, heart lurching a little as she responded in kind.

No. It would *not* do. She was as a sister to him. Hadn't he so promised Carlew?

He had just stepped away from her to stand near the sofas when the door opened, revealing a nursemaid holding a small child. At once the earl and his wife moved to speak with the servant and, after a brief discussion, returned, this time with the earl holding his tiny daughter.

"Please forgive the informality, but it appears little Grace here refuses to settle unless with her parents."

Watching Lord Hawkesbury tenderly hold his child, he had a flash of what his life could one day be. A home, a wife, children, friends. Something more than the momentary exultation of a win at cards. Something . . . permanent.

As Catherine cooed over the babe, he overheard Sophia say something about modern parenting spoiling young children these days.

Harry turned to their hostess, who seemed unperturbed by Sophia's insinuations. "I trust we will be so fortunate as to have the pleasure of listening to your wonderful music tonight."

"Perhaps." She motioned to the other ladies. "If my guests are prepared to perform also."

"One should never seek to monopolize," he murmured, glancing at Serena.

Her blue eyes held an answering gleam. "Not unless one wishes to be considered a bore."

As his lips twitched appreciatively, the countess said, "Miss Winthrop, will you honor us with a performance? I'm sure Haverstock's Seminary prides itself on its music."

"They prided themselves, but never me, I'm afraid. I play very indifferently."

"Did you not have lessons on the harp?" Carlew said.

"But for two terms. I am not very gifted at playing musical instruments."

"I would love to learn the harp," the countess said. "It seems a most angelic instrument."

"Only if played well, and I suspect angelic was the last word people thought when they heard me play."

Harry chuckled, as Mrs. Thornton said from her settee, "All this self-deprecation grows tiresome, child. Surely that expensive school was useful for something."

Serena's face stiffened. A surge of protectiveness made him clear his throat and drawl, "My maternal grandmother, the Duchess of Selby, has always held such modesty to be the mark of a true lady."

Mrs. Thornton had the decency to flush.

Serena's gaze lifted to meet his, a small smile curling one side of her lips.

"Serena does sing a little," Catherine said from her corner.

"A very little," she murmured.

"Enough to sing with Catherine and me?" the countess pleaded.

"Perhaps that much, yes."

From her extreme reluctance this seemed more than maidenly shyness. He recalled his sister also being less than willing to exhibit when asked at family functions. Some young ladies seemed aware of the limitations of their talents. Unlike—

"I'm happy to sing," said Sophy, stepping forward. She glanced at the countess. "Would you like me to begin?"

"Of course."

What followed was a less-than-perfect rendition of a Beethoven arrangement of an Irish air. But he would give Mrs. Thornton her due; she was not shy about aiming for notes that more judicious ladies would not attempt.

Once her guest had finished and resumed her seat with a slightly crestfallen look at no requested encores, the countess glanced at the sisters. "Shall we?"

They nodded, and then moved to stand beside her at the piano. Lady Hawkesbury played an opening run.

Harry settled in his seat, watching the expressions of the three very different ladies. Lavinia's piano playing was as flawless as her voice, her confidence showing in the smile that saturated her face and vocal tone. Catherine was all soft shyness, her voice adding a lower timbre to the harmonies. She sang to Carlew, his smile assuring her, as often seemed to be his way. Miss Serena, as always, puzzled him.

Clearly uncomfortable, she barely raised her eyes, her gaze lifting once to Carlew's face, and once to his own. Her vocal tone was not dissimilar to his sister's, holding a clear, light tremolo he found pleasing. When the Scotch air finished, he joined the others in applause, and, conscious of the younger girl's embarrassment, did not seek to draw further attention to her as she resumed her seat nearby.

Catherine joined the countess to play a duet, one he'd heard before, but that was played with such a simple confidence it belied the talent involved. Harry applauded as Carlew quietly praised his wife, who blushed at the attention.

Mrs. Thornton, clearly miffed at not being included, now loudly asked if she might exhibit once more. The countess graciously gave up her seat at the pianoforte, and the room filled with another performance of more enthusiasm than skill.

Now, finally, Lavinia performed, her ability unhindered by necessary deference to others, each note sure, her clear soprano lifting to the ceiling and beyond. He joined the others in generous applause at the end.

"May I request an encore?" He smiled. "I have seen many a professional from the Continent less skilled than you, fair countess."

"As have we," Catherine glanced at her husband. "Remember the concerts in Bath? The performers could never hold a candle to Lavinia. But then, few could."

"I believe our Regent might agree," the earl said, before sharing a little about a visit several years ago to the Marine Pavilion and Lavinia's performance for the future king.

The earlier tension seemed to have dissipated thoroughly, replaced by an ease as the married couples gazed upon each other with quiet affection, holding hands. The little girl lay fast asleep in her father's arms, a picture of contentment framed by familial bliss. Harry again felt that tug deep within, something that begged that it might soon be time to start thinking about finding a wife and setting up a nursery.

"My wife is talented, isn't she?" the earl said, with a tender smile at the countess that made Harry feel something else he had not felt for quite some time.

Envy.

🎋 Chapter Six

September

THE CARRIAGE WOBBLED and swayed, jerking Serena awake. She peered across the dim interior to see Jon's weary face. "How is she?"

"Finally asleep, thank goodness."

"Poor thing." She bit her lip as she watched her sister sleep in his arms. "What a disappointment for her. She's never been a poor traveler. I wonder if it was the food at that inn in Lutterworth."

"Perhaps."

She studied her brother-in-law. Past days of unseasonal heat and illness-plagued travel had left him looking less than his usual unflappable self. A fine fringe of gingery whiskers lined his face, shadows lined his eyes.

He glanced up. "Thank you for all you have done these past days."

"I'm so glad to have been able to help."

Serena had gloried in being the healthy one for a change. Apart from one incapacitating incident the day after the Hawkesbury dinner, her courses in recent months had been quite moderate. Nursing her sister this past week on their slow journey north had been small recompense for all the times she'd received assistance from her sister when migraines gripped her head and abdomen. Catherine had sickened just outside Rugby, necessitating an unforeseen night's stay at the next town before her improvement in the morning saw their journey continue. Jon had wanted to call a doctor, but Catherine was most insistent she was fine except for a troubling feeling of nausea, and after her pleading look at Serena had engendered her support, Jon was left with little room to argue. Catherine had promised to rest and see a doctor at Welmsley, if that proved necessary.

"I'm sure she will feel better once we arrive."

His brow lightened. "That won't be long now. I saw a sign to Buxton not so long ago."

She glanced down at the traveler's guide Jon had helpfully supplied her with, quickly finding the small circle denoting the spa town. "Do we pass through it?"

"I think not. But I'm sure we could visit one day if you like. It is not terribly far from Welmsley as I recall."

"I would like to see it, especially to compare to Bath. They say they have a crescent-shaped street designed to emulate the Royal Crescent in Bath."

He chuckled. "I do not think there can be too many young ladies who appreciate architecture as you do."

"Well, it *is* a form of art."

She glanced away, studying the stone walls segmenting the sheep-strewn hills in early autumn splendor. The lack of art in her life was growing less painful these days. Her fingers did not always burn to hold a pencil or try to sketch a scene, although she had been sorely tempted on the journey. As the viscount had said, this part of England held some spectacular scenery worth capturing.

"Serena."

The deep voice pulled her attention back.

Jon offered a half smile. "Forgive me, but I must speak plainly, for I would hate if you did not enjoy everything this part of the world has to offer. It concerns your art."

Her stomach tensed.

"To be blunt, Serena, your art is a gift from God. Hiding it does no one any favors, least of all you. I know you feel scarred by what happened earlier this year, but I believe abandoning such a gift is a waste." His gentle smile and tone took away some of the sting. "Do you not see? Each time you deny your gift, you let the evil continue to win."

She blinked, his words echoing around her soul. Hadn't the viscount said something similar recently? Though whether Sophia Thornton could be accounted as evil she was not entirely sure . . .

"Catherine and I have been praying for you, praying that God would restore that which the enemy has stolen away. Perhaps your time here could be a fresh start."

"Perhaps." Did God care enough to notice? He'd felt so far away in recent times. Her eyes filled.

Jon passed her a large folded handkerchief and she patted her eyes. "Thank you." She cleared her throat, motioned to the carriage. "And for allowing me to come."

"You're very welcome."

And she had truly felt his welcome, felt the love of a brother, these past weeks. After Catherine and Jon successfully persuaded Mama of the benefits of postponing Serena's come out, and that it was in everyone's best interests if Serena stayed with them for a while, Serena had spent the last few weeks enjoying a liberty she had never previously known. Safe, protected, yet independent. Prompted—and funded—by Jon, Mama had happily acquiesced to a visit to Dorset with Aunt Clothilde and Cousin Peter, whose work amongst seaside rocks had garnered him a number of interesting fossils. Away from Mama's soul-wearying presence, she had gained something of the confidence she had known when she was younger. With Mama away, and the viscount returned home, relieving her of his somewhat disconcerting presence, she'd finally been able to relax.

Until the viscount's recently reiterated invitation. This invitation had the added inducement of his father's personal handwritten solicitation as well. Her stomach tensed again. What would his parents be like?

She had met members of the Peerage before, and while Lord Hawkesbury and Lavinia were considerably easygoing, the Aynsley family was quite another matter. Caroline's father, the viscount, held no degree of warmth; his wife even less so. Would Lord Carmichael's family be stiff and formal, or would they possess something of their son's liveliness?

"I see you frowning. I am sorry if my words have—"

"No, no." She pushed her lips into a smile. "I appreciate your consideration, and your prayers. No, I'm just thinking about the viscount's family. I'm not used to staying with people I have never met."

"Then you and Catherine will be able to support each other through this great trial."

What?

He chuckled. "Don't look like that, I am only jesting. They are simply people, Serena. They eat and sleep much like everyone else. And I can say from personal experience, the Earl of Bevington and his wife are quite generous and kind. Besides, did you really think Harry could come from a family that was not so?"

"I gather he does not always care for the opinions of others, which might hold true for his family as well."

"I think you'll be surprised about how much he does value his parents' opinions," he said thoughtfully. "But enough of him. As I have to remind Catherine at times, strangers are but friends we have yet to meet."

The figure lying on his lap stirred, blinking sleepily. "I heard my name."

"Good afternoon, my darling."

As Jon murmured soft words to his wife, Serena huddled in her seat, trying to make herself invisible. Her thoughts moved to the viscount. She had not seen him since the evening of the Hawkesbury dinner, her severe menses the following day precluding a farewell to the viscount. But that had proved something of a relief. He puzzled her, this handsome charmer with his humor and consideration for others. She had found herself paying too much attention to him, laughing and smiling with him. She did not want to do so; she would *not* do so again, she told herself sternly. For if she did surely that could only lead to pain, and she had determined that no man would ever hurt her again.

She peeked across to where Catherine was smiling up at her husband, his head bent close to hers, their eyes only for each other. Her heart experienced a twinge and she looked away. If only romance might be available for all.

There was shifting in the carriage movements. Serena glanced outside. "We are slowing."

"Yes. It's quite steep here, but we are almost there." Jon gently tilted Catherine's chin. "How are you feeling now?"

"I will praise God when we finally stop."

The carriage began a careful turn, pulling between two stone pillars. Nearby stood a gatehouse, about twice the size of the one at Winthrop Manor. "I gather the house is somewhat grand?"

"Somewhat," Jon replied with a grin, as they traveled up a long drive lined with oaks.

Anticipation tingled within. "Does it have nice gardens? It is hard to see, but I imagine there is substantial parkland?"

"I think you'll find there is substantial everything here."

The trees thinned, revealing a wide, grassy parkland, immaculately maintained to resemble green velvet. Clumps of trees dotted the tops of low hills, above a string of ponds that curved to a wide lake, rippling faintly in the soft breeze. She glanced through the other window. Her breath caught. Beyond where two slopes verged, marked by a rocky peak, she glimpsed a valley beyond the hills, but before she could see more the drive was curving upward again, leaving her swinging to look behind, straining to see.

"Anyone would think you were excited to be here," Catherine said, before groaning.

"Darling." Jon's brow knit. "Can you hold on a few minutes more?"

"I'll t-try."

Serena met his worried glance and offered a smile she hoped was reassuring. "I'll stay with her when we arrive, as will Tilly. She's been wonderful these past days, more nurse than lady's maid. I'm sure our hosts will understand if we're unable to socialize tonight."

"Oh, but—"

"No, Jon. You at least know these people. I do not, so I'm sure they won't miss me."

He sighed. "I'll have the doctor come first thing—"

"N-no. J-just need rest," Catherine said, eyes closed.

Serena's silent prayers accompanied the creak and sway of the carriage as it climbed again. She peered out the window, mouth drying as Welmsley Hall revealed itself, golden in the mid-afternoon sun. Atop a hill, the house rose two stories high, centered by a magnificent dome. Banks of arch-topped windows, their glass gleaming in the sunshine, stretched between carved stone columns, whilst the roofline was adorned with battlements interspersed with Baroque-inspired statuary. Perfectly symmetrical. Perfectly proportioned. Altogether, it made for the most beautiful house she had ever seen.

"It is magnificent," she breathed.

Jon nodded, a smile touching his lips before his attention returned to her sister.

Her heart wrenched. How she hoped Catherine would feel better soon—and how she hoped their visit of sufficient duration for her to explore this grand, impressive building.

The carriage slowed then drew to a stop. A servant opened the door, and Jon exited before assisting Catherine to rise, but at her faltering motion, he swung her into his arms and moved to the shallow front steps. Serena collected her sister's reticule and her own and stepped down, as another liveried servant drew near, followed by an older man whose bearing and uniform declared his status as head servant. An exchange of words and Jon was rushed inside, followed by Tilly, who had come on the second carriage, along with Jon's valet and a vast quantity of luggage.

For a moment she stood uncertainly, the great carved stone doorway arched above.

"Miss Winthrop?"

A glance to her left and she saw Lord Carmichael hurrying towards her. She curtsied.

"A thousand apologies for my tardiness. We were expecting you yesterday." His brow knit. "Did I see Carlew carrying Lady Winthrop?"

"My sister has been unwell."

"I'm so sorry to hear that." He nodded to the footman, and then gestured her inside. "Please know we will do all we can to make her as comfortable as possible."

"Thank you." Her attempt at a smile faltered beneath his keen-eyed gaze.

"Truly, she will be well cared for." Her throat constricted at his soft words. "I suspect you might be weary as well."

"Nothing of any great import."

"Hmm." He eyed her for a moment, then motioned to the head servant, who had returned. "This is Peters, our rock." His lips curved in a smile. "Yes, that pun has been used before, but it remains true. Anything you need he will supply, won't you, Peters?"

"Of course, sir."

"And this is Anna." He beckoned forward a calm-looking lady around Catherine's age. "My mother believes every lady requires a personal maid, and I hope you will accept her services whilst you are here."

"Oh, but—"

"Please, Miss Winthrop. My mother would consider it extremely poor form if you were without. Now I expect you want to see your sister, or would you wish to see your room first?"

"Catherine, of course."

"Of course." He nodded to the assembled staff, sending them scurrying, then offered his arm. "Now, shall I lead the way?"

Serena stared at his proffered arm. It was ridiculous to be concerned about touching him. Ridiculous, and yet . . . She glanced up, catching a look of something like surprised disappointment in his eyes before he smiled gently.

"Miss Winthrop," he said in a lowered voice quite unlike his usual gaiety. "You will never be in danger with me."

Her breath caught. What did he know? Had Jon said something?

He sighed. "Now I seem to have alarmed you even more, when I only wanted to reassure. Please, forgive my unfortunate choice of words, and allow me to escort you." His brows rose, his eyes kind. "Unless you would prefer Peters to do so?"

And let the staff think the viscount had done something wrong? She swallowed, placed her hand gingerly on his outstretched forearm. "Thank you, sir."

She worked to ignore the feel of corded muscle in his arm, worked to ignore his teasing scent of amber and warm honey, as he led her through the black-and-white tiled vestibule. Their passage continued through a great hall lined with magnificent paintings, then up carpeted stairs, through another door, then along a great corridor dotted with Chinese urns and settees at even intervals. Along the way, he gave commentary about the house design, which ancestors stared from the walls, the origins of some of the furniture, which included pieces by Chippendale and Sheraton. She hoped not to reveal too much gaucherie by her astonishment and wonder. The interior was gracious, opulent, and elegant, yet obviously a much-loved family home, as evidenced by the personal touches everywhere, such as the collection of seashells displayed on a small marble table.

Within minutes she was standing outside a wide wooden door. The viscount rapped on it once and smiled as she released his arm. "See? That did not hurt, did it?"

She gulped down her reply as Tilly poked out her head.

"Oh, miss." Tilly opened the door wider to admit her. Serena turned, once more catching concern in the viscount's expression.

"Miss Winthrop, please do not hesitate to call for anything. I'm sure Carlew will remember, but I hope the modest Winthrop ladies will also come to treat this house as their home."

Gratitude at his thoughtfulness filled her chest, filled her eyes. She blinked once, twice, then gazed up at him, growing freshly aware that his eyes were a muddy sap green, fringed with indecently long dark lashes the color of burnt umber. She could see where little smile lines had creased the corners, though they weren't creased now. "Thank you, sir."

His smile hitched up one side, then he bowed, she inclined her head, and Tilly closed the door behind her.

ℜ Chapter Seven

Nearly an hour later, Serena and Jon followed a servant as they retraced their steps back to the grand entrance hall. Elaborately dressed footmen opened the gold-etched double doors leading to another suite of rooms, then another, revealing the enfilade traveling down the length of the house. Everywhere she looked, magnificence demanded her attention. Plaster-carved ceilings competed with rich tapestried wall hangings; gilt-laden tables held hand-painted Sèvres porcelain. Each piece was a masterpiece in itself, but together, while still somehow harmonious, it nearly overwhelmed her senses. How would she ever find time to fully appreciate such artistry?

Inside, nerves waged war with guilt, as she tried to believe Tilly's assurances following her earlier offer to assist Catherine. "Miss Serena, really the best thing is for madam to sleep, and for you to go tidy yourself. If you and his lordship want to be helpful, you'll let her rest."

Anna had led Serena to her room, a beautifully decorated room of soft lavender, where she found her gowns already put away and a hot bath awaiting. Too nervous to soak as she might usually prefer, she had quickly washed before allowing Anna to select clothes and dress her—and her hair. Anna had seemed to know what was appropriate, her praise of Serena's hair color and length a boost to her confidence. But it had been a long time since she'd had a maid do the things necessity had forced her to learn to do for herself.

The nerves took hold again as their passage through the house continued, Serena wiping damp hands on the skirt of her pomona green silk gown. She touched Jon's arm and whispered, "Do I look presentable?"

He leaned closer. "You look very nice. But remember, they're just people."

"And this is just a house?" She raised her brows.

Jon smiled, and they were led into a primrose drawing room seemingly twice the size of Winthrop's largest reception room. Butterflies danced in her stomach as they neared a settee, upon which two graying-haired personages were seated. At their imperious expressions, her chest grew tight. Why was she here? If only Catherine were here!

Jon gently squeezed her hand, and she lifted her chin, schooling her features to something she hoped appeared confident.

"My Lord and Lady Bevington," Jon said with a short bow. "Good afternoon. Thank you once again for your kind hospitality." His words met with nods and murmurs of pleasure at renewed acquaintanceship. "May I present my wife's sister, Miss Serena Winthrop."

Serena managed a careful curtsy. If ever there were a time to remember Haverstock's lessons, it was now.

"You are both very welcome. Please." Lady Bevington gestured to the settee.

As Serena seated herself Lord Carmichael entered. "Ah, I see you've all met. You remember Carlew's recent change of fortune, don't you? It's Lord Winthrop now, of course."

"Of course." Lady Bevington inclined her head. "I was sorry to learn your wife is unwell."

As Jon acknowledged his appreciation of her solicitude, Serena cut a look at the viscount, the recipient of a frown from his father. He shrugged slightly, and she resumed her study of the vase of roses on the low table between them. Was the earl upset with their late arrival? Or was he annoyed at his son's late entrance?

"Miss Winthrop, I trust everything meets to your satisfaction?"

"Yes, my lady." She met the countess's gaze. "Thank you for your hospitality."

"We do what we can." The older lady gave a small smile.

The lines marking the earl's forehead eased a fraction as his attention returned to Serena. "You and your brother possess quite similar looks."

"My brother?"

"Miss Winthrop is Jon's cousin, *third* cousin in fact," Lord Carmichael corrected, giving Jon a swift, amused look before returning his attention to his father. "She is Jon's wife's sister."

"I see." But his wrinkled brow suggested the earl did not.

Had Lord Bevington not heard Jon's introduction? To be sure, the family connection was somewhat complicated, their family name often confused with that belonging to the title. Her musings were cut short as a knock prefaced the arrival of two footmen and a tray of tea things.

"I expect you must be famished after your journey," said the countess. "We dine at six, country hours you know, so I trust this will suffice until then."

"Thank you, Lady Bevington," Jon and Serena echoed.

The next half hour was one which had Serena wishing she'd paid more attention to her lessons in deportment, as she strove for poise amidst the careful consumption of tea and cakes, and conversation. Eventually the earl turned to her, his acknowledgment the first since his observation about her resemblance to Jon.

"Miss Winthrop, I trust you will have a pleasant stay here at Welmsley Hall."

It sounded like a dismissal, and she was half inclined to rise, but forced herself to remain seated, to straighten her spine. "I cannot fail to do so, sir, when surrounded by such obliging staff and such a lovely house."

"You like Welmsley then?"

"It is the most beautiful house I have ever seen," she said truthfully, then smiled.

The earl's brows rose, before his features relaxed and he offered a charming smile reminiscent of his son's. "I have always felt it has a certain . . ."

The pause extended, drew out even more. Was she supposed to offer a suggestion? Was it a test? "Presence?"

"Exactly! My father spent a great deal of money reversing the rooms—but wait." He glanced at his son. "You have not shown her our treasure?"

"No, not yet."

"Then, Miss Winthrop, may I encourage you to go with my son as he shows you Welmsley's best feature." He glanced at the mantelpiece upon which rested a gold clock. "I think now a good time. You may go too, Winthrop, if you wish."

"Thank you, sir." Jon pushed to his feet. "I believe I will."

Accepting his hand, she rose and offered the earl and countess a small curtsy before following the viscount through another door and along a corridor. "What treasure?" she whispered to her brother-in-law.

"You'll see," he said with a grin.

Lord Carmichael stopped before another door, glancing over his shoulder at Serena. "Now, you must promise not to tell anyone of our treasure. It is a secret, after all, and has been in the family for hundreds of years."

"Of course." Anticipation thrummed within.

"Promise?" He raised a brow.

"Would such a misdemeanor ensure a visit from the Runners?"

He chuckled. "I somehow doubt the illustrious gentlemen from Bow Street would deem such an infraction worthy of their notice. Now, are you ready?"

At her nod, he opened the door.

To the outside. To a stone-flagged terrace. To a magnificent panorama.

Letting go of Jon's arm, she moved to the balustrade, her eyes drinking in the splendor. A vast valley, glowing golden in the late afternoon light, stretched out as far as the eye could see. Purpled ridges, some topped with woods of deepest green, others bare and craggy, created the rims of the valley bowl. A river glinted silver far below, and small ponds shone like polished diamonds, as the lowering sun lengthened velvety shadows. Her throat constricted, her eyes filling at such perfect beauty.

Serena inhaled then let out a long breath. She had once heard Lavinia talk of the power of music, where a perfect symmetry of chords and song could deeply move her soul and emotions. She now understood. It was like God Himself had painted this majestic masterpiece.

"Well? What do you think, Miss Winthrop?"

"It is almost too beautiful," she whispered.

"I think so, too."

Serena glanced across at the viscount, studying her with lips curled in one corner. Was he displeased with her reaction? She didn't gush; she couldn't. Not that she cared what he thought of her.

"Look down," Jon's deep voice encouraged.

She placed a hand upon the railing and peered down. A series of tiered gardens was carved into the steep hillside: a garden of brightly colored roses, a knot garden, a parterre. And far, far below, a series of walking trails and bridges crossed a tiny stream, which fed into a lake, beside which perched—she squinted—a Grecian-style temple.

Oh, to paint this! What would she use? Magenta, vermilion, no, carmine, then for the far-off sweep of trees, Prussian blue . . . Although watercolors could never do this justice. It should be the rich jeweled tones of oils: raw sienna, Indian yellow, Alexandria blue. The excitement grew. Not too much, of course, otherwise it would—

But . . . No.

Serena stilled, then stepped back, the view still powerfully transfixing, but her heart had dropped a little.

"Miss Winthrop?"

She forced a smile, but didn't meet the viscount's eyes, could only meet his snowy starched neckcloth. "Thank you for showing me. Your treasure is priceless."

"It makes a pretty picture, does it not?"

Serena nodded. Oh, no. It would make the most stunning landscape imaginable.

Just not one ever painted by her.

✻

Later, after their return to the drawing room, his guests' apologetic yawns compelled his mother to release them from attending the more formal dinner to eat a meal in their rooms—"for we all know that trip is arduous at the best of times, and you must be worried about your dear wife and sister." Harry removed to the library and sank into his favorite armchair, his thoughts wandering back to that moment on the terrace.

Miss Serena Winthrop. She of the tranquil aristocratic countenance and flashing eyes. Her reaction was everything Carlew had said it might be, a profound appreciation for a landscape carved by God. For some reason her response pleased him; nothing of the simpering miss about her. He grimaced. Too many overly effusive guests had prattled on, or worse, given it barely a glance, and prattled instead about the house. When that happened, he felt a sense of hurt, like he'd exposed a part of his heart and been snubbed. Like father, like son, the men of Welmsley had always regarded the house as mere audience to the orchestra of color and majesty playing across the tors and deep within the valley.

So the way she seemed to soak in the beauty—her fair hair wisping in the afternoon radiance, her eyes glimmering, that small smile— had caused his heart to glow in a way he'd not experienced for some time. He'd almost been able to see her mind ticking, planning out the shades like a true artist. Many had tried, including his grandmother, but the sumptuousness of the valley always precluded success. He could bet the Bevington silver Miss Serena would also try, and fail. He frowned, a vague memory stirring. Or was she not an artist now?

"Son."

"Father."

Something like a smile twisted his father's lips as he seated himself in the armchair opposite. Although genial, Father didn't smile too often, which had made his earlier smile at Miss Winthrop's comment all the more surprising.

"Carlew settled in?"

"I believe so."

"Is it Carlew or Winthrop? I never seem to remember."

"I don't think he's too concerned."

"Hmph." His father's brow lowered. "I don't like his wife being ill."

"I imagine none of them are enraptured by the fact."

"The doctor?"

"Peters has sent a request he attend tomorrow."

"Good, good."

Silence fell between them. The lines on his father's forehead grooved more deeply these days, the hair grew a little grayer. Father was getting old. He fought the guilt that slithered hot and sure into his chest. Perhaps he should come home more often . . . But Father had always made it clear he did not care for Harry's ideas about the estate, about investing for the future, nor did he especially care for Harry's penchant for fast living, a view he was bound to espouse in coming days—if not in this very conversation.

"You think he's here because he wants more investors?"

"Jon is here because I invited him. Whether he wants your investment I do not know. He has certainly never mentioned anything of the sort to me."

"Hmm." His father shot him a keen look. "And why did you invite her? Something your mother and I should know?"

He strove for patience. Father's desire for Harry to marry and produce an heir was renowned. "She is the sister of Carlew's wife, Catherine."

"But I still don't understand why she is here. Doesn't she have parents?"

He thought carefully. Father was somewhat punctilious about breeding, and given his antipathy to Harry's propensity for a flutter, the knowledge that her father was a known gambler might not auger well for Miss Winthrop's stay. "Her father, the late baron, is dead, and her mother is, shall we say, not especially easy."

"What's the name?"

Harry stared at him. Did he not remember the introductions from earlier? "She is Lord Winthrop's daughter."

For a moment his father was silent. Then, "Ah. The fool who lost all his money?"

"Yes."

His father eyed him sternly, but for once did not begin to sermonize on the evils of gambling hells and the like, for which Harry felt a modicum of relief.

"Is this young lady a possible candidate?"

"Forgive my ignorance, Father. A candidate for what?"

His father snorted. "Don't play the silly jackanapes with me. Should your mother be looking to hand her coronet to this young lady one day?"

"I'm afraid she is far too young for me. Why I might be called a cradle snatcher, and that would never do. And I have a strong suspicion Carlew might not wish it."

"Carlew? What has he got to say about it?"

"Well, he *is* the head of the family . . ."

"And what is wrong with our family that he should object, I'd like to know?"

"Nothing, of course, sir. He does not object, hence his pleasure at visiting." Their stay would not bode well should Father take a pet against his best friend. "I rather think he would prefer Miss Winthrop to settle somewhere closer to home." One day, in the future, to someone without Harry's own issues.

"Hmph."

He forced his features to maintain the illusion of indifference as his father scowled.

"You mean he objects to *you*? Well, the man is not a complete fool, then."

"Thank you, Father," he said drily.

"Who wants their charge marrying a gambler?"

And there it was. His smile grew strained.

"How old is she?"

"Eighteen, nineteen." He shrugged. "I'm not sure."

"That's nothing. Your mother was seventeen when I married her, at the grand old age of thirty-four, and here you are three years younger."

"Four years," he murmured.

Father's bushy brows pushed together. "She seems older."

Harry nodded. Her poise added a sense of maturity.

"And she certainly doesn't look at you with stars in her eyes."

"No, she does not." She barely looked at him at all.

"Oho! But you'd like her to."

"Father, I have no wish to be rude, but I fear your advancing years are muddling your ability to reason just a tad."

Fortunately, his father smiled—well, the corner of his mouth pushed up for a second or two. "I'm prepared to let that slide for the moment."

What, Harry's rudeness or his denial of attraction?

"Tell me, do you still have a thing for the widow?"

He felt his neck heat. "Father—"

"Well, this will be an interesting few weeks of it." Father pushed to his feet. "Perhaps your mother might finally get those grandchildren she's wanted for years."

"She already has two," Harry reminded him. His sister wasn't expecting again, was she?

"But they ain't yours, so won't be of any use to the earldom, will they?"

He bit his tongue as his father chortled and walked away.

The earldom. His spirits sinking, he thought over the exchange, and disquietude filled him as he stared out into the blackness of night.

🜲 Chapter Eight

THE FOLLOWING MORNING, having breakfasted in her room, Serena went to visit her sister, and found her sitting up in bed, nibbling on a piece of toast, a teacup and saucer on a tray over her lap.

Catherine's eyes brightened. "Good morning."

"It is now," Serena replied. "You had us quite worried yesterday."

"I did not feel at all the thing. But a good sleep helped."

"Jon must be relieved."

"Oh, yes. He was here earlier, but I sent him off to ride with Lord Carmichael. Poor Jon, he seemed quite haggard. I hope the fresh air will pick him up."

"It's good to see the rose in your cheeks. Speaking of fresh air, have you seen the view?"

"I have not left the room, so no."

"Oh, Catherine, it is simply glorious! Like something a Renaissance artist might have painted in one of those books Papa bought for me."

Her sister smiled. "Did you find it inspiring?"

"Yes—I mean, no." Her spirits drooped. "But still, when you are able, you must come see." She lowered her voice so Tilly wouldn't hear. "The earl calls it his treasure."

"How intriguing! Well, I shall soon. Jon tells me the doctor will attend sometime later today. I cannot help but think such concern a touch precipitous."

"He cares for you."

Her sister gave her sweet smile. "He does, doesn't he?"

After conversing a little longer, then waiting as her sister got dressed, Serena was finally able to introduce her to the terrace and its magnificent view. Again, her heart throbbed strangely, as if having finally recognized something she was supposed to have always known. A peculiar feeling, something like a subtle tightening then release in her soul, but one she experienced whenever she came across a scene of pure loveliness.

"It is breathtaking," Catherine finally said.

"It is pure perfection! I could make a study of the valley all day long."

"But not today," said a deeper voice.

She froze. Then turned. Joined her sister in curtsying a greeting to Lord Carmichael.

He bowed to her sister. "I am so pleased to see you have recovered."

"Thank you, sir."

"I wonder if you have had the chance to meet with my parents?"

"Not yet, I confess."

"Not to worry. They are quite relaxed about such things, and mornings can be a trifle challenging, can't they?"

"Only if you stay up too late," Serena murmured.

"I'm sorry?" He turned to her, green-gold eyes glinting. "Did you say something, Miss Winthrop?"

"Nothing worth repeating."

"I thought so." Ignoring her gasp, he offered an arm to her sister. "Now, if you feel ready, may I escort you both to the morning room? My mother and sister await you there."

Serena eyed his broad back as she followed them inside. Had he meant to sound so rude? A pang struck her. Or was she merely receiving a taste of her own ill-mannered medicine?

A short time later she was perched decorously on a striped settee, listening politely as the older ladies conversed with Catherine. Lady Melanie Rochdale appeared to be slightly older than Lord Carmichael, her early thirties at least, and boasted similar coloring to her brother, her dark hair dressed carefully, green eyes sparkling.

But where his face wore traces of a tan, hers was quite pale, giving the impression she rarely ventured outdoors. Her manners, too, were less lively than his, but still carried a measure of warmth more like the viscount than his parents. Beside her sat a small honey-blonde girl, perhaps three or four, who had been introduced as Eleanor, but whom her uncle called Ellie. She obviously adored him, her big blue eyes following him around the room, to the exclusion of anything or anyone else.

"Lady Winthrop, I trust you and your sister will avail yourselves of Welmsley's many amenities." Lady Rochdale smiled amiably. "We have very fine stables, and there are a number of excellent trails."

"I look forward to it," said Catherine.

"And you, Miss Winthrop. Do you ride?"

"Only if necessary, ma'am."

"Please, call me Melanie. Ma'am sounds too much like one is addressing the Queen."

Serena smiled. "Very well, then. And if I might say so, I prefer Serena."

"Such a pretty name. It suits you, you know. You look as poised as if *you* were the Queen. Tell me, have you made your presentation yet?"

The ease dispelled in a trickle of nerves. "No."

"I imagine you will next year then. It is terribly exciting, isn't it, Mama?"

Her mother murmured an affirmative, and Melanie continued, "I thoroughly enjoyed my first season. Well, all of my seasons!" She gave a gust of laughter.

Serena offered a polite smile, willing herself to relax.

"All the shopping, and balls, and gowns, and—"

"Melanie, if you insist on speaking of such things you will clear the room of those who claim any right to manhood," her brother said. "Indeed, I believe even now Miss Winthrop's eyes to be glazing over. Enough!"

Serena peeked at him, thankful for his intervention.

"Miss Winthrop"—no "Serena" for the countess—"Do you mean to say you do not like shopping?"

"I have not acquired the desire for it," she said carefully. Papa's finances—or lack thereof—had not left her with the capacity to indulge in any purchases more than necessary.

The countess frowned. "How extraordinary."

"And you do not like riding, I gather. May I ask what you do enjoy?"

Melanie's face wore an expression of bright interest, not condemnation, so Serena was almost at her ease to think of something other than—

"Art, I believe?" the viscount offered.

She stared at him, unease rippling within. How did—?

"Oh, you and Papa will get on famously then," Melanie said. "He's not much of an artist himself, claims he's too busy running the estate for such things." This was said with a slanted look at her brother. "But he does have a marvelous art collection, doesn't he, Mama?"

"Yes," the countess said, eyeing her son with a wrinkled brow.

"Oh, and you must have a chat with Grandmama. She really *is* an artist. Or was. Her hands are a little crippled now—"

"My dear, must you share all the family secrets?" her mother said in a weary tone.

Melanie chuckled, offering the viscount a saucy look. "Not all."

"For which I'm sure our guests will be profoundly grateful," the viscount said with a yawn. "One does not desire one's guests to be completely bored by such tedious tales." He rose. "Now, is there a small male child requiring avuncular attention? Where is Tom?"

"He went off with Peters."

"So he could be anywhere, then. Very well." He held out a hand to young Ellie. "Shall I abduct this princess then?"

His sister laughed. "Abduct away."

He leaned down, pulling the excited girl into his arms and then onto his shoulders, where she grasped his face with her tiny hands. "Ahoy there, milady." He readjusted her fingers. "This face is the only one I possess, so must be treated with care."

Clutching his niece firmly, he offered a careful bow, "Pray excuse us for a moment, while we go find a brother."

Warmth filled Serena's heart as he departed, the little girl laughing at his silly antics. How unexpectedly delightful! Her own father and uncles had certainly never behaved with her in such a free and enjoyable way. Who would have guessed the sophisticated viscount capable of such—

"Atrocious behavior," his mother muttered.

What?

"Mama, Harry is simply enjoying being an uncle. You know he doesn't see the children often."

"And whose fault is that?"

Melanie's features tightened and she turned to Catherine and Serena. "Please excuse my brother's high spirits."

"Of course," murmured Catherine.

Serena glanced at the countess, then back at Melanie. "Affection need not be excused."

The countess blinked. Melanie beamed, her approval reinforced later, under cover of the noisy return of the men and her children, with a whispered, "I knew I should like you."

Gradually the tension of the first few days dissipated. Catherine seemed better, a new light filling her eyes after the doctor's visit. Jon's relief shone in his quick wit, for which Harry was grateful after some less-than-relaxed encounters with his parents. Melanie's kindly affection had a way of layering the days with ease. Her decision to befriend the sisters was a comfort, as he was at something of a loss as to how to entertain the younger.

Apart from a visit to Buxton, during which his guests had marveled at the Crescent and its adjoining Great Stables, and the antiquity of the parish church of St. Anne, before taking refreshment at the equally timeworn Old Hall Hotel, Miss Serena Winthrop had remained cool and somewhat detached.

She did not ride. She did not read. She did not particularly care for music. But—he spied the golden head outside, descending the stairs—apparently she *did* care for the gardens.

He hurried after her now. "Miss Winthrop?"

She paused at the entrance to the rose terrace. "Oh. Hello."

"You walk alone?"

"Catherine and Jon were out driving, and I did not like to intrude upon their time." Her lips pushed up on one side. "I fear my presence provides enough intrusion as it is."

"Nonsense. I know your sister is very glad for your company."

Her brows lifted. "And you know this how?"

"Jon tells me."

"Oh." She moved away, peering at a pink rose that climbed on a trellis against the stone wall. She placed a hand on the stones then leaned close to smell the bloom, before glancing at him, edging back when she saw him watching.

He strode near, plucked the bloom and gave it to her, to her murmured thanks.

"I did not realize your interest in gardens reached such heights, or is it depths?" He waved a hand at the steps snaking down to the lowest level of the tiered gardens.

"It is quite different from Winthrop's." Her hand brushed a Buxus hedge. "The gardeners must enjoy the climb to trim such things."

"Fortunately their equipment does not need to travel with them." He led her over to the stone balustrade and pointed to a stone building half hidden by vines. "See these small buildings? Each terrace contains sufficient equipment for the staff to effectively maintain each garden."

"How extravagant."

"I prefer to think expedient," he said. "It was my idea."

She slanted a glance up at him. "You surprise me."

"By having ideas? I am wounded by such talk."

"As it is mostly *your* talk I gather you don't mind harming yourself."

He chuckled, appreciation for her wit warming his heart. He began pointing out various other elements of the garden. "See the little temple down there? A mere folly, of course, for we do not worship Diana."

"I'm pleased to hear it. To worship Diana would be folly indeed."

"Indeed." He cut another look at the sparkling blue eyes. Her sharp wit seemed at odds with her countenance, her willingness to banter surprising him as much as her humor. "It is quite lovely, although requires a fairly strenuous walk, and one I would not encourage on one's own. Perhaps when your sister is more able we could make a party of it."

"Does your mother mind if I walk alone?"

He blinked. "I . . . I don't know. I'm sure she'd prefer for you to have company, should there be need for assistance."

She gave a tiny nod. The moments stretched between them.

"Miss Winthrop? You appear deep in thought."

"Forgive me. It is very good-hearted of her to be so concerned, but I cannot help but wonder why ladies are considered so much more liable to require assistance than men."

"I beg your pardon?"

"Catherine and I used to wander the grounds of Winthrop with nary a second thought. The only time we felt endangered was when we accidentally walked into the bull yard, and even then it was only because the farmer had moved Big John minutes before. But no harm ever fell to us. Why, we only saw a grass snake once, and even then it was such a small thing I still don't know why Catherine screamed."

"I wonder if your sister remembers things that way. I may have to ask her."

Amusement tweaked her lips. "I assure you it *is* true."

"You've given me reason to expect to hear nothing but truth from you, Miss Winthrop."

Her cheeks pinked, her gaze faltered. "I will remind Catherine of such things before you ask that question. She's very obliging, you know."

"It is good to have obliging sisters."

"And that is the thing"—she met his gaze again in a look almost challenging—"I think because ladies *are* quite willing to oblige, they do not perform such things that will lead into trouble."

"You believe men more prone to adventuresome behavior?"

"Did you not visit India with Jon?"

"For a short visit, yes."

"Was that not dangerous at times?"

He thought back to the life-sapping heat, the disease, the exotic animals so filled with beauty and threat. "At times."

"See?"

He stared into the blue eyes, so filled with sweet indignation, his thoughts whirling as to why she felt so strongly about such a thing. Something deep within desired to understand.

"Men court danger, whereas women are expected to remain quiet, at home." She sighed. "I just don't understand why ladies must always be thought of as requiring assistance."

"Perhaps it is for your protection?"

She stilled, her cheeks paling, and half turned away.

"Miss Winthrop? Forgive me if have I said something to upset you."

She nodded, but refused to meet his eyes, and she moved to the steps as if to ascend. After a moment she said in a low voice, "Offering protection is all well and good, but only serves its purpose by being available when needed."

Harry frowned. She spoke as though she had been wounded in some way. But surely Jon would have mentioned something.

They proceeded up the hewn stone stairs, Harry offering his arm as they neared the upper, slightly steeper steps. Despite her mur- mured thanks, he was conscious of her stiffness with him, an appre- hension unlike most young ladies of his acquaintanceship. That tension revealed itself again when they reached the terrace and she instantly dropped her hand. His heart panged a little. What could he do to remove this unease and for her to grow comfortable with him?

"If I might return to our previous conversation—"

Her eyes widened, as if in fear.

"About young ladies being willing to oblige others." He smiled in reassurance.

"Oh."

"Does it hold true for all young ladies?"

"I cannot say."

"Yourself, for instance?"

She studied him warily. "I'm afraid I don't take your meaning."

"I simply wish to ask if you would mind obliging my sister in a small matter." His grin grew. "She requested I find you, and I meant to ask before, but got distracted by all your talk of gardens and social reform."

"My talk?"

"Not that it wasn't fascinating. It was." In part because it was the most he'd heard her speak. "Actually, it was quite interesting to learn you do not feel it necessary to scold me in *every* conversation."

"I do not do that, sir!"

"Alas, I fear it might happen again right now."

"I do not . . ." Her brow wrinkled, and she walked a few feet away, before turning, her expression haughty. "I apologize if I have given that impression."

"Now, now. I much prefer talking to the young lady of honesty, even if she does dislike me, and her comments sting at times."

She stared at him. Shook her head. "I . . . I do not dislike you, sir. In fact—" she bit her lip.

"In fact, what?" he asked softly.

"In fact, you have surprised me."

"That word again."

"Your previous manner has led me to believe you care for nothing more than how one should arrange one's neckcloth or hair or the fit of one's coat."

Was she always so incisive in her observations? "Such things are perhaps not so foolish to those who understand that being dressed respectably tends to command respect."

A contemplative look crossed her features. "Perhaps you are right. Although . . ."

"Although what, Miss Winthrop?"

"I would have thought a man's *actions* true indication of whether he deserves respect."

He strove for nonchalance as her words prickled within. Did she mean to cast aspersions on his character, or did his discomfort stem from acknowledgment that in comparison to some men—Carlew, for instance—Harry's actions had proved rather less than respectable at times?

Such discouraging musings were cut short as he became aware she was speaking again.

". . . confess I find it most puzzling."

"What puzzles you, Miss Winthrop?"

She eyed him, a question etched in her brow. "Here, you seem different, like you do not need to play the part of the foppish fellow, such as what I have observed in your warm and easy manner with your niece and nephew."

"You object?" His heart strangely strained for her response. Did she disapprove like his parents?

"Not at all. I simply find it hard to reconcile such kindly affection with the man of society I've witnessed before."

He nodded slowly. "And yet I'm not the only one causing others to wonder."

"I beg your pardon?"

"Here you are in such lovely surrounds, and I have yet to see you hold a pencil. I cannot understand why an artist does not want to produce art."

"I . . ." She gave an impatient shake of her head. "How do you know this?"

"How do you think?"

"I did not think Jon such a blabberer."

"Your sister is proud of your talent."

"Catherine?"

He nodded. "You *are* an artist, are you not?"

"I . . . was."

Was? He pushed the frown away. "But you could be again."

"I . . . I don't know."

"I hope you will, for if you are as talented as your sister believes, then perhaps you are the one to do justice to such a view." He swept a hand toward the valley.

"Oh, but . . ." She shook her head slowly, almost sadly. "No, I could not."

"Really? You would leave here without making the attempt?"

She blinked, the dark-tipped lashes seeming incongruous with such fair hair framing her face, her face with the widened blue eyes. Her beautiful, widened blue eyes.

His heart thudded. He swallowed. "This has been an extraordinary conversation, would you not agree?"

"Yes." Her brow knit, and she excused herself to find his sister.

Harry watched her leave, curiosity trailing after her, even as his connoisseur gaze noted how her simple, inexpensive gown clung to the graceful curves of her youthful frame.

He averted his eyes, suddenly hating himself. The conversation had felt too raw, too honest, yet somehow too much like a . . . like a flirtation.

His heart wrenched. And wasn't he supposed to treat her as the younger sister he'd never had?

🦋 Chapter Nine

"Thank you for coming, my dear," Lady Rochdale said, gesturing to a seat beside her. "I presume Harry found you?"

"He asked if I might assist you in some way."

"It is about Tom, really."

Serena smiled politely, brows raised.

"About something you had given him yesterday."

Yesterday . . . What had she been doing? Playing with the children, both delightful in their own ways. Tom so bold, Eleanor so sweet. Serena's interactions with young children had been somewhat limited, but she'd always enjoyed getting to know them as people. Perhaps that was due to feeling overlooked for much of her life, too.

"I see you do not ask me. Very well, I shall have to show you." She pulled a somewhat crumpled piece of paper from her reticule.

Serena's breath caught.

Yesterday. The weather had turned cool, sending billowing fog up from the valley, forcing them indoors from their game of hide-and-seek in the garden. At a loss to know what to do with them, she'd been immensely relieved when Tom started talking about a book he was reading, which made mention of a phoenix. When Ellie asked what one looked like, Serena had tried to explain, but her words could not do it justice. Tom's exasperation led him to seek paper and pencil, whereupon he completed a clumsy sketch. Serena had quickly added a couple of details, making the creature less dragon and more bird. From that, Tom had demanded she draw a dragon, which she had happily undertaken, before obliging him by making a quick sketch of their puppy, Polly, whom she learned really belonged to the viscount, but lived at their house when he was away.

"Can you please draw me?" Ellie had asked in her baby voice.

How could she refuse? So in a few quick strokes she had captured a very simple likeness. Tom had been impressed—"You know that actually looks like her!"—then demanded his own portrait, after which Ellie asked for one of both of them with Uncle Harry's puppy.

It was this last that Lady Rochdale now held. "This is your work, I believe?"

"Yes."

The other lady shook her head. "It is ridiculous . . ."

What? All the time as her pencil had flitted across the page, she had enjoyed the moment of release, as if a thousand blocked streams had given way, enjoyed the moment of spontaneous freedom, enjoyed how her fingers flew and her creativity seemed to gush forth. Considering she had not drawn anything in months, she'd thought her simple sketches actually rather good.

"Ridiculous," Melanie continued, "how one so young can be so talented."

Oh! Pleasure warmed her chest. "I am glad you like them."

"Like them? I showed Mama and she agreed you have, I believe her words were, 'an uncommon amount of talent.'"

"It is just a simple sketch," she felt the need to say.

"You should not apologize for possessing such a gift." The other lady leaned close. "I know Papa would dearly love to draw so well, but he, alas, has more desire than talent I'm afraid, much like his daughter." She flashed a smile, pulling back, eyeing Serena intently. "Something must be done."

"I beg your pardon?"

"Tell me, do you paint as well as you draw?"

"Lady Rochdale—"

"Melanie."

"Melanie. Please excuse me, but I do not see what possible relevance that has."

"You shall. So do you? Paint, I mean, as well as you draw?"

Memories arose, before Mr. Goode's attentions had grown too pronounced, when he had observed and admired her work, then arranged for her painting to be hung in Haverstock's foyer. Jon's words from a week ago chased on the heels of those memories. Why *had* she permitted someone evil to steal her joy?

Serena lifted her chin, eyeing her new friend. "Better."

"Good." Another smile flashed. "Watercolors or oils?"

"I . . . I have not had as much experience in oils. It is not considered ladylike."

"Ladylike? I'd like to know who made that rule."

Serena's lips lifted and a short laugh escaped.

"I see you agree with me. Good. I like people who agree with me."

"It saves such a lot of effort in having to see things from their point of view."

Melanie chuckled. "Harry said you had a wicked tongue."

He'd talked about her?

"Now, do you have your paints with you?"

"I . . . no." She gestured to the drawings. "These are sketches, that is all. I have not painted in months."

"Why ever not? Well, that can be remedied. I will take you to meet my grandmother. She will enjoy meeting a fellow artist."

Polite enquiry soon helped her discover the dowager countess was something of an amateur landscape artist whose defining work—a landscape of the valley—had been cut short by rheumatism. This led to Melanie sharing other tidbits of information about her family members. It seemed she relished the chance for a girlish chat.

"For you see, Mama and Papa are not terribly inclined to gossip, and Harry is not often here, and when he is, his tales of society, while terribly amusing, tend to be a little more lewd than what I want to hear."

Sorely tempted to ask just how lewd Melanie preferred her stories, Serena bit her tongue instead, as her impressions concerning the viscount shifted once more. Lord Carmichael was something of a paradox: an affectionate uncle, a foppish dandy, a gallant gentleman whose warm interest earlier had almost made her see just why Jon valued his friendship. Then to hear such an account from his sister, more in keeping with his rakish reputation . . .

Which was the true viscount?

SERENA SMILED AS she walked back to her room to rest before dinner. Lady Rochdale's manner was far more in keeping with her brother's than was first evident, their warm geniality so far removed from Serena's own upbringing. While Serena and Catherine had always been close, and their parents considerate in their own ways, cordiality had never been one of Mama's strengths. And while Catherine was all that was good and kind, she had always possessed a strong measure of reserve, proved in the way she'd hidden her regard for Jon for so many years. Her smile faded. People had often commented on Serena's impassivity. Did they really see her as being so very aloof?

She climbed the great staircase, pausing on the landing to study a magnificent painting, a Reynolds, like Papa's—she'd thought the style familiar. The oils glowed luminous, depicting a view of Welmsley from the valley; she recognized the tor jutting to one side. With an appreciative nod, she continued to her room.

Just as she turned the door handle, her sister called to her.

"Catherine! You're up."

She nodded, eyes softly shining as she gestured Serena to join her. "I must talk with you."

"Of course."

Serena entered her sister's room, surprised to see Jon rise from an armchair near the window. "Hello, Jon." She gave a small smile. "You were missed earlier."

"Carmichael?"

"Yes. He was forced to talk with me."

"No!" Catherine said, eyes filled with tease. "Did you manage?"

"Barely." She glanced at her brother-in-law.

His eyes were filled with something—but not tease. Instead he seemed concerned. "You do not mind his manner?"

"No."

"He is being a gentleman?" he persisted.

"Jon," Catherine said reproachfully.

"Of course he is. I assure you, he is being the perfect host, nothing more. Why," Serena glanced between them, "surely you cannot think he'd be anything but? He's hardly likely to flirt with me."

"Of course not." Catherine eyed her husband and nodded to the door. "Now Jon will go."

He rose, his lips pushing into a rueful smile. "I will see you both later."

"Of course."

When the door closed, Catherine sat on the bed, hands clasped. "I know he seems a mite protective, but ever since Julia . . ."

"I understand."

Julia Carlew, Jonathan's half sister, had eloped with a former friend of Jon's. Apart from a couple of letters, nothing had been heard, despite Jon employing a number of private enquiry agents to find the scandalous couple.

"But I cannot believe anyone would find *me* a threat to the viscount's bachelorhood."

"But when a man is ready to fall in love . . ." Her sister's eyebrows rose.

"Lord Carmichael? Surely not. Besides, how would you know even if he was? At Haverstock's I heard his name whispered many a time as being considered one of England's biggest flirts. I assure you, I do not find that man in any way attractive." She ignored the twinge of conscience as she continued. "And after what happened, I still have no desire for"—she swallowed—"any form of affection from any man, so you can let him know that also."

"Who? The viscount?" her sister smiled slyly.

"Jon!" She pushed down the shudder of revulsion elicited by the thought that the viscount might ever know her shame. "Now, what is it you wished to say? I gather it must be of some importance if you had to send your husband from the room. Are you asking about my migraines? I have not experienced so much as a twinge since our arrival."

"I'm glad," her sister said, patting the bed to invite her to sit. "I pray you will not see a recurrence here."

"As do I. But enough of that. You are obviously feeling much better, if you are up and able to jest. Has the doctor's medication worked?"

Catherine gave a small smile. "He gave me no medicine."

"No? You are all well then? That was quick."

"Apparently I am to suffer this particular condition for a while longer."

"Really?" Concern edged her heart. "How much longer?"

"The doctor believes another seven months."

"How can he be sure?"

Catherine's gaze connected with hers, holding steady.

Serena frowned. Why did she feel like such a slowtop? What was her sister trying to communicate? "I'm sorry, but I do not understand."

"I am increasing, Serena."

"Really?"

Light filled her sister's features as she nodded.

"Oh, how wonderful!" Serena wrapped her sister in a fierce hug. Swiftly pulled back. "Oh! I hope I have not hurt the baby."

Catherine laughed. "Of course not. But because of my illness, the doctor has advised me to forgo some of my usual activities." She sighed. "So no riding for the moment."

"That's a shame for you. I know you were looking forward to it. Still, what a wonderful reason for missing out! Jon must be thrilled."

Her sister's smile grew shyly sweet. "He is. But we have decided to keep this news only in the family, just for the moment you understand." Her smile dimmed. "After Lavinia's troubles, I do not want to deal with the curious and well-intentioned, should . . ." She bit her lip.

"Your baby will be strong."

Catherine nodded. "I would appreciate your prayers."

"You always have them."

"Thank you." She gently squeezed Serena's hand. "So, after our stay here, we will tell Mama and Lady Harkness, but only after the danger period has passed."

Serena giggled. "Somehow I cannot imagine Jon's mother as the grandmotherly type."

"No. She seems far too stylish for that."

As Catherine continued to chat about Serena's soon-to-be aunt status—"Aunt Serena is something of a mouthful"—and what role the grandmothers might play, below Serena's joy another interesting question begged for attention.

What would the viscount's grandmother, the artistic Dowager Countess of Bevington, be like?

Miss Serena Winthrop had a secret.

Harry leaned back in his chair, surreptitiously eyeing the young woman seated opposite at the dining table. The secret shone in her eyes and creased the corners of her unusually mobile mouth. She barely glanced at him, though she smiled often at her sister and Carlew—and Harry's own sister, now he thought on it.

"We are so pleased you are feeling better, Lady Winthrop," Mother said. "But Dr. MacConnell *is* excellent. Scottish, you know."

"His brogue usually gives that away," Harry murmured.

"His accent is unfortunate, but cannot be helped, I suppose. Nevertheless, I trust you will be feeling more at your ease to see some of what northern Derbyshire has to offer."

"I would certainly enjoy seeing more. I confess I did not appreciate the sights on the journey in."

"You must all come visit us at Rochdale," said Melanie. "You simply must. I know the children would especially like to have you come visit, Serena."

Miss Winthrop and his sister were on first-name basis already? His brows rose.

"You have made quite an impression with Tom. But you might have to be prepared to work."

"Melanie . . ." Father frowned.

"No need to worry, Papa. I simply mean Tom is convinced there is nothing Miss Winthrop cannot draw, and I suspect he will be asking her to sketch any and everything that takes his fancy."

"You are drawing again?" Carlew said softly to his sister-in-law.

She nodded, cheeks tingeing pink. "Only a few sketches for the children."

"Oh, Serena, I'm so pleased," Catherine exclaimed.

Harry fiddled with his wineglass. Why had she stopped? Their words made it sound as though this was significant.

"I have decided Serena must visit Grandmama," Melanie announced.

Father's brow lowered. "I'm not sure that is terribly wise—"

"Papa, you should see Miss Winthrop's work. She captured Ellie and Tom perfectly!" His sister turned to him. "You would even appreciate her skill in depicting Polly."

Harry smiled at the slightly less-than-composed-as-usual artist. "I suspect none of your subjects were fond of holding a pose for very long."

"True." Her lips curled to one side.

"I thought perhaps we could visit Grandmama tomorrow." Melanie turned to Miss Winthrop. "She even has her own studio."

She nodded politely, before turning to the head of the table. "Lord Bevington, I was admiring the Reynolds in the landing. It is quite a dramatic work."

His face brightened. "It is highly unusual, as he's not known for his landscapes. But he visited my father, who insisted he capture the view, only he refused to paint the valley . . ."

Father began his usual spiel on the virtues of this artist versus that one, but instead of the guests' eyes glazing over, Miss Winthrop was quite animated, offering carefully worded opinions on the merits of other artists and their methods. Harry found himself watching her, seeing how such talk enlivened her features, her smile flashing as she conversed with his father about various schools of art. To listen to her, anyone would think she had studied under the great masters in Venice or Paris. Father, too, seemed more enthusiastic than was his wont.

When their conversation finally wound to a halt, Mother said, "Well, this is all very fascinating, and doubtless Miss Winthrop will have an interesting encounter with the dowager tomorrow. I was thinking now that Lady Winthrop is better, perhaps we should have a dinner so you can all meet some of the notables of the district, Lord and Lady Rotheringham, and other such neighbors."

Carlew's bride blushed. "I would not wish to presume—"

"There is no presumption," Mother said. "The only presumption is when people expect an invitation to Welmsley, for not everyone is someone worth inviting."

A smile glinted in the depths of the blue eyes opposite him, though the pink lips remained still.

Yes, Mother held her ancestry dear. He fought the smile, sharing Miss Winthrop's amusement. If nothing else she seemed to share his sense of humor.

"That's a marvelous idea," Melanie said, her eyes turning to him. "What do you think, Harry? Can you think of anyone Mama should ensure receives an invitation?" Her eyebrows rose suggestively.

He pretended to flick an errant dust particle from his coat of superfine. "I'm sure I don't know what you mean."

"I'm sure you know exactly who I mean."

He eyed his sister, fighting a losing battle against the burn creeping up his neck, as he willed her not to say—

"Mrs. Milsom, perhaps?"

The blue eyes shifted back to him, now holding a faint frown.

And for the first time that name brought no feeling save for the slightest arrow of shame.

Chapter Ten

"Miss Serena Winthrop."

Serena studied the aged lady eyeing her so coolly. The little woman—for she would scarcely top five feet—held an extraordinary presence, a supreme assurance in her identity, most appropriate for this extraordinary house in which they now stood. A miniature version of Welmsley's magnificence, right down to the colonnades and dome, the building was unlike any dower house she had ever seen. The Dowager Countess of Bevington—Melanie's grandmother—might be crowned with white hair, but her voice and dark eyes snapped with as much energy as if she were three-score years younger.

"What kind of artist comes to such a locale without her supplies?"

"Grandmama!" Melanie whispered.

"No, it is a fair question," Serena said, raising her chin just a little. "Just one without an easy answer."

The dark eyes narrowed a fraction. "I see."

And for a moment, Serena thought she could. Her insides twisted.

"Well, far be it from me to enquire and thus descend into the realms of gossip as some are so inclined to do." This was said with a sideways glance at the viscount, whose eyes flashed before his face resumed his habitual polite disinterest. "I suppose you have your reasons."

The dowager glanced at the sketches her granddaughter had given her, as her grandchildren gathered close. Perhaps she was a woman of greater bark than bite.

"See, Grandmama?" Melanie said. "This one of Polly, Harry's puppy. Do you not agree it is drawn extraordinarily well? Harry was saying it is her very likeness."

"It has been done well enough, I suppose."

A strange pang hit Serena's chest. She did not think herself overly vain, and it should not matter what this aged person thought of her abilities, but for some reason she did want this lady's approval.

The viscount shot her a quick look before saying, "It's drawn so well I hope to keep it."

"What?" Melanie said. "No. Tom would never permit it. I had to almost pry this from his fingers."

"I will do another for you, sir," Serena offered.

"Would you?"

"Of course."

His eyes lit. "I should like that above all things."

His eagerness chased away the hurt. She offered him a small, quick smile that he returned.

The dowager sighed. "Well, I suppose if you must, there is no point in wasting such ability on inferior materials. Come."

Serena questioned the viscount with her eyes. He nodded, tilting his head to the heavy oak door, so she followed his grandmother through it.

Into paradise.

The large room was glorious, the windows that lined three sides creating a light-filled space perfect for painting. Either side of the door were several tall cupboards, in which she guessed painting supplies were stored. Canvases were stacked against another cupboard, the painted surfaces revealing an artist of no mean talent. An easel was set up in one corner, before which stood a table set up with a still life: fruit spilling from a large ram's horn.

Serena's heart began a strange thud, as a mix of admiration and envy clamored within. "This is truly amazing," she said in an under-voice to the viscount.

He smiled, which caused a new, and very different, feeling within, one she determined to ignore. "Count yourself most fortunate," he murmured. "She rarely lets anyone outside the family in here."

The dowager turned, frowning. "What are you whispering about?"

"Only your magnanimity in permitting me to see your studio, my lady."

The older lady sniffed. "I only bother showing it to people I feel have some appreciation for what truly matters."

"There is nothing quite like the feeling of expressing one's creativity," Serena offered.

"Yes . . . perhaps." The dark eyes shifted to her grandson then back. "I gather you're still young enough to not know better."

The viscount cleared his throat. "And young enough not to hear such intimations."

Serena fought the blush heating her cheeks as she motioned to the unfinished canvas. "Lady Bevington, pardon my assumption, but I was given to understand you prefer landscapes?"

"Of course I do. But the out-of-doors do not agree with me as they once did. So, I am stuck inside painting bowls of fruit. Bowls of fruit—I ask you!"

"I understand completely. I particularly loathe painting busts, and vases of flowers," Serena agreed, thinking of the exercises she'd been set.

"Exactly! Flowers should be captured in their natural surrounds."

"And portraits should be painted of people, not merely of their sculpture, which contains little of the essence of a person."

"I agree. But when one's fingers refuse to cooperate with one's mind . . ." The dowager sighed and held out her fingers, the knobbly knuckles displaying signs of rheumatism.

"Still life it must be." Sensing any offer of sympathy would be instantly dismissed, Serena moved closer to examine the canvas. "You have captured the pear well. I always have trouble making the shape look less symmetrical."

"Pears are easy. It's the pineapples I detest."

Serena chuckled. "I have not been in the happy position of having too many pineapples available as props in my art classes."

"You should remedy that here. Welmsley has a pinery. You are welcome to enjoy one."

"Thank you." She glanced at a wide-eyed Melanie, and at Lord Carmichael, who nodded.

"It is a shame one must forgo the far more pleasant scenes available outside." The dowager shot Serena a narrow look. "I suppose you've been told about my life's work?"

"About capturing the valley? A truly awe-inspiring feat."

"It would have been, had I been able to finish it. Now I cannot stand to look at it. Always reminding me of what I could not complete." She jerked a nod to the cupboard in the corner. "It's in there, if you care to take a look."

Now both grandchildren had wide eyes. Melanie muttered in an undertone, "Grandmama must really like you; she *never* shows her canvas outside the family."

A minute later, Lord Carmichael had cleared away the multitude of canvases stacked in front and Serena was staring at the painting of the valley, the breadth and scale of it drawing breath from her body. A glory of color half filled the canvas. Sketched-in details revealed the tor and garden temple yet to be painted . . . She tilted her head. If it were her painting, she might change a few details—the river looked a little flat, and some of the trees seemed a little oddly shaped—but the level of skill in evidence filled her with deep appreciation. "It is remarkable."

"Hmph. Anyone who paints such a vista would receive such praise."

"I only wonder how you could not fear to attempt it."

"Fear is a commodity I have never had much use for, I'm afraid."

Serena stifled a chuckle at the unconscious irony, lifting her gaze to encounter the viscount, who seemed similarly amused, his dimple dipping in and out. That strange sensation tugged warmth in her chest again. She quickly returned her attention to his grandmother. "It puts me in mind of the Reynolds above the landing."

"I still remember the day Sir Joshua Reynolds came. Your grandfather"—she nodded to Melanie and the viscount—"was tremendously thrilled to have an artist of such caliber here. He believed it would distinguish the Peaks as one of England's finest locales. And when it was finally revealed, at a ball for nearly five hundred guests, it certainly caused a sensation."

"Does it take long to travel to the valley?"

"Not as long as before Reynolds came. His visit prompted the cutting of all those steps down the cliff. Have you been there?"

Serena nodded. "But no lower than the first two terraces."

"Visit the temple. There is a lovely spot there, well worth painting." She sighed, her gaze straying to the window.

Serena's heart panged with compassion. How frustrating it must be to be hindered by health from doing all that one wanted. "You have a lovely outlook here," she said, motioning to the gardens sloping to the woods.

"But not the same. However, my son assures me that even if he cut a swathe through the trees I should still not see the view of the valley."

"Could you not live at the Hall if you miss it so much?"

"Experience has taught me that it is not advisable for mothers to live with their married children. Too much room for conflict, you see."

"I understand," she said, thinking of the challenges Catherine faced with both Mama and Lady Harkness stating their opinions loudly and often.

The dowager chuckled. "There! A sensible girl. You've got a fine one there, Henry."

"Grandmama, we are not—that is," his cheeks tinged red, "we do not—"

"Perhaps you ought," she said, glancing at Serena.

"Miss Winthrop *is* very lovely—"

Her heart gave a painful throb.

"But rather young to be thinking of marriage," continued Lord Carmichael, refusing to meet Serena's eyes.

"Nonsense!" The older woman held a frown in her brow. "I know he can be something of a rattlepate, but you cannot do better than my grandson. He'll be earl one day, and owner of the Hall, and an estate of nearly twenty thousand acres. What have you got to say to that, eh, Miss Serena Winthrop?"

"Only that his countess will be a fortunate woman."

"But not you?"

Serena managed a stiff smile. "Ma'am, I suspect your grandson has as little inclination for matrimonial manipulation as I do."

The dowager stared at her. A creaking sound tinged with amusement soon rasped into a dry chuckle. "Well! You do have a tongue on you. Good! I have never been able to abide milk-and-water misses." Her gaze grew sly. "And neither has my Henry here."

And it was all Serena could do to keep her head high and not glance at the handsome man standing beside her.

ARMED WITH A wealth of materials and canvases from the dowager, Serena found the next few days a frenzy of plans and painting. Whilst Catherine and Jon were pleased to sightsee in the carriage, Serena had pleaded to be freed from social obligations in order to paint.

"But dearest, are you sure?" Catherine had said again this morning, prior to an expedition to the estate village of Welmsley. "I should not want you to feel lonely."

"I am not lonely, and truly, I would hate for others to feel obliged to keep me company, just as you would hate to know I felt obliged to accompany you if you insisted I ride."

"Oh, I could never do that."

Serena had raised her brows.

"Oh. Very well. If you are—"

"Sure? Yes, I am. Now go. Don't keep Jon and the others waiting."

Serena now hurried down the steps, accompanied by Anna and a bemused footman carrying the easel and prepared canvas. Down one flight to the rose garden. Another twenty steps to the Tudor-style knot garden. Another twenty steps to the French parterre.

Her heart thumped with excitement. The past days had proved wonderfully freeing, a kind of healing release, at once invigorating and relaxing, as the questions in her brain quieted to a single focus: the picture. Nothing else mattered. Catherine had insisted Anna's presence was necessary because she knew Serena's tendency to forgo everything else in her desire to create artistic perfection. Serena was sure Anna did not mind, seeing as her duties consisted of ensuring she ate and carried a wrap, leaving plenty of time for mending and reading. Only one question stole into her content: Why had she avoided the very thing that gave such joy?

Following the dowager's advice, she had visited the temple, agreeing wholeheartedly that its location beside the lake was as evocative as it was charming. The previous days had been spent sketching ideas, preparing the canvas, refamiliarizing herself with the nature and texture of oils, and developing her colors to those which best approximated her imagination. For while she wanted the painting to be realistic, she also desired it to possess more than a hint of romantic idyll, so she planned to include some Grecian figures.

Discussing her concept the previous night after dinner with the dowager—whose attendance at evening meals was due entirely to her interest in the new artist, or so Melanie said—she'd been cautiously optimistic. "But how much experience have you had in painting goddesses? They are not exactly thick on the ground these days."

"If in fact they ever were," the viscount had murmured, his eyes twinkling.

Serena had removed her gaze from his then worked to ignore the look of speculation in his grandmother's. "I think it can work, and if not, then I'll paint over it. That is the joy of working with oils."

"I simply believe it important to paint from experience. Emotional connection to the subject will always enhance the authenticity of its depiction."

"Perhaps Miss Winthrop worships such creatures?"

Serena had looked at the viscount then, giving him a frown she was sure would not be amiss on his father's face. In fact, so obvious was her disapprobation, Melanie had laughed, asking what Harry had done to incur Miss Winthrop's displeasure.

The episode was hushed over, the viscount apologetic, but still she could not help wonder what he truly believed. For herself, painting again seemed to have drawn her closer to God. She held a new appreciation for the Master Craftsman who had created such beauty, who had given something of His own nature through enabling humans to create also. And outside in the cooling autumn, inhaling the fresh scent of roses and cut grass, hearing the trill of birds, she felt such peace steal across her soul, it was like her heavenly Father stood beside her, like He could speak, and she would hear His voice.

He had felt far away for far too long. Shut out, no doubt, due to the walls she'd built to protect herself from further disappointment and pain. But this locale, this ability to breathe again, meant she felt a renewed sense of security to let down her barriers and let Him in once more. She believed again. Could almost dare trust God with her future once again.

A twinge passed through her chest. Where *did* the viscount stand on matters of faith?

"Excuse me, miss?" Davis, the footman gestured to the easel. "Are you happy with the placement here?"

"Thank you. That will do nicely."

He nodded, then spent the next few minutes arranging the easel, her stool, the canvas, and her paints as she'd previously indicated. Once satisfied she did not require anything further, he executed a small bow and returned to the steps to make the long ascent.

"You are sure he does not mind?"

Anna smiled. "Mr. Davis would wonder at your asking, miss."

Serena arched a brow. "I'd noticed he does not seem averse to spending time in your company."

The maid blushed. "He is quite kind."

Serena laughed and turned her attention to her painting.

Her painting!

Sighing with happiness, she studied yesterday's line work, nodded, then dipped the dowager countess's flat-topped hog bristle brush into the pot containing Prussian blue.

❧ CHAPTER ELEVEN

"I CANNOT FIND her anywhere. Where could she be?"

Harry glanced up from his newspaper. Catherine's brow was wrinkled, she was biting her bottom lip.

Carlew patted her hand. "I should think she is still off painting. You know how she can be."

"Yes, but I do not like the look of those clouds over there."

Harry followed her glance and frowned. Those types of clouds were not the sort to float by without delivering. He pushed to his feet. "Lady Winthrop, I gather your sister remains unaccounted for. Would it alleviate your concern if I were to conduct a search?"

"I do not want her to be late for tonight's dinner, but I'd hate for you to be disturbed."

"You would rather remain perturbed yourself? Come, I would not have you worry." He glanced at Carlew. "I shall run down through the gardens and see if I can spot her there. I feel sure she is down near the lake, seeing that is her preferred location this past week. Perhaps if you stayed here to assure your wife?"

Carlew nodded. "Thank you."

Harry hurried from the room, and shrugged into a sealskin cloak designed for conditions in the Midlands where the weather could turn so quickly. He couldn't account for his eagerness to go; he didn't especially relish getting wet. But today's tour of the village of Welmsley had ignited fresh dissatisfaction, and he could not help being glad for a reason to escape the confines of the Hall and all its reminders of his inadequacies. As he hurried down the steps, he felt the first cold drops from heaven. He swiped a hand over his face and upped his pace, quickly catching up to a slight figure dressed in black, struggling to descend the now slippery steps.

"Anna? Why are you not with Miss Winthrop?"

"Oh, sir! She said she'd nearly finished and sent me back up, but then when it looked rain-like, I thought it best to return with this." She held up the large umbrella.

He pulled it from her grasp. "Return back above. I'll see to her."

A loud rumble of thunder filled the air. The maid jumped, her eyes wide, her body trembling. "But sir—"

"Your willingness to be of service does you credit. Now go."

"Should I send Davis to help?"

"And have him caught by rain showers, too? No."

He hurried down the next flight as the sky grumbled once more. Thank goodness the maid had not protested long. He did not think himself capable of dealing with two hysterical women in the rain.

By the time he reached the bottom the spitting sky had determined on something more intense. He jogged in the direction of the lake, cutting across the weaving path in the shortest route possible. And—

There! A figure was dabbing frantically at the canvas, even as the rain fell and thunder rumbled ominously above. He pounded through wet grass. Why was she not frightened?

"Miss Winthrop!"

She startled. Glanced up, strands of damp hair stuck across her face. "What are you doing here?"

"My question exactly." He picked up her paint box, pulled the canvas from the easel.

"Sir, I do not wish to leave—"

"And I have no wish for you to be struck by lightning. Please."

"But—"

"Now!"

Her lips pushed out in a pout equally frustrating and enticing. He fought the disquieting thought as he handed her the canvas. "Go over there, to the temple. It should be open."

She nodded, and after finally folding down the easel, he hurried after her. By now the rain was sheeting down, accompanied by several drawn out peals of thunder in rapid succession, of volume enough to send a shiver down his spine. Despite his heavy cloak, rain dripped past his collar, sticking his shirt to his back as he raced the final few feet to the temple.

He clambered up the folly's three shallow steps to where she stood shivering, her hands holding the canvas firmly. "Is it locked?"

She nodded.

He dropped his burden, wincing as he heard the sound of tinkling glass.

"The paints!"

Stifling a curse, Harry twisted the door handle—to no avail.

"Still locked?" came the voice laden with sarcasm.

He shouldered the door, once, twice, before it splintered open.

"That seems a little drastic."

He eyed her, all thoughts of temptation gone. "Would you please get inside?"

"With you?"

Harry muttered another oath under his breath. "I will stay out here if you are that concerned about propriety."

Her blue eyes narrowed, and with a flounce worthy of a half-drowned peahen, she moved inside.

He picked up the paint box, the chinkling sound reminding him of his clumsiness. As apparently it did her.

She pulled the box from his grasp, kneeling at his feet. "I cannot believe you were so careless!"

"Says the girl who likes to paint in the rain."

She glanced ferociously upward. "I lost track of the weather."

"And caused your sister worry."

"Catherine's worried? Oh."

"Yes, 'oh.' But it seems this is not the first time you've been so caught up in the moment to become inured to other people's feelings."

"I beg your pardon?"

Harry gazed down at her, her snapping eyes and rosy expression so far removed from her usual tranquil countenance that he couldn't help it. He smiled.

Her brows knit together, and she seemed to jerk back slightly, before she glanced down at the opened box. "Oh no!"

He crouched down across from her, the smashed bottles splintering guilt across his heart. "I'm sorry."

She gave a deep sigh, her chest lifting up then down under the thin fabric of her gown. He blinked, pushed away, as a dozen raw emotions battled in his chest. He would *not* be attracted to her. He was a gentleman; he needed to act like one. He busied himself by standing the easel upright and fixing the stool so she could sit.

"The yellow ochre is half gone. And the madder is nearly empty."

"Madder?"

"It is a type of crimson. Made from crushing the roots of the madder plants."

"Madder plants?" He stared at her.

She met his gaze, made an impatient sound. "*Rubia tinctorum?* The common madder?"

He nodded as if he understood, and gestured to the stool, but she shook her head, intent on discovering what other damage he'd inflicted upon her paints. Amidst her sighs and groans, he moved to where she'd hastily leaned the canvas, and paused, his skin prickling.

The temple scene was remarkable, her painting holding a vitality similar to her drawings. If he closed his eyes then opened them, staring only at the painting, it was as though he stood outside gazing upon the scene. Even his grandmother, whom he'd long considered to be one of the best amateur artists he'd known, could not compare. "This is lovely."

She pushed to her feet, frowning as she studied the canvas. "I don't think the lake is quite right. And," she pointed to a white smear, "the rain has quite carried away my Grecian figure."

He swallowed, as words about *her* figure draped in white sheets sprang to his lips. But she was innocent, he was not, and nothing could come of this . . . this . . .

He clenched his hands.

"Lord Carmichael, are you quite all right?"

"Yes."

"You don't look it."

"I suspect we neither of us look our best at this precise moment in time," he muttered.

Her gaze dropped as she pulled the damp strands of her hair into a semblance of order. "Thank you for coming to my aid. I'm sorry I wasn't very gracious."

He lifted an eyebrow.

"Or not gracious at all?" Her lips curled to one side. "Please forgive me. I am disappointed for your grandmother's sake that I've broken her paint pots."

"*You've* broken? I thought I managed that feat."

"Well, they were my responsibility. And they're quite expensive."

"How expensive?"

She named a figure. He smiled. "I think I can safely afford to replace all the paints at that price and still have enough remaining for a new door for the temple."

"But I could not ask you to do so."

"You did not ask, and I would certainly not expect a guest to have to pay for my clumsiness. The very thought is anathema!"

Her lips twitched, but she kept a straight face as she said demurely, "I thank you, sir."

He smiled before offering her his cloak. She needed something over her gown, for her own—and his—protection.

"Oh, but I could not have you get chilled."

"Again, my very thoughts spoken aloud. Would you truly have me behave so disgracefully as to see a guest at Welmsley catch cold, sicken, and possibly die, simply for the want of a—relatively—dry cloak? Please, do not place such a burden on my conscience."

She chuckled, an enchanting rippling sound that warmed his heart. "Thank you, then. I accept."

He carefully placed the cloak around her shoulders and moved to hook it closed at the top. Standing so near, he could detect her scent, something like roses and the sharper tang of linseed oil. His senses stirring, he heard her breath catch, and his fingers paused from their clumsy endeavors. He glanced down. Wide blue eyes were fixed on his.

"Sir, I do not wish—"

"To be cold, yes, I know." Hurrying his movements, he internally sighed with relief as he finally clasped the hook and eye together, and her wet, somewhat diaphanous, gown was covered at last. "That better?"

She nodded, enshrouded by the voluminous cloak to look like an ancient Norse enchantress. "But I hope you are not too cold."

"Thank you, I am not." Rather, he felt a little warm.

She moved backward, but the extra length of his cloak tangled beneath her feet and she slipped. Jerking forward he grasped her arm and pulled her upright, too close to his pounding chest.

Harry stared into eyes as luminous as a starlit sea, gazed at pink lips and wished to learn their softness, wished for the first time he was not her host, that he did not know Carlew, that his best friend had not charged him with the responsibility of protecting his sister-in-law, that she was simply a lady whom he could kiss without any stain of guilt at all.

He drew back.

Her smile was tremulous. "I . . . seem to be much in your debt this afternoon, my lord."

"Not at all." He cleared his throat, hoping the slight squeak went unnoticed. He shifted to the window, glancing at the rain still pouring from the sky. "It seems we shall be here a little longer."

Her little sigh curled disappointment in his heart.

"What is the purpose of this place, anyway?"

He glanced back at her. "The temple was built as a folly by my grandfather, and used as a summer house." Amongst other things. But he would not share about the many rendezvous the temple of love had seen.

"It is very quiet."

"Except when heavy rain is falling. I never noticed how loud it could be."

"You probably had your mind on other things." The look she shot him was innocent—wasn't it?

He swallowed. "I wonder, would you tell me about what first drew you to your art?"

"I . . . I have not thought on my reasons at great length."

"Then perhaps just share a snippet?"

She stared at him, her lips pushing into a small pout, before she licked her bottom lip in a way that again tugged desire from deep within. "I . . . I have always enjoyed creating. I love being able to create something from nothing." Her gaze dropped, her eyelashes dark against her cheeks. "I imagine it is how God felt, creating the world."

"You imagine yourself as God?"

"Of course not!" Her eyelids lifted. Scorn flashed in the blue depths of her eyes.

"Forgive me."

Her eyes flickered then she nodded. "I simply mean I can understand what is said in Genesis, how in the beginning, before God created, the world was empty and formless." Her gaze grew searching. "You do know your Bible, sir?"

A question, not a statement. "Of course."

"Do you believe it?"

He smiled. "You begin to sound like Carlew, my dear."

She stared at him a moment longer, something like disappointment clouding her eyes, her features. "You are not a man of faith."

Statement, not question.

"I . . . I—"

"If you cannot answer, then your answer is obvious." Her lips pursed in such a way that he knew she was disappointed.

"I do not meet your brother-in-law's high standards."

"No."

The word shafted home, piercing his heart. Now *he* knew disappointment.

Her lips curled to one side. "Not yet, anyway."

He managed a wary chuckle, wondering at this chit of a girl. Most young ladies' chatter left him wishing for a pack of cards and far more interesting turns around a table. It was rare to meet someone who drew forth pieces of his heart he'd had no intention of sharing, whose conversation could hold his attention as much as her face did.

"So we have established you enjoy art as a way to emulate God."

"To glorify God, not be like Him," she corrected, eyes narrowing.

He felt the invisible cord of connection between them drawing thin, and hastened to get in her good graces once more. "And was someone the inspiration for your art?"

"Lavinia."

"The Countess of Hawkesbury?"

"I used to sometimes see her outside, sketching or with her watercolors. I liked the freedom such activity gave her."

"Like my grandmother."

"Yes. I gather Lady Bevington has not always adhered too closely to social convention."

"Such keen powers of observation." Her cheeks tinged pink at his words, and he was strangely glad he seemed to hold the power to disconcert this cool miss. "But you stopped."

She stiffened, staring at him wide-eyed.

"My dear Miss Winthrop, I do not mean to cause embarrassment, but I gather ceasing art was not by choice."

"You . . . you do not know?"

He shook his head.

She turned away, moving to the window where the rain pattered ceaselessly.

His neck prickled with foreboding as the silence stretched, as she stood unnaturally still. What could it be? Such talent would not cease from high expense; Carlew could certainly afford to pay. Was it her mother's doing? Her sister's? No. There was some mystery here.

"Forgive me. I would not wish you to share if it distresses—"

She jerked her head no.

Quiet filled the little room again. Experience had shown the temple's ability to block the outside world. Somehow the persistent rain, the cocoon of shadows, made this feel a space safe for sharing intimacies far more important than any he'd ever imparted or received before. What had stolen away her passion?

He did not realize he'd spoken aloud until he heard her whisper, "My . . . my art master."

What? "He would be a fool to not recognize your talent."

She shook her head once more.

For a moment he struggled to understand. Surely she didn't mean . . . ? No. Dear God, no.

Something white and hot quickly swelled within, raging through his soul. So this was why Carlew had warned him away. This was why she had no inclination for society, why she seemed skittish with men, with him. A thousand questions burned; he swallowed them. Poor girl. The poor, sweet, beautiful girl.

Harry slowly unclenched his hands. "I am very sorry."

She shrugged, her back still to him.

He wanted to do something, to say something, to help her feel better, to take away her pain, but nothing sprang to mind, except a kind of enormous relief that he had never acted on any impulse to hold her—or kiss her. "You have my word that I will not speak of this to anyone."

"Thank you."

Harry turned away, fingers clenching again. What had Carlew done? What would Father have done had someone tried to hurt Melanie? Emotion rose in his chest again. Men like that should be horsewhipped! Should be strung up by their—

"Lord Carmichael."

He pivoted to see her looking at him, that half smile curving her lips.

"You may ask Jon what measures he took, though I don't believe they were quite so extreme."

"I said that aloud?" At her nod, his neck heated. "I beg your pardon."

"Why?" Her eyes flashed most unserenely. "That is exactly what should happen to men like him."

He chuckled, and a few seconds later she joined in, their shared laughter bouncing around the little room, breaking the tension. "You are not quite what I expected, Miss Winthrop."

"Not so meek and mild?"

"No."

Their gazes connected once again, and for a moment, something warm twined between them, curling tenderness in his heart, swirling something that felt like hope. He blinked, stepped back, away from her, away from danger, and glanced outside. "The rain has ceased."

"Oh, good." Her lips twisted into a half smile. "Not that I haven't enjoyed your company, my lord."

"I could never dream such a thing possible. I always endeavor to please."

"Would it be rude of me to admit I am not surprised?"

He grinned, relieved to see the sparkle back in her eyes. "Not only rude, but unladylike," he dared tease. "Yet refreshingly honest."

They shared smiles, and another moment of connection. Yes, Miss Serena Winthrop was refreshing, her honesty something he'd never encountered with a young lady before. The fact that she would dare entrust him with such vulnerability only increased his esteem for her. What strength of character must she possess to have undergone such a trial yet still be able to smile? Harry looked away, conscious of a tumult of emotions within. He'd long found her outward appearance appealing, but what he'd witnessed these past weeks in her kindness to her sister, her patience with Melanie's children, her quick wit, and her trusting him just now, made her seem like she had become an unlooked-for friend. It was ridiculous, considering their disparity in age and fortune, but this surge of protectiveness, these tender feelings she evoked, made her seem infinitely more precious.

His heart panged. If only Carlew had not extracted such a promise from him. He drew in a deep breath, then cleared his throat. "Are you ready to return?"

The blonde head nodded. "At the risk of more unladylike honesty, I must confess to feeling rather hungry." Her habitual composure dissolved in a gasp. "And isn't tonight the night of your mother's important dinner?"

ℜ Chapter Twelve

Welmsley had so far proved relatively informal, so it came as something of a shock to realize just how different tonight's dinner would be. Serena descended the grand staircase to discover the guests waiting in the hall. She glanced around: Catherine, Jon, the viscount—how had he managed to change so quickly and look so debonair?—Melanie smiling up at her plain blond husband, the earl and countess, and a dozen others whose expressions ranged from hauteur to—from the younger males at least—something approaching admiration.

These last she ignored, moving to her sister's side. Catherine's wide-eyed surprise at her earlier ramshackle appearance had necessitated hurried explanations while she exchanged her sodden gown for this far more elegant one and allowed Anna to quickly make something of her damp hair. She smoothed the cream silk skirts, lifted her chin, and approximated a look of coolness.

Peters appeared, dressed impeccably as ever, and sounded a gong. "Dinner is served." Melanie slid to her side and began a quick recitation of names and pedigrees as the guests walked into the dining room.

The earl offered his arm to the diamond-drenched Viscountess of Rotheringham, whose husband escorted the countess. The married couples were separated as tradition demanded and entered the room paired off according to rank, Lord Carmichael taking in a Mrs. Milsom, whose pairing left Serena feeling a kind of loss even before Melanie was escorted away.

"Excuse me, Miss Winthrop, may I have the honor?" Mr. Craven-wood, a gentleman of minor rank—second son of a neighboring bar-onet, so Melanie had whispered, but of very good fortune—held out his arm.

"Thank you." She took his arm, working to suppress the nerves in dealing with a young man whose appreciative eyes upon her entry had made her freeze inside. Would she forever feel uncomfortable with gentlemen? Although she did not feel quite so with Lord Carmichael . . .

The next-to-last to be seated, she glanced around the table, noting her position between Mr. Cravenwood and the blond and taciturn Lord Rochdale. Sighing internally, she pasted a polite smile on her face and focused on the magnificent table. A rococo epergne centered the table, intricately decorated with gilt-laden birds and flowers, topped with a silver pineapple, the symbol for hospitality. Low vases of white roses—doubtless fresh-picked from the tiered garden—sat between heavily festooned silver candelabrum of beeswax candles. The family crest adorned the gleaming silver cutlery, and similarly marked the gold-and-turquoise Sèvres dinner service. A dozen delectable aromas teased her senses from the multitude of dishes, while above, a great chandelier complete with ormolu sunbursts shimmered candlelight through the sparkling crystal and across the guests and table.

Grace was said, a prayer that sounded as if the earl spoke regularly to his heavenly Father, then the white soup was served. Soon the hubbub of conversation and clank and clatter of spoons and forks made it easy for her to withdraw from the polite civilities and observe the lady seated opposite.

Mrs. Lillian Milsom was a curvaceous brunette, dressed in a chili color known as Aurora, with a smile as wicked as her repartee. Compared to her vivid plumage Serena felt as insignificant as a sparrow, a sparrow dressed in white, perhaps, but a sparrow nonetheless. Rubies the size of pigeon eggs glinted at Mrs. Milsom's breast, drawing the notice of the men gathered—save Jon, the earl, and, somewhat surprisingly, the viscount. Courteous as ever, he gave attention that was all decorous, but in other moments, he seemed quiet, almost distracted. Was he also thinking about this afternoon?

Mrs. Milsom seemed to notice Lord Carmichael's lack of interest as she leaned closer to him, her low-cut gown displaying her buxom figure to advantage, murmuring in undertones suggestive of intimacy. More than one glance was sent across the table, as she eyed Serena with a look half disdain, half speculation.

For her own part, Serena endeavored to appear unruffled, but her usual poise felt strained tonight, stirred by the strangest afternoon she'd experienced in a long while. Her joy at painting had been severely tried by the viscount's unfortunate clumsiness, but it was the ensuing conversation that had really played havoc with her emotions.

Her insides twisted uneasily. Had she erred in sharing something of the truth of her pain? Had her admission given him a disgust of her? Is that why he refused to look at her now? She could hardly account for why she had been so revelatory, save the viscount had seemed strangely trustworthy, strangely safe, someone whose open kindness helped her to see him as deserving the regard Jon held for him. What kind of man could irritate her so much then look at her so kindly she wanted to weep? Why did he seem to treat her as a little sister one minute and then the next stand so close, his eyes dropping to her lips, almost as though he wanted to kiss her?

And why, for that matter, did she want him to?

She winced internally, hitching her lips higher to maintain the aloof smile. What a fool she was, a ridiculous, romantic fool, to think such things, especially now he knew something of her story. Granted, they had exchanged some long glances and shared amusement at some quips, but in every other way they were too dissimilar. He did not even believe in God! What kind of man did not believe in God? No, she did not even truly know his character, so the fluttering feelings he evoked had to be quashed. He might have made her feel safe—for a few moments at least—but he was all wrong for her.

Serena peeked through her lashes to where he sat, between Mrs.

Milsom and Catherine. He looked extraordinarily handsome tonight, dark hair swept to one side in casual elegance, neckcloth neatly tied, white teeth flashing as he laughed. Serena fingered her small string of pearls, a gift from Papa when she turned sixteen. Modest, especially in comparison to some of the other gems on display tonight, but at least she looked far better than the drowned rat she had resembled this afternoon when they had eventually made it back to the house. She fought another shiver as the memory rose.

All the long hike up the stairs, the viscount had kept up a steady patter of silly stories, even as they were caught in yet another rain shower. They finally arrived on the terrace, sodden, red-faced yet laughing, to be greeted by a group of early arrivals, chief amongst them the beautiful Mrs. Milsom.

After kissing the viscount on both cheeks she'd leaned back, surveying him with a smile. "Well, I certainly did not expect to see you looking quite so *dishabille*." Green eyes had flickered over Serena's odd ensemble. "And you found a little friend to play with in the rain. Hello."

Serena, aware her appearance was causing whispers among the guests, had drawn herself up and eyed her with all the coolness she could muster. "Good afternoon." With a nod for all and sundry, she turned to the viscount. "Thank you for your assistance, sir. Now, if you would give me the paint box, I would be much obliged."

But he had refused, saying, with a glint in his eye, "I shall endeavor to remedy my earlier recklessness, and ensure you have what you need for tomorrow."

"Where will you find more madder?"

"I believe I am acquainted with a lady who might just have cupboards of spare paints hidden away."

"Well, if you are charming enough, perhaps she might give it to you."

"Do you doubt my ability to charm, Miss Winthrop?" He'd looked deep into her eyes.

Her heart had thudded. "Not at all, sir. Your expertise in such matters is widely known."

For a moment, something like hurt had flashed in his expression, before a smile appeared. "Apparently not expert enough. Now *there* is a challenge."

Mrs. Milsom made it very plain that she did not appreciate their banter, as she continued to make loud comments about their state of dress. Her obvious interest in the viscount had prickled confusing disappointment across Serena's heart, making her wonder if the viscount had ever visited the temple with her, and if so, just what they had got up to.

Chewing the inside of her bottom lip at the indecent thought, she tore her gaze away, only to encounter Jon's troubled expression. She pushed her lips up to reassure him, but while he offered a nod and a small smile, his brow remained knit. Was he that concerned over her absence this afternoon?

Her gaze dropped to her plate, the half-finished pigeon pie curling ribbons of nausea through her stomach.

"Miss Winthrop, I see you do not care for pigeon," Mrs. Milsom observed from across the table.

Serena stiffened, conscious all eyes now attended her. As Mr. Cravenwood drew her attention to a plate of gammon, Mrs. Milsom said *sotto voce*, "It takes a sophisticated palate to appreciate such things."

Heat filled her chest, but Mr. Cravenwood was insisting on serving her more food, so she turned and offered him a smile. "Thank you, sir, but I am quite satisfied." She glanced back to catch the viscount's frown before he averted his face. What—?

"Miss Winthrop, I understand you are fresh from the schoolroom," Mrs. Milsom said.

Serena glanced to the end of the table where her hostess sat. Lady Bevington appeared unperturbed by conversation occurring across the table, so she returned her attention to the woman in red. "Yes." She could not resist adding, "At Haverstock's."

"Oh." The surprise on Mrs. Milsom's face suggested that Haverstock's reputation extended as far north as here.

"Serena is an excellent artist," Melanie said, seated two seats from Mrs. Milsom. "Her sketches have an energy to them rare from one so young."

Why all the emphasis on her youth? Serena's smile grew tight.

"Oh, sketches," Mrs. Milsom said, in a manner that suggested sketching was for mere beginners. "I imagine them to be quite pretty."

"Pretty? Lillian, you make it sound as though she does nothing better than what you and I can manage. I believe you quite mistake the matter," Melanie said, a militant gleam in her eye. "I have shown her work to a local *artiste* who quite agrees with my appraisal, and is prepared to support her work in whatever way possible."

Serena smothered a spurt of laughter at the exaggeration of the dowager's comments. Still, she appreciated the gesture.

"My sincerest apologies, Miss Winthrop," Mrs. Milsom said in a tone neither sincere nor apologetic. "I did not mean to cast aspersions on the quality of your work."

Did you not? whispered the imp within. She glanced at the viscount, her usual partner in enjoying the foibles of others, but he was studying his wineglass. Hurt edged her heart. She pushed it aside, smiled sweetly at the woman opposite. "I'm sure you meant something very different, Mrs. Milsom."

Vertical lines appeared momentarily on the beautiful face, as nearby several loud throat clearings took place.

Green eyes narrowed, but nothing more was said, releasing Serena from the confusing undercurrents at the table.

Later, after the tablecloth was removed and the dessert course consumed, conversation sputtered to a stop and the countess rose to signal the ladies' departure. A footman helped move out Serena's chair, and she followed, catching Jon's eye. He gave her an encouraging smile, his look in stark contrast to the viscount who had virtually ignored her all evening. Her feelings dipped, and as she settled into a seat in the drawing room amidst the burble of conversation, she worked to remind herself of her earlier convictions. She would not entertain ridiculous notions about that ridiculous man. Hadn't his lack of faith made him ineligible?

"Miss Winthrop?"

Serena blinked, mind racing to remember what her hostess had been saying.

"You have played the harp for us earlier this week. I wonder, would you play again tonight?"

"If you so wish, ma'am." Her skill was limited, but much to her relief, she had acquitted herself tolerably well.

The countess smiled. "Mrs. Milsom has an excellent voice, so we must prevail on you, too, Lillian."

"I'd be delighted," the brunette purred. "I've no false humility in being averse to exhibit."

Because, Serena thought unkindly, that lady lacked humility of any kind, real or assumed.

The ladies' conversation forced a shifting of seats, Serena's safe haven next to Catherine removed as the countess called for her sister to join the titled ladies and Mrs. Milsom in a conversation about the delights of London. Fortunately, Melanie hurried to Serena's side, her eyes revealing something of her agitation.

"You should not mind her, you know."

"I beg your pardon?"

"Oh, don't give me that queenly stare. You know who I mean. Lillian."

"I do not see what you mean—"

"That woman has always had her claws in Harry. I cannot stand her, she's so selfish and vain, but she knows how to wheedle her way into Papa's ear, and because she is the daughter of the Earl of Hardwicke, Mama cannot find fault."

"Why you think I'm in need of this information, I cannot possibly fathom."

The green eyes, so like his, danced. "Can you not?"

And Serena strove to ignore Melanie's implications—and the disquietude prompted by her words.

"Well, I think that went well. What say you, Henry?"

Harry glanced at his father. After port had been drunk, they had rejoined the ladies in the drawing room for musical performances, followed by tea, after which the ladies had retired, leaving him fighting his thoughts, as well as his lethargy. "Tonight has been most pleasant."

"Pleasant? I doubt your mother would think such mediocre praise counted as success." He frowned. "Are you ill? You've been very quiet all evening."

"I am quite well, thank you, Father." Harry dredged up the last vestiges of enthusiasm he could muster and turned to Carlew. "Your wife is quite an accomplished pianist."

"She has less confidence than she ought, but I believe both she and her sister would own musical ability as being rather less than their greatest strength."

No. It seemed the younger sister's greatest talent—apart from the obvious—was her ability to penetrate his thoughts, leaving him edgy and uneasy. Carlew's appraising gaze drew awareness that he required some form of answer, so he nodded.

"Miss Winthrop is your sister, sir?" Cravenwood asked.

As Carlew explained something of the complexities of their family tree, Harry studied the young man. Handsome, with his dark red hair and blue eyes, he'd made no secret of his admiration of Serena during dinner, despite her less than enthusiastic encouragement.

The Viscount Rotheringham hefted his considerable weight as he shifted in his chair. "She is a pretty thing. Rather too cool for some, eh, Carmichael?"

This was said with a guttural chuckle that sounded more lewd than he expected Carlew would find comfortable. Or in fact that *he* was comfortable with.

He opened his mouth to give the man a set down when Father said, "Harry has always preferred ladies to be a little more open in their manner." He shot a look at Carlew. "Not that there is anything wrong with your sister's conduct."

"I consider Serena's conduct to be exactly as it ought," Carlew said stiffly.

"Exactly so," Rotheringham said, clearing his throat. "Exactly so."

"She seems almost angelic to me," Cravenwood said, looking to Carlew as if for approval.

Carlew's brows lowered, a simple yet effective method of dampening the boy's pretensions, judging from Cravenwood's deflating features.

A swirl of something like envy twisted through his gut, as again he wished the ties of obligation to be removed. But if he expressed to Carlew something of these feelings concerning Serena, would his friend look at him like that, as one might eye a toad?

Harry sipped his wine, thoughts veering between self-disgust and reproach. How could he even think like this, knowing now why Carlew had garnered his pledge to protect her? But how could he not, when everything about Serena made his every sense come alive? Tonight she looked so lovely, an innocent, lustrous pearl amid a table of lesser gemstones, it was all he could do to not look at her. He'd had to *fight* to not look at her. He was aware of Serena even when he wasn't looking, his ears straining for her low voice, conscious of her graceful movements, making him barely able to keep up with Lily's conversation.

His gut twisted. Why had he fostered that relationship as much as he had? Aware as he was of Miss Winthrop, he was equally aware of Lily's efforts to recapture his attention. Once he'd quite enjoyed their interludes; now it felt as an iron yoke around his neck. Lily had always possessed a confidence that matched his own, a disregard for certain social conventions, but now he felt uncertain about so many things, and her blatant self-assurance seemed almost barbaric in comparison to the cool poise of the younger lady. No, Lily had always taken a little too much for granted.

"Carmichael? Come now, boy," Rotheringham said with another wheezy chuckle. "Tell me more about these mines of yours."

He forced his attention to the conversation, forced himself to speak of his dreams in front of his disapproving parent, trying to engender enthusiasm for something that felt like another lost cause. He glanced at Carlew, another pang sliding within. As much as he wished for his friend's investment in his hopes, he'd have to somehow encourage Carlew to leave. Serena must go, else Harry would need to.

The conversation soon veered to the price of wool and other things, leaving Harry free to continue his ruminations. Somehow he had to master this attraction to Serena, because he couldn't stir up anything more. He'd kissed too many women not to recognize the interest in her eyes, to sense her attraction to him was growing deeper by the day, just as his was to her. But he'd rather be shot than be the cause of more pain in her life. And wouldn't that be the result of any further interaction? No, as attractive as he found her, as much as he'd wondered whether he'd found in her a friend, honor demanded he not taint her with further disappointment. Isn't that what his father always thought him to be?

His thoughts darkened, yet he forced himself to act his part, all the while conscious of feeling like a snared hare, caught by this foppish, fleshly reputation he'd cultivated over many years, bound forever to expectation and obligation, even as the morals of the Winthrops whispered freedom for the man he wanted to be.

CHAPTER THIRTEEN

SERENA BREATHED IN the fresh air, once more marveling at the view. She'd done a rough sketch of the valley before deciding such magnificence could scarcely be captured in the few days she had remaining. Following Welmsley's formal dinner, the past week had been spent finishing her painting and planning out the next in the sketchbook kindly given her by the dowager. It would not be long until the Winthrop party would conclude their stay, even though she'd heard the earl and countess press for a continuation. But though he hid it well, Jon seemed increasingly keen to leave, confirmed this morning by Catherine when Serena dared ask concerning their date of departure.

"For Jon seems quite distracted, and I wonder if some strain has come between him and Lord Carmichael, as they do not seem so close as before."

Catherine had bit her lip, drawing further enquiry.

"You have seen it too. What do you know?"

"Serena, dearest, has . . . has the viscount ever said anything to you?"

"He has said many things. As I have to him."

Her sister's dark gaze remained fixed on her.

"Oh, of course not! We have had this conversation, have we not? Why do you persist in thinking something exists between us when nothing does?"

"Would you like it to?"

Serena blinked, the bluntness of her sister's question felling her façade of indifference.

"You *would* like it to." Catherine shook her head. "I can read it in your eyes."

"He does not believe as we do."

Her sister nodded slowly. "And he does not seem to value what we hold dear."

The back of her eyes burned. She blinked. Swallowed.

"He is not worth your emotions, Serena."

"I know," she muttered.

"I agree he is quite charming, but you have seen him act so with Mrs. Milsom. That is his way. I do not like to speak ill of others, but neither do I wish to see my sister hurt, and much as I like him, I find him an unsteady man, without any real sense of purpose."

Serena nodded, sore at heart to hear her own misgivings spoken aloud.

"I will encourage Jon to leave soon, before your emotions become even more entangled."

Entangled . . .

As much as she wished to deny it, the confusion that had snuck up in the night, littering her dreams, had left her feelings in a parlous state. She was most assuredly entangled, desire mingling with romantic fancy, leaving reason and sense far behind.

A series of squeaking calls from a lonely peregrine falcon drifting far above the valley broke into her reverie. She blinked, her heart echoing the bird's search for its mate, and glanced down at the sketchbook. Lord Carmichael gazed from the pages, his dimple marking his lower cheek, his lips curled in that half smile she knew so well.

Heat traveled up her neck to fill her cheeks. She must have things quite bad if she drew his picture unconsciously! Perhaps Catherine was right to insist they leave soon.

"Here you are!"

Serena jumped, closing the sketchbook hurriedly as Melanie drew near.

"Now, now. There is no need to panic. I'm not your art master, am I?"

Her mouth dried. Had someone said something?

"Why do you look at me so? Truly, I did not mean to alarm you, Serena."

"I . . . I am sorry."

"No matter. Now, what have you been drawing here?"

She moved as if to possess her sketchbook and Serena snatched it away.

"One imagines the drawings within are not of mere flowers?" Melanie chuckled, her eyes assessing. "Never mind. I'm sure you have a good likeness. Oh, if my brother only knew what turmoil he induced in so many a maidenly breast."

Surely her face must be glowing bright red! Serena cleared her throat, willing her features to return to normalcy. "Was your sole intention in searching for me merely to torment?"

"Ah, no. And I must beg your forgiveness for such a breach of good manners." Her smile grew. "Especially if you are to agree to my proposal."

"And what proposal is that?"

"I want you to paint my children's portrait."

"I beg your pardon?"

"You heard me. I have just come from Grandmama's and seen your painting. It is quite lovely."

"Thank you. But it is not quite done."

Art was a cruel master, refusing her sleep until she finished. She still had to add the figures, though the dowager had said not to do any more, saying it was quite perfect as it was. Lady Bevington had gone on to show her own painting, positioned from the lake's other side, before adding, "But I think I prefer yours. It has a greater sense of drama."

But her next question, that of what Serena would paint next, had stumped her. What she'd like to do was paint the valley, but they would leave soon, so that was impossible now. Beginning a new work would scarcely leave time for it to dry.

"Serena?" Melanie's face hovered close. "Are you thinking on my brother again? No? Merely thinking on your fame and fortune as an artist? Exhibiting at Somerset House?"

"I thank you for your belief in my ability, but I am a landscape artist, not a portraitist."

"Nonsense. You're anything you want to be. Do not set your limitations when you have yet to experience new things."

"But we are leaving soon—"

"Hence my request. Truly, I would like you to paint my children, for I have not seen anyone else capture my children's vitality so well. Not even Grandmama," she added in a hushed voice.

"You are very kind—"

"No, I am quite determined. If you do not paint them, then nobody shall, and my darling angels will go to the grave without anyone remembering their beauty."

Serena managed a chuckle. "You are quite similar to your brother, aren't you?"

As soon as the words escaped, she wished them unsaid, especially as Melanie's eyes sparkled and she opened her mouth—then closed it, giving her head a little shake.

"My parents are to blame for this levity, you know."

"How so?"

"They have so little—levity I mean—what reserves Harry and I have were mined deep in our childhood, encouraged by our grandmother."

"The dowager countess? She does not seem—"

"Overly fond of the ridiculous, I know. But when Grandpapa was alive she was extremely good fun. It has only been in the last few years that she has become less so."

Serena nodded, thinking of how her mother had changed after Papa's passing. "Death changes those left behind."

"Yes. But let us not talk of death, but far more pleasant things. Please, what can I do to ensure your willingness to paint my children?"

"Besides not tease me so unmercifully?"

"Apart from that." Melanie grinned. "I will tease him instead—"

"Oh, please do not! Not concerning me, anyway."

She sighed. "Very well. I will behave. Now, what will it take? May you come visit? Stay a few days? Oh, that would be marvelous! We could invite your sister and Lord Winthrop too—"

"Jon wishes to return to London soon."

"Even better! Then you won't be shackled by their expectations when Harry comes to call."

Serena began gathering her belongings. "I'm afraid I won't be able to—"

"No, no! Please." Her friend's expression grew serious. "I will not speak of him again."

"Not *ever* in my company if you wish me to stay."

"So you will come?"

Should she? Part of her longed to visit, to see more of the world, but would she be able to hide her feelings if Lord Carmichael did call? She *had* to; there could be no future there. Catherine had always said Serena's countenance was like a mask . . . She gave a reluctant nod.

"Wonderful!" Melanie beamed. "When? Tomorrow? I'm sure Mama won't mind if you come then. Oh, you cannot believe how excited I am!"

"I have some idea."

Her friend's laughter was like balm to Serena's heart, her excitement obvious as she clapped her hands. "To think, my children will be the first people in England to have their portraits captured by such a talent!" She drew Serena close for a hug, then pulled back. "I sincerely believe you will be an enormous success, my dear. I look forward to seeing your pictures hanging in the Summer Exhibition."

Serena allowed herself to be pulled close again, as she fought the new burn in her eyes. To be successful with her art was a lovely dream, but to gain success with mastering her heart . . .

❦

"You're going to do what?"

Glancing at the subject in question standing next to his sister,

Harry caught the glint in her eyes before her features smoothed to their customary coolness. At once the ungracious tone of his words rose, mocking his claims of gentleman.

"I beg your pardon, Miss Winthrop. I am surprised by my sister's actions."

She gave a nod then glanced away, the action twisting pain in his heart. Gone was the feeling of camaraderie, the invisible ties between them severed, the aloofness he'd first known her for once again as evident as the frown on Melanie's face.

"I don't know why you find it such a problem. I simply asked Serena to paint Tom and Ellie and she agreed."

He glanced at Miss Winthrop, catching a wisp of a smile on her face before it vanished.

"Harry, why does this bother you so?"

Because he could not have her stay. Miss Serena Winthrop, remaining close at hand but forever out of reach.

It was agony.

He rubbed his forehead and turned to Carlew. "I thought you wished to return to London?"

"I will send word to my men of business. They are capable, and if it allows Serena to help your sister, then we are happy, aren't we, Catherine?"

"Of course," the brunette said softly.

He thought quickly. Somehow he needed to be elsewhere. For if Carlew stayed, then he'd be obliged to continue to play host, which would necessitate visits to his sister, which would necessitate seeing—

"I . . . I'm afraid when I learned of your plans to return south, I made plans also."

"What?" Melanie cried. "You cannot go just yet."

"I cannot stay. I . . . I have made other arrangements."

"Not with the Milsom creature?"

"Melanie." He scowled at his sister.

Carlew coughed. "Pardon my interruption in what seems to be a family matter, but I had wondered if our extended stay might provide another opportunity for you, Carmichael."

"I'm sorry?"

"If you could be persuaded to amend your . . . plans"—his grave face relaxed into a smile—"I wondered if perhaps you might show Catherine and me something of these mines of which I've often heard you speak."

"You really wish to see them?"

"Of course. You should know by now I'm always keen to seek new business opportunities, and if these prove as productive as what you have suggested, then perhaps we could come to an agreement."

Hope flickered, his spirits lightening. "I would love to show them to you. They are not far, near Castleton. And I do think the possibilities could be quite lucrative, if managed the right way."

"And mines must be managed the right way, for they are nothing without workers willing to work."

"Of course." Although how any man could wish to work in such dark, dank environs was beyond him. "Their conditions must be as good as anywhere."

"Or better?" Carlew said, one brow rising.

"Or better." Harry nodded, glancing at Lady Winthrop. "And you are sure you would both wish to come?"

"I must admit the idea of traipsing around in the dark does not exactly thrill me," she said. "I would be content to remain here—"

"Or you could stay with us also!" Melanie said. "I'm sure Serena would love to have your company."

The younger girl's face lit, causing another odd pang in his chest, as she said softly, "I always love your company, Catherine."

"Then it's settled. I get to keep Serena and Catherine while you get to have Lord Winthrop."

"You do recall these are people you refer to, Melanie, and not your toys?" he drawled, to a general round of laughter. He glanced quickly at Serena; her smile remained, as did her averted gaze.

"It is not very far, is it?" Catherine asked. "I should not like to be apart for long."

"Why ever would that be?" Melanie said with a grin.

Lady Winthrop turned a rosy color, prompting Harry to say, "You must forgive my sister. Sometimes I cannot quite believe she is older than me, and the mother of half-grown children, when her own manners can be *so* appalling. But you see, she's been this way since a girl, and I can attest there have been many times when I, too, have had to overlook some of her more audacious remarks."

Now the chuckles grew—from all save his sister—and he chanced to glance again at Miss Winthrop. The blue eyes finally met his, the sparkle eliciting a glow in his chest, before he remembered his pledge and looked away.

He *would* conquer this. He must!

"Carmichael?"

Carlew's voice drew his attention to his friend's face, whose forehead now grooved. Did he still suspect Harry's conflicted emotions? He swallowed, aimed for a jovial tone. "Yes, old man?"

"I think your plan is a wise one"—the blue-gray eyes hinted a warning—"and cannot help but think the sooner we leave the better."

"Naturally. I shall make the arrangements while you write your letters to London, and we shall endeavor to visit the mine in the next few days."

"Excellent." Carlew's brows tipped up again. "I do have one more question, my friend."

"Which is?" Hopefully nothing to do with Miss Winthrop.

"Are you sure such plans won't interfere with your previous arrangements?"

His nonexistent plans to escape? His neck heated under the assessing gaze. "Positive."

❦ Chapter Fourteen

ROCHDALE, THE FAMILY seat of Melanie's husband, was all that was peaceful and lovely. The well-tended gardens and prospect of a glassy lake were far less dramatic than Welmsley's view from the hilltop, but still held a restful beauty. In a way, its quietude gave some explanation for Melanie's at times hectic personality. Serena did not wonder at her friend's desire for company. The estate was somewhat isolated, Lord Rochdale was of a reticent nature, and her children were often with their nanny. Serena imagined Melanie's life without regular visits to her former home would be quite dull indeed.

She studied the shrubs politely lining the garden, their strict planting out every ten yards saying something of the order that Lord Rochdale seemed to prefer. Holding up her pencil, she thumbed the place indicating the exact space between the sycamore and limes, before carefully translating that to her page. Attaining the correct perspective was most important in a landscape, and her time waiting for the gesso preparation to dry for the children's portrait had been well spent, planning a far more tame landscape than the one she'd envisaged from Welmsley's terrace.

For that painting, doubtless to forever remain in embryonal stage, she had already sketched a scene, even going so far as to label the paint mixes she would have used: venetian red, flake white, Naples yellow, yellow ochre, verdigris, and the tiniest amount of French ultramarine. The colors worked well in most landscapes, and with the addition of burnt umber, her palette would have sufficient variety for every tree and tor. But such planning had now proved pointless.

Ignoring the strange pull in her heart, she bent closer to the page, tracing the curve of the lake carefully. The scent of grass wafted closer, the tickle of a light breeze lifting her hair softly. The day was growing surprisingly warm, the heavy painting apron she wore adding to a feeling of stickiness. The past few days had been quite sunny for October, the air filled with the weight that usually preceded thunder.

But sunshine did little to brighten the recesses of her heart.

He did not like her. That much was evident by his making excuses to stay away. By his refusal to look at her. By his fobbing off Melanie's invitation to dinner last night. Had she done something to upset him? Been too forward? True to her word Melanie had not said a word or even sent one teasing glance Serena's way. But contrarily, she now wished for the chance to talk and release this growing pressure within. Sometimes it seemed her internal atmosphere was reaching a stage where great gusts of wind and rain might not occur from only the sky. To have the chance to be heard and be reminded as to why he was everything wrong would surely help. Wouldn't it? Oh, why did she even *care*?

She stabbed at the paper, wincing as her efforts tore a tiny hole.

"Careful, dearest, else you will need to start over."

"Hello, Catherine," she said without looking up, as she struggled to fit the tiny triangular flap back into the page.

Her sister placed a hand on her shoulder, and Serena stilled, just as when they were children. The action had always had a calming effect.

She breathed in deeply then slowly released her breath. A measure of peace nudged her heart. "Thank you."

Catherine moved to the nearby bench where Serena had laid her supplies. "Your painting is not working well?"

"It's not that."

Her sister's brow puckered. "You have not got your pains?"

"No."

"I had wondered, seeing as you seemed well enough at Welmsley, whether coming here would be wise. If they should happen again—"

"Then I will hide in my bedchamber for several days like last time. I cannot live wondering when pain will strike."

"I know. It's just . . ." Catherine bit her lip.

"Awkward to explain for you, awkward and embarrassing for me, without any cure." Her spirits slumped further. How could any man ever wish to have a wife who was most likely infertile, let alone one who had suffered such inappropriate attentions?

"Dr. Hanbury did suggest that it's helpful to avoid stressful situations."

"I know." Hadn't nearly every attack stemmed from something physically or emotionally challenging?

"And eating more fruits and vegetables might alleviate some of the symptoms."

"Which I attempt to do. And go for the walks he suggests." Serena motioned to the paint box and other artistic accoutrements lining the bench. "These did not arrive by themselves."

"You did not ask a footman to help?"

"When I can fend for myself? Of course not. Now, enough of me. How are *you* feeling?"

"I still grow weary too easily."

"But the nausea?"

"Seems to be easing." Her sister's cheeks pinked. "I don't know if I'm being immodest to talk to you of such things."

"Oh, but it is perfectly modest to discuss my physical condition?"

Catherine smiled. "But dearest, you are not married."

Nor was she likely to be. Serena gave a strained smile and returned her attention to the canvas.

When she next looked up, it was to see her sister still regarding her. "Is there something I can do for you, Catherine?" Serena's eyebrows pushed up. "Is Melanie's chatter proving to be less than conducive to your peace of mind?"

"She is all that is generous, and I could never abuse my hostess by implying otherwise."

"In other words, yes."

Catherine chuckled. "She is talking with Lord Rochdale, so I took the opportunity to visit you."

"To escape, you mean."

"Serena!"

"What? I simply speak the truth."

Her sister's brow creased. "Do you?"

She stared at her. "Of course. How can you think otherwise?"

"It . . . it is simply that you have seemed a trifle out of sorts of late."

"I'm sorry. I did not realize. I suppose it is the painting. I remember now why I prefer landscapes—nature doesn't tend to wriggle like small children."

A smile touched her sister's lips then was gone. "It is not that." She shook her head. "You miss him, don't you?"

"Jon?" She smiled brightly. "Of course. But probably not as much as you—"

"Lord Carmichael."

The words bored into her heart as much as Catherine's penetrating dark gaze. She shook her head, glanced away, picked up her pencil, fiddled with the sketchbook as she blinked against the burn. Of course she missed him. Missed his laughter. Missed his ability to make her laugh. Missed the shared appreciation for the ridiculous. Missed his smile with the silly, dear dimple.

Her sister's arms enveloped her, the tender action causing her eyes to fill. "I have tried, you know." She gulped. "Tried to remove him from my heart, but he still lives there."

"Oh, my dear . . ."

"I tried to follow your advice—whenever a thought of him came to mind to think on something else—but it doesn't help." She drew back, wiped a hand over her damp cheeks. "I try to remind myself about why it wouldn't work, but . . ."

Catherine sighed. "I'm sorry."

"As am I."

Somewhere came the sound of birdsong, the hush of the breeze in the grass, a ruffling of sketchbook pages.

"You have prayed?"

"I've asked God to take these feeling away, for me to regard him as a brother, but it—"

"Doesn't work, I know."

"You do?" She eyed her sister. How could her impossibly good sister know such things?

"I'm not saying prayer doesn't work. It does. But until our heart truly hears truth we can continue to be led by our emotions." Catherine gave a small smile. "When I was in Bath and believed Jon to love another, I grew miserable, still smiling on the outside, but within . . ." She gave a little shrug.

"How could you ever think such a thing? You know he has always loved you."

"I know that now, and he reminds me almost daily, but circumstances, and misunderstanding certain things—on both our sides—had led us to believe we neither cared for the other."

"Which was far from the truth."

"Very far," Catherine agreed. "But I still persisted in my despair, until Aunt Drusilla reminded me that God's word is truth, and that if I believed it, then I should act that way. No, not act. *Live* that way."

Something like hope tingled across Serena's soul.

"Her words propelled me to ask God for some verses to help, and I was reminded of the words of Jesus, that He has come to give us life to the full." Catherine smiled. "I believe you should ask God for verses to comfort you."

Touched, yet somehow not wanting to admit to how right her sister was, she forced a chuckle. "You make it sound like a bereavement."

"Which the loss of love can feel like, can it not?"

Ouch.

"Hello! Serena, Catherine!"

At the far-off voice and sound of barking, they exchanged glances, and Serena plopped her bonnet back on, hoping it might shade some of the telltale signs of emotion doubtless still on her face.

"You look fine," Catherine murmured, as their hostess drew near, Polly scampering about her feet, before a quacking from the reeds drew canine interest away to the lake.

"Here you both are!" Melanie glanced at the sketchbook in Serena's hand, her gaze straying upward. "How goes the planning?"

"Nearly there." She managed a smile that did not feel completely artificial.

"Good, good. Rochdale has just told me he must leave today for Manchester for a few days on business. I was thinking to cheer ourselves up that if this weather holds we might enjoy a little jaunt this afternoon. You know the Blue Cave is not terribly far, and the children have been begging for a little excursion."

"But the painting—"

"Does the canvas not require time to cure? I'm sure Grandmama has said things like that before. And it would only be one afternoon. Surely you could manage one afternoon."

Catherine caught Serena's glance and gave a slight nod. "Will we meet Jon and Lord Carmichael there?"

"What a good idea! I'll have a message sent. I'm sure Lord Winthrop would be *very* happy to see his wife again."

"Oh, yes, but—"

"Serena"—the dark head now studied her—"are you quite well? Your nose seems a little red. I would not like our resident artist getting sunburned before she's really begun."

"I shall endeavor to wear my hat more often. I do not like to work with it on, as it seems to slip and mar my concentration."

"Perhaps a headband of some description might be in order? I see you have Grandmama's painting smock already."

"She said I might." After Lord Carmichael had insisted Serena wear one following that afternoon in the rain, and had begged his grandmother for its use.

"Grandmama seems to have taken quite a fancy to you. She didn't even make a fuss when Harry broke those paints, like she would have with the rest—Oh! I'm sorry. I was not to mention—"

"Your grandmother is very kind."

"Hmm. Yes." The green eyes peered curiously. "Are you quite sure you are well? I would not have you working—or gallivanting on picnics—if you are sick."

Was this her excuse to avoid seeing him? "I am perfectly fine. Although sometimes I do experience a degree of pain which renders me somewhat dysfunctional. And I—"

"Oh, do you experience painful menses, too? It's terrible, isn't it? Hopefully it won't detract from your enjoyment of our special guest."

"Guest?"

"Yes." The green eyes widened. "Didn't I mention it? Luncheon is almost ready, and we're expecting visitors."

"Wonderful," Catherine said. "And who might we expect to see?"

"Someone to cheer up our dear friend here," Lady Rochdale said, glancing at Serena before giving a brilliant smile. "Mr. Cravenwood."

Serena pasted on a responding smile. "Wonderful."

The village of Castleton held the pretty, scenic quality that Londoners claimed epitomized the best of English countryside. More importantly, it possessed the richest seam of Blue John in the land. Beyond a row of stone cottages lay a small canyon, through which a path led to near vertical bluffs, across which the silvery seams ran thickly. From his seat at the village public house, Harry could see the weathered cliffs that had provided a very different treasure to the view his father valued so highly.

Forking in another mouthful of mutton, Harry chewed over his dining companion's earlier reaction on their walk through the upper reaches of the mine.

"I thought you said this was blue?" Carlew had said, peering closely at the rock face.

"Only when cut."

"And has it use beyond jewelry?"

"Smelting, for use in manufactories."

Carlew's questions and Harry's explanations had continued for the next hour, until the unseasonably warm weather—and hunger—had forced them inside the public house. Here it was cool, the dining area dim, the view partly obscured by the thick foliage against the window. Harry swallowed another mouthful of the bitter-tasting liquid and nodded to Carlew. "How is the venison?"

"Very good, thank you." His friend's smile curved to one side. "But we are not here to talk about food, are we? So come, tell me why, in all these ventures to different mines, you talk of your plans but never of your father's?"

Harry swallowed. "To be honest—"

"I always prefer that."

"I'm afraid my father has little time for my ideas."

Carlew frowned. "I did not gain that impression at Welmsley."

"Because he has a social front for visitors, and quite another for his son."

"But why?"

Harry thought back, back many years, to when the tension had begun. "I was at Eton, then went to Oxford, as you know. We met . . . when? Halfway through that first semester?"

Carlew confirmed this with a nod.

"You might not have known that my father did not like my preferred course of study." A waste of time, and talent, and money, Father had said, too many times for him to count. "Of course I disagreed—"

"Of course," Carlew murmured.

"But as he was footing the bills I thought it expedient to transfer my studies to something more akin to what he wished. Fortunately, I have always enjoyed the classics, so my study of Greek and Latin was not thought frivolous."

"Very useful subjects, indeed."

"Aren't they?"

They shared grins.

"And your original area of study?"

"Chemistry, with an interest in natural science and geology."

"Ah."

"Yes. Far more practical for the future of the estate, yet the thought of his son reduced to something he thought grubby . . ."

"One does not get *quite* so dirty poring over Greek manuscripts, dusty though they may be."

"No." He drained his glass. "I'm ashamed to say I've hidden my passion for rocks and minerals for far too long."

"A forgivable sin."

Harry nodded. "So, even though Father did not approve, I took great joy in spending time with my grandfather whenever he visited the mines. Unlike some of the family-owned mines around here, the Bevingtons have always treated their workers with a degree of consideration. We have needed to, as our family holds the title to at least three different mines, two of lead, one of fluorspar. I enjoyed learning, gaining a sense of the skills needed to manage them—Grandfather was always very practical in his instruction."

"I remember a similar process when I was learning about business under Harold Carlew. He might not have been my biological father, but he fathered me in more ways than I realized."

Of course. Lord Jonathan Winthrop's father had died before he was born, his mother remarrying so soon that her son had borne his new father's name—which caused no end of speculation over his true parentage whilst at Oxford. Such a very distant cousin attaining the barony had proved something of a shock to those mourning the passing of the previous Lord Winthrop, namely Catherine and—

No. His heart tripped. His hands fisted. He *would* master this! He must! He forced his thoughts back to the matter at hand.

Carlew frowned. "If you don't mind my asking, why is your father so opposed?"

"I do not know. I've wondered if he and Grandfather had a falling out, or if Father never realized a great portion of the family wealth came from underground. Perhaps education raised his sights to such a civilizing degree that he forgot how that education was paid for. Regardless, he has always preferred the finer things of life, like his art, and his books, and music. Anything less he had no time for."

"Or anyone less?"

Harry jerked a nod, his gaze falling before his friend's too-discerning eyes.

"I'm sure he does not feel that way."

"I'm sure you cannot be so sure, old man, but I do appreciate the sentiment."

The sounds of the public house filled his ears, as he waited for Carlew to finish his pastry and meat. He glanced out the ivy-fringed window. What would his life have been if Father had supported his early desires? How different a man would he have become?

The clank of cutlery on plate drew his attention back to his friend, now leaning back in his chair, eyes watchful, brow furrowed.

"So the pomade-wearing, gambling sophisticate would really prefer to be a humble miner after all."

"Pray don't advertise the fact."

Carlew chuckled. "Why can't you just tell him that's what you want to do?"

"Because . . ." he swallowed. "Until I know this path is feasible I remain unsure."

"You'd truly be content to continue with all your drinking, and gaming, and flirting?"

That stung. He glanced away as he suddenly saw how his life must appear to Carlew, to Father, to Serena. His dandyism. His attempts at sporting glory. His gambling. His flirtations. His stomach grew queasy. It must appear he had no penchant to settle down to anything. What kind of blackguard must she think him?

"Carmichael, you've stood as my friend since Oxford days, and I'm forever grateful for your kindness when whispers made life almost unbearable. But let me speak plainly: Do you really think pursuing such things will bring satisfaction in your life?"

The sounds of the public house faded away, the moment suddenly seemed endowed with heavy import, as if this next answer might determine the course of his life.

"Of course not," he muttered.

"Then why not change your life's direction? Determine to live for more."

Harry traced the rim of his wineglass, avoiding his friend's gaze. "I . . . I have admired the passion that drives you."

"That passion stems from something fundamental in my life. I may have wealth, a degree of power, and a wonderful, wonderful wife, but something more is needed to give direction."

He glanced up. Carlew held his gaze, expression sober.

"Another plain question: Do you still believe in God?"

"Yes."

"Do you let that belief determine your actions?"

"I . . ." No.

Carlew's countenance did not alter, though his eyes held no condemnation. "Do so, my friend," he said softly.

But how? He must have looked his confusion, for Carlew continued, "Seek His will first. Ask God what He would have you do."

"And a great voice from the sky will tell me what to do?"

Carlew smiled. "Probably not. Although you may feel an inkling, a prompting, to do things differently than before."

God knew Harry needed to do things differently from before.

"Let Him show you," Carlew said, "and obey His leading, and your paths, your life's direction, will be made straight."

He nodded stiffly. Asking God for help might seem something of a crutch, but it surely couldn't hurt . . .

"If I may, your father does not seem particularly enamored of your current lifestyle."

"Father won't be content with anything I do."

"What would satisfy him?"

"Apart from the obvious, you mean? Marrying, preferably Lily so the Milsom lands will join with ours, taking an interest in the estate, and all that? That's the thing. I *do* believe pursuing mining is a way to take care of the estate. It might not involve sheep, but it has potential to be far more lucrative than the wool off some poor beast's back."

"And your father does not see it."

"He has no wish to."

"So you study the classics, develop a fashion sense, build a fearsome reputation in the gambling hells of London, come visit me in India, all to what end? To please other people?"

"I wanted to see *you*, old man." Harry grinned. "It could not be helped that there are some rather interesting mines in that part of the world."

"I'm touched." The humor glinting in Carlew's eye belied the dry response. "But you know you cannot live your life forever hiding your true ambitions."

"Perhaps. But it has been easier to pursue such things than stay here, frustrated because I cannot finance my plans nor pretend to be the person Father always wished me to be."

"You mean you would rather avoid the confrontation."

Coward. He could almost hear the word.

Harry shook his head. "It would kill him to admit he was wrong."

"And it's not killing you to be living a lie, pretending that you care for nothing when, in truth, you care more than you dare admit?"

He shrugged, but the denial ached somewhere deep inside. Add that to the other bruises he wore there.

"What is it you truly wish to do?"

"Truly?"

Carlew nodded.

"I want to see the mines succeed again. I know they still can produce, I feel it in my bones. Call it my lucky streak, or what you will, I just know. But with cheaper imports, Father is not convinced, and does not want to waste good money on what he thinks is a gamble."

"I can see his point."

He frowned. "You are not being entirely supportive, old man."

"Do you want my support, or my honesty?"

"Honesty," he muttered.

"Then let me be honest. From what I've seen these past two days I can quite understand how your father feels. The mines are indeed in a sad state; without proper equipment and close management, the workers lack motivation to excel, and so of course they are not producing as well as they might."

"But if someone were to invest, then it would improve."

Carlew eyed Harry. "Perhaps."

"But that is where you come in. You're the finances, I'm the brains."

"Not the best way to put it, I should think."

"Humble apologies." Harry inclined his head. "But why should you not invest?"

"Because I would want a greater proof than just whatever your bones may be feeling."

"Such as?"

"Reports, deeds, mine certifications." Carlew mentioned half a dozen other legal documents. "Show me these and I will see what I can do."

Harry leaned back in his chair, impressed. He could see why Carlew made a formidable businessman.

"That is, however, provided your father does not object."

"He barely pays heed to what the estate and mine managers say, much less finds reason to object to them." It seemed the day-to-day operations of any part of the estate were beneath his father's notice, as long as the coffers continued to be fed. "I doubt he will consider your involvement of any interest." Harry's involvement on the other hand . . .

Carlew nodded, his eyes still searching, as if he wanted to read something Harry wasn't sure he wanted seen.

"Was there something else, old man?"

"This running of your mines, *is* that all you desire?"

A fair face flashed into mind.

He pushed it aside, dredged up a smile. "It is all."

All he could have.

And definitely all he deserved.

Chapter Fifteen

"Miss Winthrop, may I hold the parasol for you? Is this position better? I should not like you to have the sun in your eyes. There, is that better now?"

"Thank you, Mr. Cravenwood," Serena muttered.

She scowled at her sister, seated beside her, Catherine once again barely able to restrain her laughter. For the last hour, Mr. Cravenwood, somehow also seated next to her, had been so industrious in his attentions and nonstop chatter, she had barely had a moment of quiet to think. She glanced across the carriage at Melanie, who mouthed an "I'm sorry" before giving a little smile that suggested she wasn't really, and returned her attention to the chatter of her children, seated either side of her.

"Mr. Cravenwood, perhaps you might feel more comfortable seated at the front?" suggested Catherine.

"I am quite satisfied here."

"But it is a little confining, is it not?" Serena said sweetly.

He looked at her, nonplussed, so she bit back a sigh and fixed her gaze outside.

At least the view made the trip worthwhile. This part of Derbyshire was exceptionally pretty. Long, low hills, spiked with the rugged peaks that gave the district its name, gave way to little valleys, like miniature versions of Welmsley's "treasure," dotted with clusters of sheep. Verdant green vales contrasted with the treeless moorlands, whose magnitude seemed able to cleanse her soul in a manner she'd not experienced since leaving Welmsley's spectacular view. There was something about the wildness, the barrenness, that seemed to call to her, to beg her to not settle for constraint and conformity. Perhaps Melanie's idea for an excursion was not all bad.

"Mama, are we nearly there?" Eleanor said sleepily from her perch beside her mother.

"Nearly."

Melanie wrapped an arm around her daughter, the loving gesture twisting emotion around Serena's heart. Catherine, too, studied the sweet-faced girl, wearing a smile that suggested she dreamed of one day soon cradling her own child.

"I see Castleton ahead," Tom shouted, twisting in his seat.

"Thank you, Thomas. We are not deaf, although such clamor might encourage one to deafness."

"Sorry, Mama."

Melanie smiled. "I trust your husband and my brother received the message."

"You do not know?"

"It does not matter, save for your sake, of course, Lady Winthrop. If they are not there we still have Mr. Cravenwood to lend us his support."

"I have always wished to see the cavern," said Mr. Cravenwood. "I understand it is quite something of a tourist locale, even though it is still being mined."

"Fluorspar is a most remarkable substance," Catherine murmured.

"So very attractive," agreed Serena. "And I'd like to see where it can be found."

Over luncheon Melanie had pointed out a number of pretty ornaments carved from the striking mineral. Ripples of purple-blue and yellow-gold seemed to glow in the autumn sun. It had made Serena wonder about Lord Carmichael's words, spoken months ago, about her eye color. She frowned. Surely he didn't think her eyes yellow . . .

"Miss Winthrop?"

The eager face of the gentleman beside her stole into her musings. "Yes, Mr. Cravenwood?"

"Would you allow me to escort you down the cavern's steps? I understand it is quite steep, and I'm sure you would appreciate assistance."

"Thank you, sir, but I believe your assistance would be better given to my sister here." She sent Catherine a thin smile. See how *she* liked being fussed over—especially when she was the one whose condition meant a fuss should be made. "That is, of course, unless Lord Winthrop is there. If he is then I wouldn't advise it."

"Oh. Is he a jealous man?"

"Of course n—"

"You can't expect me to answer that, can you?" Serena said, interrupting her sister. "Let me just say that I know for a fact that he has faced a charging elephant."

"Has he really?" Tom's eyes were huge. "Uncle Harry never had things like that happen to him."

"That we know of," his mother added, with an air of reflection.

The carriage had now drawn into the village, a collection of pretty stone buildings encircling a village square. As the vehicle made its stately procession down the main street, a number of locals stopped and stared, Melanie and her guests seemingly the town's chief tourist attraction. Serena wasn't sorry when they eventually pulled up near a cleft in the hill.

"Is this it?" Tom said, leaning out the window, disappointment in his voice.

"Aye, Master Tom," said the coachman. "This 'ere be it."

"It doesn't look especially prepossessing," Catherine said, doubt crossing her brow.

"It still be Blue John Cavern, my lady."

Melanie ruffled her daughter's hair, gently stirring her awake. "Are you ready to see the cave, my precious?"

"Yes." The little girl peered over the edge of the door. "Look! Isn't that Uncle Harry?"

Serena's heart skipped a beat. She tamped down her excitement and smoothed her features into calmness. Just because she had not seen him for a week was no cause for goose-ish behavior now. She would not give him—or anyone else—the satisfaction of knowing he perturbed her equilibrium. Because he didn't. At all.

⁂

"Uncle Harry! Uncle Harry!"

Harry stared at his sister and her party. "What on earth are you doing here?"

"Surprise!"

He fought for his gaze not to drift to the young woman seated opposite her, who was even now being whispered to by . . . Cravenwood?

"Harry? You look a little flustered. Have we come at a bad time?"

Ignoring the speculative look in his sister's eyes, he bowed to the vehicle's other occupants. "I'm so pleased you could come, ladies, gentleman." He frowned. "Wait, isn't this my carriage?"

"That you scarcely use. It was the only one large enough to fit us all in, and even then it was a little squashy, wasn't it, Serena?"

The blue eyes refused to meet his, leaving him feeling a mix of relief and regret.

He glanced at the young man beside her, whose attentions made his intention plain. Again, that wretched feeling wrenched his chest.

Carlew assisted his wife's descent, his tenderness evident in the softly spoken words, their shared secret smiles. How he wished . . .

"So, Harry, tell them what they'll find in this famous mine of yours," Melanie said.

"Yours?" Cravenwood said.

"It was deeded to me by my grandfather."

"The dowager's husband?"

The low, clear voice curled gladness in his heart. So she *was* still speaking to him . . .

"The same," Melanie said. "Now, shall we have our tour?"

"Oh, but it is quite steep. I really do not think it suitable for Ellie, and perhaps some of you ladies might not care for it particularly."

"Nonsense," began Melanie. "I—"

"If you do not mind, I should be very happy to wait here," said Lady Winthrop. "I sometimes find enclosed spaces a little frightening."

"Then I will stay, too," said Carlew. "I have seen the mine already and, while interesting, I confess to preferring the company of my wife above ground."

"Oh, but . . ." Miss Winthrop bit her lip.

"We can look after Ellie if you would like, Melanie. Her little legs might find it a challenge."

"Would you?" His sister's face brightened. "That would be very kind."

"Not at all."

"Then that leaves us four and Tom. Mr. Cravenwood, might I oblige you for your arm? You seem a strong young man . . ."

Their voices faded as they moved toward the cave entrance, followed by Tom, leaving Harry standing near Serena, Carlew and his wife having moved with Ellie back to the carriage.

"Miss Winthrop?"

It was only the second time he'd spoken to her directly since their escape from the rain. He held out his arm. "May I?"

Her glance slid from his arm to his eyes, and he found himself gazing into their depths. A thousand words came to mind: apologies, excuses, promises. He said nothing.

She placed her hand on his arm, her touch seeping through his shirtsleeve to heat his skin like fire. He almost felt to hold his breath as they passed through the cave entrance and immediately began the steep descent. Soon he had to remove her hand, to walk in front for her safety, in case she slipped on the smooth steps. Along the tunnel were tiny nooks stuffed with candles, now alight, revealing a giant, shimmering spiderweb of gleaming ore.

He stopped, held out his hand, drawing her closer as he held a flickering candle up to the silvery seam. "See the traces of blue?"

"Yes." Her gloved hand touched the rock face. "It is hard to believe such beauty lies behind something so dull and gray."

"Things are not always what they seem."

"No."

He guided her to the next landing, his emotions swirling. Despite the innocuous conversation, the sense of strain lingered. What could he say to mend the breach? What should he say? Perhaps his escorting Serena through dark tunnels was more than another of Melanie's sadly impulsive ideas, and was actually a test from God to see if Harry could box these feelings.

Well, he would!

Well . . . he would if the darkness had not heightened every sense, if he couldn't hear her soft breathing, catch the scent of roses when she moved, feel her hand in his and wish . . .

No.

He gritted his teeth.

Ahead he could hear Tom's shouts, and some muffled conversation between his sister and young Cravenwood. But he cared for nothing save for whatever words might fall from the lips of the woman beside him.

"Sir, your grasp is too tight."

"I'm so sorry." He shook his head at himself, releasing his hold. What kind of gentleman was he? He was every kind of fool, every kind of—

"Lord Carmichael."

He lifted the lamp the better to see her face.

"Would you mind? I still need your assistance." She held out her hand.

"You mean—?"

"I might not mind rain and storms, but like Catherine, I find something rather eerie about dark places."

"And yet the One who created the world above also created the depths beneath, filling it with unseen treasure."

"Unseen treasure." The candlelight flickered shadows on her face. "I like that."

"I believe He has blessed the earth with precious gifts for our use."

Surprise lit her expression. The luminous blue eyes seemed to search him for the longest time. Finally, she gave a small nod.

He helped her down another steep step. Lifted the lamp to point out another sparkling seam.

"Lord Carmichael, do you truly believe that God created such things?"

"Yes." At the rise of her eyebrows he continued, "Does that surprise you? I know my reputation is not always synchronous with that of a man of faith, but I do believe in God."

"I am pleased . . ."

"But? I sense a but, Miss Winthrop."

"But is not reputation built on actions which reflects one's character?"

His heart wrenched. How many times in one day must a man hear of his shortcomings?

"Sir"—one gloved hand touched his arm—"that was rude. Please forgive me."

He drew in a musty, earth-scented breath. "It was not rude. Merely honest."

"Perhaps brutally so."

"Perhaps." He sneaked a look at her. Her brow was creased. "What would you suggest to help one's reputation change?"

She shook her head.

"I know my reputation is hardly flawless, and there have been things I have done of which I'm not proud." Why did the darkness induce honesty?

Still she hesitated, her forehead pleated.

"Please, Miss Winthrop. I would value your opinion."

"I . . . I do not claim to be an expert, but I've observed those whose character I admire, people like Catherine, Jon, and Lavinia, their character is revealed not just in their words but in their deeds. Their actions make for good repute."

Her implication was clearly that his actions did not. Lunch soured in his belly.

"I remember Lavinia's father—he was the minister for a long time in St. Hampton Heath—he often said there are many believers, but few followers." Her head tilted as she glanced at him with a small smile. "But if one wishes to change, then belief in God is the starting point to good actions, wouldn't you agree?"

He nodded, unable to speak as her words swirled around in his heart. Change.

The whisper within echoed Carlew's earlier comments. Was this some of God's prompting? Something of His direction? To rebuild his reputation and become a man deemed trustworthy and honest? Someone Carlew—and Serena—could respect?

He would change. The thought firmed into purpose. He believed; he would trust. He *would* change. God would help him. *Lord, help me . . .*

She gave a tiny smile, turning from him to examine the rich seam sparkling in the candlelight. "It is a beautiful stone."

"And rare. The only place it is found is here and one other nearby hill." He held her hand carefully as they descended the last few steps. "The Duchess of Devonshire has an extensive mineral collection, including some wonderful ornaments made from Blue John. I believe some was even inlaid around a fireplace."

"Does that not defeat the purpose? I would think the chief attraction is seeing light ripple through the different colors."

"Light inhabits true beauty."

Her eyes searched him, before she gave a slow nod. "I agree. Darkness can hold beauty, but also an unsettling quality. Light can be considered an expression of God."

"Who is Light, and in whom is no darkness at all."

She looked up at him as if in surprise.

"I believe that is from the Bible," he said.

"Yes."

Was that approval in her eyes? He wished he could read her expression, but she had turned away to examine the seam once more, reaching out a hand to its silvery streaks. "There can be much to appreciate in such hidden depths."

Did she speak of him or the mine? He settled for a safe, "Yes."

"I have seen some handsome examples of fluorspar at your sister's. She has a lovely urn."

"I believe that was a present from my grandfather at her coming of age."

"And did you receive something when you turned one-and-twenty?"

He grinned. "Yes." Something rather larger. "The deed to the mine."

THE RETURN TO the top was much faster, and he couldn't help but notice the relief on both Carlew's and his wife's faces when Serena emerged, prompting his sardonic, "See? No harm done."

"We did not expect any."

Harry raised an eyebrow, sourly pleased to see his friend redden, before Melanie's reappearance demanded attention once more.

"Well! That was an experience I won't hurry to repeat."

"Getting dirty in the dark is not to everyone's taste, I suppose."

Melanie grinned. Mr. Cravenwood snorted.

Now Harry's own neck heated. "I did not mean—"

"Why do you like the caves, Lord Carmichael?" Serena looked at him innocently, saving his blushes, although that twinkle in her eye—

He forced his thoughts away and talked of his family's involvement in the local industry over many generations. "And I hope one day to see mines like this resume their full productivity."

"Have you talked with Papa about this?" Melanie frowned. "I did not think him keen."

Her words pricked his confidence, deflating his hopes. "I . . . well, we'll see."

Miss Winthrop glanced to Melanie before her gaze settled on him. "You wish to be responsible for them?"

He nodded.

"I'm so glad."

"Really? Why?"

"Because good deeds require doing, don't they, Lord Carmichael?"

Her half smile for him ignited fresh resolve. He *would* make this work. He would speak with Father. If he had to gamble his own inheritance to do so, he would make this work.

She believed in him.

Chapter Sixteen

"Miss S'ena, Miss S'ena!"

Serena glanced up from her canvas to smile at the little girl. "Let me guess. Mr. Monkey is making you wriggle again?" The tiny blonde nodded, prompting her chuckle. "He sounds a very naughty Mr. Monkey."

"Mr. Monkey is not a he. Mr. Monkey is a girl."

"My apologies."

"Honestly, Ellie. Don't you know anything?" Tom said loudly, with a shake of his head and a glance at the clouded heavens. "A mister can't be a girl. A miss means a girl, like Miss Serena, see? A mister is a *man*."

"Unless he is a goose."

Serena jumped, heart thudding as the viscount came into view, trailed by an excited puppy.

"Uncle Harry! Uncle Harry!" Ellie jumped from her carefully arranged position on the garden seat to be thrown above her uncle's head and caught safely.

He glanced at Serena. "Have you ever noticed this one's habit of repeating one's name? I begin to wonder if I have an invisible twin that only she can see."

"Uncle Harry, Uncle Harry, can you tell Tom that Mr. Monkey is a girl?"

Lord Carmichael nodded to his nephew, as he said seriously, "Mr. Monkey is a girl."

Tom shook his head. "You're just saying that."

"As I was commanded, yes. You will find it sometimes best to just agree with the ladies, even if you know them to be wrong."

"A harsh indictment on our sex, my lord."

"Would you prefer me to disagree, Miss Winthrop?"

The eyes—sap green, tinted with ochre—locked with hers, his smile curling to one side, causing tightness in her chest. She swallowed. "I . . ."

"It's S'ena, Uncle Harry. S'ena!" the childish voice piped below.

"Xena?" He smiled. "One can only trust you will be as hospitable as your name suggests."

"You know Greek?"

He dipped his head. "Honors at Balliol, Oxford." His gaze met hers again. "Things are not always as they seem, Xena."

The little voice piped up again. "It's *Miss* S'ena, Uncle Harry! *Miss* S'ena! She's a girl."

"That she most certainly is." He smiled, his dimple reemerging.

More of that peculiar fluttery feeling filled her heart. He was behaving so affably today, it was enough to make her think—

"Stop it!"

The squeal snapped her attention back to the children, Tom holding the soft monkey toy in one hand as he raced away to the lake, chased by his small sister and a barking Polly.

"Thomas and Eleanor!"

She jumped.

"Come here." The figures stilled, as the deep voice continued. "Now."

Serena peeked up at the serious-faced viscount. He caught her glance. "My apologies for startling you. I trust the imps have not been so wild the entire time."

"No, they have been very well behaved."

"You're sure?" His brow furrowed. "I would not have them distress you."

"Thank you, but it is good to know what to expect with children. I need the practice, you see." At his upraised brow, heat touched her cheeks, and she hurried on, "For when my sister—Oh! I was not meant to say—"

"So that explains Carlew's decided look of self-satisfaction." He grinned broadly. "Never fear, Miss Winthrop. Your sister's secret is safe with me."

The warmth in his eyes gave curious reassurance to his words. She felt she could truly trust him.

"Serena!" Melanie's voice called, prompting an internal sigh. Would she never get this painting finished?

The viscount leaned closer. "But I would avoid mentioning it to her."

A chuckle slipped past her frustration.

"And speaking as one who often fought with his sister, one can never know what to expect with small children," he added in an undertone as the children approached.

She watched him as he gently but firmly, reprimanded them. Impeccably dressed as always, he looked the epitome of the gentleman as the sunshine gleamed golden strands in his dark hair. More than superficial handsomeness, today she could see character carved in the firm lips, a new light in his eyes. Tenderness showed in how he comforted little Ellie, holding her close as he spoke quietly to her brother. Just how she imagined Jon might father his and Catherine's children. She blinked away the burn. Something had changed. Was it her, or was it him?

She swallowed, slumping in her seat, as memories of another man's subtle transformation took hold. People changed, they could wear a façade, and hurt—

"Oh, is my brother disciplining my children again? I declare, that man is beyond ready to be a father." Melanie's head tilted, her eyes sparkling as she smiled at Serena. "I don't suppose—"

"Please don't suppose."

"Very well." She sighed. "Harry, are you behaving?" she said in a louder voice.

"More than your children are." He glanced at Serena then back at his niece and nephew. "I want you both to sit very still and do exactly what Miss Winthrop asks."

"Miss S'ena."

"Yes, Miss Serena."

Her skin tingled, despite the bright sunshine. He spoke her name as though with a caress.

He inclined his head then offered an arm to his sister. "I think it best we leave the artist to her work."

"Er, yes. I suppose so."

He moved Melanie away, his gaze catching Serena's, his half smile catching her heart.

She swallowed the sudden dryness in her mouth. "Thank you."

"Oh!" Melanie turned. "I was going to see if you wanted to join us shortly for luncheon. Mama and Mr. Cravenwood are here—"

"Oh . . ."

"Do you want your children's portrait finished or not, Melanie?" Lord Carmichael asked. "If so, you simply must refrain from interrupting. Mother will be content talking with Carlew and your sister, so you need feel no obligation there, Miss Winthrop," he said, before turning to his sister again. "Melanie, I'm sure the children are not needed for luncheon just yet, and could remain a little while longer. As for Miss Winthrop, send some food out for her with a servant, but whatever you do, don't tell Mr. Cravenwood where she is, else the painting will never be completed."

"I suppose you're right."

"Yes, I am. I'm so pleased you finally brought yourself to admit it."

He winked at the children, offered a bow to Serena, and escorted his sister away.

Serena exhaled, then turned around to see both children gazing at her. "Are you ready to resume now you've had your run-around?"

They nodded, moving into their respective positions, and she picked up her brush to touch up the grass with saffron yellow.

"Miss S'ena, Miss S'ena."

She frowned. How could she best capture the highlights of the sun? "Yes, Ellie?"

"Why do you look at Uncle Harry that way?"

Her gaze flew up to meet the children. "In what way?"

"Like Mama looks at Papa?"

"Don't be silly, Ellie. It's because she likes him."

"Do you like him, Miss S'ena?"

She ducked her head behind the canvas. If the children had noticed, who else had?

"Miss S'ena? Miss S'e-e-eena!" persisted the girl in a singsong voice. "Do you like Uncle Harry?"

Serena coughed. "Of . . . of course I do."

"Good. We like Uncle Harry, don't we, Tom?"

"Yes." Tom's face screwed up. "Will you marry Uncle Harry?"

She gulped.

"We like you too, Miss S'ena!"

"Thank you, Ellie. I like you both as well."

"So will you?" Tom asked again.

Really, why must she paint the world's two most determined children? She wiped her brow. "I . . . er, no."

"Why not?"

What could she say both honest and reasonable to young children? "He should ask first."

"Then you'd say yes?"

"I . . . I don't know, Tom."

"I'm gonna tell Uncle Harry to ask you, Miss S'ena."

"Please don't, Miss Eleanor," Serena managed.

"But then you would be our aunt," Tom said wisely. "And we'd see you nearly all the time. You'd like that, wouldn't you?"

She peeked over the top of the canvas at the two adorable children, both gazing at her so seriously as Serena had asked, Ellie still clutching the toy monkey Tom said Uncle Harry had given her two years ago. Her throat thickened. "I'd like that very much indeed."

Gray clouds dappled the skies but she could not stop. Serena was in her element, the painting taking on a life of its own as her brush worked with great speed. Two servants had brought out a large umbrella with stand, followed a short time later by another servant with food. Each time their presence had startled Serena from her artistic absorption, at which the children laughed, prompting her amusement, too.

Their nanny, a placid older woman—whose sudden appearance had caused yet another jump—had collected them for a couple of hours or so, to have luncheon and speak with their grandmother, and for Ellie, perhaps a short sleep.

Serena hoped they enjoyed their break—they had been very patient after all—but rest was the furthest thing from her mind. She cleaned her brush, smearing it dry on the rag she kept for such a purpose. It would stain her hands, but no matter. So she would appear at meals for the next few days with paint stains. It could be worse.

A dab of vermilion, tinted with white, blended until the perfect skin tone was reached. She nodded. Lovely. She retouched Ellie's face, working to capture the tiny, adorable pout, such a contrast to the deep eyes, peering out so seriously. When she was satisfied with the facial features she moved to capture the expression in the eyes. There. The tiniest dab of lead white to highlight the iris. Sparkling. Elfin. Such a contrast to her brother.

She leaned back, picked up a slice of bread, chewed it as she studied his image. Tall, like his uncle, with the dark hair and green eyes that identified Bevington legacy, also. It was hard to believe such an earnest look could come from one so prone to mischief. But she liked the lad, liked his forthrightness, even if she did not appreciate his every word.

Her cheeks warmed again remembering the earlier inquisition. Would she marry Uncle Harry? What was she supposed to have said? How should she have answered? Thank goodness they hadn't asked if she *wanted* to marry him! How could she answer *that* question honestly? And even if she did, her opinion might count for little if Jon and Catherine did not approve . . .

No! The bread fell to the ground. How she hoped the children were not inside telling all and sundry that "Miss S'ena" wanted to marry the viscount! Her heart wrenched. Oh, the embarrassment! Why hadn't she asked them not to say anything? Although, perhaps telling them what *not* to say would only put it in their minds again. And the sooner everyone forgot the better.

The better for everyone.

Serena shook her head. She could do nothing about what the children may or may not say. Best to shove those thoughts to one side and concentrate on what she was supposed to do. Paint this portrait.

She studied the picture. An amalgam of portrait and landscape, she found the balance between grass, lake, and sky and serious child poses quite pleasing. Despite the autumn color, she had painted to give the suggestion of spring, of youth, of freedom, yet somehow constrained by the social mores of the day, evidenced in the posture of the children. What did it need? What would make it truly sing?

During the next hour or so the painting gradually took on the form she'd imagined in her mind. Two children enjoying a lovely day, their pose relaxed—as indicated by the inclusion of Mr. Monkey and Tom's open atlas—yet serious. Another dab here. Another speck of white there. Now the lake was forming before her eyes: smooth, glassy. She added in a small rowboat, one occasionally used for fishing by Tom, under strict supervision, so Melanie had informed her. Another dab, another. There! Perfection.

"Miss S'ena, Miss S'ena."

She smiled, bending forward to gently apply the tiniest crumb of ultramarine to Ellie's white smock. How sweet the little girl was. Even with her partiality for unanswerable questions.

Leaning back, she surveyed the picture. Satisfaction bloomed within. How very lifelike—

"Miss S'ena, Miss—"

Serena blinked, frowned. The voice sounded so far away—was it even real? She looked up from her canvas. No, Ellie was not in her seat or chasing her brother. She rolled her shoulders to release the aching muscles. Glanced behind her. Still no young girl. Where—?

She looked over at the lake, just as a small hand vanished underwater.

No . . .

Breath constricted. Horror curdled within. She leapt up, knocking over her easel and paint box, and rushed to the lake's edge. Stepping into the muddy depths she staggered towards where the small rowboat was now drifting away.

"Miss Serena! What are you—?"

"Get your uncle! It's Ellie!" she screamed at Tom.

As she plunged deeper, knee height, thigh height, hip height, she looked around frantically. No ripples broke the surface. Where had Ellie gone? "Lord God! Help!"

Tears burned. She wiped her eyes, her skirts hampering movement. "Lord, I'm so sorry! I didn't realize—Please help me—"

Recriminations chased her as she stumbled further into the icy lake, until it was up to her chest. Her feet slipped, knocking her under. Gasping, she pushed to the surface. Sucked in breath. Then plunged under again.

Her heart knocked against her ribs as she desperately scanned the murky water. If she did not move much, then the mud would not be further stirred up and perhaps she'd see—

There!

A glimpse of something white propelled her forward. Dear God, *dear God*, let her not be too late! Struggling for air she broke the surface again. Vaguely heard shouts, barking, a splash, but she would not stop. She knew now—

Holding her breath she plunged back under, wiping hair from her eyes as she desperately searched the darkness. *Thank God!*

Two steps closer and she grasped Ellie's hand and tugged. Like a frozen mermaid, the little form floated toward her, eyes open, mouth closed, still.

Fear ricocheted within. No. No! She could not be—*Oh, God!*

Lungs burning, she clasped the body close, pushed up. But her skirts refused the action.

No! *Lord God, do a miracle!*

Movement caught her eye.

The viscount. Swimming strongly. White shirt plastered to his chest. Horror straining his features. He motioned to Ellie and Serena passed the tiny form to him. He kicked to the surface.

Freed from the extra weight, Serena broke the water's surface, sputtering and gasping as she moved toward shore. Her feet alternately sticking then slipping in the mud as the wet and wheezing form of Mr. Cravenwood advanced on her.

"Are you all right?"

Was he serious? "Get a doctor," she managed to croak.

"Miss Winthrop, please—"

Panting, she pushed him away, away from her line of sight to the viscount, who now had Ellie on the shore. "Is she . . . is she . . . ?"

"I don't know."

Somehow the sunlight seemed to make the water colder. She shivered, her steps slowing, as Melanie raced towards the scene with a heart-piercing scream. Serena stumbled in the mud. "Lord God, please help!" she muttered. "Please help . . ."

"Of course."

Before she knew what was happening she was being picked up and carried to the shore. As she struggled against the arms pinioning her, the old panic rose, fears of another man, holding her, forcing her to himself against her will—

"Put me down!" She writhed, clawing him to escape. "Put me down!"

The little crowd around the motionless child shifted, giving her a glimpse of the viscount as he glanced up, his pale face unreadable, before he bent to his task again.

Her heart wrenched. She elbowed her captor's chest. "Put me—"

"Mr. Cravenwood!" Catherine hurried to her side, frowning at her rescuer. "Release her immediately."

"I was just trying—"

"Trying, I know. Please. Now."

He released his hold, and Serena wriggled free, trembling as she hurried to Catherine's side. Her sister drew her into a close hug. Slowly the wild tremors wracking her body calmed.

"Shh, dearest."

"She was . . . she was . . ."

"Shh." Her back was rubbed as her sister's soothing voice continued. "You are safe now."

Serena released a shuddery breath. "But Ellie . . ." Her eyes filled with tears. "Ellie!"

Breaking free from Catherine's comfort, she stumbled to the huddled group. Melanie knelt, wailing next to her daughter's prone body. The viscount continued his desperate ministrations. Around her servants murmured, interspersed with soft tears. Slightly beyond, next to a whining Polly, Tom stood, white faced, attention fixed on the scene as though he couldn't believe his eyes.

Serena pushed past the crying nanny. "How is she?"

Melanie glanced up, her face stark and terrible. "This is your fault."

Her breath caught, her stomach growing queasy with that truth.

Around her the mutters grew as Lady Rochdale was helped to her feet. "Ellie came to see you. You let her drown!"

"I didn't know! I didn't see—"

"You should have!"

Serena wiped away the trickling tears. "But . . . I just saved her!"

"Harry did. You let her drown."

Dear God! "I—no. You are mistaken. I did not—"

"You did!" Her voice broke. "You let my poor sweet baby—"

"Melanie."

The heartbroken mother looked down at her brother.

"She lives."

Relief whirled within. Faces blurred, noises faded, the scene slipping, sliding into . . .

Darkness.

CHAPTER SEVENTEEN

OUTSIDE, THE COOL night air brought welcome relief. Harry stared into darkness, out to the treacherous lake, coolly smug under a quarter moon. Inside, however . . .

Emotions tangled in his head, twining with his memories, refining, redefining the awful horror of earlier. Laughter. Horror. Joy. Fear. Hope. Despair. How could a day of family, friends, peace, and artistic endeavor end in such near tragedy?

He swallowed his wine, the dregs swishing as the images kept coming.

Serena, chest deep in the lake, sobbing. The lake's muddy murk. Ellie's doll-like body. Melanie's keening despair. Tom—poor Tom—silent and guilty. Cravenwood, carrying a mud-stained Serena, panic in her voice and face.

His fingers clenched.

How bizarre that in the midst of everything today his heart had jarred at that image.

Serena . . .

He drew a deep breath of cleansing air, and the events continued their relentless march across his brain.

Serena's shock at Melanie's accusations. The jolt as he realized his prayers for Ellie were answered. Serena's body, slumped on the ground. His heart clenched anew.

He closed his eyes, rested his head on his hands on the table.

Dear God . . .
His throat swelled. His eyes burned. He swallowed.
Thank You.

⁂

"Good morning, dearest."

"G'morning," Serena mumbled.

"Are you going to open your eyes?"

She pushed open her eyelids. Glimpsed her sister. Shut them again. "There."

"Come. Sleep much longer and you won't rest tonight."

"I don't care." She pulled the bed linen closer to her chin, rolled to her side. "So tired."

"I know. But surely you must be hungry. Look, here's some tea and toast for you."

"I don't want to go down. I can't bear facing Melanie, and . . ."

Him. She swallowed. Huddled deeper in the bedclothes.

"Dearest, nobody is blaming you."

"They were yesterday."

"But that was in the heat of the moment."

"How could they even think such a thing? I know I should have paid more attention"—regret gnawed again—"but I'd *never* let someone drown! I don't know what that says people think about me, if they believe that I could permit such a thing."

"I think it says more about them. You must allow for a mother's natural anxiety." Like their own mother, whose proclivity to worry was well known. "Here, sit up and have your tea."

Serena groaned, her limbs protesting as she shifted back against the pillows and accepted the cup Catherine handed over.

She nodded her thanks, sipped her tea. Warm sweetness trickled down her throat, easing the dryness caused by her long sleep. "Has Melanie forgiven me?"

At her sister's pause, she glanced up from studying the milky brown liquid.

Catherine's brow knitted. "Let's just say she's not holding you responsible for Ellie wandering off."

Ellie. Her heart twisted. "And is Ellie going to be all right?"

"The doctor says it's early days, but she had a good night's sleep, so Melanie said this morning." Catherine shook her head. "Dr. MacConnell was away at a distant farmhouse helping deliver twins, so he couldn't rush here immediately."

She nodded. Her head felt heavy, thoughts swirling sluggishly, too fragmented to form. Her stomach tensed, released.

"How are you feeling?"

Serena coughed. "Like I could spend a week in bed."

"You poor thing. It must have been shocking."

"I *honestly* did not know she was there. The first I saw was her hand sinking." Her eyes welled. Tears trickled over. She wiped the moisture away. "I was terrified."

"As were we." Catherine sat on the edge of the bed, held her hand. "When Tom returned yelling about Ellie and the lake, everybody rushed outside, but the viscount was quickest. I saw his face when we noticed you so far out. He turned white. Oh, Serena, I was so frightened for you." She squeezed her hand. "I didn't know him to be such an athlete, but the viscount was out there in a flash, running, swimming . . . We could see nothing. How ever did you find her?"

She shuddered, as visions resurfaced of the child, white, suspended. "I was . . . I was praying, asking God for help. I knew roughly where she had disappeared, because of the boat, so I went there, but . . ." She drew in a deep breath. Exhaled shakily. "I was *so* glad to see him."

Catherine gave her a careful hug.

"I was holding Ellie, but my skirts were so heavy. If he hadn't come when he did I might have—" She swallowed as the full horror of what might have eventuated roared through her mind. "Oh, thank God!"

"He saved your life *and* poor Ellie's."

Lurching emotions prevented anything but a nod.

"Poor girl."

Poor family. She shuddered again.

"Drink some more tea."

Serena obeyed, savoring the comfort. "And how are you? The drama did not harm you, I hope?"

Catherine smiled. "I still felt nauseous this morning, so I gather everything is as it should be."

"I'm sorry."

"Don't be. I count this a trial well worth rejoicing in."

Serena nodded, her smile fading as the events from yesterday crowded in. Another shiver wracked her body as the guilt swooped in again. Ellie could have died! The stress might have affected Catherine's baby. Oh, how wretched was she?

"Dearest? Are you worried about the painting?"

"The paint—Oh no! The portrait! I think I knocked it over." Her eyes blurred. "It must be spoiled now, and to think it was the last image of them happy—"

"Hush now. It fell over, but landed on its back. The painting itself was not damaged."

"Oh, thank goodness."

"Thank God."

"Yes. Thank You, God." If only Ellie was not damaged, either. *Please God, heal her . . .*

She swallowed the remaining tea. Nibbled at a piece of toast. Forced her aching limbs to move as Catherine helped her dress. "I don't want to go downstairs."

"I know."

"I don't want to see them. I don't want to see the accusation in his—their eyes."

"Nobody is accusing you."

Serena forced a watery smile at her sister's denial. Yes, someone still accused.

She accused herself.

❦

The morning held a strange quality, a cross between a sense of mourning and a profound sense of joy. How could they be sad? His night had been one of half-whispered prayers and praise. He'd even scrounged a dusty Bible from the library, flicking to the Psalms where he found a wealth of verses reflecting his heart over the past few days.

Sorrow that gave way to repentance, igniting hope that cleansed away the stains. Somehow this near tragedy had proved a catalyst for his heart to seek God as it hadn't since university days. And even though things still seemed somewhat shaky in Melanie's world, he had confidence now that God would bring good from this, just as Carlew had prayed last night.

The door to the morning room opened, admitting Melanie, holding a sleeping Eleanor. "I could not stay upstairs, my thoughts preying on me."

He stood, offered to relieve his sister's burden, but she shook her head. He smiled wryly. He did not envisage his sister relinquishing her motherly attention anytime soon. "How is she?"

"She still has not woken."

"She will."

A tear raced down her cheek. "But what if she doesn't? What if she's impaired in some way? She's my baby girl, I cannot stand to lose her."

"She is alive, Melanie. Be thankful."

"Oh, I am. But I just cannot help think—"

"Think on good things."

"Like what? How is any of this good?" Melanie sank onto the settee and settled her daughter snugly in her lap, pressing her damp cheek to the child's hair.

"She's alive, Melanie. She could have died but she didn't."

"No thanks to—"

"Do not say it," he warned.

"But I must! If Serena had been watching for her none of this would have happened."

He leaned back in the seat, thankful the room remained empty of others. "I did not realize you employed her for that role."

"What?"

"Does Ellie not have a nanny?" he persisted.

"Foolish woman," she grumbled. "Chasing after a stuffed toy when she should have been watching my daughter."

"At your request, as I recall."

She flushed, her eyes narrowing.

"I do not think you can blame her, or Serena." She opened her mouth to speak so he hurried on. "In fact, I thought you had asked Serena to paint your children's portraits."

"Well, yes . . ."

"Was there some secret clause of which I'm unaware that the artist is also responsible for the well-being of the children?"

"Of course not."

"Then how is this her fault? You've seen her at work, oblivious to everything save her art when she's in the depths of creativity. There was no way she would have been aware." He shook his head. "We had a multitude of adults inside, all of whom could have checked on Ellie's whereabouts, but did any of us? No. We were all too willing to think a four-year-old girl would simply do what she said she'd do, and run back to Serena. How is Serena at fault for not being aware of your daughter's intentions?"

Her eyes snapped. "You cannot blame this on poor little Ellie." Her hand protectively cupped the child's head.

"And *you* cannot blame poor Serena. You weren't out there in the lake. You didn't see her desperation. She nearly drowned herself! Dear God, if I hadn't got there when I did, she would have! Is that what you would have preferred?"

A beat. "Of course not."

"Then, please, do not speak of your blame of her anymore. Especially to her. You might not have noticed, but she was crushed when she thought . . . when she . . ."

"I know." Her eyes narrowed a fraction. "I must admit to a certain level of surprise."

He gazed at her wearily.

"I certainly did not think you preferred her over your own family."

He blinked, before anger stirred once more. "Are you serious? You think this a game where I take sides?" He leaned forward. "Your children are *your* responsibility, Melanie. Yes, they have a nanny, and perhaps Rochdale is frequently away, and you might prefer adult company at times, but they need to hear from *you* when they have crossed the line. And that is something both you and Rochdale know, and something I say because I love my family."

His sister glared at him, but for once did not argue.

He slumped back in his seat. "Come. I don't wish for harsh words. Not when there is so much to be thankful for."

"You keep saying that."

"Aren't you *glad* no one died? Aren't you thankful Mother had already left and wasn't here? Can't you see how much pain that would have caused her—and you?"

Melanie nodded, a tiny smile twisting her lips. "She would not have been of great assistance."

Or any. He let that slide. "And Tom. Aren't you thankful he was not involved?"

"But I was."

Harry swiveled to the now-opened door. "Tom! How long were you standing there?"

The boy crept into the room, shooting a quick glance at his mother and sleeping sister before coming to stand before Harry's seat. "I . . . I'm sorry, I didn't mean—" He gulped.

"Didn't mean what?"

"I'm the one who told her about the boat. Ellie was talking about it earlier, and I . . . I dared her to hop in. But I didn't know she'd do it. Or that she'd fall. Or get so . . ." His eyes filled with tears. "I'm so sorry, Uncle Harry."

"You're forgiven." He pulled the boy close, hugged him, feeling the little shudders as the boy sobbed out his shame. Over Tom's shoulder he caught Melanie's reddened eyes. Perhaps now wasn't the best time for her to start disciplining her children appropriately.

The door opened again to reveal Carlew, Catherine, and Serena.

His heart leapt. *Thank You, God.* She was all right. Even if she seemed as pale as Ellie. He smiled his hello, but Serena's gaze had bent to the children, her glance shifting between them as she bit her bottom lip.

"We seem to be interrupting," Carlew said, taking a step back. "We'll leave—"

"Don't go." Harry frowned at Melanie who had neither moved nor greeted her guests. He returned his attention to the Winthrop party. "Tom here is simply expressing his relief."

"We've all done that, Thomas," Catherine said kindly. "There have been many prayers prayed over your sister's health these past hours."

"That's right." Harry thumbed away a fat tear sitting on his nephew's cheek. "God has shown Himself most faithful."

"Indeed He has," Carlew said. He nodded to Harry before turning to Melanie. "Lady Rochdale, I'm sure at this distressing time you do not need the additional burden of guests, so if it's convenient, we plan on taking our leave tomorrow."

"Oh!"

No. Dismay flooded his soul. If she left, how could he ever prove himself, how could she ever know—

Melanie's gaze caught his before she slowly turned to Serena. "But . . . but what about the painting?"

All eyes swiveled to Serena. Although her features remained composed, he caught the tinge of pink on her cheeks. "I . . . I did not imagine you wanted me here anymore."

"Why?"

"Because of yesterday." The pink deepened into rose. "I . . . I'm so sorry, Melanie. Truly, I did not know—" Her eyes sparkled, and a watery line traced along her nose. "Please, please forgive me."

Melanie's mouth twisted, her arms clutching Ellie jerked a little. She shook her head. "There . . . there is nothing to forgive." She cut him a look before returning a strained face to Serena.

"Truly? You cannot know how heavy this weighs on my soul. I would give anything to change what happened."

"You would not have rescued Ellie?" Harry said.

She blinked. "Of . . . of course I would have."

"You would have preferred your painting to be less than the remarkable effort that it is."

Golden eyebrows lifted, knitted. "You have seen it?"

"It is truly extraordinary."

Her blush renewing, her gaze dropped to the floor.

"I know! You would prefer that someone other than Cravenwood hauled you from the lake?"

"Yes. I mean, no. I mean, sir, you are deliberately misunderstanding—"

"And I suspect you are filled with self-recrimination. The only trouble is, so is young Tom here. And, I suspect, Melanie. And I'm sure Nanny feels this was her fault, too. And I also feel guilt for what happened yesterday. So what should we all do? Blame one person in particular? Offload our guilt onto their shoulders? Or should we all accept a degree of responsibility and decide to be more aware of our actions and their consequences next time?" He smiled, grasped Tom's shoulder. "I was reading the Bible last night. I don't believe God wants us burdened with guilt all our lives. And if He is so willing to forgive, then we likewise must forgive others, and ourselves."

Serena's gaze connected with his for the longest time, before she finally murmured, "Thank you."

Warmth chased away the clouds inhabiting his chest. He exhaled, caught Carlew's nod, Catherine's smile, and turned to his sister.

Melanie wiped her cheeks. "That was . . . beautifully said, Harry."

He raised a brow, tilting his head the slightest degree toward Serena.

"Oh!" Melanie gave Serena a tremulous smile. "I do hope you'll forgive me for what I said yesterday. I was not thinking . . ."

"Of course."

"And I do hope you will stay until the portrait is completed, if . . . if not longer."

"We would not wish to impose—"

"Nonsense. I would dearly love the painting to be completed." She smoothed a trembling hand across her daughter's brow. "But only if you wish to, of course."

"I would love to." Serena moved closer, touching Tom on the shoulder before kneeling to look at the sleeping girl on Melanie's lap. She stroked Ellie's hair, whispering soft words he strained to hear. Was it a prayer?

Melanie shifted, and Ellie yawned. She blinked sleepy eyes several times then stared at Serena.

"Hello, Ellie," Serena said.

"Miss S'ena, Miss S'ena!" She yawned again. "Are you painting today?"

His eyes blurred. Thank God. *Thank You, God!*

"Not today, precious girl. But perhaps tomorrow."

Melanie choked out a sob and her breathing stuttered as she turned it to laughter.

Ellie rubbed at her eyes, as the room filled with sniffles and cleared throats. She looked around the room, catching his eye before turning back to Serena. "Miss S'ena, Miss S'ena."

"Yes, dearest?"

His niece tilted her head and gave the mischievous smile he so well remembered. "Has Uncle Harry asked you to marry him yet?"

CHAPTER EIGHTEEN

SERENA FROZE. A smatter of chuckles around the room put paid to her very slim hope that nobody else had heard Ellie's *extremely* unfortunate remark. Heat crawled up from her chest to fill her cheeks. What to do? What to say?

Fixing her eyes on Ellie she said, "He has not."

"Oh." The baby lips pushed into a pucker, before her gaze shifted beyond Serena's shoulder. "Uncle Harry, Uncle Harry?"

"Yes, dear child?"

"Are you going to ask Miss S'ena to marry you?"

She would not look at him. Could not look at him—though part of her *craved* to see his face.

A loud clearing of throat suggested he found the impertinent question as awkward as she had. "I am *thrilled* to see you back to your monkeyish ways, young Eleanor."

Oh. Her heart dipped. She worked to keep her features neutral and not betray her disappointment at his answer—especially with his sister eyeing her from such close proximity.

"Speaking of simians," the drawl continued, "where is that abominable creature I brought back from India? Don't tell me Mr. Monkey has climbed a tree?"

"No-o-o." Ellie laughed. "She's prob'ly in my bed."

Serena pushed to her feet, pretending not to see his hand offering assistance, as Melanie murmured to Tom about retrieving the soft toy. The movement caused the room to tilt slightly.

"Serena?" Catherine placed a hand on her arm. "You look pale. Are you quite well?"

"Of course."

"Do you wish for the doctor again?" Jon asked.

"No. Thank you." She offered a smile to reassure. She would be well. Soon. Probably.

Tom returned with the stuffed toy, his little sister's delight causing another round of hurriedly brushed wet eyes.

"I have never understood why she prefers that toy above all else," Melanie complained. "Not dolls. No, never dolls. But that little defurred orange creature remains a favorite."

"Perhaps it has something to do with the giver?" the viscount suggested with a grin.

"Are monkeys really that color in India?" Tom asked.

"Not that I saw, but perhaps you should ask Lord Winthrop here. He spent a far longer time there, and may have seen all sorts of things I did not."

Tom's expressed interest soon had Jon touching on some of his experiences with the Indian wildlife. Thankful for the change in subject, Serena fought to maintain her composure, fought to keep her eyes from straying to the man who had positioned himself near her left. But she remained acutely aware of him all the same. It was as though her senses strained to know him, her skin prickling with awareness, her ears catching every sound he made, from his words to the faintest rustle as he moved. Her sense of smell also seemed to have gained new appreciation for him, and as she breathed she caught the slightest tang of his cologne: warm, rich, sweet, tantalizing.

"Serena?"

She blinked, returning her attention to her hostess. "I beg your pardon?"

Melanie's brow creased. "Perhaps when the doctor comes to check

Ellie he should also see you. That was quite the feat you performed yesterday."

Was that accusation in her eyes? It seemed . . . not. The tension in her stomach abated slightly. "I am not in the habit of having such adventures, 'tis true."

"Uncle Harry has," said Tom. "He once swam across the Thames."

"In London?" Catherine said, wide-eyed.

"In Oxford. Which is not so very wide, but neither is it a feat for you to emulate, young man," he said, ruffling Tom's hair. "The person who did that was quite foolish."

"Poor Harold," his sister murmured, tease in her eyes, which seemed to elicit a glare.

"Why did you do it, Uncle Harry?"

Now she did peek at him. His ears were red. "I would rather not say."

"It was for a bet, wasn't it?" Melanie said, eyes glinting to suggest she was not completely immune to her brother's discomfort. "How much did Harold win?"

"Melanie—"

"We've all done foolish things in our youth," Jon's deep voice interrupted the viscount. "I'm sure none of us would like all of our past misdemeanors brought to light."

"But when someone like my dear brother here has so many to choose from . . ."

Serena caught the flash in Lord Carmichael's eyes, the muscle throbbing in his jaw. Her stomach twisted. Was he upset? What could she say to ease things? She smiled at Tom. "Your uncle seems to have chosen a gift exceptionally well for your sister. Did he also bring you a present from his travels?"

The boy's eyes lit as he explained about a real, working telescope that, along with his uncle's recent birthday gift of an atlas, was one of his two favorite gifts of all time.

She nodded, pleased to have turned the conversation to something better than damaging the viscount's character, listening as the nephew's stories confirmed her earlier conclusions about the uncle's generous, affectionate nature.

"You know," Tom's face crinkled, "Mr. Cravenwood has never been anywhere interesting. At luncheon when you were all talking, I asked him where he'd been, and the best he could come up with was Edinburgh."

"No!"

"It's true, Uncle Harry." The boy nodded, before turning to Serena. "I bet even you have gone somewhere more interesting than that."

"Even I?" She smiled. "I'm afraid the most interesting place I have been is your uncle's cave."

"The cave?" A new voice said from the door. "What is this about a cave?"

※

Harry's heart sank as his parents, accompanied by Grandmama and Lily Milsom, entered the room, the two older ladies moving straight to Melanie to cluck over a now wide-awake Ellie.

"We thought it best to visit, after your note," Father said. "Lillian just happened to come to visit as we were setting off, and was most concerned to hear the news."

"Yes, I simply insisted on coming to see you all." She sent Harry a questioning look. "I admit I was somewhat surprised to learn you stayed here last night also."

He forced a smile but didn't answer, her insinuation not worth pursuing.

"Well, I'm pleased to see my granddaughter appears quite well. Nothing like what you'd indicated, Melanie." Mother's brow creased.

"She seems to have made quite the full recovery."

"No doubt thanks to numerous and persistent prayers," Harry said.

The room seemed to take a collective breath. He met his parents' startled gazes, saw the approbation in Grandmama's eyes, the confusion in Lily's. Had it been that long since he talked of spiritual matters?

The round of greetings and rearranging of seating continued amongst further questions concerning the incident. To her credit, Melanie seemed to be accepting part of the blame, and did not once link Serena's name to culpability. Perhaps there was hope for his sister yet.

"So am I to understand, Miss Winthrop, that you were instrumental in rescuing my dear little namesake?" Grandmama said, having wrested Ellie to her own lap.

"I . . . I only did what anyone else would have done."

"Yes, somehow I rather doubt that." Grandmama cast a none-too-subtle glance at Lily.

"You appear *quite* the heroine," Lily murmured, in a manner opposite of laudatory.

Serena stiffened, prompting him to say sharply, "She almost drowned herself, Lily."

"Very careless," she muttered in a voice low enough for only his ears. "I wonder, Miss Winthrop," she said in louder tones, "just how you were the first to be aware of the poor child's dilemma?"

"Miss Winthrop was outside painting."

Her glance was shrewd. "Thank you, Harry. I'm sure the girl can answer for herself."

Her expectant look drew Serena's own raised brows. "I was outside painting, it's true." Her tone, her look, remained mild yet cool, but he thought he detected faint color on her cheeks.

"I just find it odd how someone can be so fixated on some paints to grow completely unaware of the real world."

"Ah, but you are not an artist, are you Mrs. Milsom?" Grandmama said. "You don't have an artistic bone in your body, if I remember correctly."

Lily flushed, and seemed to withdraw her claws, even as she perched on the settee with a smug expression, as if she hadn't just made such accusations.

The atmosphere grew stilted, Serena's discomfort obvious as Lady Winthrop made enquiries as to the health of both older ladies. Such gentilities were cut short.

"Henry, what was this I heard before? Tell me you did not go to the Blue Cavern?" His father's frown underscored the condemnation in his voice.

Tension twisted through his chest. "I could, but that would be a falsehood."

Father snorted. "I trust you didn't drag all these good people down there with you."

"There was no dragging involved. Everyone who visited went willingly."

"I simply cannot understand the attraction of a dirty hole in the ground," Lily said, her brows lifted at Serena before she shot Harry a sly look. "Or perhaps I can."

He focused his attention on Tom as he shared his thoughts on the adventure underground. Harry snuck a look at Serena's unruffled countenance. Was Lily correct? Had Serena only agreed to the expedition to be near him? No, he could not credit it. She was unfailingly honest, and he'd never witnessed her behave in underhanded ways. But why, then? Was it something that piqued her artistic disposition? Or did something—someone—else interest her?

His heart skipped a beat. He glanced at his niece, placidly sucking her thumb as she clutched the orange abomination to her chest. His thoughts tracked back to Ellie's earlier comment, when Serena's customary implacability had cracked and she'd appeared as flustered as he'd felt. During the hubbub surrounding his parents' arrival, he'd quickly queried Tom as to why on earth Ellie would say such a thing. Out had tumbled a somewhat convoluted explanation, but the general gist had filled his heart with hope.

That was, until he remembered she had refused to look his direction.

Lily continued her interrogation of Serena. "You must have quite soiled your gown, my dear."

"Yes. However, as Melanie has very obliging laundry staff, it appears none the worse, nor am I." Her expression remained cool. "I would hate to be thought too delicate to experience the amazing opportunities to be had in this world."

"Well said," Grandmama nodded.

"Delicate?" Lily's brows rose. "*Quite* the opposite."

"We enjoyed the experience, didn't we, Serena?" Melanie said, in a louder voice. "The mine might be dark and dirt-laden, but seeing where such beauty"—she gestured to the Blue John urn—"originates was quite exciting and informative."

"Fool nonsense." His father's scowl lifted a fraction as he nodded to Melanie. "How's the girl?"

Harry frowned. Explanations concerning Ellie's health had already been made. And certainly Father could see for himself.

"Much better, since we sent you word."

"Good, good." He shook his head. "I still can't understand how you let her go like that."

At his sister's drooping posture, Harry cleared his throat. "And doubtless that will remain a mystery. Now, Grandmama." He smiled. "I'm so glad you're here. Miss Winthrop's portrait of the children is well worth seeing."

"Surely it cannot be finished already?" Grandmama looked at the pink-cheeked artist.

"Not quite, ma'am."

"Well, then, I should be very pleased to see your progress."

"Shall we go now then?" Harry rose. Now he could repay Serena's earlier kindness in turning the conversation from his youthful misconduct and remove her from the awkwardness of dealing with his parents' interrogation—and Lily's.

"May I come, too?" Lily asked. "I should very much like to see this famous portrait."

"I thought you did not care for art," Melanie said. "I wonder why you would wish to see it now?"

As he cut his sister a stern look, Lily stood, clasping his arm. "I imagine people are permitted to change their minds, aren't they?"

Her smile, her steady gaze tilting up at him, it was like she was waiting for him to say something. He cleared his throat. "I believe it was Virgil who said something about a woman's changeability."

Her eyes flashed, but her smile widened. "Perhaps, but when important matters of the heart are at stake . . ." Her clutch tightened.

He stared at her, her gaze penetrating the dim recesses of his mind. No. Surely she didn't mean—

"Uncle Harry, Uncle Harry!"

He subtly removed his arm from Lily's possession, thankful his niece's outburst gave excuse for him to shift away to meet the little girl's wide eyes. "What is it, Ellie?"

"Miss S'ena."

He swallowed, uneasiness sliding within. "Yes?"

"You haven't asked her yet."

"Asked her what?" Father said with a frown.

"You haven't asked Miss S'ena to marry you."

Above the gasps and muttered exclamations, the high-pitched voice continued. "She's the one you have to marry. We like her best."

His whole body froze.

"How unfortunate for you, child," the lady beside him said, before glancing at him, her fingers once more finding his sleeve, digging into his arm like claws. "Especially as your uncle has always expressed a preference for the lily." Her lips pushed up in a glittering smile as she surveyed the room. "Yes, Henry has asked to marry me and I have finally accepted him."

❧ CHAPTER NINETEEN

One week later

THE BUMP AND sway jolted Serena from sleep. No, not sleep. Repose, perhaps, but definitely not anything that could be considered as refreshingly satisfying as sleep. Whenever she closed her eyes it seemed the final days at Rochdale haunted anew. How could he—?

No. She blinked. Best to not think. Just not think. Otherwise the hurt would crash in again, and—

No. She pushed upright and, catching her sister's worried glance, forced up her lips.

"You slept awhile."

Serena didn't correct her. "Are we nearly there?"

Jon nodded, pointing to the fields outside. "Hatfield."

"Good." She gazed unseeingly through the dust-coated window.

"Dearest, are you hungry? There are still a few apples."

Serena turned, nodded, accepting one of the Ashmead's Kernels Melanie had insisted they carry away with them. She bit into the sweet, juicy flesh, an explosion of sunshine in her mouth. The action triggered a deeper, belly-rippling spasm, reminding her of her lack of food over the past few days. But then, her pains never induced her to eat.

Serena finished, wiping her hands on the handkerchief Catherine supplied. She glanced at her sister, whose dark eyes were underscored by shadows. "How have you been feeling?"

"Better than the trip north. But that is nothing to you. How have *you* been feeling?"

"Better than five days ago." Serena eked out another faint smile.

"Poor thing. You had Melanie quite worried you know."

She nodded.

The pains had not consumed in such a manner for months. One minute, desperately adding the finishing touches to the children's painting in order to leave the Peak District and all reminders of the viscount. The next, clutching her middle as physical agony pierced her from within, reminding her again why she would never have children, like those who had stared at her in horror before they raced off with cries of "Mama! Mama!"

Melanie had been decisive and kind, ensuring the attention Serena would not have anticipated in those minutes after the lake incident. But Serena's bedridden state meant forgoing the visits of goodbye from all save the dowager countess. She had demanded entry to Serena's bedchamber, to examine the painting so she said, but really to enquire about that last extraordinary day in the drawing room, when the world had tilted so dramatically.

Innocuous conversation about art, framing, and London had swiftly moved to a far more dangerous discussion about the viscount, her grandmotherly disapproval well evident in her mutterings about "that woman."

"Can you believe him to be such a fool?"

Serena had stared at the delicate blue flowers papering the walls, unable to formulate an appropriate reply.

The dowager had sighed. "I know. And I really thought—" Her dark eyes snapped back to Serena's face. "Do you like him?"

She blinked. Raised a brow.

"Oh, don't look at me like that, girl. I'm not someone you can fob off with such a cool air. Tell me, for it makes a difference, do you admire my grandson?"

"I do not know why you ask such a thing, especially when he is betrothed to another."

"Because I've seen you two together, and wondered."

Ice had stolen inside. How enamored had she appeared? She swallowed. "I did not think my conduct—"

"Your conduct was unexceptionable. It's Henry's I wondered over. He seemed more . . . settled, I suppose, and I'd hoped—I'd wondered if you and he had reached some form of understanding."

"There was no understanding." She writhed within. Thank God Catherine wasn't witness to this.

"Then you do not care for him?"

"He . . . he has great charm," she said carefully.

"But you do not love him?"

Cheeks heating, she managed, "I do not know him well enough for such things."

The old lady harrumphed. "You think that love is something one chooses?"

"I think real love develops from esteem of another's character."

"And you do not esteem my grandson?"

"As I said, I do not know him well—"

"Tosh. Don't give me such missish explanations. What can you object to?"

She lifted her chin and eyed the dowager countess. "I find . . . a want in his steadiness of character, and cannot choose to align my heart with someone I do not know will prove trustworthy."

"Well!"

Her insides roiled. Had she grossly offended her by such bluntness?

Then the older lady laughed. "You are an original, my dear." She had sighed. "I do hope you will see his good qualities before too long."

"Pardon me, but I do not know why you should so wish such a thing, when he is betrothed—"

"His father has intended him for that Lily creature since before you were born. That does not mean it is the right decision."

"I fail to see what this has to do with me," Serena had finally managed.

"Do you?"

Heat filled her cheeks, and she desperately hoped her face had not disclosed the fear such words stirred.

Somehow, thankfully, the conversation had moved back to London, the countess being so kind as to recommend an artist in whom she might find a beneficial instructor.

"Monsieur Despard knows everyone. I will write to him and let him know your direction, if you like. Then if you—oh, and I suppose Carlew—approve, then he might be able to visit you. You'd like him, I'm sure."

Her stomach roiled again, as memories arose of her last art master . . .

She shivered as the coach dipped alarmingly.

"Dearest? Are you uncomfortable? Would you like this blanket?"

"Thank you, Catherine, but I am quite comfortable."

Her sister's brow wrinkled. "You seem concerned. Are you worried about London?"

"No," she lied, offering a bland smile.

"I'm sure it will be better than what you expected. And you can resume your art again."

She nodded.

Jon eyed her, the faint frown in his eyes since that torrid day easing a mite. "We must restock your supplies. Do you have a preference for such a place?"

"Ackermann's," she said automatically. "But they are expensive."

"Ackermann's it is."

As usual Jon's smile fueled a trickle of comfort within. She nodded and turned to study the buildings outside. Perhaps London would not be so bad after all.

Derbyshire

The strain in his heart over these past days seemed nothing compared to that which echoed in the current atmosphere. Harry glanced around the drawing room, for once devoid of Lily, who had returned to the manor Frederick Milsom had built for her all those years ago.

Seated opposite were his parents, their pleasure in his engagement now gone, judging by their facial expressions. To one side sat his grandmother, whose displeasure in the actions of the last week was almost as tangible as that of his sister, whose vociferous opposition had left him in no doubt as to *her* feelings concerning the proposed viscountess.

"But, Henry, I don't understand. Why now, after all these years, has she finally accepted your proposal?"

The answer was as plain as the scowl lining his sister's face.

"Exactly. She's finally jealous. And why is that?"

Because he'd had the misfortune to fall in love with a young lady he was not allowed to.

He hoped Carlew knew the sacrifice he was making. But somewhere deep, deep within he knew he was not right for Serena. She was too young, too innocent. And he was too scarred by experiences she need never know about. Lily had been the first girl he'd thought he loved, hence his proposal during Oxford days. Her preference for the much richer and more handsome Frederick Milsom had been one he understood, Milsom's untimely death prompting the words he now wished had remained unsaid: that should she ever decide to marry again, his offer was always open . . .

A fool. For a few moments at Rochdale, as Carlew offered quiet congratulations, the questions in his friend's eyes had almost made Harry wish for a horse to ride away.

But he could not. He'd made a promise. And it was ungentlemanly, dishonorable, to back out now.

Even if he felt trapped.

His father's frown deepened, prompting another sigh within. But recent tales of his exploits in younger days, embarrassing though they may be, had prompted the reminder: he was done with cowardice.

"Father, forgive my bluntness, but I sense disapproval in your scowls."

His father shook his head.

"No? My mistake. I apolo—"

"Why must you persist in this mine business?"

Harry exhaled slowly, glancing around the room. His mother and sister held still, but his grandmother leaned forward in her seat, face fixed as if for battle. He returned his attention to his father. "Forgive me, but I was under the impression the Blue Cavern was in my name?"

"So it is, but—"

"Of course it is," Grandmama snapped. "Your grandfather wanted *you* to have it."

His father shot Grandmama a dark look before returning his attention to his son. "I fail to understand why you feel the need to invest funds into something that is clearly past its prime."

Harry kept his mouth closed, working to control the spurting anger within.

"This Carlew fellow, has he promised to invest? I cannot see dear Lillian agreeing."

"No. Dear Lillian has not agreed." Because he would never ask her. He would rather be hanged than accept funds from a wife he did not want.

"But Carlew?"

"Once again, Father, I remind you this is *my* mine, and as such, the matters of business concerning it are my prerogative."

"But not if you require estate funds to support it. I will not allow it."

"I have my own inheritance."

"Which is tied up until you marry."

His heart sank. "Then I suppose I will wait a while longer."

"How much longer, Henry?" Mother asked. "Surely you have kept Lillian waiting long enough?"

He tilted his head at his parent. Did she truly believe it was his fault Lily had said no all those years ago?

"You mean he's kept *you* waiting," Grandmama said. "I know you and George want to see the line secured, but marrying that woman is not wise."

His gaze flicked to the older woman. She studied him with a deep look of concern. "You should not marry where you cannot love."

"What nonsense!" Father snapped. "Henry loves her. He's always loved her, ever since they were children together. I'm relieved to see he's come to his senses at long last and will make an honorable woman out of her."

His insides clenched. Surely Father didn't suppose Lily was his *par amour*? He cleared his throat, about to protest his innocence when the memories arose. The temple. Her manor. The London house. A sick feeling twisted past the chill as his history clawed past the honor he now wished to wear.

Father was right. Regardless of her eager complicity, Harry did owe Lily the respectability of his ring.

He glanced at his sister. Her eyes now held an expression of sorrow, as if she could see all his bad choices and understand some of his reasoning, but was unable to do anything except offer her pity. Her pity stung almost as much as his self-recrimination.

"So does this mean you will not engage in more fruitless discussion concerning the mine?"

Harry eyed his father. "Yes."

For the moment, anyway, he thought. His father exhaled in obvious relief while his grandmother muttered her disappointment.

Resolve strengthened within. The next discussion he had concerning the mine would not be fruitless, for he would be financed. Carlew *had* to help him. And once he could focus on seeing the mine return to productivity and profit, when he could see the legacy of the Bevington estate assured for the future, perhaps, one day, he might forget the young lady he could not have, and grow to like, if not esteem, the one to whom he was betrothed.

❧ Chapter Twenty

London
January 1818

"Mademoiselle, may I suggest you 'old the brush like so?"

Her skin prickled as the art master drew close, but the little French man merely made a minute adjustment then stepped away, humming under his breath as was his way.

Serena exhaled. Thank God Monsieur Despard seemed quite oblivious to her in any capacity save as *artiste*. The past ten weeks had firmed the middle-aged art master into everyone's favor. Jon's approval had been won the moment *le monsieur* had agreed to visit the house in Berkeley Square and conduct lessons with Serena in the presence of Tilly. Mama approved because Jon did, and as she now wished to live with them in London, Mama was quick to agree with whatever he said. Catherine's support was garnered when she heard of his exclamations over the quality of Serena's work, and thus proclaimed him "a sensible man." Serena's initial fears had been put to rest by his professional conduct, and the fact he knew his craft so well.

No more was she to use the squirrel-tipped brushes, *non, non*. Instead, mademoiselle must use *le* hog hair, "for they caress *le* paint so much more." Such pronouncements had startled her at first, but as Serena grew used to his ways, she learned to smile and enjoy such avowals instead.

M. Despard worked happily on his own canvases in the little room at the back of the Carlew mansion, so the large salary Jon paid him seemed nearly moot. A talented landscapist, whose exhibitions had garnered him mild acclaim, M. Despard seemed to find his primary work in assisting those of the gentry who could afford his services. To have received the dowager countess's high praise had opened the door; Jon's willingness to pay a high salary had kept it open, but Serena's skill had secured his passion.

She placed the brush down then stepped back, eyeing the work dispassionately as *le monsieur* required. A misplaced brushstroke here. A slightly odd rendition of verdigris there. Tame Hyde Park could use a tad more drama . . .

"I thinks *ze* trees needs to tell a story, no? The trees, they say nothing to me."

"Perhaps because it's winter?"

He made an impatient noise.

"It needs a focal point?"

"*Oui.* Something to draw *ze* eye, to make the casual observer stop to say, 'Now *zis* is worth *ze* attention, not like those boring ones. I must be at *zis* park, because it makes me feel . . . ?"

"Relaxed?"

"Tell me, *ma chère*, do you find visiting *ze* Park unwinds you?"

No. She found every visit stressful. The people she was forced to greet, to smile at, to engage with in polite inanities. "I believe it is supposed to be relaxing," she offered.

"Then you do not feel it. When you feels it, then you can paints it." He nodded. "That is why the dowager loved your portrait of *ze leetle* children, and recommended you to me. You understood them, and could capture the very thing that made them unique."

She nodded. God bless "leetle" Ellie and Tom. They had written several letters over the past months, via Melanie, the first containing an apology regarding the series of unfortunate remarks made by Ellie. After the abrupt jolt such admissions made her feel, she had chosen to overlook her discomfort and reply to their—and Melanie's—letters with the friendliness their kindness deserved. Even if some of what

Melanie wrote about brought a lump to her throat when she thought about it overly long at night, and made her wonder why Jon never mentioned his friend at all.

"I want you to feel *ze* easiness, mademoiselle." M. Despard clapped his hands, glanced at the corner of the room. "Miss Teelie. You must accompany us to *ze* Park. Go and get your mistress's cloak and bonnet. Go now. Now! We must be there before the shadows overly alter. Go!"

At Tilly's worried glance, Serena chuckled. "Thank you, Tilly. I imagine we'll only go for a short walk."

When Tilly had left, M. Despard shook his head. "Is there something wrong with *zat* girl? Is she simple? She never listens the first time. I repeat myself over and over and over. Pah!"

"It may have something to do with the fact she's employed by my brother-in-law and not you, monsieur."

"Perhaps you are right. But I thank the good God above that you at least have sense enough to know to obey. But then, you are *une exception*." He sighed. "I do not know too many young ladies so willing to trust poor Despard."

"How many other young ladies have you instructed?"

"Two? Maybe three? But they were all simpletons, like your Teelie there. I promised myself I would not teach *ze* little girls anymore, but then you changed my mind. It is rare, *ma chère*, to have such focus combined with such talent to know what should be exactly where."

Serena smiled, his praise as warm balm. She was learning to trust her own instincts—at least when it came to art. She cleaned her hands of the worst of the oils, removed her painting apron and cap and hung them on the hook installed for such a purpose. There was no point changing her gown; the pelisse would cover it, her gloves would hide the paint residue on her fingers, and likely as not they'd return for more endeavor in the little studio. M. Despard had led her on more than one spontaneous excursion in the past weeks, necessitating a startled Catherine's company the first few times, before she realized his purpose was not nefarious but merely to illustrate the particular shade or line of a tree.

Tilly returned, carrying Serena's blue pelisse and matching bonnet, cloak, and gloves. Soon the trio was walking along Mount Street then right onto Charles, before another left took them onto Grosvenor and towards Hyde Park. Serena drew in welcome crisp air, savoring the tang of dead leaves and smoke, for once devoid of the wintry bite she'd experienced on other such expeditions. She was now as familiar with the walk as she was with the Frenchman's humming.

Thank you, God, for the dowager countess's recommendation.

A tall, dark-haired gentleman walked toward them, well dressed in the flamboyant style she used to associate with—

No. She curled her fingers into fists and averted her eyes from the stranger, whose widened glance and smile had coiled the old distrust within. Hurrying after the art master, she placed a hand on his arm. His step faltered then he resumed at a slightly slower pace, this time pointing out the architectural details of the buildings lining Grosvenor Square. Gradually the tension ebbed away, and again she prayed blessings on both the dowager and the man beside her.

These past weeks had been made far more endurable thanks to M. Despard.

The focus he demanded had almost made her forget the man who seemed to have none.

Derbyshire

"Lord Carmichael, might I turn your attention to an inspection of the farmstead?"

Apparently. Harry bit back the acerbic remark and nodded to Welmsley's estate manager, nudging his horse to follow. Thank God the air held no ice-laden wind to make today's excursion more challenging than it already was. Thank God also for Thurston, who had shown a remarkable level of patience these past weeks as Harry had slowly acclimatized himself to his new responsibilities. With his hopes for the mine at a stalemate, he'd forced his thoughts to the present, something it was becoming increasingly apparent his father should have done long ago.

His lips tightened. The estate had received even less attention from his father in recent years than he'd previously realized. While Father's art collection had increased both in number and value, the value of the lands had simultaneously decreased. The Bevington estate was land rich but asset poor, and even the lands were growing poorer by the month. Thank God for his grandmother's advice. If he'd ignored things, who could say how much longer the coffers would bear up? Thurston had expressed no modicum of relief when Grandmama's advice prompted Harry's initial visit to the estate office, even if his words had been couched with caution.

"I would not wish to upset your father, Lord Henry."

"And I have no desire to upset him either, so perhaps if we keep this between ourselves?"

The gray-haired man had looked at him before emitting a small smile. "Aye. As you wish. It is rare for him to enquire after estate business anyway."

"And one day I will become earl, so I had best start learning all I can."

So the initial visit had become two, then three, then more as the extent of the dilemma became apparent. And besides, without investment for the mine what else was he going to do?

He ignored the spurt of resentment at Carlew and tried to listen as Thurston spoke on other estate affairs, but his thoughts whirled away like a scattering flock of crows. What else *could* he do?

Spend time with Lily? Join his mother and his betrothed in planning a wedding? He'd rather dye his hair blue. He'd managed to delay the wedding a few more weeks but Mother was insistent it needed to happen before Easter. But what could he do? Caught in a web of his own making, where Lily was as much both spider and fly as he, what could he do? He'd wracked his brain for hours trying to see a solution, but nothing came. He'd even searched the Bible for verses to give direction.

Nothing. It was as if the universe was conspiring against him. Why, even little Ellie and Tom no longer regarded him as their favorite uncle, so Melanie had—vindictively, he'd thought—informed him when he last visited. Rochdale's boring, balding brother, also visiting, now held that status, so she'd said. The disappointment crowding their eyes and in their too-short hugs made him think back to Ellie's loudly expressed preference as to his wife, and caused more than one pang of regret things had not worked out differently.

He shook his head as the horses trudged down the hill. Lily *would* make a suitable wife. Doubtless they would get along nicely. She knew the area well, knew what would be expected, knew his family, knew him intimately. He winced.

"Aye, you see it too, do you, sir?"

"I beg your pardon?"

Thurston pointed to a track where long muddy grooves ran alongside the peat. "The peat be washing away in the rains. It needs addressing, else the hill will one day slide away."

Harry chuckled, then saw the estate manager's frown. "You're serious."

"Aye. The grass on top can only hold so much. It's the peat that helps stop the river flooding and protects the fields. If the peat goes, then much of the land suitable for sheep will be lost also."

"Is my father aware of this?"

"He's been told, sir."

"But has done nothing."

"I don't like to speak ill of the master, but . . ."

"Aye." Harry frowned. "What can be done?"

"If we divert some of the channels, then when the rains come they won't wash away the roots. They be fragile, you see."

For some reason, the mention of fragility made him think of her.

He tried not to think of her too often, to school his thoughts away, for thinking overly long made him sick at heart. He'd never thought Serena as precisely delicate, but she seemed to have become more so in that final week, her fainting, then that time closeted away due to some mysterious illness nobody talked about. He hoped that was all it was, but he'd seen her face when Lily had made her announcement.

Seen the moment of shock before her features closed into customary aloofness. It was the next day she'd succumbed. Pride, stupid pride, still whispered it was his fault, that he was the reason for her pain. Then she was gone. Gone, without saying goodbye.

His chest burned.

Gone.

"My lord?"

He cleared his throat. "How do we divert? Would rocks or soils prove helpful?"

"I be thinking, if we dumped sandstone, that quite nearly matches the existing ground cover. The trouble is finding the quantity. And the weight, of course."

"What about the mine dumpings?"

The man slowly nodded. "Aye. That might work. It needs be something the soil will adhere to."

"You've seen the weeds and how quickly they envelop the shale hills. I think it could be an answer."

For the first moment since his grandmother's interview he felt a flicker of enthusiasm.

Perhaps here was something he *could* do. Perhaps he might never have the natural passion for the lands as some men did; his preference would always be for the wealth that existed underground. But the estate required learning, and Thurston seemed a reliable teacher. He had worked the Bevington lands since Grandfather's days, and what he did not know was most likely not worth knowing.

Carlew, too, had seemed impressed on the occasion they met, three days before they'd departed. Since Carlew had inherited his title and lands in Gloucestershire, Harry had seen how his passion for setting things right led him to adopt ridiculous levels of study and hard work, and hours spent in the saddle learning about agriculture, this on top of his usual business commitments. Carlew's conversation revealed he had come across men like Thurston, estate managers, both good and bad, and his summary after the meeting was that Thurston was solid. And though he might be clutch-fisted at times, to give Carlew his due, he *was* a quick read of a man's character.

Character.

His spirits dipped in conjunction with the hill as memories arose of his friend's assessment. Did he continue to think him irresponsible? Would he think so if he could see him now, inspecting the lands like the landowner he would be one day? Would Carlew still hold out against allowing Harry to dream of—

No.

His fingers tightened on the reins. He would not live according to other people's expectations *all* the time . . .

Except it seemed he did.

As if sensing his tension the stallion's ears pricked and he tossed his head.

Harry gently rubbed him between the ears, nodding to Thurston when the man glanced his way. Now the farmstead was revealed, nestled in the hollow of the hill, its fields marked by snow-edged stone walls, the hills crisscrossed with age, like an ancient face.

Only Grandmama's words had stilled his restlessness when he'd returned to discover Carlew's abrupt departure had meant forgoing a final goodbye to Miss Winthrop.

Somehow Grandmama had glimpsed past the pretense to see his heart. She'd stared at him, the keen dark eyes as piercing as when he was a boy and he'd broken one of her favorite figurines. He'd felt the same level of nerves and shame, sure he was in trouble, though for the life of him he could not imagine what he'd done to incur her most recent wrath.

Upon his enquiry, she'd snorted, "I did not take you for a fool."

He'd swallowed the immediate retort, praying for wisdom to see past her ire to the truth she thought she saw. Grandmama did not get upset easily, and he'd learned over the years whenever she did it was usually with good cause. "What is it that displeases you?"

"I do not understand you at all."

"I'm sorry, but at this moment the feeling is mutual, Grandmama."

She'd snorted again. "You could have made that girl an offer and then you would not be caught in such a bind."

"I scarcely see my wedding Lillian as a bind," he'd lied.

"You're not a simpleton, though you're acting as one. What is it then? Some misplaced sense of honor?"

"Grandmama, you of all people know the situation."

"That you offered, and she rejected, and she took up with that fool Milsom because he had more wealth than you? How could you suggest such a scheme? An open-ended proposal? Who has ever heard of such a thing? Such foolishness."

"Your loyalty *is* touching," he'd said drily.

"Why have her when you could have Serena?"

He'd stared at her, before saying evenly, "Because she would not have me."

"She rejected you?"

"She did not need to. Carlew had made it very clear he did not want me engaging Serena's affections."

"Well, your methods were deplorable. Of course she was captivated."

His heart had kicked. He'd lowered his gaze. "Has she . . . did she say something?" he said in a low voice.

"She didn't need to. It was written over her every expression."

He winced within. "I did not mean to . . ."

"Because she is so young? Because of Carlew? I cannot understand why he would object."

"He . . . wishes for someone without my reputation."

"Ah." She'd frowned. "But can't you prove yourself now?"

"What is the point? I once, no, twice made Lily an offer, which she has at long last accepted."

"That can be undone. Tell me, do you truly love her?"

"Miss Winthrop?"

Her mouth had sagged open, her face in that moment seeming quite, quite old. "There is my answer. I *am* sorry, Henry."

Her sympathy clogged his throat.

"Dear boy, if you choose not to renege on your offer, which I strongly urge you to do, then can I suggest you take this time to turn your attentions to the estate. Your poor grandfather would be ashamed to see how little interest our son displays, and I can only hope that the future will be brighter in your hands. But that will never be until you learn just what being Earl of Bevington involves."

He had promised.

She had nodded. "And Miss Winthrop?"

"Is not for me."

Grandmama sighed. "I wish your father had never become friends with that silly creature's father."

"Lillian's?"

She eyed him sternly. "She does not love you as you deserve."

"Oh, I think she does." He managed a ghost of a smile.

"I think you're going about this all the wrong way." She shook her head.

His anger had suddenly slipped the reins of self-control. "What would you have me do? Beg Lily's forgiveness and run off to London to plead for Carlew and Serena to overlook my reputation and somehow convince them I have changed? Such irregular behavior would *surely* convince them of my character."

"Do you believe your running off to London will demonstrate such things? No. Better to make your apologies to Lily now, before it becomes any more public, then stay and prove to everyone, including yourself, that you are the man of faithfulness I know you are."

Her words touched him, but he said roughly, "Surely breaking an engagement would only show my lack of faithfulness."

"Or else it shows a man prepared to live differently than he'd imagined as a foolish youth."

In that moment, in his grandmother's drawing room, his world had seemed to tilt and turn, as a thousand possibilities swam before him. Something within seemed to call, some deep impulse begging him to be more, to *be* the man his grandmother believed him to be. A verse he'd once read echoed faintly, something about putting off the foolish things and pressing on to a higher, upward call. His heart stirred uneasily. In all of this, he hadn't dared ask a crucial question. What did God want?

"My lord?"

He blinked. Realized they'd passed the farm gates and entered the yard, where he was now being stared at by Thurston and Farmer Woodcott and his expectant family.

"Good day, m'lord." The farmer nodded.

"Good day, Woodcott, Mrs. Woodcott."

"Good day, sir." The brown-haired woman curtsied.

"I hope the wintry weather has not affected your health adversely," Harry offered. "It's been quite bitter lately."

"Thank ye, m'lord, but we be well," Woodcott said, ruffling the hair of his youngest.

His wife curtsied again. "If I might, sir, the news has reached us, and I offer our congratulations."

"Congratulations?"

"On your engagement to Mrs. Milsom."

Oh. He forced a nod, his heart sinking.

Congratulations on the worst mistake of his life.

CHAPTER TWENTY-ONE

London

"You can do better, *ma chère*. This line is all wrong. And where is *ze* sparkle? I know she has not much, but you have made Teelie seem so flat. You have no passion for painting her picture."

"Sorry, Tilly." Serena offered an apologetic smile over her shoulder.

The maid glanced up from her stitching and gave a little shrug. Serena turned around to see M. Despard glancing through her sketchbooks. "Oh, monsieur, please—"

"*Non.* Here, let me see . . ."

Embarrassment crawled within. How many sketches had she completed? Abandoned?

"*Oui, oui! Zis is tres bien!* Who is *zis* fellow?" He pointed to a picture of the viscount.

"Nobody."

"And yet he appears on page after page after page. Monsieur Nobody indeed."

She moved to grab the book but he shifted it from reach.

"And for this nobody man, Mademoiselle has a tremendous imagination. Look"—he stabbed the page—"you 'ave even managed to conjure a dimple in his cheek. How did you imagine such a thing, *ma chère*? Did it come to you in the midst of a dream? No? I 'ave rarely seen such detail on a real person, let alone an imaginary one. No, this Mr. Nobody is very fortunate indeed."

Her cheeks heated. What if Tilly heard? Worse, what if she reported back to Mama? "Monsieur," she said in a low voice. "I do not want—"

"Ah. Of course." He drew closer, turning his back so the maid could not see the page he held. "He is your secret lover?"

"No!"

"You secretly love him?"

"Monsieur!"

"Aha! It is true. Where, where is *zis* man? Tell me at once, for him you must paint."

Serena shook her head.

"Your Mama does not approve? Your brother perhaps?"

She did not bother to correct his oft-stated misconception. "He— No."

"Then where, where is he?"

"He . . . he is not in London."

Melanie's latest epistle made it very clear the viscount was remaining in Derbyshire until his wedding. As always, that word made her heart hurt, but the pain did not hurt so much now. It felt more like a bruise might feel when pressed, a tender ache. But she would recover with time. She had to.

M. Despard was frowning. "Can we not get him here? For him you simply *must* paint! For him you have *ze* passion."

She shook her head again, as moisture burned her eyes and throat.

"*Ma chère!* Ah, please do not distress yourself. Despard is *ze* clumsy oaf. A thousand apologies."

"Miss Winthrop?" The sketchbook was closed with a snap as Tilly's worried face appeared. "Are you quite well?" The maid cast a suspicious frown at the art master.

"I am well, thank you, Tilly. I would appreciate a glass of water for us both, if you would be so kind."

"Of course, miss."

When the door closed, the art master pulled his chair close. "Mademoiselle, I understand *ze* lover's tiff. I offer my condolences."

"He was not my lover."

"But you cared for him?"

Her gaze lifted to his brown eyes, large with sympathy.

"I see. But he does not care for you?"

He was marrying someone else, wasn't he? "No."

"Then he is an imbecile! Only a fool cannot treasure such a lovely young lady, so *ze* imbecile he must be. And surely, we should not paint an imbecile."

A chuckle pushed past the pain.

"There. That is better. Now." He resumed flicking through the pages. "Would you prefer to paint your sister? *Non? Ze* Monsieur Baron Winthrop?" His teeth glinted. "Your mama?"

"*Non.*" The thought of asking her mother to pose for hours on end? Being stuck in a room with her for said hours? "*Non, non, non.*"

He laughed, a funny, whinnying sound that was rather endearing. "You do not wish to paint anyone else?"

She slipped the sketchbook from his hand and flicked back to the page. The viscount, as she'd imagined him, standing tall, half smiling, with a portion of that dramatic valley beyond. She could see it now. Could see him now. It would be magnificent—if the idea of painting him didn't hurt so much.

"You still hold for him *ze* passion?" the art master's voice came softly.

She nodded.

"*Ma pauvre chéri.*" His fingers snapped. "Could this not be *ze* remedy? *Ze* medicine? *Ze* passion, *ze* brokenness, expunged by *ze* painting? Then it is no more. Poof! It is gone."

She stared at him. What he referred to had happened before. When she had become too emotionally attached to someone—her stomach grew queasy—the best remedy had involved painting until the emotion lived in the canvas, not in her heart. She imagined it to be similar to Lavinia's playing of music, or going for a good long ride as Catherine and Jon seemed to prefer. For her it was art. But the last time she'd sought such release had involved her former art master. And look where that had got her . . .

"Mademoiselle, *ma chéri*, I do not pressure you."

"I know. It's just . . ."

The door opened, admitting Tilly with the glasses of water. "Here you are, miss. Monsoor."

"Thank you."

"*Merci*, Mademoiselle Teelie."

"Oh, and miss? Her ladyship wants to know how much longer you'll be. She mentioned something about shopping."

Shopping? Her heart sank. "I thought I told Catherine I did not need to go."

Tilly shook her head.

Serena stared at her. "I did not say that?"

"No, miss. It's the other Lady Winthrop who wishes to have you accompany her."

"Mama?"

"Yes, miss."

Her spirits slumped. Shopping. Being forced to buy unnecessary things—on Jon's money, no less. Being forced to talk with people she cared not for, and who did not care for her. Being forced into artificial politeness with artificial poseurs.

Or . . .

She glanced back at M. Despard and gave him a tiny smile that vanished as she returned her attention to the maid.

"Thank you, Tilly, but my mother is well aware that Monsieur Despard is employed as my instructor for the next two hours. I cannot dream of disappointing him, not when he is in such high demand."

"Oh, but miss—"

"I know Mama will understand. But perhaps you can mention I said that Lord Winthrop is paying for such things, and as such, his funds should not be ill-used. Besides"—she smiled at her instructor again—"we have a great deal of planning to do."

"*Oui?*"

"*Oui*." She nodded as the concept firmed in her mind. "We must paint *ze* passion of the valley."

"Oh, but miss!"

"Thank you, Tilly. That will be all." She opened her sketchbook again. "Now, monsieur, we have work to do."

❧

Derbyshire

"I tell you it will not work!"

Harry stared at his father, whose most recent fit of apoplexy had turned his cheeks bright red. "Father, if we do nothing the fields will be rendered useless."

"What do I care about a silly farmer's fields?"

He drew in a deep breath, slowly exhaled. "You might not, but their livelihood depends on our careful management of the estate. And the estate's livelihood depends on the rents we collect from them. If they do not prosper, neither will we."

"I repeat, why should I care?"

His father's baleful glare caused Harry's neck to prickle. Sometimes, more often of late, he barely recognized his parent. Fits of rage, slamming fists on the table, this was not the man he grew up knowing. Something was clearly amiss.

"Well? You seem like you have all the solutions, Henry. What have you got to say now?"

"Father, people will hear you."

"Let them hear! I have nothing of which to be ashamed."

"I do not understand—"

"No, you never did. You might have got honors in Greek and Latin, but in anything beyond your own self-interest you have always failed."

The accusations slammed against the good intentions barely capping his own anger. "Father, I am trying—"

"You have always been trying," his parent muttered.

It took some effort not to grind his teeth.

"Oh, go on," Father said. "What have you got to say for yourself?"

"Only this. Forgive my bluntness, but one day, you will die, and I will become earl. And I am sure you do not want your legacy to be that of the seventh Earl of Bevington who allowed his estate to decline because he could not be bothered to care."

Father's eyes widened, before narrowing into tiny slits. "Get out."

"Why? So you can look at your precious paintings? You would not have so many if it had not been for Grandfather taking such an interest in the estate's affairs over the years. Do you forget that?"

"Do *you* forget to whom you are speaking?"

"I am sorry, sir, that you do not appreciate my plain speaking. But the time for plain speaking is well overdue."

"Yes, it is! You speak of estate affairs and I ask you what estate affairs have you ever interested yourself in apart from your foolish women and your stupid mines!"

He stiffened. Swallowed. "Lillian is not foolish—"

"She is if she marries you!"

He eyed his parent some moments before offering a bow. "Good day, Father."

"That's right. Run away, like the little boy you've always been," his father jeered. "Go find that poor girl and convince her you've been hard done by. Why she wishes to marry you when plainly you do not love her I do not know."

"Isn't this what you wanted? The Milsom lands combined with ours?"

"You're a fool. While you're at it, go sob to your grandmother. She never liked me enjoying the finer things of life."

Harry bit back another retort and escaped as his father's complaints chased him into the hall. His mother moved towards him. "Henry? What on earth—?"

"Not now, Mother."

He strode away, anger pumping through him so hard it felt as though sparks might fly from his fingers. He hurried outside, out onto the terrace, but for once the view did not comfort. He leaned his hands on the stone balustrade, heaving in the cool afternoon air as if it might dissipate the fog inside. He glanced down, saw the whitened knuckles, and consciously unclenched his hands. As he continued his slow breathing, the fire dancing embers across his eyes, burning his lungs, pounding his heart, gradually, gradually died.

Heavenly Father . . .

The prayer was almost an unconscious one these days, said in a multitude of places, multiple times each day. A reminder he was not alone, that Someone far more powerful was in control, regardless of what his earthly father might do and say.

These past few weeks, as his father's opposition increased, he had needed to remind himself of this truth very often. To place his trust in the One he read about in Psalms. "I lift up mine eyes unto the hills, from whence cometh my help. My help cometh from the Lord . . ."

The Lord . . . "The Lord who made heaven and earth," he murmured. "The Lord who is thy keeper. The sun shall not smite thee by day"—his lips twitched, though his earthly father might want to—"nor the moon by night. The Lord shall preserve thee from all evil, he shall preserve thy soul."

He rested his elbows on the balustrade, his head slumping into his hands. How he needed such reminders that he was not alone. For where else could he turn?

Mother and Grandmama refused to see Father's changing personality as anything but another mood. His grandmother had even gone so far to say that her beloved George had become much the same.

Horror pricked him anew. Would he too succumb to this state of unreason? Was this to be another family legacy he wanted no part of?

"Heavenly Father . . ."

Who else could he turn to? He closed his eyes. Made an effort to still his heart, still his questions. After several minutes focused heavenward, he felt a measure of peace lodge in his soul. *Lord, direct my paths. Help me. Show me what to—*

"Harry!"

His sister's voice drew up his head. "Hello, Melanie."

"We heard your argument with Father."

Marvelous. "I'm sure there is something wrong with him."

"There is something wrong with both of you." She frowned. "I do not like to see you muttering to yourself all the time."

His lips twisted to one side. Muttering prayers was his offense. "I'm not muttering to myself, exactly."

"Then who?" She glanced around. "I don't see anyone else around here."

Melanie had never been one for faith. "I . . . I find it easier to clarify my thoughts when I speak them aloud."

"I have read that is a sign of a diseased mind. Careful. I don't want my favorite brother locked up in Bedlam for want of clear thinking."

"Father . . ." Frustration laced his sigh.

"He does not seem to like you overly much at the moment."

"I'm trying to learn the estate management, but it seems as if every suggestion I make is met with flat refusal. I don't understand. He is being illogical, wanting me to settle down, then objecting to everything I do. He even called Lillian a fool."

"We know."

He frowned. "You heard?"

"Yes. We all did. Mother, Lillian, and I were having tea in the saloon." The saloon that shared a wall with his father's study. "I'm afraid we heard everything."

Everything.

"Wait. Everything? Even the part about—?"

"Yes, even that."

He groaned and resumed his slumped posture. "Dear God."

"Yes, I think you better start praying, for I spy a lady with an axe to grind."

He peered past his sister and straightened, as the sight of an offended *fiancée* strode toward him. *Dear God . . . help me.*

"Dearest Henry," Lillian said with a tight smile. "I had wondered where you were."

"You need wonder no more," he managed, in a sad attempt at levity.

"You may leave us, Melanie," she said, eyes not moving from his face.

Melanie shot him a look then hurried away.

"So you are not at your grandmother's yet?" Lillian's smile grew tight, her words and tone leaving him in no doubt just how much she had heard.

"As you can see."

"I'm sure you'll be over there shortly, once you've heard what I've got to say."

His smile grew strained.

"I had wondered at your reluctance to set a date for our wedding. Your father was right in that I was a fool to think you cared for me. Once upon a time you cared, perhaps, but not now." Her smile dipped, disappeared, as her eyes grew hard. "I should have realized it when I saw you with that little girl."

Now his smile departed.

"I am still prepared to marry you, because I quite like the idea of being a countess. And it makes sense, as everyone can see, that our lands should finally join, but I will *not* stand to be made a mockery. So, if you have any thought of her, or anyone else, you must not act upon it, do you hear? I will not stand for it."

She seemed to be waiting for an answer; he gave none.

"I am not unaware of your family's fading fortune, Henry, and I have connections of my own to ensure my name remains unsullied. So, I repeat, do you have any thought of her?"

He swallowed. "I presume you refer to Miss Winthrop?"

"Of course I do!"

Her eyes blazed with a fury that tugged at the knot of trepidation. This was why he regretted reiterating his proposal after Frederick Milsom's death, why he even found it difficult to kiss her these days. Her moods were as capricious as his father's. He needed someone steady . . .

Someone gentle.

Someone who spoke truth, believed truth, like he was trying to.

He frowned. "Do you believe in God?"

"What?"

"I know you attend services, but have you ever thought how the Bible is relevant for today?"

"Are you mad?"

"Not mad." He smiled, genuinely. "I have merely seen the light."

She made an expression of disgust. "Now you speak as one of those Evangelicals who preach in Hyde Park. Tell me I am not going to align myself with such a man!"

Harry stared at her. Hope flickered across his soul. Something within whispered of faith.

"Well?" she snapped.

He offered her his most gracious bow. "Dear Lillian, you are not going to align yourself with such a man."

Her brow lowered. "Wait. Do you mean—?"

"Yes. I find myself reneging on my proposal of so many years past. I do not wish you to be burdened with a husband you cannot respect."

"I didn't say I don't respect you."

"You didn't have to."

She flushed.

"I will send the notice to the papers. The wording shall be . . . discreet, of course."

"But I haven't agreed! I do not accept this—"

"And yet you were so quick to accept my hand before."

"I . . . I love you, Harry."

"No, you don't," he said gently.

"But I have always loved you."

"Which is why, years ago, you refused me to marry Milsom."

"I do not want this." Her eyes flashed. "You cannot do this to me!"

"We do not always get what we want, Mrs. Milsom."

Her hands curled into fists. "If you so much as speak to her, I'll make sure she knows all about what you and I used to do."

He shrugged, offering a faint smile. "I'm sure there's nothing you can say that she doesn't already suspect anyway."

"Then you *do* plan on seeing her. I warned you!"

"Truly, it will make no difference. She will not have me anyway."

With another bow, he hurried from her gasping outrage. But not to his grandmother's.

Instead, he turned inside, back to his father's study to inform him of the news, before his wavering courage fled.

Only after much shouting and threats did he later linger in the shadows of the Grecian temple, frustration churning beneath the lonely, hopeless future Father predicted for him.

Only then could he reflect upon the many people who would not get what they wanted today.

Or ever.

Chapter Twenty-Two

London
February

"I CANNOT BELIEVE it has taken until now for you to be willing to accompany your poor mother to the shops."

"I have been busy, Mama."

"Too busy for your own mother? I've hardly known what to say when the likes of Lady Harkness ask concerning you."

Serena said nothing, unwilling to confess to the truth, but so thankful for her brother-in-law's decree that her art lessons continue unhindered. It had not been without many squawks of protest from Mama, of course, but Jon's simple restatements of his intention seemed to conquer Mama's complaints in a way her daughters had never managed. Or maybe it was he merely ignored her. Regardless, it had become a real wrench to force herself away from the secret painting.

It had become a secret, something she worked on without Tilly's company, which necessitated being without monsieur's company as well. But each afternoon, when her mother and Catherine rested, she would paint and create and allow the wellspring of emotion to live in her canvas. She would paint and remember his smile—a smile that had no doubt caused scores of ladies to throw themselves at his feet over the years, but one she could not forget, the twist of his lips so mischievous sometimes, heartrendingly wry at other times. She would paint and remember the scent of him, the way the aroma of his sweet earthy-warm cologne seemed to curl into her heart and make her wish she could paint his very essence. She would paint and remember his buoyant spirits, his humor, his tease, his affection for his grandmother, his kindness to his niece and nephew. She would paint and remember the laughter lurking in his eyes, the way his gaze had fallen to her lips, almost like he wanted to . . . No. Her eyes filled. She would never know now. She would paint and remember instead that day in the lake, the time he looked at her so coldly, the way he'd turned away. As she painted she would paint out her emotions—her esteem, her burgeoning hopes, her disillusionment, her secret sorrow. Her love.

Each morning she would show the French art master her progress. He would hum and make suggestions, and then she would commence work more appropriate for the eyes of her family. For she knew they would not approve, neither the painting of a male figure (though he be fully clothed!), nor the man whose figure it was.

"Serena, tell me what you think of this lace. I am not sure that it as fine as this one . . ." As her mother droned on about a multitude of other boring fashionable fribbles she considered necessities, Serena's thoughts churned on. They had still heard nothing. Surely letters should not take so long to arrive from Derbyshire. She would like to know something of how Ellie progressed, and Tom, and the dowager, and—

She forced her thoughts away to nod at something her mother said. But they wound back in, as sleek and slippery as the silver ribbon the shop assistant unfurled before them.

Yesterday she had learned something of why Jon did not speak of his friend anymore. He had refused investment in Lord Carmichael's mine.

Upon overhearing his conversation with Catherine, Serena had been caught in a quandary. How to find out his reasons without appearing to assume too much interest? In the end, it was Catherine who had noticed Serena's concern, who had asked Jon to explain.

"I did not think him so securely settled that he would continue to care so much. Reopening the mine is not a short-term thing, it affects many people for many years."

"So you did not think him consistent?"

"No."

Serena had cleared her throat. "How long would he need to prove his consistency? Three months? Twelve months? Five years?"

Jon had lifted his gaze to study her intently. "You think I'm harsh?"

"I think you've dismissed more than one friend not sharing your innate dependability."

His eyes had widened, even as a muscle twitched in his jaw. After a moment or two he had said, "You speak of Hale?"

Major Hale, the man who had run off with Jon's sister, Julia. "I do not know him—"

"No, you do not."

But she knew Hale was a wanted man. She swallowed. "I . . . I have heard through Melanie that . . . her brother has these past months been trying to manage the estate."

He gave a hollow laugh. "Trying would be right. That estate needs someone with a firm hand, not soft ones."

"You despise his attempts?"

He blinked. Studied her. "Why do you care so about Carmichael, Serena? You know he's to marry Mrs. Milsom. You know they share a past."

"I know." Her heart knotted, as memories resurfaced of the intimate looks passed between the viscount and his neighbor, looks that suggested they'd shared more than just a past.

Catherine looked up from where she'd been quietly embroidering. "I do not like to see your friends depart either, Jon. You need them."

"And they might need you," Serena said quietly.

He frowned, his glance sliding between her and his wife. "Perhaps."

"We all need people beyond our families to share our hearts with."

He was silent for a moment, then, "You are right, Catherine. I . . . I should not be so quick to judge. I will write him in the morning."

"Thank you, Jon."

He'd seemed caught in Catherine's approving smile before his own faded and his attention returned to Serena. "I still do not wish for him to engage your heart."

"What does it matter, Jon?" Catherine said. "He is already engaged."

Serena smiled blandly, to cover the little throb of pain that reminder always brought. He *was* already engaged. As was her heart. Though she hoped her painting might remedy that soon . . .

"Serena?"

She blinked. Forced her attention back to the present, back to the shop, back to her frowning mother.

Mama sighed. "I don't know why I ask you to accompany me. You clearly have no interest whatsoever in your appearance." She picked up Serena's left hand. "Look. Paint."

She tugged her hand away. "Yes, Mama."

"Can you not remember when we are to go shopping for gloves, it is preferable for one's hands to be clean? Do you want the clerks talking about you?"

"Do you really care what they say?"

"Of course not!"

Serena swallowed a smile and dutifully followed her mother to the next counter of the busy store. It seemed as though hundreds of ladies were shopping today, accompanied by a multitude of maids and footmen, all being waited on by dozens of assistants. The hubbub filled her ears, the jostling and scent of sticky, pushing bodies swelling her desire for the calm of her studio.

"I cannot believe the crowds here. So ill-mannered!"

"I'm sure they would not have come had they known *your* intention of doing so, Mama."

Her mother's brow lowered. "Well, perhaps. But I think they came because the prices are so good. Can you believe how little they charge for lace?"

"Mama, you know Jon can get us anything for less than what they charge here."

"Of course! But that doesn't mean one should forgo the enjoyment of finding a bargain."

"Of course," she murmured.

In addition to a new pair of gloves for Serena, Mama also selected several pairs of silk stockings and a new fan for herself. As their purchases were being wrapped, Serena heard a voice she recognized, and her heart sank.

"I think, Sophy, you will find this suits dear little Lucien so much better."

She had to get Mama away. Her loathing of Lady Milton was such that there would likely be a scene far more conducive to shop clerk gossip than the paint on Serena's fingers. She laid a gentle hand on her mother's arm. "Mama, could we please go back to look at the slippers?"

"Whatever for? You said before you had no need for another pair. Why have you changed your mind?"

"I . . . I thought perhaps a new pair might go well with my new gloves."

"You are an odd creature. Very well, then." Her mother began to move. "Oh, look! That linen would make the perfect baby shawl for Catherine. Don't you agree, Serena?"

"Serena?"

She closed her eyes, prayed for strength then turned to meet Sophia Thornton's blue-eyed gaze. "Hello, Sophia." Her false smile slipped. "Lady Milton."

"Serena." The cold eyes sent a shiver through her soul. But better that than the look Lady Milton was giving Mama.

Sophy glanced at the fabric Mama still held. "Ah. One can only wonder what the purchase of such lovely soft linen must mean."

"It is quite lovely, isn't it?" Mama agreed. "We thought it would—"

"Make a lovely shawl," Serena hurriedly interjected. "Oh! Look at the time. Please excuse us. We must go. What a shame."

"I beg your pardon? I thought Catherine must be expecting."

"Really? She is not the only married lady we know who might be thought to be in an interesting condition." Serena eyed Sophia's less-than-svelte midsection before smiling her sweetest smile.

Sophia's face pinked.

"I thought a place like Haverstock's would curb some of a young girl's more vulgar statements," Lady Milton said, her gaze sweeping up and down Serena.

"You never went to Haverstock's, did you, dear?" Mama said to Sophy.

"I . . . er, no."

"That must have been very disappointing for you all, but they are *quite* select about whom they accept, you know."

Lady Milton's face suffused to match her daughter's, her eyes snapping furiously.

"If you'll please excuse—" Serena began.

"Are you in town for long?" Sophy asked Serena.

"For a few months—"

"Serena," interrupted Lady Milton, "you may tell your mother that we saw the Hawkesburys last week."

"Sophy, you may tell *your* mother that Serena stayed with the Earl of Bevington's family in Derbyshire over autumn."

Lady Milton's eyes flashed, and her chins wobbled with suppressed outrage. "Serena, you may inform your mother that a lady of her age does not appear to advantage when wearing such colors."

Mother drew herself up. "Sophy, you may tell *your* mother that we are shopping for Serena's come out."

"What?"

"You're going to be presented to the Queen?"

Two dismayed faces turned to Serena, their expressions echoing that within her own heart, but she would not give them the satisfaction of knowing Mama's statement distressed her as much as it did them. Even if her come out wasn't to be until next year.

"She is looking forward to it, aren't you, dear?"

Serena glanced between her Mama's proud expression and the profound dissatisfaction worn by the other two ladies.

Lord, please forgive me.

"Yes."

Derbyshire

"Tell me, how is your father today?"

"Much the same."

His grandmother frowned, cutting her venison into tiny squares. "I did not think he would continue this grudge so long. I am grieved for you, Henry."

Harry nodded, her sympathy making him feel less than the man he needed to be. He concentrated on cutting his own meat into manageable pieces.

Some days he wanted to pack up and leave for London, but then sense would whisper and he'd stay. Duty demanded he remained. Responsibility. Legacy. How could he up and leave when his father's care for the estate had dwindled down to almost nothing?

"Have you seen Melanie lately?"

He swallowed. Nodded. "Two nights ago. I had dinner with them."

The broken engagement had only deepened the estrangement between father and son. Father no longer acknowledged him, the pale eyes glossing past whenever he was in the room. It made for icy dinner conversations, so much so that Harry had started taking the occasional meal at Grandmama's, or Melanie's, or even sometimes one of the tenant farmer's on one of his longer visits to the farms. While his relationship with the estate dependents was slowly improving, he did not like the questions, then the lack of questions, about why it was the son and not the earl fulfilling such obligations. But his father's refusal to acknowledge his responsibilities only deepened Harry's resolve to do more.

So, the tenant visits continued, a slow, drudgery of a task made more pleasant by the fact that he was outside and enjoying Derbyshire. It might be cold, some would say bleak, but the landscape still remained a canvas of loveliness created by the Master Artist. One sure to be appreciated by another masterful artist, if only she were here.

"Henry!"

"Forgive me. You were saying?"

Grandmama frowned, but he sensed it was from concern rather

than his breach of manners in not attending. "I was asking about the children. How are they?"

"Friendlier these days." He managed a small smile. "I don't know if Ellie will ever forgive me for . . ." For not asking Miss Winthrop to marry him. Regret gnawed within.

"I'm sure your current mood is not due to what your niece thinks of you regarding an engagement—or the lack of one."

She raised her eyebrows but he would not bite. He lowered his gaze and continued pecking at the meal. Heard her sigh.

"Henry, why do you persist in this? You are becoming dull, and if there's something I cannot abide in my grandson, it is when he is dull."

He glanced up. "I am sorry my slow spirits displease you. Would you prefer a joke? I'm sure if I try I can remember one Tom told me—"

"No. I do not need to hear such things. What is it that depresses you?"

He stared at her. Chuckled. What did not depress? No money, no life, no love, no distractions, no prospect of anything changing. The better question was what didn't depress him? He had God, he supposed, but even His promises seemed a little weak at the moment.

"I have had a letter from the solicitor," he finally offered.

"And?"

"And it seems the estate is fast approaching parsimonious measures."

"What?"

He smiled thinly. "I do not know what Father has been doing, but the estate has little beyond the land value at this time."

"No!"

"Yes. Unfortunate, is it not?" He swallowed a sip of wine. "Now can you understand my lack of hilarity?"

"What will we do?"

He permitted himself a small smile at her use of the pronoun. His grandmother's support was better than none. "You know Father refuses to speak to me. I went to his study today and asked about the finances and he ignored me. I cannot see what I'm to do. Thank

God I have Thurston's support, and I'm grateful that the bankers and solicitors are prepared to talk with me, but as for finding out where the money has gone, I cannot until Father speaks."

"Your mother?"

"Refuses to involve herself." His smile faded. "I would admire such loyalty in a wife, but not when it goes against my cause."

"Dear boy."

His grandmother stared at him and, unable to cope with the commiseration in her eyes, he lowered his gaze to his plate.

What could he do? What should he do? Was there any way forward? Where was God in all this? The darkness rushed in again, weighing heavily upon him, stealing away his feeble grasp at a lighter mood.

Harry finished the meal, making his best efforts to lift his grandmother's spirits, but his grin felt garish, like a painted clown whose smile was fixed because it was his job to make others laugh. Where was the person to make the clown smile?

He hurried his steps back to the main house, trying to ignore the answer to that. He knew exactly where she lived. Melanie had told him, but just as with his grandmother, he refused to act. What was the point? She would not return. Carlew had made his sentiments very clear, and he could only imagine the impact his broken engagement would have on his prospects with that very upright man. He scarcely expected to hear from Carlew again. Since his refusal to support the mine Carlew's letters had grown as rare as the sighting of a golden eagle. Not that Harry could blame him. Daily he was made aware of his shortcomings; daily he worked hard to compensate. But it was never enough, would never be enough, *he* would never be enough—

"M'lord?"

He almost stumbled into the footman. Straightened, as the man gave apology. He waved a hand to dismiss him. "That was my clumsy fault."

"You have a letter, m'lord."

"At this time?"

The footman coughed. "I gather it was important."

"Thank you." He tried a smile to cover the dismay. Probably another creditor demanding payment. Was it coincidence the number of businesses which had suddenly requested payment since his engagement to Lillian was called off?

He shook his head, walking past the silent rooms, to where another footman waited outside the library.

"The earl?"

"He's inside, my lord."

Harry nodded, and kept walking to the drawing room next to the terrace. Empty. Perfect.

He lowered into a seat, braced himself for what the contents might reveal, and opened the letter. He skimmed the contents, then reread it more slowly, and his eyes began to burn.

Perhaps God was not so far away after all.

CHAPTER TWENTY-THREE

A TOUCH MORE carmine. Maybe a dash of umber . . .

Serena stepped back, tilting her head to see the nearly finished canvas. From the terrace of Welmsley, Viscount Henry Carmichael stared back at her, his handsome face twisting in the smile she'd seen so often. One hand rested on a pillar—how many hours had she spent on that left hand?—the other rested casually by his side. Behind, she'd included just a hint of the valley's majesty, a scene she'd needed to convince M. Despard as being true.

"But it is fantastical! *Mon Dieu*, the heavens themselves must smile to see such glory."

"It is very lovely."

"And he will be *ze* earl one day?"

"Yes."

"Oh, but to see such a place . . ." His grin had taken on a sly look. "Perhaps he will prove to not be the imbecile we once thought, *non*?"

Non. Any thought of him beyond the subject of her painting must be ruthlessly quashed. No good could come of pining after someone who had made his intentions so very plain. She returned to her perusal of her painting, then dipped her brush into the palette and applied the tiniest smear of carmine. There. The tree beyond seemed more finished.

An hour later, she waited as the art master surveyed the portrait.

Each day he had much to say, but lately the critiques were fewer, the praise more. One day she hoped he would stand, stare, and find no fault.

"Ah, *ma chère*." Her breath suspended. "I think you have captured *ze* dog to perfection."

Pleasure escaped in a smile. Adding Polly had been a midnight inspiration two nights ago.

"But perhaps you need add a little something 'ere," he said, pointing to the pillar.

Serena shook her head. So the fault-free day was yet to come.

"You do not agree?"

"Pardon, monsieur, I was thinking of something else."

"But you cannot! You must only think of your painting, your masterpiece. Now, do you not think this pillar a little bare?" His black brows pushed together. "Normally I would suggest adding another figure, but you composed your painting in a way that such a thing becomes impossible."

She studied the picture. "If I had placed the hand more centrally then it would not be so bad. But I utterly *refuse* to paint his hand again."

"It is *ze* hand." He moved closer to the canvas, scrutinizing carefully. "You have done a marvelous job, but . . ." He peered at her. "Does he wear a ring? A signet?"

She thought back. For all his dandyism, he had never seemed to affect a ring. "I cannot remember."

"No matter. I suppose when you next see him you can look."

Her stomach tensed. When she next saw him, he would be married. To Lillian Milsom. She shook her head.

"Then we need something else. Hmm. What do you suggest? What is *ze* imbecile's interests?"

"Please don't call him that," she said in a low voice.

"But he must be, if he marries someone other than you. But—no more. What shall we place 'ere instead? What did you say his interests be?"

"Mining."

"But you have already placed a mine in *ze* background. We want something to suggest his character, his love—what a shame you cannot paint yourself into *ze* picture."

"Monsieur . . ."

"What about a favorite flower? Do you know what they are?"

The answer swept across her, stealing her breath.

"Mademoiselle, you know?"

As she nodded, sadness teased within. "Oh, yes. I know this has been his favorite for a long time."

So she began to plot how she would add his favorite flower.

The lily.

White's Gentlemen's Club, London

"Carmichael."

"Carlew." Harry rose, shook his friend's hand. "You look well."

"I would say the same, but it would not be true. What on earth has happened to you?"

He offered a wry grin. "What has not, you mean?"

His friend frowned. "Let me order, then I want you to tell me everything."

Half an hour later Carlew was finishing his turbot as Harry finished his story.

"I did not think your father so overbearing."

"Neither did I." Harry fiddled with the vegetables remaining on his plate. Why anyone thought cabbage a suitable vegetable for such an elite establishment . . .

"Carmichael?"

He glanced up.

"I am pleased to hear of your endeavors." Carlew took a sip of wine. "It is not easy, I know, especially in the face of hostility. But I did not have to live with the people who opposed me, neither were they my close family. I do not envy you."

"I confess there have been many times I have wished to return, to escape back here."

"But you did not."

"No."

"Because?"

"Because I understand my duty lies up north. I cannot let the future be destroyed because of my father's present inability to lead appropriately." Harry swallowed. "And . . ."

The sandy brows rose in silent query.

"And I believe God would have me stay."

"God?"

He nodded, a smile twisting his lips. "I commend you on your ability to hear, old man."

"You have been praying?"

"I have been trying. I . . . I sense something of God's direction sometimes when I read the Bible."

Carlew's gentle queries prompted more about his renewal of faith, and his friend's face split into a wide grin. "I am so pleased for you."

"I am, too."

His own smile slipped, echoed in Carlew's fading joy.

"But you remain troubled. You say you feel led to stay in the north, so what brings you to London?"

"Bankers."

"Ah."

After Harry shared a little more, Carlew shook his head. "I am sorry, my friend. I will pray God gives you wisdom."

"Thank you."

Carlew pushed aside his plate. "Now, to brighter news. Tell me, how is your *fiancée*?"

He blinked. "You have not heard?"

"Apparently not."

"Mrs. Milsom and I are no longer betrothed."

"What? I beg your pardon. I thought this a settled thing."

"And I was sure you would have heard the truth by now." He played with his wineglass. "It was in the newspapers."

"I'm afraid I do not read much beyond the business notices. Forgive my curiosity, but I am surprised. Was this a mutual decision?"

"She was not best pleased."

"You called things off?"

What followed was another story, told to Carlew's murmurs of disbelief.

"You *have* had a tough time. I'm sorry to hear it."

He nodded, emotion cramping his throat, clamping his lips.

Carlew met his gaze. "And I remain sorry for the coolness that sprang up between us. If I had known—but I gather you've been so busy, you probably did not feel it worth your while to inform us."

He could have said something to the effect of not knowing if Carlew even stood as his friend anymore. He chose not to. "I was glad for your letter."

"I'm ashamed it took me so long. If it hadn't been for Catherine and Serena . . ."

His foolish heart quickened, but he schooled his features to neutrality. "Catherine remains well?"

"She will be glad when the babe is born." Carlew picked up his water glass, drained it, eyed him over the top. "Serena is well, too."

That name! He forced his fingers to unclench beneath the table. "I—" He cleared his throat. "I imagine she has found London better than she expected."

"She works almost daily with your grandmother's former art instructor. Quite a talented man, if a little . . . shall we say Gallic at times?"

He fought the envy spiking hot and strong. Was this man handsome? Wooing her with his French endearments? He forced himself to say, "I'm sure you are beating her suitors away with a stick."

Carlew chuckled. "She is well able to do that with those icy looks she gives, remember?"

Oh yes, he remembered.

"Most of the young men have managed to get the message, but there are a few persistent gentlemen. We may see one of them prevail."

He hated them. Hated them all. Striving for nonchalance, he

glanced away and asked, "Any meet with the Winthrop seal of approval?"

Carlew did not answer, forcing Harry to finally meet his friend's steady blue-gray gaze.

Still the odd perusal continued, until his friend leaned back in his seat and gave the slightest of nods. "Carmichael, do you have plans to attend the season this year?"

"Only if my father's health and matters concerning the estate permit such a thing."

"Would you care to join us for tea the next time you're in town?"

"Tea?" Usually only ladies had tea.

"Yes." Carlew smiled. "Tea."

What? Why? Oh . . .

He gulped down the emotion, managed to stutter an acceptance, all while trying to come to terms with the approval—not warning, not pity—he could finally read in his friend's eyes.

Berkeley Square

"Mademoiselle . . ."

Serena's pulse thudded loudly in her ears as she watched M. Despard study the painting, his bottom lip tucked in, arms folded in characteristic fashion. He had not seen it for several days, and feeling her work had finally attained that elusive quality of completion, she'd not dared touch it, so the paint had dried over Sunday. But would he agree? The longer the silence, the more hope bubbled furiously within. Would today be the day of praise?

He cleared his throat. "*Ma chère?*"

"Yes?"

"*Tres magnifique!*"

Air she hadn't realized she'd been holding released in a whoosh. "You truly think so?"

"I truly think so." He gesticulated. "You have captured *ze* lines, *ze* depth, *ze* colors, but more importantly, you have captured him. I can tell what kind of man he is by his eyes." He shook his head. "To 'ave such a gift at such a young age? *Non c'est pas possible!*"

Warmth bloomed across her chest as the muttered French phrases continued. "*L'incroyable . . .*" He turned sharply. "You must show."

"I beg your pardon?"

"Such a gift should not be buried—how you say—under a bushel? *Non*, it should be shouted to the treetops!"

Laughter rippled through her. "Shouted *from* the treetops, monsieur."

He made an impatient gesture. "I do not care. *Ze* trees themselves would applaud if they could. Your talent simply *must* be exhibited."

"But sir—"

"No but, but, buts! I refuse them. *Ma chère*, when I say it must be shown, it is because I only wish I 'ad your talent at your age."

"What you say is very kind, but I do not wish to have others see—"

"But why not? You 'ave created something *ze* most beautiful, something any artist would be proud of, something *ze* very man himself would be proud of—"

"No. No, no. He is *never* to see this. We agreed, at the start, remember? This was my painting to release my emotions, not to reveal them to the world. Nobody else is to see it."

"But mademoiselle—"

"No." She eyed him firmly. Waited. Finally he nodded, and relief pushed past the faintest strain of disappointment.

"You will permit me to frame?"

"What is the point of framing a work no one will ever see?"

"What is *ze* point in painting a work one will never see?"

She stared at him, thankful for Tilly's absence again, as his words challenged her insecurity. "You really think it good?"

"Mademoiselle, *zis* picture could make your reputation as a portraitist! If you were to exhibit, you would be inundated with requests."

"You are not serious."

"But I am." His expression grew wistful. "You do not know what it is like to have *ze* dream but not *ze* means, to want the world to know but be forced to smile and pretend *ze* scraps you 'ave are enough."

She stared at him. Of course she knew.

"You cannot know what it is like to be forced to work for others when all I want is to work for myself. *Zis*"—he gestured to her painting—"*zis* could set you up forever."

She frowned. "I would earn money?"

"*Ma chéri*, do you know how much *ze* best artists get paid?"

He told her. Her jaw sagged.

"But they would not pay me such sums."

"Not at first, no. But as your reputation builds, as you become more acclaimed . . ."

She would not need to rely on Jon and Catherine's goodwill. She would not need to hope her looks and lineage enough for a man to overlook her past and wish to wed her. Indeed, she would not need to marry at all.

"Please, I beg of you. You could be *ze* making of me if you are successful. Many people would wish for poor Despard to teach them, too. I will not tell them they will never paint as well as *ma chère* because she contains more talent in her *leetle* toe than they could learn in a lifetime. Besides, what could it hurt? People need not know it was you. You have no signature, and from what you say, he seems happy in *ze* north. He need never know it was you."

"But what if he found out? He would . . . hate me."

"*Non, non.* Why would he? Would he not be proud of your talent?"

Non, non—the words echoed in her brain. She swallowed. "Jon and Catherine would never let me."

"Who will tell them it is you? Would they even know? Do they go to the exhibition?"

"Not usually."

"Then *please* let me see if we can show. Who knows? They might be such imbeciles they do not want your work. But what can you lose by *ze* attempt?"

She blinked. She had nothing. No *fiancé* to lose. No prospects. No fortune. Barely any family. What *was* the worst that could happen?

Despite the disconcerting feeling that she had been manipulated more skillfully than Michelangelo might wield a brush, she found herself nodding. Found herself being hugged. Found herself being exclaimed over.

The door opened. "Excuse me, Miss Winthrop? There are visitors here for you."

She sighed. "Thank you, Tilly, but if it's that silly Lord Franklin again, I am not hurrying." She spoke to M. Despard. "The last time he stayed for nearly half an hour. It was excruciating. He had the nerve to describe my eyes as cornflower blue! I doubt that man has ever seen a cornflower, let alone know the hue."

"Excuse me, miss, but it is Lady Rochdale and her children and—"

"Ellie and Tom are here?" Hope lifted her heart. "Oh, in that case . . ." She stripped off her mobcap and apron and hung them on the pegs by the door before turning to M. Despard. "Do what you must with the painting. I must go."

"This is *ze leetle* girl whose life you saved? Of course you must go." His brows pushed together. "Wait. Despard remembers. *Zis* is the sister of *ze* man we discussed before?"

"*Au revoir, monsieur.*"

He laughed and bowed, and she turned and followed Tilly up the stairs.

"Miss Winthrop, Lady Winthrop has asked that you change."

"Oh, it is only Melanie. She'll quite understand." She picked at the paint staining her fingers. Sometimes it took days for the oil to disappear. Never mind. Catching a glimpse of her refection in the hall mirror, she tried smoothing her hair, but it would not submit. Perhaps she should—oh, never mind. The footman was opening the drawing room door, and it was too late.

Smile on, she entered the room, then stopped. Her mouth dried.

Oh, *dear God*, no.

CHAPTER TWENTY-FOUR

NON, NON, NON, no!

"Ah, Serena." Mama's smile held a frown. "Did you not get my message?" She turned to their guests. "She can be a trifle absent-minded at times, with those little daubs of hers."

"Surely you cannot possibly refer to her magnificent art as mere daubs, Lady Winthrop?" Melanie rose, smiled. "Hello, Serena."

"Good afternoon." She offered a curtsy, refusing to look at the man—

"Miss S'ena, Miss S'ena! We missed you!"

Before she knew what was happening, a little body was hugging her. "Hello, Miss Eleanor. I missed you, too." She knelt down and smiled at the brother. "Hello, Master Tom."

"Hello. Have you been painting?"

"Can you tell?" She waggled her fingers and gently released Eleanor.

"You have paint on your cheek, too."

"I do?" She placed a hand to where he pointed and sure enough . . .

"Oh dear. What are we to do with you?" Mama said with a sigh. "Pray excuse her, my lady, my lord. Serena, do go and put on something more appropriate."

"She looks well enough as she is, Lady Winthrop."

"You are too kind, Lady Rochdale. Serena, come and greet Lord Carmichael here."

She pushed to her feet unsteadily, and drew closer to the viscount as a mouse might walk hypnotized toward a cat, staring into his green eyes. For a moment the world seemed to hold still.

He was here. Gazing at her like she was him, cautious, as if disbelieving, waiting, sure that a too-long look might cause someone else to comment and thus pierce this lovely fantasy.

Him. Here. The epitome of her dreams. The very subject of her painting . . .

Her painting! Oh, heaven forbid anyone want to see her artwork! She dropped her gaze, cheeks heating. "Good afternoon, my lord."

"Good afternoon, Miss Winthrop."

Somehow she managed a curtsy, somehow she managed to find a seat, somehow she managed to gather enough remnants of her shredded dignity to affect something approaching composure. But the pulse thundering in her ears suggested just how fragile her façade might prove, especially if Melanie embarked on another of her none-too-subtle bouts of teasing.

Dear God, help . . .

"The viscount and his sister have graciously condescended to visit us for tea. Is that not lovely?"

"Lovely," Serena murmured as Catherine passed her a steaming porcelain cup and a sympathetic smile.

Her thoughts rushed. Why was he here? Why had she not known about this visit? She frowned. Had Catherine told her, and she'd somehow been too focused on her painting to truly hear? Or had Catherine's recent pains distracted her from informing Serena about a social call of such significance?

As Melanie, Catherine, and Mama carried the conversation, she stole another glance at the unexpected visitor. Her heart twisted. Despite the smiling countenance, he seemed gaunt, wearied, his eyes holding nothing of the spark she remembered. His effort to engage in conversation seemed to drain him, his answers too slow, his responses too brief, a far cry from the lively raconteur bubbling with wit that she remembered, the confident sophisticate that she had painted. What had bruised him so?

She glanced at his ungloved hands. No ring. Her memory had not been completely faulty. But—her heart thudded painfully—if he was visiting without Lily, did this mean he was not married then? Oh, *why* wasn't Mama asking the right questions!

Catherine cleared her throat. "Lord Carmichael, how are your parents?"

"My father has been a trifle unwell but seems improved of late, thus releasing us for a visit to London."

"Please send them our good wishes."

"Of course."

She would not ask about his betrothed. She would not! The tension coiled within as the exchange of politenesses continued. She tried to focus on the children, tried to focus on the beautiful fabric of Melanie's gown, but all she could think of was lilies. Lilies! Her hands clenched— "And how is Mrs. Milsom?"

As soon as the words slipped out, she heard a collective gasp. The viscount's jaw twitched, he did not meet her eyes as he said quietly, "I believe she is well."

Believe? Did he not know?

Melanie chuckled unpleasantly. "We will not be sending her your good wishes."

Serena glanced her confusion across at Catherine, whose groan and white face told a different story. Heart pounding, she rose and went to her sister's side. "Catherine, are you unwell?"

Her sister looked heart-stricken. "Dearest, I . . . I meant to mention, but I forgot. It is inexcusable of me. Oh, forgive me." Her face pinched in pain.

"Catherine?"

Serena stepped out of Jon's way as he crouched before his wife, murmuring softly to her, before glancing at the room. "I'm sorry. You'll have to excuse us. Catherine is unwell."

"Of course," Melanie said. "We should probably leave. I trust she will feel better soon."

"Thank you." Without further ado, Jon swept Catherine up in his arms and carried her from the room.

Serena moved to follow, when Mama said in a querulous tone, "She needs her mother, not her sister."

No, she didn't. She swallowed the words and said tightly, "Mama, I really feel she and Jon will be well—"

"Oh, what would you know?" And before she could restrain her, Mama had hurried away also.

She blinked against the burn, wished her cheeks did not feel on fire, and turned to their guests. "I . . . I beg your pardon."

Melanie chuckled over her teacup. "Never mind. We know all about parents prone to causing moments of difficulty, don't we, Harry?"

They exchanged a glance that made Serena wonder just what difficulty their parents had created. To ease her tension, Serena focused her attention on the youngest visitors and soon learned about Mr. Monkey's adventures in London and the recent visit Tom had paid to Bullock's Museum, all the while agonizing over the strange reaction to her enquiry. But she would not ask again. Truly, she would not!

Melanie placed her cup on the table. "Now, Serena, before we leave, may I make a request?"

"Of course."

"I would simply love to see what you've been working on."

"Working—? Oh. Oh!" The vault of her chest seemed to vibrate with loud hammering. What if they saw his picture? What would they say? "I . . . I'm afraid it is not finished."

Melanie smiled broadly. "It does not matter. I'm sure we would all find your art as appealing as ever."

Oh no, they would not.

"Please, Serena?"

Mama wandered back into the room, her look of discontent suggesting Jon had successfully barred her from Catherine's bedside. "What is the trouble now?"

Melanie explained, leading to Mama's shaken head and "Oh, go show them your silly pictures, Serena. Why you spend so much time on them I'll—"

"Lady Winthrop."

Serena's gaze snapped to the viscount, whose deep voice and intent look had quelled Mama into open-mouthed silence. Expectancy filled the room.

"You do your daughter's talent and skill a great disservice by dismissing her work thus."

Serena's eyes heated, her throat clogged.

"Surely, ma'am, you are aware that her artistry is such that she is in demand as a portraitist. My own sister here requested your daughter paint her children, and the resulting picture is one much admired."

"But she is only a girl."

"She is a remarkable and talented young lady, and it would behoove you to recognize her as such."

Serena lowered her gaze, unable to let him see how much his words of affirmation affected her. The air seemed to stretch, to crackle, as the air she held tightened her lungs.

"Miss Winthrop?" She lifted her eyes to meet his muddy green ones. "Would you be so kind as to show us something you've been working on?" His lips curled to one side. "Please? For everyone's sake?"

Non, non, non, non, non, her heart screamed.

"Yes."

⁂

How could he not speak up?

Harry followed the white-clad figure down a series of steps, round a corner, then down another corridor, certain she could lead him to the icy deserts of Siberia and he would still happily follow, would still feel warmth in her company.

Since she'd entered the room, it was all he could do not to drink in her every feature. But he would not be caught blatantly staring, so after that one hungry look, he'd forced himself to observe the walls, the carpet, the children, his hostess. But in that moment of yearning, he'd noticed numerous things. Her pale cheeks when she first spied him. The blueness of her eyes with their striking luminosity.

The spots of red on her fingers, though she tried folding one hand on the other. His gut clenched. How he longed to hold her hands, hold her—

"Here we are." Serena did not look at him now. "I am not sure if Monsieur Despard is still here. I will see—"

"Oh, it does not matter. We can come, too. Do you remember Despard, Harry? Oh, perhaps you don't. You were away at the time, now I recall. He taught Grandmama whenever she visited London."

Serena seemed to flinch as his sister entered the room, her two children chattering behind.

He murmured, "I am sorry for my sister's pushiness."

"You are not the only one."

Their eyes met. His heart kicked at the wry humor he saw in the blue depths.

With something like resignation she preceded him into the room, then stopped so abruptly he nearly collided with her.

"Oh, thank God," he thought he heard her whisper.

A dark-haired man strode toward them from a large table covered in paper for wrapping purposes. "Ah, mademoiselle. *Ze* matter from before has been dealt with."

"Packed away?"

"Ready for *ze* framers."

Serena's shoulders sagged. "Thank you."

He bowed. "These are your friends, I see?"

As Serena gave the introductions, the little man's dark eyes scanned Harry before giving a little smile and nod. "*Tres bien. Bonjour,* Monsieur Viscount."

"You know me?"

"You'd be surprised how well." The Frenchman's gaze slid to Serena, who now stood holding Ellie's hand as she pointed out features on the landscape.

His heart leapt. Serena had mentioned him? He hoped she had spoken well . . . Harry moved to join his niece to study the picture, a landscape, quite recognizable as Hyde Park, but—he frowned—not a trace of carmine to be seen.

"She is *ze* artist *tres formidable*, eh?"

"Yes."

The art master moved slightly, giving him another of those piercing looks, before again shaking his head with a little smile. "Truly remarkable, though perhaps, I hesitate to say, a trifle idealistic."

Serena glanced at him before looking at Despard. "You think the likeness isn't true?"

"I think you are a superlative artist, with *ze* eye for re-creating what you 'ave seen that is parallel to none."

Harry frowned, glancing between the pair. They seemed to share a hidden message.

"I think it a very good likeness," Melanie said, after peering at the picture. "Although I'm surprised, Serena, that you've reverted back to landscapes after your portraiture work before."

"I . . . er . . ."

"Ah, Madame Rochdale, but that is *ze* way a true artist works. Sometimes a little of this, sometimes a little of that." He turned to Harry with that unnerving smile. "Sometimes a big bit of that."

Before he could ask the strange little man his meaning, the door opened and Carlew strode in. "Ah, you're still here. I'm so glad."

"How is Catherine?"

"She is feeling better now, resting comfortably." He turned to Serena. "She would like to talk with you at your earliest convenience."

"I could go now, if you like."

Her eagerness to depart caused another twist to his heart. Did she dislike him that much?

"Later, when our guests are gone." Carlew met Harry's gaze. "So, what do you think of our prodigy?"

"She is as talented as ever."

Carlew nodded, pride suffusing his features as he smiled at his sister-in-law.

"Tell me, Serena, do you spend much time in the Park?" Melanie asked. "I would imagine there are all sorts of young men who would enjoy escorting you there."

Serena's cheeks flushed. "I . . ."

"Melanie," he warned in an undertone.

She grinned at him before turning back to the younger girl. "If you lack enough desirable company, perhaps Harry here could take you for a drive."

"Melanie, I should not like Miss Winthrop to feel obliged."

Serena's rosy cheeks darkened in hue, even as her chin tilted. "Like the sense of obligation you now feel, sir, to ask for something you do not wish."

He stared at her. "But I do wish to take you driving."

"But Mrs. Milsom . . ."

Harry glanced at Carlew. "Did you not tell her?"

"Tell me what?"

Melanie laughed. "Oh, you poor dear. Did you not know? Harry is free." She smiled slyly. "And free to take you driving, Miss Serena."

"I . . . I do not understand." Wide blue eyes turned to him. "Are you not engaged?"

"No."

"Thank the Lord," muttered Melanie.

A wealth of emotion passed through Serena's eyes, and her lips seemed to tremble before her countenance grew composed once more.

"Lily and I should never have been engaged," he said in a low voice, heart throbbing with explanations, with apologies. But right now was not the time, this room was not the place. The moment still felt too raw, too fragile.

Serena's cheeks paled, but her shy smile and the new light in her eyes fueled fresh hope in his heart. Perhaps he had a chance, after all.

"Perhaps not so imbecilic, after all?" he heard the Frenchman murmur.

Her smile stretched, but her gaze remained on Harry.

"I do not understand," her mother complained. "What is happening? Why do you look like that, Serena?"

"I wish to take your daughter driving tomorrow, Lady Winthrop."

"Serena? Oh, I suppose it will do her good to get out. She's spent long enough in here, no matter what Jon says."

Harry possessed himself of her hands, her soft paint-smudged hands, his eyes still not leaving hers. "Would you like to go, Miss Winthrop?"

"I . . ." She moistened her bottom lip, her beautiful, soft-looking pink lips. "I would, if Jon does not object."

"And why should he?" her mother said loudly. "*I* do not object, and I am your mother, after all. Of course you can go, Serena!"

Carlew cleared his throat, forcing Harry to relinquish Serena's hands and face his friend.

"It seems I bow to a higher authority." Eyes intent, Jon glanced at the ceiling, and smiled.

The constrictions around his heart finally eased. Perhaps Serena's mother thought Carlew meant he bowed to her wishes, but Harry knew the authority his friend truly meant.

A heavenly authority.

The Lord, who made heaven and earth.

The Lord, who was his Lord. And Serena's.

Harry's smile threatened to burst his cheeks. "Thank you, Lord Winthrop," he said, with a graceful bow, but genuine gratitude. *And thank You, Lord.*

❦ Chapter Twenty-Five

She lived in an impossible dream.

Sweet chestnuts flashed by as the phaeton's wheels rolled smoothly through Hyde Park. Chilled air nipped at her ears, threatening to bite through the silky squirrel muff she held. The scent of spring blossoms mingled with the far more enticing fragrance of the man beside her. She stole another look at him. Pinched the inside of her wrist. Yes, still real.

Every waking moment—and some sleeping ones also—Serena wondered how it was that Lord Carmichael was here in London, beside her in a carriage, at church, at dinner, smiling, laughing, like the past few months of separation had never happened. Like there had never been a coolness between himself and Jon. Like he had never been engaged to his childhood friend. For some reason he'd thought it necessary to explain to her about the ill-fated match, and this, coupled with Jon's and Melanie's words later, meant she could now understand, could even sympathize with his situation, faced with the trap Mrs. Milsom had so carefully walked him into. His words made her feel—somewhere very deep inside—almost glad for the experience, as he seemed different now.

His gaze seemed less bright yet more content; his laughter less brittle, more whole. He was less of a flirt and more of a . . . man. Despite the troubles Jon had alluded to, difficulties with his father and the bankers, the viscount owned a new confidence that owed less to social polish and more to genuine heart. He truly seemed to care. This was revealed in his warm countenance, the way his eyes lingered on her in a manner always respectful, never too long, but always long enough for her to know he was aware, and willing to fulfill her slightest wish, be it ever so humble. He further demonstrated his care in how he listened, how his words seemed more measured, like he spoke not to reply but to understand. Her words were not many, centering mainly on art, and home, and gardens, but in recent days she had felt him slowly becoming the person who understood her most. Even more than Catherine.

Serena smiled as a butterfly flapped tiny white wings past the lead horse. Poor Catherine. So apologetic for not telling her about the broken engagement, pains having chased all other thought from mind. Poor Jon, thinking Catherine had told her, not wanting to stir up emotions best left mending. Poor Melanie, promising her brother to not mention it in her letters, assuming Serena knew anyway. But what did it matter now?

Her smile dipped. But what would it matter in the future? For while the viscount seemed happy to escort her on carriage rides and talk and smile, he soon would not be. This dream would prove impossible as soon as he saw the painting with the lilies.

She cringed again.

"Miss Winthrop?" The green eyes turned to her, smudged with concern. "Are you cold?"

"I . . . thank you, I am not."

"You are sure? It is no trouble to turn around."

"Thank you, no." She smiled.

She heard his catch of breath, felt a warm dizzying sensation as he returned her smile warmly. For a moment they seemed surrounded by light, and hope, and promise. Heart thumping, she had to drag her gaze away from the tenderness in his. Good heavens! Was this near unbearable sweetness what Catherine meant when she spoke of being in love?

Love she knew. Well, knew what it *should* be. The Bible spoke of love proved by actions, through kindness, forbearance, lack of envy or pride. She saw it modeled in Catherine and Jon's relationship, wanted it herself one day. But this, this gush of deep emotion in his company . . . How could *this* end well? Especially when her actions in painting his picture had been motivated by something rather more self-seeking than seeking Lord Carmichael's blessing. Her spirits plunged.

The horses continued their trot around Hyde Park, then across to Kensington Gardens. Century-old plane trees, planted by Queen Caroline, shaded their progress from the weak afternoon sun. Daffodils waved golden heads as if in salutation. To the right she caught glimpses of flashing blue, the Serpentine winding its way through the green. An approaching carriage offered widened eyes, nods, and a "Good afternoon, Carmichael," and though he slowed and offered his own acknowledgment, the viscount did not stop.

He turned to offer a small smile when they were well clear. "I hope you don't mind my lack of introduction. I don't really want the rest of the afternoon taken up by Buffy Snorestream demanding to know the intricacies of every member of your family tree, even though I'm sure it is riveting, and they are all thoroughly lovely people."

"Oh, it is, and they are." Her chuckle joined his. "Buffy Snorestream?"

"Lord Burford Snowstrem to his parents; Buffy Snorestream to anyone who has ever endured a conversation with him. He's such a gossip you do well to avoid him. He's probably now stopping the next carriage, demanding to know about the beautiful mystery lady who gave him such a cool look."

Her heart performed a somersault. He thought her beautiful?

"I do like those cool looks of yours, Miss Winthrop, except when they are directed at me, of course. When that happens, my heart shrivels and I want to curl up somewhere and die."

"You are full of nonsense, sir."

"You do not believe me?" His gaze grew wistful. "I wish you would."

Her chest tightened, and she shifted her attention away, slowly releasing her breath.

"Perhaps you don't believe everything I say, but believe me when I say you do not want to waste your afternoon with Buffy."

"Not when I could waste it with you?"

"Exactly."

She smiled, peeking across to see his grin. The dimple had returned, just as she had painted it, the skin tone smudged with the faintest darkness on the jaw that occasionally glowed golden in the sunlight. Yes, her memory had not been completely faulty.

He cleared his throat. "Why do you look at me so intently, Miss Winthrop?"

"Oh! I'm sorry." She snapped her gaze away, her cheeks heating.

"I do not mind at all. It can only make me hope—but enough. I will confess I much prefer your intense perusal than that of Despard's."

She swallowed. Well she knew why M. Despard studied the viscount. "He . . . he is an unusual man." It was not a lie; the Despards of this world were few and far between.

"But you still have not answered my question."

What would he say if she told him the truth? Panic clawed up her throat.

"Miss Winthrop?"

"I . . . I am glad you are here." Again, not a lie.

She glanced across to see his smile deepen, a new light appearing in his eyes. "At last. Now, that was not so hard to say?"

But while true, it wasn't the truth. She swallowed, summoned courage, and finally dared touch on the question she'd only spoken in her bravest imaginings. "I . . . I was wondering if you've ever been painted."

"Why?" His look grew warmer, more intense. "Are you offering?"

She could say nothing.

His attention returned to the horses. "I confess such a thing has appeal. It would mean you spending hours in my company, gazing into my eyes—"

"Sir!" Propriety demanded a protest, but the thought nonetheless evoked a fluttering in her heart.

He laughed. "I suppose I will need a portrait one day." His nose wrinkled. "There is one of Melanie and me when we were children, but that won't suffice. No, I'd be quite happy to have my portrait done. And even happier if it be by your hand."

"Sir, no. I am but fresh from the schoolroom."

"I do not think of you so."

His gaze was respectful, his tone such she could not read innuendo.

Serena's heart thudded. If he truly thought of her as a young lady, perhaps these drives were leading to something like what Mama hoped and believed.

He snapped the reins. The horses picked up speed. "Of course, I should not like to appear pompous."

She smiled at the thought. "Of course not."

"Or terribly squat."

"Never."

"Or overly handsome. A *little* handsome, perhaps, but nothing so over the top as to generate despondency in the average man's heart."

"Your thoughtfulness towards others does you credit."

"I *am* very thoughtful, and so glad for your perception of the fact. So, you would have me appear a little handsome? I would want a faithful representation, so nothing as to be unbelievable."

"A touch of handsomeness, noted."

He glanced at her again, his eyes growing serious, almost pleading. "I think I can trust you to see me as I am, and more so, see who I want to be?"

A myriad of images twined together. The flirt. The joker. The generous uncle. The miner. The friend. The hard worker. The believer. The suitor—

Her breath caught.

"You . . . you would truly trust me to paint you?"

"I would trust you with everything, Miss Winthrop."

She stared at him, as a thought tickled the edges of her mind. Was this God's means of providing an escape from her dilemma?

"I can see the brain ticking, but what conclusions it draws I do not know." He grinned. "Are you wondering how much to charge? I would say the moon, but unfortunately I could not afford such a price."

"I would never ask to be paid."

"Have you learned nothing from that inestimable business brain of Carlew's? Your paints cost something, the canvas, your time. Grandmama has said more than once that the frames alone can cost more than everything else—"

"But—"

"But I imagine you would paint for the enjoyment of it, for the love of it?"

"Yes."

"Would you paint *me* for the love of it, I wonder?"

She studied the trees again, willing her face to coolness, but her cheeks disobeyed, flushing with fire. "I do not know what you mean."

He gave a soft chuckle. "How I wish you did, my dearest Miss Winthrop." He snapped the reins and turned the horses to home.

Already somewhat familiar with the concentration and attention with which Serena approached her art, it still came as something of a surprise to see how committed she truly was. It seemed the soft smiles and moments of intimacy of yesterday's drive were almost forgotten as she briskly set to work, quickly sketching and then outlining him and blocking in color, amidst consultations of M. Despard and a sketchbook she guarded jealously. Harry had tried to peek inside but she'd snatched it away so violently he wondered if the secrets inside should best be preserved. Such animation from the normally cool Miss Winthrop was enough to make him wonder—to hope—that the contents might somehow pertain to him.

"Lord Carmichael."

He snapped to attention and smiled at the young lady before him. "Yes, Miss Winthrop?"

"I need you to maintain the pose I showed you earlier."

"The one with the imaginary pillar?"

"Remember I am trying to portray you on the terrace at Welmsley. Although I'm sure I can never do the valley justice," she added in a mutter.

"I'm sure you can. You are extremely talented, would you not agree, Despard?"

The art tutor spoke something appropriately Gallic and complimentary, Serena seeming to drink in his confidence in exact reverse of the way that she ignored Harry's attempts at gallantry. A pang of envy slithered within, quickly followed by renewed sympathy. While blessed with talent, she seemed cursed with self-doubt—was it any wonder she preferred to hear the praises of a known *artiste*? Yet her self-doubt proved—he smiled wryly—another way they were compatible.

"There. Perfect."

She was gazing at his face, a small frown etched between her brows. "Don't move."

But it was hard not to react, when she adjusted his hand and fire seemed to leap between them at the touch. Was it just his hopeful imagination, or did that color highlighting her cheeks signal her own response to his nearness?

The door opened and her mother walked in, necessitating a greeting and bow from him, and a muffled sigh from her daughter.

"I have come to see how you are getting on."

"We've barely started, Mother."

"Then what have you been doing all this time?" Lady Winthrop settled herself on a seat in the corner.

Harry's spirits sagged. So, it would not just be Serena he would need to charm, but her mother as well.

"Sir?"

His attention snapped back to Serena's face. Her frowning face.

"I beg your pardon, Miss Winthrop." He stood again, working to approximate the pose from before. "Is that better?"

She cast him a withering glance before resuming her frenetic pace at the easel.

"I hope this coat was appropriate."

"It's fine. It brings out the color of your eyes."

He smiled.

Her frown deepened. "Stop smiling like that."

He lowered one side of his mouth a fraction. "Better?"

"No." She drew nearer, peering at him. "The other side."

"Surely it doesn't matter which side of his face the viscount smiles, Serena," her mother said.

Serena's hands clenched, then unclenched. "It *does* matter," she muttered.

"It is *ze* question of *ze* balance, madame," Despard said in an apologetic tone.

"Well, I do not think you should treat his lordship so dismissively," Lady Winthrop continued, eyeing her daughter, who flushed.

Protectiveness fired within, forcing him to say, "Madam, we mere mortals cannot interrupt the artist while she is at work." Her mother mollified, he turned to Serena. "Forgive me. Would you show me how you want me to smile?"

She drew closer, and he could feel the tension emanating from her.

"I wish I knew what would make you smile, Miss Winthrop," he said softly. "Would dancing with you at the upcoming Leavenworth ball win me a smile?"

"I don't have time for balls," she muttered. "But getting this painting done on time might do so."

"I was not aware there was a time frame for doing so." Her head snapped up, her eyes wide, like she was worried. He smiled. "I certainly have no such requirements, I assure you."

She bit her lip, the weight she seemed to be carrying an almost tangible thing.

"Serena? What are you doing? What are you talking about over there?"

Serena's sigh burrowed into his heart, eliciting his compassion. "Give me one moment," he murmured to her, before moving off the platform and approaching her mother. "Lady Winthrop, I wonder, have you ever had the opportunity to study an artist at work before? No? My grandmother was always extremely focused on her work and found interruptions to be decidedly inconvenient."

"Oh, but I'm not interrupting—"

"Because Miss Winthrop has scarcely had the chance to begin." He waved a hand at the canvas and smiled, holding out a hand which she accepted, and he gently encouraged her to stand. "Perhaps it might be best if you returned later. I can assure you that I will treat your daughter with all due respect, and with the chaperonage of Monsieur Despard, there can be nothing untoward taking place."

She studied him a moment before releasing a small moue of protest. "Very well."

When her mother had finally exited the room, Serena's shoulders sagged. "Thank you, sir."

"I am glad I could assist." He moved to his place and resumed his position. "Now, you were going to show me how to smile?" He tweaked the left side of his mouth. "Like this?"

"No." She drew near and touched his face. "Like this."

His breath caught. She was so close he could feel her breath on his skin, could see the fringe of golden lashes tipped with darkness, like a fan of gold dipped in soot, could see the perfect plumpness of her parted lips—

"There. What do you think?" She stepped back, and turned to the Frenchman, who gave a decided nod.

"*Tres bien.*" He peered at the sketchbook, and nodded again. "*Oui.*"

Why did it sound like they had planned this? He supposed she needed to, but it seemed a little odd . . .

"Monsieur, do not frown."

"Sorry," he said, working to smooth out his brow.

He eyed Serena, who had joined her tutor in examining the sketchbook, and was once again peering at him.

Sometimes, like now, he could sense she was looking but not really seeing him, was seeing, perhaps, a vision of potential, of a work completed. He understood; he could see the mines, had long dreamed about the family mines fulfilling their potential. Until his dreams had recently been enhanced by something else. By someone else.

"Lord Carmichael," that someone else called. "Stop smiling!"

"Please forgive me," he said. "Some people just seem to bring it out of me."

Her gaze narrowed, and he bit back a laugh, and settled in for a delightful few hours of Miss Serena's company, of seeing her, hearing her, being with her, scowling focus and all.

Chapter Twenty-Six

"I CANNOT HELP you. I'm terribly sorry, Lord Carmichael, but measures such as these require your father's signature. So, I cannot help you."

The words from his visit to the banker today swam around his brain even as he forced himself to smile, to dance, to chat, to engage with those around him. He glanced at the blonde head chatting to young ladies nearby, the worries in his heart easing as she looked up and smiled.

He returned the look, warmth glowing in his chest. After her initial reaction, he'd thought perhaps Serena might not attend the Leavenworth ball. But it seemed even great artists were required to bow to the wishes of family sometimes, and she'd been forced to lay aside the brushes for a night away from the painting that so consumed her.

Thank God for Catherine, for insisting her sister have an evening devoted to dancing.

Thank God for Jon, whose approval at Harry's interest let him gently pursue Serena unfettered.

Thank God for Serena—and daily, he did—for her smiles and their shared humor had a way of easing the strain of worries originating farther north.

He studied her now, dressed in a gown of palest blue, embroidered with cream and gold flowers. That she enjoyed his company, he was sure. That he wished to be part of her future, he was sure she did not yet believe. But he was determined. Yet he would not pursue aggressively. While he longed to touch her, to hold her, to kiss her, such imaginings only led to a fire he could not easily dampen. So in the lonely hours at night, he forced himself to pray blessings on her, to pray for strength for himself, to plead for wisdom for the financial straits in which Father had placed him.

"My lord?"

"Ah, Miss Winthrop, how I wish I were."

She blinked. Smiled. "I was going to ask if you were unwell, but clearly you're feeling better now." She turned and moved as if to return to her previous companions.

"Oh, but I am unwell."

"What?" She pivoted, studying him, a small crease between her brows.

"I am wishing to be somewhere other than this noisy house with its noisy guests." He moved closer. "I wish you were painting me as before."

The blue eyes met his, lit with an answering smile. "As do I."

The world around them seemed to shrink until it consisted of just their two, twinned smiles, shared memories. It had happened before, during their painting sessions, even as art master, maid, and sometimes even sister or mother attended. Apparently no number of chaperones could thwart this blossoming bond between them.

Harry moved closer, dipped his head. "Did I mention how lovely you look in that gown?"

"A few times, yes."

He laughed, as his sister approached, trailed by a bored-looking Lord Rochdale.

"Serena? What have you been saying to that brother of mine to make him so happy? Whatever it is, do more, please. He has not seemed so gladsome for months."

Harry cleared his throat. "We were discussing how beautiful she looks."

Serena's mouth sagged. "We were not! You make me sound vainglorious, sir!"

"When you are anything but. My apologies."

She nodded, turning as his sister said, "Well, you do look quite ravishing, my dear. It's not every debutante who can get away with something other than white, but you are something out of the ordinary." Melanie turned to her husband. "Isn't she, Rochdale?"

"Isn't who what, my dear?"

"Oh, for heaven's sake!"

As Melanie quietly berated her husband, Harry caught the wisp of laughter in the poised Serena's eyes. "I believe you would make a remarkable poker player, Miss Winthrop."

Blue eyes flashed. Twin roses appeared in her cheeks. "Do not speak with me of gambling."

Her gaze dropped, along with his hopes. He was a fool. Of course she wouldn't appreciate such things. Not when her father had once held London's reputation as the worst gamester from the West Country.

His sister glanced at him, Rochdale having kissed her hand then slipped away. "Alas, poor Harold."

He scowled at her for her use of the long-despised nickname from his younger days, usually uttered whenever his sister had mocked his misdemeanors.

Serena looked between them. "Who is Harold?"

"Someone Melanie used to know."

"Used to know?" His sister enquired with a lifted brow.

"Didn't I tell you? That man has died."

"I'm sorry," Serena murmured.

"That seems a sudden thing," Melanie said.

"No, it's been coming on for a while." Renewed faith had killed the old nature, but some of the practices seemed to take longer to die than others.

His sister held a wicked gleam in her eye. "I trust he is completely dead?"

Serena frowned. "How did he die?"

"He . . ." He swallowed, gazed into her eyes. "He was overcome by a malady of the heart."

"How tragic."

"It was. His dissipated youth gone"—he snapped his fingers—"gone, in an instant."

"Will he be much missed?"

"Perhaps in certain quarters, by the likes of Buffy Snorestream and company. But as for me, I shall endeavor to endure his passing with fortitude."

Melanie chuckled and moved to rejoin her husband, who led her into the dance set that was just forming. Harry offered his arm to Serena, and they moved from the bustling ballroom to a slightly quieter alcove, where he stopped to pretend to examine a camellia in the floral arrangement.

Serena's brow smoothed, her glance when next she looked up held shrewdness. "Harold, did you say?"

"I didn't. That was Melanie."

Her smile flickered, then she moved to study a flower of her own. "You mentioned a malady of the heart. Were the doctors unable to help?"

"Completely ineffectual."

"Yet you seem . . . rather relieved at his passing."

"I think many, including you, would feel the same."

She did look up then. "Poor Harold."

"Yes."

"I hope you don't miss him terribly much."

"Alas, I cannot. Not when I'm suffering a malady of the heart myself."

"You?" Her smile touched her eyes. "Can nothing be done for you, sir?"

He sighed, using the moment to inch closer, touch her gloved hand, reveling in her smile as he did so. "I fear the only person able to help has proved most impervious."

"Perhaps that person might have a change of mind?" She tilted her head to one side, revealing the beautiful lines of her throat.

"Tell me, Serena," he said in a low voice, "do you ever change your mind?"

"Sometimes." The widened eyes now sparkled like jeweled seas.

"And would this be one of those times?"

"I . . ." The sapphire eyes seemed to dip to his lips before flicking up again.

His heart kicked. Angling his body to screen her, he leaned closer. Closer . . .

"Serena! Is that you?"

He pulled back abruptly, heart thudding, as a young lady hurried to Serena's side. She introduced her as a school friend, Miss Caroline Hatherleigh. He bowed, and then bowed again to her insistence on dragging Serena away to see her mother.

Leaving him alone. Frustrated. Longing for more.

"Carmichael!"

Harry turned, his heart sinking. "Where's that sumptuous creature you were with earlier? Hiding behind the flower pot, eh?"

Harry affixed a smile to his lips. "Buffy. Hello."

"Who is she? You simply must introduce me."

Whatever he said now would fast become fare for society's chief rumormonger. "Miss Winthrop."

"Winthrop? I don't seem to recall the name. She's not related to that fool from that godforsaken place out west, is she? I seem to recall a Lord Winthrop—"

"Lord Winthrop is one of my closest friends. She is a distant cousin of his. Tell me, how are your parents?"

"Oh, fine, fine. And how is your dear father? I heard he's not well."

"No."

"Such a shame, such a shame." The portly man took a pinch of snuff then delicately coughed. "I imagine you're looking forward to taking over the reins, so to speak?"

"I don't think anyone truly wishes for their parent's death, do you, Buffy? If you'll excuse me." He bowed, and moved away, hoping the interrogation would stop.

But Buffy waddled alongside him. "Are you searching for your young lady? I believe she is with Lord Aynsley's daughter. She's pretty enough, but not quite in your Miss Winthrop's style."

Harry lifted a glass of champagne from a passing footman's tray, shoved it at his friend. "I must be going."

"Is it true you were seen exiting the bank today?"

"It might be." *Dear Lord, give me an escape!*

"This wine is not terribly good."

"Because it is champagne," he muttered. "Excuse me," he said in a louder voice, adding something about retrieving Miss Winthrop for the next dance.

Harry hurried away, relieved to find her in the next chamber, her cool expression as she listened to the chattering Aynsley ladies lighting as she spied him. He offered humble apologies but that he must steal Miss Winthrop away as she had promised him this next dance.

"But I did not," Serena murmured as they moved to the ballroom from where the strains of music came.

"You should have. I would rather dance with you than anyone else."

Her cheeks tinted, her eyes enlarging as they entered the room. "Oh, but sir, it is a waltz!"

"Exactly."

The next half hour was the most exquisite of his life. The world seemed to blur, his attention, his every sense fixed on Miss Serena Winthrop. She was a diamond in the midst of lesser jewels, everything light, clear, and true. Warmth filled his heart, certainty filled his soul. Miss Serena Winthrop was everything he wished for: pure and passionate and clever. Someone who understood him; someone who shared his faith, his humor; someone who—like Grandmama—seemed to believe in him. How he wished it was time to speak of his feelings; he ached with the very effort of holding back. But caution prompted him to withhold a declaration. She wasn't ready. Yet.

Too soon the music concluded, and Carlew was ushering his sister-in-law home, leaving Harry feeling forsaken, like the candles had been snuffed. He wandered from the ballroom, unwilling to dance with anyone else, his worries crowding in again—money, Father, the estate—and nearly cursed himself when he bumped into Buffy once more.

"Aha! I see you were having a nice time with your lady friend."

Harry's smile tightened. Why did that expression make him feel slightly nauseous? "Your powers of observation do you credit, Buffy."

"Tell me," Buffy said, rubbing his hands together, "can we expect an announcement soon?"

"I'm sure there are many announcements to be made, but whether they are ones you might expect or ones affecting me I simply cannot say. Oh, look!" He pointed over Buffy's shoulder.

As Buffy turned to look, Harry murmured an "Excuse me" and ducked into the adjoining saloon. The saloon set aside for gaming. He heaved out a breath. Buffy never condescended to enter such venues.

"Well, well! Carmichael. We haven't seen you in an age."

"Which is why we've all been richer."

"Where have you been, old chap?"

He nodded to his acquaintances, mentioned something about Derbyshire, the estate.

"Here to try your luck?"

"If he is, there goes our luck."

He stared at the table, stacked with banknotes and two dice. The old itch began to tingle. Here was money. Here was solution. His prayers might've worked regarding Serena, but they hadn't for the estate. The coffers remained empty. His mine remained closed. He had always been lucky. Had God given him this gift?

"My lord," Lord Ashbolt eyed him. "Are you going to play?"

He glanced around the table at faces he could read with his eyes closed.

Somehow a chair slipped under him, and he lowered into it automatically.

Just one round. Just one turn.

Apparently the old man still had some life in him, after all.

❧ Chapter Twenty-Seven

Berkeley Square

"Now MOVE A little to the right. There. Hold."

"Like this?" the viscount grinned, striking another pose.

"No! Are you going to be difficult or shall you let me do my work?" Why had he chosen to be so fey today of all days? He'd barely stopped grinning since the ball ten days ago.

"Really, Serena," Mama said from her corner of the studio. "Must you speak so to Lord Carmichael? It seems immeasurably rude to address a future earl in such a common way."

Serena gritted her teeth as the viscount chuckled and murmured yet another apology. She was already behind. She needed this done. Needed this done yesterday! Oh, why had she agreed to balls and picnics and the like when the painting remained incomplete?

"Steady, mademoiselle. You must let *ze* discontent go."

"Will you escort her from the room, then?" she muttered under her breath.

M. Despard chuckled. "You will have time. Just apply patience."

But patience, so long her friend, seemed to have fled. Painting the viscount had caused quite the uproar when he had first mooted the idea to her mother, but she had quickly been won over by his charm. Unfortunately, his charm had won Mama to such an extent that she now preferred to be in the room whenever Lord Carmichael arrived for their portraiture session. Of course she insisted it was for propriety's sake, for dear little Serena needed a chaperone after all.

Serena huffed out a breath, stabbing the canvas with her brush. What did Mama think the viscount could actually *do* while M. Despard remained within the studio? But Mama's topics of conversation these days had narrowed down to two: the upcoming birth of her grandchild, and her oft-expressed hope of having a future earl as a son-in-law.

"Careful, *ma chéri*. The canvas needs *ze* tender touch, like a woman." At the sound of muffled laughter from the front of the room, the Frenchman turned. "Would you not agree, monsieur?"

"Undoubtedly."

At the viscount's grinning countenance she felt the tension fractionally dissipate. Perhaps Mama's presence here wasn't so bad. Not when it permitted time with him, and—her heart thumped loudly, reminding her of her purpose—opportunity to produce another portrait like the first.

Except it was *not* like the first. She frowned, her paintbrush swirling the vermilion and white into skin color, then bent to carefully approximate the left hand that had caused so much trouble before. With this painting, she found herself second-guessing so much more, not just the precise tone of hair color, but how she'd painted his carefully disheveled waves. And his left hand: Were the fingers splayed evenly on the pillar, or had she left more space between the smallest finger and ring finger? She pushed at the dull ache rimming her forehead.

"Miss Winthrop? Would you like to rest a moment?"

No! She swallowed, found a smile. "No, thank you, my lord. I'd like to continue, if you please."

"As you wish."

She ducked behind her canvas, conscious of his eyes watching her, at times humorous, at times thoughtful, like now. Oh, how she'd like to rest, but last week's news had put paid to that.

Now she applied a thin layer of white, ensuring an appropriate play of light, even as her thoughts raced. Under the joyous shock of learning her work would be exhibited next month at Somerset House lay a multitude of questions and regrets. Why, oh why, had M. Despard not sent it away for safekeeping at a different framer's? Why had M. Despard's framing friend permitted two Royal Academy judges to see her work? Why had they agreed to send it for inclusion? She was a near novice! Chief question of all: How on earth could she complete this painting by the end of next week, in order to exchange it for the one already marked for inclusion?

The thump in her head magnified. Her pleas to touch up the previous picture—simply to paint over the lilies—had fallen on deaf ears, so she'd labored, morning, afternoon, even snatching time late last night, trying to repaint the picture to a similar high standard, trying to finish before the final date for submissions. Pressure filled her heart, filled her thoughts, affecting her right down to her shaking fingertips. Everyone would know what the lilies represented—or, more precisely, whom. It was tantamount to announcing Lord Carmichael's engagement to Mrs. Milsom. She could not embarrass him so. The viscount's reaction if she were unsuccessful in exchanging the picture was something she dared not contemplate.

"Miss Winthrop?"

She glanced up, heart skipping as she met the smiling green gaze. "Yes?"

"Please don't frown. It makes me feel like you disapprove of your subject matter."

"The only thing I disapprove regarding my subject matter is his constant need to talk."

"Serena!"

"Sorry, Mama," she muttered, to the viscount's soft laughter.

"Mademoiselle, perhaps a *leetle* less of zinc? Monsieur's hand has not leprosy, *non*?"

She sighed, picked up the rag, and carefully dabbed away. It would not move. The light and heat beneficial in helping her previous painting dry so quickly had already dried this one. Tears burned.

"Here. Permit me?"

Serena nodded, easing from the stool to stretch as M. Despard gently removed the layer of mismatching paint. Her back was sore from holding position for so long. She rubbed her forehead, unwilling to meet the sympathy she was sure to see in the viscount's eyes.

"Miss Winthrop?" His voice drew her attention to his face. Sure enough, his brow was knit. "Are you unwell?"

"I have a slight headache, that is all."

His frown lines deepened. "Shall we be done for the day?"

"No! No." She smiled to cover the panic she knew laced her voice. "I'm happy to go on."

"But I'm not, not if you have a headache. Monsieur Despard, surely you'd agree that an artist cannot paint well when he is not feeling quite the thing."

"I . . ." The Frenchman glanced at her. "I would normally agree . . ."

No!

"Oh, Serena, do close your mouth. 'Tis not ladylike."

She bit her bottom lip, the pressure in her head sharpening to that of a thousand stabbing pencil points. A hazy-bright sensation swam before her. Breathing past the pain, she grasped the table.

"Miss Winthrop?"

She shook her head, but the very movement deepened her discomfort. The familiar ache, so long a warning of the onset of her pains, rippled across her insides. She gasped, clutching her midsection.

"Mademoiselle?"

The room seemed to tip and tilt. She would *not* fall. She would *not* faint in front of him! She had to finish—

"Serena?"

Strong hands held her arms, the scent of amber and warmed honey touched her nose. Strong. Too strong. She pulled away, nausea swelling within. Had to get away. "Excuse me."

Another desperate tug and she was finally released to stumble to the door.

"Serena, where are you going?" Mama called, as if from far away.

Now the pain shrieked within, crippling her movements to all save a bending motion. She gasped, bracing as the pain came again. And again. Stupid, *stupid* pain that meant she'd likely never have children. Nausea threatened to escape. Tears leaked from her eyes.

"I've got you."

The words whispered close to her ear before she felt those same strong arms lift and carry her from the room, away from the studio, along the passage through the hall, and up another flight of stairs. She closed her eyes, savoring the cooler air that brought relief to her body, but which could not bring relief within. Saltwater slipped down her cheeks, past her lips. She would never finish the painting now.

"Serena?"

Catherine's voice, far away.

"Bring her into this room."

The viscount's low voice rumbled in his chest, against her ear. She couldn't make out his words. Could barely think, save that somehow, in his arms, she felt strangely safe.

Her head tipped slightly. Now she could hear, could feel, the steady thump of his heart.

She whimpered, though she wanted to wail, as she was finally laid on a soft mattress.

His heart. His admiration. His love.

It would all, so soon, be . . .

Gone.

White's Gentlemen's Club

"Raise."

Harry upped his stake, growing impatient with the game of Brag. It seemed they'd sat here for hours, though perhaps that was the effect of the company. Ramsey and Billington were gamesters of long duration. Ashbolt, tonight's dealer, a man whose conversational skills were never high. Harry's success at the Leavenworth ball had fueled their desire to regain their blunt, and his erstwhile habit refused his denial. He'd wager none of the other men seated here had a head so filled with distraction.

Three days ago, he'd finally held Serena in his arms, but her swoon had led to scenes and sensations nothing like he'd imagined. Panic. Helplessness. Convulsions.

Then today, her sister's explanation.

He clenched his teeth, wishing now he'd never agreed to play for such high stakes, as Catherine's words from this afternoon ate into his concentration. Today's visit, his third since the incident, a third visit with flowers for a patient he did not see, had at least been leavened by the absence of Serena's mother, which seemed to free Jon's wife to an honesty he hadn't anticipated. An honesty he'd now rather not know.

"Raise."

Harry matched the previous call. He had good cards, he could afford to go higher. Besides, wasn't he always lucky?

His lips twisted. Except in love, it seemed.

On his previous visits, his gentle enquiries as to Serena's health were glossed over politely. But not this afternoon. Catherine had stared at him, her sad, intent expression raising the hairs on his neck.

"What is it, Catherine?"

She'd sighed. "I do not wish to say this, but she's insisted."

"Serena?"

Catherine nodded, seemingly unfazed by his use of her sister's name. "She . . . she is very appreciative of your flowers, sir . . ."

He braced internally. "But?"

"But she thinks it best if you do not visit anymore."

Hurt pounded his chest, forcing him to clear his throat. "Why?"

"Her illness—"

"You said she has migraines."

"Th-they are related to a deeper issue."

Issue.

His hands formed fresh fists.

Her problem was such that should he marry her, Serena would never present him with issue.

"Carmichael?"

He blinked. Refocused on the faces around him. The game. "Raise."

Eyebrows shot up; he ignored them. Let them sweat. Heaven knew he'd spent plenty of time sweating today.

His thoughts returned to the Berkeley Square drawing room, whose calming green tones did nothing to assuage the storm brewing inside.

"You mean she cannot have children?"

Catherine nodded.

"But how can you know?" A memory spiked, along with fresh pain. "I"—he swallowed—"I did not think the art master had forced himself—"

She'd gasped. "You know?"

"You mean he did?" Nausea swirled.

"No! No. He did not. She is innocent, Henry."

Breath he had not even known he'd been holding released.

"The doctor believes the severity of her pains is related to an inability to bear children." Catherine's eyes grew shiny. "She does not talk about things overly, she is a very private person, which is why it surprised me that she wanted you to know." She sighed again. "But she said she wants you to be fully cognizant of your . . . choices."

His choices.

Somehow through the shock he'd managed to utter polite nothings, take his leave and stumble here, back along the once well-trodden path. His mind spun. Why had Serena insisted on having such intimate details revealed? Her mother would likely collapse upon learning he knew. Serena's eligibility would be next to nil should word get out. What member of the Peerage wished to marry a barren woman? How could any estate cope with a family line sure to die?

How could his?

"Carmichael? You do not look well."

Harry gritted out a smile, deflecting the question with another flick of his wrist.

Why had she told him?

He peered at the men seated around the baize-covered table. How many men here had marriages where children were born out of wedlock because one or the other had fertility difficulties? How many smug wives had known, or even just suspected, such a thing? Why then had Serena insisted Catherine tell him?

"Fold."

Harry glanced from Ramsey to look at his cards. Forced himself not to frown. His cards were not good. Not good enough for this deep play.

"My lord?"

What should he do? Pass or play? Pass on Serena, or—

"Carmichael?"

He looked up. Saw Ashbolt eyeing him narrowly. Panic scratched his heart. "Play."

Ashbolt's teeth glinted as he doubled the last bet, the sovereigns shining gold under the candlelight.

"See." Harry swallowed. Threw his cards into the middle of the table.

Saw Ashbolt place down his cards.

He fought to maintain composure as the table swam before him. *How* much had he lost?

Oh, dear God . . .

He flicked at an imaginary piece of lint on his sleeve, unwilling to meet the mix of commiseration and smug satisfaction he knew the other men's faces would reveal. He cleared his throat. "Gentlemen, please forgive such appalling play on my behalf."

"Not at all," Ashbolt said, eyes hard and hawk-like. "Care to play again?"

"Forgive my inattention, but how much am I currently owing?"

"Ten thousand."

Bile shot up his throat. For a second he felt himself sway.

"You do not look so very well, Carmichael," Ashbolt said with a gloating smile. "I imagine you now know how we've all felt over the years."

"I'll grant it's not the most pleasurable feeling."

"Perhaps not as much fun as time spent with that widow you're so friendly with?"

Harry ground his teeth.

"Play again?" Ashbolt smiled without friendliness. "Chance to recoup?"

Chance to recoup or chance to further stamp Welmsley into ignominy?

Something within him urged him to stay. To win. To get his head in the game. To show Ashbolt and his miserable friends that he could do it. The voice insisted that if he focused, Harry could win again. *Needed* to win again, to save the estate from financial ruin.

But something else whispered he leave. Forgo his pride. Save himself. Save his reputation. Save the estate. Remember his faith.

Choices.

His choices. God's choices.

Oh . . .

After summoning pen and paper, he scribbled his vowels. Pushed back his seat. Stood. Smiled. "Gentlemen, thank you." He nodded to Ashbolt. "You may expect payment tomorrow."

"I can?"

Heat surged through his chest. "You doubt my word?" he said softly.

"Of course not."

"Merely hinted at it."

Ashbolt's cheeks reddened. "There have been rumors, my lord, about the Bevington estate—"

"And you believe them? My, my! What things amuse such . . . minds. But I suppose when one's family is so distinguished there will always be those who cannot help but display their ignorance and envy." He bowed to soft gasps. "Pray excuse me, gentlemen."

Without a backward glance he walked from the room, his steps deliberate and unhurried so as not to give the impression of desperation and escape.

He paused in the brighter light of the hall as a sudden wave of responsibilities crashed over him. He needed money. Had to speak with his banker. Should speak to Carlew. Should write to Father. Should eat.

"Carmichael?" Lord Hawkesbury stepped into view. "Are you quite well?"

"I hardly know."

"Care to join me for dinner?"

Harry stared at him. So much to do. So many questions. Aromas wafting from the dining room tempted him to stay. But he did not wish to see Ashbolt and his cronies again.

His stomach rumbled.

Hawkesbury smiled. "I'll take that as a yes?"

He nodded, following Hawkesbury as he walked past a dozen gossip-laden tables through to a more private dining room beyond.

Somehow between ordering meals and exchanging pleasantries he calmed enough to answer the earl's concern. "It is nothing."

"Ten thousand pounds nothing?" The earl raised a brow. "I confess I've never been a gambler—could never afford to be—but I hardly think such an amount to be sniffed at."

Harry looked up from his soup. "I don't sniff, exactly. I . . . I am not used to losing."

"Forgive me, but I thought you had quit?"

"I had. That is, I tried." The hazel gaze prompted further honesty. Thank God for the relative privacy of this table. "I needed the money," he muttered.

Needed the money he no longer had. Now he needed even more. He shook his head. "I used to be able to play recklessly and still win, but now . . ."

"Something weighs on you."

What didn't? He scraped together a smile and over the course of the meal, quietly confided something of Welmsley's troubles. Anything more personal he could not share; he would not share.

"I did not realize things were so dire. I am sorry, my friend."

"I'm sorry also." Fresh revulsion filled him at what he'd cost the estate. "I thought I'd changed." He shook his head, guilt twisting through him like a miner's spiraling bore.

"I have seen you at services. You have seemed . . . more engaged."

"Yes." He pushed his plate away, sipped his water. "I've been challenged to trust God."

"Through gambling?" Hawkesbury smiled.

Strangely, he didn't feel any sense of the earl's judgment or condemnation. He shrugged.

"I understand how easy it is to fall back into previous patterns of behavior," Hawkesbury said. "My wife has had to deal with a husband who still far too easily reverts to his old proud and sarcastic self."

"It seems a wife is very good antidote for one's pride."

Hawkesbury eyed him keenly. "'Get thee a wife,' Shakespeare's Benedick would say. Get thee a wife."

Harry's gaze faltered, lips tightened. How could he? The only candidate he wanted for that role had shocked him nearly senseless.

"Forgive me. I fear my words bring more sting than salve." Hawkesbury waited as their plates were cleared away. "As one follower to another, may I remind you of our Lord's grace? Nothing is impossible for those who believe."

Like God healing a woman of infertility? He stilled. Wait—

"Your past mistakes need not define you. Indeed, as believers, we are called to lay aside every weight, every burden, the sin that so easily besets us."

Harry played with his untouched wineglass. "I fear I'm burdened and beset."

"You need not remain so. Allow God to help you throw it off. He is our help, is He not?"

The quiet hum of the dining room filled his ears as the psalmist's words penetrated his heart anew: I lift up mine eyes unto the hills, from whence cometh my help. My help cometh from the Lord . . . The Lord is thy keeper . . . The Lord shall preserve thee from all evil, He shall preserve thy soul.

God help him, he *would* change. God would help disentangle Harry's mess.

The hazel eyes studied him. "You have the means to pay?"

"Yes." From his winnings from the night of the ball. A tight smile formed. Thank goodness for Ashbolt's greed that night.

"May I offer some advice?"

Harry jerked a nod.

"If London has the means to ensnare, then why stay?"

"You think I should return north? Lick my wounds?"

"Return north, and remember who you are." Hawkesbury smiled gently. "And who you are no longer."

He nodded. Resolve firmed. The future Earl of Bevington was going home to stay.

✳ Chapter Twenty-Eight

Berkeley Square

"But it is too late, mademoiselle. I'm terribly sorry."

Serena stared at him. No. No! *Why* had she become ill? Why had it taken over a week to recover? If the painting was not exchanged, the viscount would think she'd made mockery of him. He would hate her. She pulled the mobcap from her head. *Oh, heavenly Father . . .*

The Frenchman's eyes softened. "I did everything I could. I wondered if I should finish your work, try to emulate your style, but I fear they would know it was not *ze* artist original."

Her eyes filled. She blinked. Blinked again.

"*Ma chère*, do not cry! Perhaps it will not matter. While your work is superb, as you are a beginner, it will likely be—how you say?— skied. It will be very hard to see from the floor when it is up so high near the ceiling."

The thought, far from being insulting, gave a modicum of comfort. She swallowed. "You think so?"

"*Oui*." His dark eyes flickered. "But no matter. People will not to know it is your work."

She shook her head. "But the viscount will. We spent days on re-creating the exact painting. Of course he will know!" She dragged in a breath. Another. Oh, what had she done?

"Shh, shh. Calm yourself, mademoiselle. You cannot even know if he will attend."

"Of course he will!" And most likely invite her to view the exhibition with him, too. That is, if he still wished to be her friend. She sank to the stool. Catherine had mentioned the interview she'd reluctantly given him. His shock. His dismay. He may send flowers still, but all hope of anything beyond friendship must have faded now he knew her secret. Which was only fair. He could not marry her now. He should not. It was only right that she made him aware. She dashed a hand over her eyes.

"*Ma chère!*"

A hand patted her shoulder. Serena dragged in a shaky breath. Straightened her spine.

"Shall I request the painting be removed?"

Hope flickered in her heart. If the painting were removed, all her problems vanished—as would all hope of being recognized for her talent. Not that she cared for that. Love demanded she think of what was best for the viscount. "Do you think they would?"

"*Oui, oui.* Artists often demand their painting be removed rather than have it hung from *ze* rafters. It is *ze* loss of prestige. Everyone wants their work displayed on center line, or as close as possible. If it is not, *le artiste* might feel his value, his reputation—*pah!*" He shrugged.

"But that is only the great artists."

"*Oui.* It is unheard of for a novice to request a painting be removed. But it is also unheard of for a novice to exhibit near *ze* center line. And it would be a crime for it not to be shown."

She chewed her bottom lip. *Heavenly Father, what do I do?*

"Please, mademoiselle. Do not live in fears."

Was that what she was doing? How long had she allowed fears to master her? Surely it was time to master her fears. "Very well, then."

He gave an exclamation of delight and clapped his hands. "Perhaps *ze* lilies won't be so very noticeable hung up high. One can only hopes."

She slowly nodded. One could only *hopes* indeed.

THE OFFICIAL LETTER to one "Mr. S. Winthrop" caused no small amount of confusion at first, before the seal's initials revealed the sender as the Royal Academy of Arts. Catherine's huge eyes and intake of breath as she handed the envelope to Serena told her everything.

Just as M. Despard's friends had informed him weeks ago, the work "The Passion of the Valley" had been selected as one of the pieces for this year's summer exhibition. This was an honor, etcetera, etcetera, chosen from nearly six thousand submissions, etcetera, etcetera . . . and "Mr. S. Winthrop" was invited to attend the vernissage—the varnishing day—in three weeks' time. Enclosed were several tickets for the artist and friends, etcetera, etcetera, etcetera.

"Serena!"

She glanced up from reading the letter at the shocked, delighted faces. She forced a smile. "Monsieur Despard entered it."

"You never told us!"

What could she say that was not a lie? "I did not know he would, Mama."

"You mean he entered your painting without your permission?"

"He . . . he thought it had merit."

"And obviously he's not the only one," Catherine said. "How wonderful for you!"

"Congratulations, Serena." Jon smiled warmly. "We are tremendously proud of you."

"'The Passion of the Valley.'" Catherine frowned. "I do not recall seeing that one."

For good reason. Her every emotion was on full display. "It . . . was one of the earlier ones."

"What is it of?"

"You'll see." She gritted out a smile.

"Is it similar to the one of the viscount?"

"Somewhat." God forgive her.

"What a shame you could not finish his picture." Mama sighed. "I quite enjoyed having that young man come here so often. He has quite an air about him, don't you agree?"

Her spirits sank.

"Serena?"

"Yes, Mama?"

"Don't you agree? He's such a handsome man. And wealthy. And a viscount!"

Serena nodded, surprised her mother refrained from rubbing her hands with glee.

"I trust we'll see him again soon, now you are well?" She peered expectantly at Serena.

"I . . . I could not say."

Catherine frowned. "Mama, you can hardly expect her to invite him to call."

"She did before."

"That was my invitation, ma'am," Jon said mildly. "I have not seen him of late."

"He must still be in Town. His bouquets arrive every day." Mama's brow puckered. "Surely he would tell us if he intended to leave."

Serena caught Catherine's worried glance. She shrugged. This *was* what she wanted.

"What is this, Serena? Why do you shrug? 'Tis most unladylike." Mama frowned, glancing between them. "Is there something you are not telling me?"

Her mouth dried. She would *never* tell Mama the viscount now knew her secret.

"Mama, will you be here when we interview for a nanny?" Catherine said.

Her mother's thoughts happily diverted, Serena shot her sister a thankful look before murmuring an excuse and leaving the table, returning to the studio. She wandered around the room, lifting then replacing brushes, straightening paint pots. The studio now seemed too empty, too vast, too quiet without M. Despard and his gentle humming. She turned the nearly finished canvas to the wall, unable to look at her failure. For a world without the viscount in it—

A tap at the door revealed Jon. He was holding the letter, which he proffered. "Serena, you do not seem overjoyed by this great honor."

"I . . . I am, of course."

"I do not sense it."

She turned away. Oh, that she could confide in him. Oh, that he would understand, this big cousin who was like the big brother she had never known. Oh, that he could help—

"Forgive me, Serena, but is something wrong?"

Her eyes blurred as she returned her attention to his face. "The picture."

"Which picture?"

"*His* picture."

"Carmichael's?" At her nod he smiled. "It is a shame it is not yet finished—"

"No. I finished it."

His brow creased. "I do not understand."

"I . . . I did it from memory, weeks ago."

He blinked. "That is the picture entered?"

"Yes," she whispered.

"You painted the viscount from memory?"

She nodded, hating the smile she could see in his eyes.

"I'm sorry, but why is that a problem?"

"What? You do not think it terribly brazen?"

"He should be honored to be held in such high regard," he said in a serious tone.

Her eyes filled. She shifted so he could not see her crumpling face.

"Serena, something is obviously troubling you. Please tell me. Perhaps I can help."

She shook her head, biting her bottom lip to stop the tremble.

"Serena?"

Drawing in a deep breath, she steadied her voice to something approximating normality. "You cannot."

"Please?"

She swallowed the burn in her throat. "At . . . at the time I did not know his engagement had ended . . ."

"The one to Mrs. Milsom?"

"How many engagements has he had?" She peered up at him.

"Not a single real one, if you ask me," he said drily. "But I digress. Tell me about the painting."

"I . . . I painted some flowers next to him."

"I'm afraid I still do not understand. What sort of flowers?"

"Lilies."

Jon stared at her, before his lips twitched.

"It's not funny."

He made a noise that sounded suspiciously like a chuckle turned into a cough. "Can it not be painted out?"

"Monsieur Despard and I have tried to access the painting, but without success."

"But if you could?"

Hope flickered. It had not been varnished, so . . . "Yes."

"Then that is what we'll do. Unless of course you'd prefer to withdraw the painting altogether?"

She stared at him. Not if it could be remedied.

"I thought not." He smiled. "Leave it to me."

Gratitude rushed through her chest. "Thank you, Jon. I've been so worried."

He peered at her. "Is that what the rush was with the previous painting? You were trying to do a copy?"

She nodded.

Jon chuckled. "I don't think Carmichael knows what a jewel he has in you."

Her cheeks heated, and she looked away. "He does not have me. He cannot."

"Not yet, perhaps—but . . . Serena? What is it?"

In a quiet voice she was very pleased did not shake, she told him what she'd asked Catherine to say. At his inhale of breath she turned to see his stunned expression.

"Well! I . . ." He shook his head. "You have no wish to marry him?"

She bit her lip.

"But you cannot know if your condition is as dire as you seem to believe."

"And you cannot know otherwise," she flashed.

"Serena, I do know that with God all things are possible."

She swallowed. "But not this."

"Even this!"

She shrank at his tone.

"Please . . ." His voice had gentled, and now he drew her close for a brotherly hug. "Please do not worry."

But how could she not?

"I cannot make promises regarding Carmichael, but I will do whatever I can to retrieve your painting, my dear."

"Thank you," she whispered.

And the ball of shame crowding her chest for so long eased a fraction.

Chapter Twenty-Nine

Derbyshire

THE VALLEY GLOWED bright and verdant far below. Harry leaned his folded arms against the balustrade and gazed down, the familiar sight fading from his focus. He'd thought running to Welmsley would solve things, would give him space to sift the weight of emotions in his heart. Would give time to seek God's direction and purpose. Would fill his days with estate business and distraction.

But everywhere he walked he saw her. Exclaiming over the view on the terrace. Painting near the Grecian temple. Walking through the gardens. Stooping to peer closely at a flower, as if trying to ascertain the exact pigment one should use to capture the blossom. It was similar to those first weeks after Grandfather's death, when he kept expecting to see him stride through the corridors or to hear his voice in the stables. The old pang hit him. Grief never really healed; it could only become a bruised memory.

He blinked, and the view refocused. He *could* see Serena here. Regardless of her condition, he wanted her as his wife, his countess one day. Nobody else filled his heart as she did; nobody could. Save God, whose presence and truth crept into a little more of his heart each day.

"Heavenly Father, what should I do?"

His mind flicked back to the words he'd read this morning, the first book of Corinthians, chapter thirteen. A description of God's charity towards him; a picture of how God wanted him to treat others. Including Serena. Love that suffered long, that was not puffed up nor sought its own, love that bore all things, believed all things, hoped all things, endured all things.

Love that never failed.

He now understood why Carlew and Catherine and even Hawkesbury seemed content. How many years had they had this divine revelation of God's amazing love? How different would his life have been had he not sought his own way, his own pleasure, his own pride? Would matters have been better with his father? Indubitably. Would he have avoided this reputation from which he longed to be freed? Most likely. Would Serena and Carlew and others know him as trustworthy, someone they could safely invest their hearts and lives with? He'd like to think so.

But regret was an empty emotion. He could not live in the past. Learn from it, certainly, but wallow in remorse? No. There was too much to consider regarding his future.

He moved from his position at the window overlooking the valley and entered the drawing room where his grandmother sat, her knobbly hands moving restlessly. "Ah, Henry." He came near to press a kiss to her cheek and she grasped his arm. "Have you seen your father?"

"I was about to look for him."

"Good, good." She sighed, looked down, then squinted up at him. "I meant to ask earlier. How is that lovely young girl?"

"Miss Winthrop?"

Her lips pulled up. "Always so quick, aren't you? Yes, the artist."

"She is very busy. Well, she was, until she grew sick."

"Oh dear. I hope she's feeling better. I do like her."

"Yes." Grandmama's sentiments were hardly a surprise.

She peered at him. "Yes, I thought so, too."

"I beg your pardon?"

"Will you make her an offer?"

He blinked. Forced a smile. "Grandmama, I do not believe that is of anyone's concern save my own."

"Stuff and nonsense. It's of concern to everyone. If you marry the wrong gel, it can have dire consequences for the estate."

Such as the line dying out. The ounce of peace from earlier crumbled.

"Henry? Why do you look like that?"

"I . . . I thought she was the right one—"

"I knew it!"

"But something has come to light which gives me pause."

"Yes?"

Half hating himself for exposing Serena's secret, he quickly told her.

His grandmother sat back with a frown. "You mean she willingly availed you of this information?"

"Yes."

"Is she mad?"

He looked at her. "I beg your pardon?"

"She's either mad, or she loves you very much."

His heart kicked.

"But what do I do?" He cringed. How much did he sound like Tom, pleading for advice?

"You have prayed?"

"Of course."

"And what did God say?"

"I am not a prophet. I do not hear voices."

"Thank the good Lord for that. We have enough trouble as it is," she muttered, shaking her head. "Did you feel inclined to read a particular passage in the Bible? Did any verses quicken to you?"

The love chapter. He nodded.

"What did it say? If we desire relationship with God, surely we should expect to hear Him speak, even if only through the holy Scriptures. So, what did it say?"

Love patiently, with kindness. Bear all things. Hope and trust, protect and persevere always. Love others as God loved him. Serena. His father. He stared at her. "Love."

She smiled. "I hear an answer there."

More than one, actually.

"Dear boy, surely you would prefer to marry where there is no deception, where the girl is clearly not self-seeking, but seeks your benefit above her own?"

Put like that . . . "Well, yes."

"If God is guiding your paths, then surely He is able to provide for the future of the earldom also?"

"Yes." Her words seemed to swell within, chasing out the doubts. "Yes, He is."

"Yes, He *is*." She smiled, her face wrinkling into a thousand precious lines. "I am proud of you, dear boy."

He kissed the top of her head. "I'm thankful at least one person here is."

"You'd be surprised. Remember, your father is not as well as he could be."

"I should find him." Pushing to his feet, he excused himself and headed to the hall, where the footman indicated his father was in the study. He moved to the doorway, paused. Two days ago, the last time he'd dared enter his father's sanctuary, Father had given such a tongue-lashing at his impertinence he'd been reminded of boyhood episodes of naughtiness. He wasn't a child, but neither was he sure if his battered emotions could cope with much more abuse.

Noiselessly, he opened the door, and stilled.

His father stood at the safe, stuffing something inside. Harry peered in the dim light. What was it? Father had shown him the combination upon his coming of age, but when he'd checked on his last visit, it contained nothing of any consequence, apart from the usual papers.

Father moved around the swung-open painting then bent to retrieve something from the desk. No, not from the desk—from underneath the desk?

Harry stepped forward. A floorboard creaked.

"What? Who is it?"

He moved closer to the window. "It is Henry, sir."

"Henry?" His father peered at him. "Who are you?"

Harry stared at him. Hadn't Father snapped at him over the breakfast table not two hours ago? "It is Henry, your son."

"Son? You're not my son."

"Father, it is me, Henry." He moved closer, managed a smile.

"Get away! Get away, I say! I don't know who you are, but I refuse to have some stranger in here with me. Peters! Peters!" he called.

How could his father remember a butler but not his own son? Harry pinched his lips tight, working to ignore the hurt rushing through his body, then stilled. Why was Father holding so many banknotes?

"You called, my lord?"

"Peters, this man is an imposter," Father said, pointing. "Remove him now."

"Of course, my lord."

The butler shot Harry a sympathetic look and beckoned him to follow. Once in the hall with the door closed, Peters murmured, "I'm terribly sorry, my lord, but your father has good and bad days. Today seems to be one of his bad."

"He does not know me?"

"It would appear he does not know anyone on his truly bad days, I'm sorry to say."

"But my mother?"

The butler coughed. "Her ladyship is not unaware of his tendency to forget, but she is rarely in his company, and tends to choose to be elsewhere when he falls into such a state."

"I . . . I did not know."

"It has been much worse of late, I'm afraid."

"He has not seen a doctor? I would have thought Grandmama would insist."

"She did, but, ahem, your father was not very cooperative."

Harry nodded. "Send for one now. Oh, and where is my mother?"

"In the morning room, sir. But, if I might say, his lordship's moods can vary. You might find you could walk back in there now and nothing would be amiss."

Harry chuckled without humor. "That would be the day. Send for the doctor anyway. I wish to speak to my mother."

"Very good, sir." With something that looked a little like relief and a lot like respect the butler nodded and moved away.

Harry whirled around, facing the study door again. Would Father recognize him this time? He knocked firmly on the door.

There came a scuffling sound from within. "Enter."

He reentered the room, head up, as if his father's condition did not wound him.

"Who are you, and what do you want?"

Harry stared, sorrow twisting within. "I am Viscount Carmichael."

His father frowned. "Carmichael. I seem to recall that name."

"I believe it is one of your family names, sir." A soft sound at the door drew his attention. He motioned to his mother to remain where she was.

"Really?" his father continued, as if lost in thought. "Are you telling me we are related, young man?"

"Yes."

"Hmm. What are you? A distant cousin?"

He cleared the burn in his throat. "Your son."

"Hmm. It doesn't seem likely. You look nothing like my son."

He ignored the jabbing pain. "What does he look like?"

"Oh, he's a small chap, only so high." Father held a hand at waist height. "He went away to school, but we haven't seen him in an age."

Now the heat burned his eyes. "I'm sure he misses you," he managed to say, his voice cracking.

"You believe so?" His father's face brightened. "I hope so. He was always such a funny chap. A sweet boy, and clever, even if he doesn't care much for art and such things."

Behind him, Harry could hear his mother's soft sniffles. He swallowed the pain. "I believe you would find he has a new appreciation for such things." He stepped closer, closer again. "That is a Rembrandt, is it not?"

"Very good! Yes, it's one of my favorites, which is why I have it here." He caressed the frame, before glancing back at Harry. "What did you say your name was?"

"Henry, Viscount Carmichael."

His father's forehead furrowed. "Do you know my son?"

"I know him very well."

"Can you tell him to visit again soon?"

Fresh emotion clogged his throat. He could only nod.

"A sweet boy."

Harry bit his lip to stop the trembling, felt a soft touch on his arm. He turned.

"Come," Mother said, and led him away.

He strove for some kind of dignity in front of the servants as he crossed the hall into his mother's favorite room. Flowers filled a multitude of vases, as if Mother wanted to blot out the sad reality that lived in the room across the hall. He sank into his seat, sank his head into his hands, and exhaled, working to check his emotions. "How long has he been this way?"

"For weeks."

For weeks. Weeks while he'd been away, enjoying London, enjoying the company of—No. He glanced up. "How are you?"

Her eyes were shadowed. "I am . . . managing."

"What does the doctor say?"

"Dr. MacConnell believes it best for your father to stay quiet, without too much noise or change. He can get quite frustrated when things are not as they usually are."

"Why did you not tell me?"

"I have not seen him so bad before. He recognizes me, and your grandmother. Most of the time he recognizes Melanie also, and when he doesn't, it is never as obviously bad as that."

"What should we do?"

"What can we do? The doctor is adamant he should remain quietly here."

"While the estate flounders? Mama"—the old word slipped from his tongue—"we cannot continue like so."

"Will you return then? Stay?"

Stay, and not renew his attentions to Serena again? What did love demand he do?

He swallowed. "If I am to be earl, then yes. I need to."

She gave a long sigh, her shoulders slumping. "Oh, I'm so relieved. You need to be here, Henry."

"I know."

Never had words tasted so bitter in his mouth.

Berkeley Square

"I cannot like it, Jon. She needs to be told."

Serena stopped outside the breakfast room, listening as the deep voice murmured a reply. Who needed to be told? Mama? Herself?

"I cannot believe he would do such a thing! I thought he'd changed," Catherine said.

Her heart sank as Jon's deep rumble came again. She strained to hear. What was that? White's? High stakes? Debt?

"Serena? Why are you standing in the hall?"

At Mama's voice, the conversation within ceased immediately. Cheeks aflame, she tossed her head, lifting her chin as she entered. Catherine looked up, her puffy face almost as distressing as her wide girth. Poor thing. Surely it must be any day when Serena's niece or nephew made an appearance. Her gaze slid Serena a warning about their mother, who had followed her into the room.

"Serena, girls who skulk around houses are highly unlikely to find themselves considered fit to contract an eligible union."

She bit back the chuckle at her mother's warped logic. "I beg your pardon, Mama."

"Hmph." She eyed Serena's attire and sniffed. "I do wish you would dress more appropriately. What if the viscount should happen to call?"

Her heart twisted. "It does not seem likely, Mama. He hasn't called in nearly a fortnight."

She exchanged glances with her sister. Nor would he, now he knew the truth.

"Yet he still sends these flowers every day." Mama's brow furrowed.

"Why would he do that unless he wished to remain in your good graces? No, I am sure he will visit soon, so why don't you go and exchange that old gown for one of your new ones?"

Jon cleared his throat. "I believe the viscount has returned north."

"What?"

His gaze rested on her, laden with sympathy. "I was at White's and saw Hawkesbury. He informed me Carmichael suddenly decided to return home on the Monday of last week."

The day Catherine had told him. Hopes Serena hadn't known she still entertained crumpled. She sank into a seat, fixing her attention on the floor, unable to meet anyone's eyes.

"Well, I imagine he has responsibilities up there. One would, when one will be an earl one day." Mama tutted. "Now there's no need to look like that, Serena. Compose yourself, please."

"Mama, would you mind terribly if we postpone today's outing?" Catherine said. "I'm not feeling quite the thing."

"Of course you aren't, my dear."

As Mama clucked over Catherine, Serena obeyed Jon's gesture and followed him from the room into the library he claimed as his domain—and where they'd be safe from Mama's ears.

He gestured to a chair and seated himself. "I am terribly sorry, Serena, but the news is not good."

"So I gathered."

He looked startled. "I meant regarding the painting."

"Oh."

He shook his head. "I have contacted the trustees, but they are adamant it cannot be removed, unless one has the status of Gainsborough."

"And it cannot be retouched?"

"I mentioned that, but it seems your best chance is next Friday, on varnishing day. Forgive my ignorance about how these things are done, but perhaps if you were to paint it out and leave that part unvarnished—"

"No, it would look odd. The varnish seals the paint, and might alter the colors slightly. The varnish itself can crack if not applied correctly, which would draw even more speculation."

He sighed. "Does it really matter?"

"Because he is home? You think he won't see it?"

For some reason, the thought he would not see her painting filled her with more pain than the knowledge he had run from her and her condition. She turned to study the book-lined cases.

"Serena, I do not wish to be the bearer of bad news, but Catherine insists you know the following, so you can make up your own mind."

Something cold stole over her soul. "Is it about Lord Carmichael?"

"I'm afraid so."

"Tell me." She turned, met the steady blue-gray eyes.

"He was gambling recently."

Her stomach twisted. No.

"I know how you feel about such things."

"Because of Papa."

"I understand." He patted her hand. "If I might say in his defense, he did lose quite heavily, which suggests his mind was on other things. Perhaps he wasn't thinking clearly."

"But that is not a defense! I thought he had changed. I do not understand how he could when he knows our situation. I thought . . . I thought he cared." Wretched heat filled her cheeks.

"Yes."

"Why does he still send those bouquets?"

"He is a conflicted man." Jon sighed. "Apparently there was talk he would see Mrs. Milsom."

Her heart clenched. "Who said that?"

"A Lord Ashbolt? Says Carmichael mentioned something of the sort that last evening."

"But . . . but that is only talk."

"Perhaps. But the gambling wasn't."

No. Her throat grew tight, her fragile hopes flitted away.

"Serena, I hate to burden you with this, but I could not bear to see another young lady whom I care about have their life destroyed by a reckless man."

Like his sister Julia's life had been. A shiver ran through her.

"I cannot believe I've chosen my friends so ill." Jon snorted. "I *hate* knowing I'm responsible for bringing these men into the lives of those I most care about. I am so sorry."

"Jon, no." From deep within she dredged up a smile, feeling as though her face might crack. "You are not responsible for this foolish girl's vain imaginings. I managed that all on my own."

"Encouraged by Carmichael, I'll warrant. I really thought he had changed."

She nodded, the tightness within forbidding speech.

"So back to your painting. Does it matter if the lilies remain?"

Her eyes blurred. "I suppose not."

Not if he truly were reconciled with Mrs. Milsom. Her heart gave a painful wrench. What did any of it matter anymore?

Chapter Thirty

"GOOD HEAVENS! HE'S returned!"

At the sound of her mother's excitement, the lethargy weighing on Serena since her conversation with Jon three days ago lifted. "Who's returned?"

"The viscount!" Mama waved a thick cream card. "It says it right here. Look!"

Serena frowned as she saw the direction. "Mama, this was addressed to Catherine."

"It was addressed to Lady Winthrop. I still hold that title, if you please."

"I don't think Catherine will be best pleased."

"What won't I be pleased about?" her sister said, waddling into the saloon and sinking heavily into a seat. She looked expectantly at Serena, who could only shrug helplessly as Mama snatched back the card.

"Look! We've an invitation. Let me read it for you: 'Viscount Carmichael requests the company of Lord and Lady Winthrop, the dowager Lady Winthrop, and Miss Winthrop at Bevington House, Cavendish Square, for dinner on Thursday night.'" Mama handed it to Catherine. "I was not even aware he had returned! But now he's here, I'm sure he'll be asking for your hand, Serena!" she crowed.

Serena fought for composure as confusion melded with the panic within. Why had he suddenly returned? Why invite them to dine if he still cared for Mrs. Milsom? Would he insist on seeing the portrait? *Oh, dear God!*

"Oh, how can you look so calm, child? A viscountess! You could be a viscountess!"

"Only if I married him, Mama."

"Well, of course you're going to marry him, child."

She arched a brow. There was no "of course" about it. Even if he did ask, she was unsure of her answer. He'd made several choices neither she nor Jon could comprehend. How could she ever trust him?

"Oh, don't look at me so," her mother huffed, so Serena turned to her sister.

Catherine rested one hand on her belly as she read the gold-edged parchment. "This was addressed to me, was it not?"

Mama's cheeks took on a pink hue. "I was mistaken."

"Were you?" Catherine's gaze narrowed on Mama before she turned to Serena. "I cannot attend, of course, but do you wish to?"

Serena shook her head. "It is the night before the exhibition opens. I would rather save my energy—"

"For goodness' sake, Serena," Mama snapped. "A viscount invites all your family to dine. Of course you are going to go."

"But—"

"Enough! I don't want to hear another word about the silly exhibition. Now, you will wear . . ."

As her mother outlined her choice of gown and accessories, Serena turned her focus to her sister. Catherine said in a low voice, "I, for one, am *very* sorry my condition makes it impossible to see your work."

"If you deliver soon then perhaps you can see it later. The exhibition runs for six weeks."

"When I should still be in confinement."

"But we need not always do what social conventions suggest."

"No," her sister said thoughtfully, before turning to their mother. "Mama, please stop lecturing Serena on what to wear. She's quite capable of choosing appropriately."

Her mother's jaw sagged. "I'm prepared to overlook your comment, dear girl, on account that it is a very warm day."

Catherine gave a tight smile. "You are all graciousness."

"Hmph. Well, write an acceptance, then. Do you think Jon will wish to attend?"

"I do not know, Mama," Catherine said, the snap in her voice and eyes most unlike her usual placidity. "But it would seem odd, wouldn't it, if you went without him, especially as you are barely acquainted with anyone except the viscount. You would not wish to attend without Jon, surely."

Hope flickered in Serena's heart. If Jon didn't attend, she could likely avoid going, too, and avoid all the confusion that thoughts of the viscount seemed to evoke.

"Well, I wish the viscount would visit here then, and bring some of his family," Mama said petulantly. "Then there would be nothing untoward if we should attend without Jon."

It seemed Serena's prayers and Catherine's hopes were ignored as Mama's wish came true the following day. The viscount, accompanied by Melanie and the dowager countess, condescended to visit Berkeley Square to pay their respects to Lady and Miss Winthrop.

After a warm embrace with Melanie and the dowager, Serena shot a quick glance at the viscount. He did not meet her eyes, but she could see the strain on his face. Her heart gave a painful thud. Something seemed quite wrong.

"You seem surprised to see us," he said to Catherine, after the usual greetings had been exchanged.

"Not at all," she demurred. "I understood you had only recently returned north."

"Family commitments bring us back." He exchanged a wary look with the two ladies of his party.

What family commitments? Serena looked between her guests.

"Tell me, dear girl," the dowager said, "how is your painting going? Henry tells me I simply must see this marvelous painting you were completing of him."

She stared, fear wrinkling within. "I . . . I'm afraid—"

"She was not able to finish that one," Mama said. "But you might be interested in knowing Serena's great news. Shall you tell them, Serena, or shall I?" Without pausing for Serena's answer she continued. "My dear girl has a work included in this year's exhibition!"

"Really?" Melanie said, light filling her eyes. "How marvelous!"

"Oh, my dear!" the dowager said, the first smile of the visit creasing her face. "Is this true?"

Mama passed around the letter, leaving Serena to stifle her annoyance at the presumption. How dare Mama object and make such a fuss, and then pretend to be so proud?

The viscount finally turned to her, his muddy green eyes unreadable, as he held the letter his sister had passed him. "May I read this?"

She managed a nod, glad he'd had the courtesy to ask.

He skimmed it quickly, his face lighting up like his sister's as he glanced up and smiled. "My heartfelt congratulations."

She stifled the traitorous thump her heart gave and willed her features to neutrality. How could he smile at her so warmly if he did not care for her?

He stood and passed her the letter, his fingers accidentally brushing hers, causing her to freeze. As the room stilled, he said in a soft voice, "I am so pleased to see you looking so much better than the last time we met, Miss Winthrop. I trust you received my flowers?"

"Yes. Thank you."

"She enjoyed your flowers and notes *very* much, my lord," Mama said.

A smile touched his lips, touched his eyes, his gaze not moving from Serena's face. "Is that so?" he said gently. "For it would seem you are displeased to see me."

"Not displeased, my lord. Merely surprised." And confused. And anxious. And worried. Surely he could not look at her so intently if he had reconciled with Lily Milsom? Would he now insist on accompanying her to the exhibition? Surely he would notice . . .

Her chest grew tight, her head felt dizzy.

He quickly glanced at Catherine, now listening to Melanie talk of the children, before his attention returned. "Miss Winthrop," his voice was low, "I was concerned to hear of your . . . illness, but I can assure you it does not alter my feelings towards you at all."

What? The room spun. No. For his sake she would not let him charm her. She would not! "You cannot mean that."

"I assure you, I do."

"But Mrs. Milsom."

"Means nothing to—"

Further conversation ceased as the door opened, and all eyes turned to the footman's entrance with the tea things. All eyes, except Lord Carmichael's.

He drew nearer still, his brow creased. "Miss Winthrop?"

She blinked. Drew herself up. "Mr. S. Winthrop, according to this." She tapped the letter.

"Never, *Miss* Serena," he murmured, eyes intent on her.

She shivered within.

"Harry, have you finished cajoling yet?" Melanie said with a smirk. "Serena, I trust you will be able to come to dinner tomorrow night. The children are dying to see you again."

All eyes now swung to her expectantly. Oh, the pressure, the pressure . . .

"I . . . would not want their deaths on my conscience," she managed.

"Good."

The viscount nodded, his eyes sober once more. "I'm very pleased you can come."

She kept a polite smile pasted on. If glad, why did he look so grim?

As they left, he pressed her hand again. "You will come tomorrow?"

"I said I would."

He exhaled, before saying in an undervoice, "I—that is, we need you . . . need your help."

What could give rise to such concern?

He lifted Serena's hand to his lips, his touch sending a fresh shiver through the length of her body, sure to keep her awake half the night, wondering, wishing, hoping. In a louder voice more like his usual manner, he said, "I congratulate the artist of the moment." He released her fingers, gave her a skin-tingling smile. "Would it seem excessively inappropriate to say I am extremely proud of you?"

"Perhaps not *excessively* inappropriate, sir."

She forced out a smile. What would be inappropriate was any pride he'd feel in her when he realized how she had accidentally made him look to be a fool.

Bevington House

The sound of the carriage outside hurried his footsteps to the window. At the sight of Carlew handing out his mother- and sister-in-law, relief expanded within. He'd wondered at her coolness, her avoidance of his eyes. Was she that upset he'd returned to Derbyshire without speaking to her? And her question about Lily—surely she didn't still think such a thing possible? The questions had haunted him last night, had distracted him from the man whose position at the head of the table was in name only, whose presence was the reason they were here in London.

"Is Miss S'ena here?"

"Yes, Miss Eleanor."

"Has she painted any other children yet?"

"You will have to ask her, Master Tom."

The door opened, and their guests were announced: Carlew, grave as ever; then Lady Winthrop, fluttering a fan, eyes darting around the room; and finally, her cool-eyed daughter.

His mouth dried, his heart thumping against his chest. The times he'd seen Serena in evening dress were too few. Her gown of cream and gold was everything stylish, yet she wore it with such careless grace. Her hair was dressed with tiny yellow flowers, and a pearl necklace nestled at the base of her throat, in that little well just made for—

He shook away the thoughts. She made a delectable vision of spring.

"Good evening." He bowed, received the curtsies and bow in return.

"Miss S'ena! Miss S'ena!"

The cool expression dropped away as the young girl flung herself at her legs. She leaned down. Smiled warmly. "Good evening, Miss Eleanor."

Ellie laughed, tossing her blonde curls. "That's just what Uncle Harry said."

Serena's pale face pinked, her eyes slanting to him.

"Not quite what I said, but never mind." He drew near. "Thank you for coming."

"We cannot stay overly late, as I need to be at Somerset House early tomorrow."

"Which is why we brought dinner forward. That, and so two rascals could say hello to one of their favorite people."

"Tell me about that Despard character," Grandmama said. The light in Serena's eyes quickly warmed, as did the conversation—and his hopes. A few minutes later, as his parents and Melanie engaged Carlew and Lady Winthrop in talk about the season, he was finally able to approach Serena. She was studying a landscape of Surrey, a picture Father had banished from Welmsley, on account of it being too dark.

"Tell me, Miss Winthrop, what do you think of the interplay of light in this particular composition?"

"I find the use of chiaroscuro most effective in adding a sense of drama to the scene."

Chiaroscuro? "Ah, yes, my thoughts exactly."

A smile crossed her features.

Heart lifting, he drew nearer, but stopped as she seemed to freeze. "Miss Winthrop? Is something the matter?"

She shook her head in the slightest of movements. "Why did you say you needed my help?" she murmured.

He glanced over his shoulder. They were out of earshot of the others. "My father has not been well. You might be aware we have had some issues with the estate?"

"Which necessitated your gambling?" The blue eyes flashed.

"I thought it did. I was wrong."

She eyed him narrowly. The icy glare gradually abated. "I *despise* gambling. My father lost most of our money through trying to get rich at the expense of others. You can have no idea . . ." She shook her head, before adding in a low voice, "It was only later that I realized how much my father had deceived us, and realized that a gambler's words cannot be trusted. I do not *ever* want to be placed in such a position again."

Shame coiled in his heart. He pushed it away. Christ had set him free. But at least now he understood her disappointment; it was not because he'd left without farewell. "I . . . I have rarely lost before, and to my shame never realized just how grim the consequences can be. I should have trusted God, not my past success."

"Yes."

"I'm sorry, Serena. I hate that I've disappointed you."

"It's just—" She shook her head again. "You cannot know what it is like to feel yourself deceived by a person you thought loved you, to have everything you have ever known ripped away due to one man's addiction."

Couldn't he? Perhaps not addiction, though he understood the widespread pain a man's illness could render, such as his father's rapid descent into dementia. "I am sorry."

"I just want to know that I can trust . . ."

You. He could hear the unspoken word, see it written in her eyes. The lump in his throat doubled. "Please forgive me," he said hoarsely.

"I . . . no."

No? Disappointment pierced within.

"No." She exhaled. "I shouldn't stand in judgment." She looked down, revealing the soft swirls of her earlobes. "There is nothing to forgive."

Relief seeped through his chest. But their connection still felt so tenuous. What would it take for her to trust him again? He sighed. He had nothing but honesty. "I'm afraid it is not simply financial issues I have had to contend with." She peeked up, a frown clouding her eyes. "My father's illness is why I have brought him to London to see doctors other than our local quack, who, while I'm sure he is a very good man, has not got the same wealth of experience as others."

"What is wrong with your father?"

"He does not remember things." Like taking money from the safe to hide in boxes in the garden beds. Thank God for Peters's keen-eyed observations, which had restored several thousand pounds to the estate. But how many other boxes remained undiscovered? He sighed. "He barely remembers me."

She blinked. "He has forgotten his own son?"

"Yes."

"Oh." Her features softened, she placed a hand on his arm. "I'm so terribly sorry."

He despised the eddying pleasure that her touch and sympathy drew from within. "It goes without saying that we have not spoken of this outside the family and doctors."

"Of course." She nodded. "So what is it you wish me to do?"

"Speak to him tonight of art. Remind him of who he is. He is so used to being at Welmsley, every other place is quite foreign, even here, in the town house he has visited so many times. Nobody talks to him like you do about art, not even Grandmama. I would consider it an enormous favor and would be in your debt."

"Well, of course I will."

"Thank you." The gush of gratitude dwindled at her puckered brow. "Miss Winthrop?"

Serena glanced up at him, eyes wary.

"Something seems to trouble you."

"I . . . you . . ." A soft sigh released. "You mentioned about being in my debt."

"Forever indebted to you." His lips curved. "Ask whatever you will of me and I will honor the obligation."

She hesitated, chewing her bottom lip. Her perfectly shaped, perfectly kissable—

"Would you . . . try to be understanding at the exhibition?"

"As to why you did not paint me?" He grinned. "Of course."

Something like a wince crossed her features. "You . . . you will remember saying so in upcoming days?"

"Absolutely."

She nodded, an odd smile on her face, before murmuring, "I can only hope so."

The gong sounded, and they moved to the dining room, where she was seated at Father's right hand. Through the remainder of the evening, Harry watched her skillfully draw his father into conversation. The discussion of art and architecture led to an exchange about the design features of various London landmarks, such as the artistic merits of St. Paul's versus Westminster Abbey. Father's sparkling eyes made it seem he was almost completely better, if occasionally absent-minded.

His father peered at her now. "So you prefer the Palladian style to that of the Tudor?"

"Yes, my lord. I much prefer the symmetry and grace it entails."

"I have a house, you know. Welmsley. You may have heard of it. It was designed by Adams." He nodded. "You will have to come visit it one day."

"Thank you, my lord. I should be honored."

Serena's glance slipped past his father to find him, the shiny sympathy in her eyes reflected in the twist of her lips, her sympathy burrowing deeper into his affection. The tender spaces of his heart reserved for her enlarged yet again.

"Welmsley?" Her mother said. "Isn't that where you—?"

"Yes, Mama. I believe it must be one of the loveliest houses in all England. Now, have you tried the chicken? Lady Bevington, I hope your chef is amenable to sharing recipes, as I'm sure this would be the very dish my sister would enjoy." She smiled at Jon. "Wouldn't you agree?"

The rest of the meal passed without incident, any breach in social polish quickly covered by Serena or himself, something his mother seemed aware of, as she met Harry's gaze with an expression akin to relief and looked on Serena with what could only be considered approval.

Later, when it was time to leave, he clasped her hand. "Thank you, Miss Winthrop. I am, as I said, in your debt."

"It was no trouble."

He drew her hand to his lips, savoring the softness and scent of roses, savoring the intake of breath. He glanced up. "Will I see you tomorrow? May I collect you for the exhibition?"

She shook her head. "I attend early with Monsieur Despard for the varnishing."

"Then I hope to accompany you once you have finished." As her brow knotted, he pressed her hand warmly. "Please say I may."

After a moment's hesitation she finally nodded, they arranged a time when he would collect her, and he made his farewells. "Good evening, Miss Winthrop. And thank you so much for your kind services to my family."

"Good evening, Lord Carmichael."

"Do not worry about tomorrow." He gently squeezed her hand. "You will astound them all."

"That is what I'm afraid of," she murmured.

Jon handed her into the carriage and Harry watched them leave, waiting until the carriage turned past the corner. On his return inside, his father remained calm, his mild manner more like the man Harry remembered. Concern eased within his chest.

"It was wonderful to hear him talk of Welmsley again." Mother's eyes welled.

He wrapped an arm around her shoulders. "Miss Winthrop was very patient."

"She is a jewel, Henry." Grandmama eyed him. "A jewel."

One he wished to care for amongst the Peak's treasure for his remaining days.

"I'm certainly looking forward to seeing her painting tomorrow."

"Indeed." He smiled, heart warm with gladness. "I'm sure tomorrow will amaze us all."

❧ Chapter Thirty-One

Somerset House, London

"Mademoiselle, please be thinking about how much you want to charge."

"But I do not want to sell it."

"But you could make much money. Most every other painting will be for *ze* sale. It is one of *ze* best ways for *le artiste* to find acclaim."

Serena nodded, M. Despard's question joining the others spiraling through her mind. Yet another early morning challenge on this day of vernissage. She trudged behind him up the long, winding staircase leading to the exhibition hall. Despite the fact that he carried her equipment, he seemed to leap ahead like a gazelle, whilst her steps felt heavier than lead. Where would the painting be hung? Probably very, very high, as unknown artists were wont to be. But if so, how could she reach so high to repaint and varnish? M. Despard had mentioned scaffolds and ladders, but the thought of clambering so high, especially in the company of so many strangers—so many men—had kept her awake half the night.

Or perhaps that had been the effect of last night's encounter with Lord Carmichael. His request, odd though it had seemed, made perfect sense when she saw his father's piteous state. Poor man. Her eyes pricked. Poor Lord Carmichael. How wretched to not be known by a parent. Her lips twisted. Although after last night, she would prefer perhaps a *little* time when she was less noticed by her own.

Mama could barely stop talking during the carriage ride home about Serena's success. "Oh, my dear, he could barely take his eyes off you!"

For once her mother was correct. That knowledge, coupled with the memory of his lips on the back of her hand, had sent a fresh shiver through the length of her body, and kept her dreaming the other half of the night, wondering, wishing, hoping . . .

He would forgive her.

Dear Lord, please help him forgive me. She sighed.

M. Despard paused, looked behind, his mouth falling open, before he hurried back. "Mademoiselle! A thousand apologies. I did not know you were so far behind."

She grasped the bannister and pulled herself up. "I did not know I would feel so strange." Like a great flock of starlings had taken residence within and were wheeling and whirling away.

"It is an honor, that is true. Now, you are sure of *ze* plan?" At her nod, he grinned and almost danced the final remaining steps to the great doors at the top. "*Entrée*, Mademoiselle Winthrop."

She entered the space and stopped. The walls in the square-shaped room were covered in paintings: portraiture, landscapes, still life, the frames so close they were often touching. Three, four, sometimes five paintings hung from the floor to the ceiling far above, beneath the high, arched windows spilling light. She stumbled toward a plush red settee in the middle, her senses reeling. There was so much to take in, especially after the bland walls of the steep climb before. Portraits of royals, dainty farm landscapes, naval battles, scenes of ancient allegories—and somewhere was her painting.

She scanned for the viscount. "Can you see it, Monsieur Despard?"

"*Oui.*"

Serena followed his pointing finger to the opposite wall where the viscount smiled down at her. Just above center line. Oh . . .

Stunned, she slumped into the seat as her art master clapped his hands. "*Très magnifique!* What an honor for you, *ma chéri.* How many men three times your age would kill for such an honor!" He turned, wiping his eyes. "You cannot know how proud this makes Despard."

He held out his hand, and she took it numbly, and he drew her closer to where the painting glowed. Placed between an enormous, heavily gilt-edged framed portrait of a Grecian bathing scene and a rather insipid portrait of a brunette, the colors of the valley in her painting—the standard ninety-inch-by-fifty-five—seemed to glow in the morning sun. She looked up, inexplicable wonder filling her chest. Had she *really* painted such beauty? It seemed impossible. Surely her memory had not been so faultless. For it seemed as though a smiling Lord Carmichael could step down from the wall at any moment, hold her in his arms, and—

"Despard!"

Serena broke from her fantasy as an elderly gentleman drew near.

He gestured to the painting. "Do you know the artist? 'Tis a wonderful work. Full of vibrancy and passion."

M. Despard grinned, and bowed to Serena. "Monsieur Kentell, may I introduce Miss Winthrop?"

The white-haired gentleman nodded, his attention returning to the Frenchman. "Yes, but who is the artist? And who is the subject? I note in the catalogue it is described as 'The Passion of the Valley,' and he is 'A Gentleman.'" He gave a guttural laugh. "I'd like to know what favors this gentleman permitted to induce such adoration in the artist."

Serena gasped.

M. Despard frowned. "You much mistake *ze* matter, Kentell."

"You know the artist?" The older man gave a lecherous smile. "I would have not thought such a thing quite in your usual style."

As her friend's face reddened, the heat rose in Serena's chest. "How dare you insinuate such things?"

Mr. Kentell blinked. His smile fell away. "I beg your pardon?"

"Neither this gentleman," she gestured to M. Despard, "nor that one," she pointed to the picture, "have ever engaged in anything such as you imply. It is excessively rude and vulgar to suggest otherwise."

"Hush, *ma chéri*," M. Despard said.

Mr. Kentell's eyes now resembled cold blue marbles as his gaze swept her simple attire. "You, young lady, look like you should return to the schoolroom." He turned to M. Despard. "Just what is she doing here?"

"I am the artist," she said.

"You?" He made a choking sound. "You are but a schoolgirl."

"And I am but her art master," M. Despard said. "A wonderful work, as you said. Full of vibrancy and passion." He smiled at Serena. "A compliment indeed, from one of the trustees."

"No. No, no." Mr. Kentell shook his head. "I refuse to believe—"

"Check *ze* catalogue, *mon ami*. You will see this portrait was painted by none other than my *leetle* friend here."

Kentell flicked through the pages, tracing the hundreds of entries, a heavy frown wrinkling his brow. The lines plunged deeper. "It says a Mr. S. Winthrop is the artist."

"Meet Miss S. Winthrop."

"But . . . you are not a man."

She eyed him coldly.

"His abilities of surveillance do not fail," M. Despard muttered. "Nevertheless," he said in a louder voice, "*zis* is *ze* artist, and she would like to finish *ze* varnishing."

By now several other gentlemen were drawing near, their murmurs and speculative glances causing Serena's skin to heat and prickle. As her art master continued to argue, she turned to where he had stored her supplies and grasped the brush with a trembling hand. Lifting her gaze, she studied how the other artists varnished the higher-placed paintings. Just as he'd said, she would need to climb a platform and be raised many feet in the air. She grimaced.

"Mademoiselle?" M. Despard's face held an angry cast. "It would seem *ze* gentlemen 'ere are not believing us when we say *zis* is your work."

"But it is!" She glared at the men, some of whom stood with their own scowls and crossed arms. "I painted it."

"You? A little schoolgirl could not paint so well."

She studied the hard faces, and M. Despard's despairing one. "We cannot varnish?"

"It appears we cannot." He sighed. "Not until we can prove it is your work. You are unknown, you see 'ow it is?"

"Oh, I see how it is." She eyed the men. "You do not believe I can paint because I am female. Yet, is it not true that two of the Academy's founding members were ladies? Would you object to Miss Kauffmann and Miss Moser's works, too?"

"We do not object to the *work*, Miss Winthrop."

"Just my word?"

Kentell bowed his head. "You are so young."

Fire raged through her chest. She breathed in. Out. Forced her trembling fingers flat against her gown. "Very well. When I prove my authorship, will I be permitted to varnish?"

The men glanced between each other. "We do not permit ladies to climb so high."

What? "So even if I were to prove I had painted it, you would not permit me?" They shook their heads. "Would you permit Monsieur Despard?"

"But he is not the artist."

She uttered a broken laugh. "You are impossible!"

"Perhaps we should take it down—"

"*Non, non, non!*" M. Despard threw his hands in the air. "You cannot be so imbecilic! To remove one of *ze* best works in years?" He turned to the other artists, some of whom had ceased their work and were watching the display on the floor. "Would you wish to see your work removed simply because these fools did not believe it was your own?"

There was a chorus of "No."

"Then can we not permit this young lady's work to remain?"

Another man pushed forward. "Whoever is responsible has captured the image exceptionally well. Surely such artistry should not be penalized."

"*Merci, monsieur.*" M. Despard gathered their equipment. "We shall be back, *messieurs*, and you will all know 'ow talented Mademoiselle Winthrop is, and will eat *ze* words."

Serena followed as the Frenchman whirled away in outrage, her cheeks hot, her chin high. How *dare* her word be suspected? How *dare* these men make such accusations? Such insinuations?

Outside, at the top of the stairs, she drew in cooler, fresher air. A few early visitors looked at her curiously, so she hurried after the art master, whose Gallic mutterings and gestures were causing more than one raised brow.

"Such imbeciles! They do not believe Despard? I 'ave half *ze* mind to return to France and never darken English shores again."

"Monsieur, we can return. I have my sketchbooks, and my notes."

"I doubt *ze* fools will even believe such proofs! But we can try, I suppose." He muttered something she was sure was a French curse.

"But, monsieur—" She touched his arm. He slowed, stopped. "What about the lilies?"

"*Mon Dieu!*" He slapped a hand to his head. "I forgets. I'm sorry." He moved to go.

"But if the viscount sees them—" All her hopes would dissolve.

He shook his head. "I'm so sorry, *ma petite*, but you heard them. *Ze* lilies will need stay."

"But—"

"Come." He grasped her hand. "You must return as quickly as possible. When does your cavalier come?"

She placed a hand to her mouth. The viscount. So eager to see her work. So desirous to be her escort. So soon to be flung into a cesspool of innuendo.

Her eyes filled with tears.

❦

Harry grasped Serena's hand as she exited the carriage, his fingers firming, refusing to let go. Finally, they were here. He'd felt her nervous energy since Berkeley Square, almost a strange reluctance to attend, revealed in the slanting glances and incomprehensible answers to his sister's and grandmother's questions.

Serena's dismay at their accompanying him had been apparent, the cool façade she so often wore melting into widening eyes and flushed cheeks when he had first mentioned his guests.

"But, sir, I must tell you something—"

"You cannot in the carriage?"

She shook her head. "Not with the others . . ."

He knew a moment's impatience. He stifled it, forced himself to calm, to listen. "My dear, whatever it is, I am sure it is not worth this much anxiety."

"It's about the painting!"

"Did you get the chance to varnish as you wanted?"

"No, no." Her eyes grew shiny. "They would not let me, because I am female."

"Fools. How ridiculous to think they permit a woman to exhibit but do not let her finish."

"They did not even believe it was my work."

"What?"

"I have to take this for proof." She held up her sketchbook. "But that is not the—"

"Are you two *still* in here?" Melanie entered the room, hands outstretched. "Serena, Grandmama and I are so excited to be visiting with you. Although not as excited as someone else here, eh?" She sent him a candid look, bringing a smile to his lips. "Is your sister coming?"

"Mama has decided she and Catherine had best remain home." He'd caught the fleeting look of sadness in her eyes. "Jon also, as he's quite concerned about Catherine's health." Her brow furrowed. "Perhaps I should stay—"

"No, no." Melanie gently tugged her to the door. "Grandmama is in the carriage. You must come. We want to celebrate such an accomplishment with you."

Serena had paled, shot him an uncertain look, before finally agreeing.

He glanced at her again as they crossed the courtyard to the entrance hall. "I'm sure your sister will be feeling well soon."

She nodded, her gaze averted, and clutched the book closer.

Melanie raised her brows at him as he paid the shilling apiece for their programs and entry. He shrugged, handing out the pages.

"I'm looking forward to seeing your name here," Melanie said kindly.

"They . . . printed it as Mr. S. Winthrop."

"Silly of them," Grandmama said. "I think the world should know how great an artist a woman can be."

They joined the long crowd snaking their way up the stairs. This, the opening day of the Summer Exhibition, always drew society's cream. The stairwell was hot, noisy, the smell of unwashed bodies forcing him near Miss Winthrop. "This is a sad crush."

Her head angled up, her eyes searching him, her bottom lip caught.

He smiled. "Don't be anxious, my dear. Your work is honored. You should feel proud. I most certainly do."

"I hope you still think so when you see it."

He frowned as she turned away. What was her hesitation?

"Carmichael." An old acquaintance from Oxford days shot him a smirk as he descended. "Well, well."

He nodded, angling his body to shield Serena from view as the beefy heir to a dukedom eyed his companions before the crush of people forced him to descend.

"A most uncouth man," intoned Grandmama. "His father was just the same. No notion of propriety."

Gradually he became aware of other glances, more curious, being leveled at him from others descending the stairs. They finally reached the top, where the room filled with paintings dazzled. His heart leapt, his gaze immediately skimming the walls to find her work.

"I imagine yours is near the top?" Melanie said, craning her neck at those pictures tilted forward for better display. "It is hard to see."

"I am sure you will recognize it," Serena murmured.

He glanced at the wall to his left. The center line held the royals, as usual. Famous dukes, actors, Wellington. Below were smaller pictures, mostly landscapes, a few hunting scenes. Near the top windows the paintings consisted of a myriad of people he did not recognize— fortunate, because at the angle they were positioned, some were in shadow. He imagined it was a shame for those who had worked so hard to have their pictures nearly beyond view. But still, an honor to be included, especially for those like Serena, who were so young and new.

He scanned the uppermost sections of the remaining walls. Nothing he even vaguely recognized.

"Have you seen it yet?" Melanie asked. "Serena?"

He looked down. Serena wasn't there. His heart thumped loudly, until he recognized the green of her pelisse, over in the corner next to Despard. They were talking to some men, showing them her book. Of course.

"Excuse me," he said, leaving his grandmother to his sister's care. He shouldered through the crowd, some of whom refused to move, but when they did, they glanced at him and gawked. He frowned at their pretension, but all the while grew more conscious of the increasing number of glances he was receiving, both speculative and amused. His neck collar grew damp. How long would it take to live down his colorful reputation?

He neared Serena in time to hear one of the men say, "But this could be anyone's work."

"Would 'anyone' just hand their sketchbook to me?" Serena asked. "Sir, please—Oh!"

She jumped as he planted himself beside her, eyeing the men with something he hoped approached his grandmother's well-worn look of disdain. "I can vouch this is her work."

The men's eyes widened, one of them gaped.

So being heir to an earldom was good for something after all. Harry nodded to Despard before turning to smile at her. "She is a magnificent artist, would you not agree? So talented, so gifted, someone truly special." He dragged his gaze away to face the men. "But then, you must agree, if you permit her work to be displayed."

"You . . . You're a gentleman."

"I'm touched you can recognize one."

"No. A gentleman."

He frowned. "A gentleman. Yes." He glanced at Serena. She'd closed her eyes, her lips moving as if praying. He gently grasped her arm. "My dear?"

Her eyes opened. Her skin held a waxy sheen, like she might faint. He wrapped an arm around her and felt her body sag. He eyed the men and snapped, "I trust you now believe Miss Winthrop is the artist she claims to be?"

Her sketchbook had fallen to the floor. He tucked it under his arm, the jostling crowds would ensure it would be trampled in no time. "Come, my dear. Let me find you a seat."

Leaving Despard to continue his discussion, Harry gently deposited Serena on one of the central settees. "I'll find a glass of water."

"Thank you," she said faintly.

He threaded through the crowd, retrieved the water, and was returning when his passage was blocked by a slow procession of shrill ladies. "I'm sure it is him. Just fancy!" They glanced at him, eyes widening, before they tittered. "It *is* him!"

Again he felt a shiver of unease. Why was *he* the object of attention? He frowned, pushing past them.

"Carmichael."

He turned, his heart sinking. "Hello, Lillian."

"How are you?" Her gaze tracked down his body, her smile widening. "You look well."

"As do you. Please excuse me."

"I saw your grandmother earlier."

"Really?"

"And your sister. Of course, they didn't seem pleased to see me."

"I really must go—"

"I saw your painting."

He frowned. "My what?"

"Your painting." She sidled closer. "It is magnificent. Such sophistication." She fluttered her eyelashes. "I confess to no small amount of surprise to learn you still care."

"I'm terribly sorry, I do not understand. There must be some mistake."

Her eyes glinted. "Oh, there's no mistake. Look." She pointed to his right.

Above the milling heads and preposterous hats, just above the center line, he saw it. Only it wasn't a picture of Hyde Park. No, the subject was far more familiar.

A face he saw every day in the mirror.

CHAPTER THIRTY-TWO

"I HOPE YOU'RE not terribly displeased," the cooing voice continued. "I'm certainly not."

He pushed past her, his steps slow yet steady, the painting holding him transfixed. She had painted him standing with his dog, with the unmistakable faux Grecian temple at Welmsley to one side, and the autumnal blaze of color lining the valley on the other.

The scene was melodious, such as might be seen in a hundred other paintings. Only the picture held a strange hypnotic quality, something perhaps to do with the contrast between the gamboling dog and the wry twist of Harry's lips, and a haunting, pensive look in his eyes.

The hairs on the back of his neck rose.

How had she captured his soul?

"I hope you're not terribly displeased?"

Same words, different voice.

He glanced down, mechanically handed Serena her water, which she accepted with murmured thanks, before the picture reclaimed his attention. "I thought it unfinished," he said in a low voice.

"I . . . I painted this before the other one."

"I do not recall you painting this. How . . . ?"

How had she depicted his heart? *Here* was the man he wished to be, a man who wore wisdom in his eyes as well as he wore a coat made by Weston, a man capable of being amused by his own flaws as well as by those around him, someone connected to his heritage, his future. He peered closer. Why, she'd even included a mine down in the valley.

"Oh, Serena," Melanie breathed, joining him. "It is . . ."

He joined his sister, and now grandmother, too, in silent admiration. Not only did the painting display excellent technique and composition but the vibrancy, the life she'd instilled in her portraits of Melanie's children was once more evident.

As was the love. His heart glowed. Surely nobody could doubt the intimacy flowing between artist and subject. How else could she paint the very essence of his heart?

Around them, a ripple of conversation seemed aimed at them, a few pointing fingers, giggles and pointed remarks eventually eating into his awe.

He glanced down at the artist, still watching him, her teeth nibbling her bottom lip. Surely she must care for him?

"You do not disapprove, my lord?"

"How can I? It is truly magnificent." He smiled as she exhaled, gladness washing over his heart at her obvious relief.

She licked her bottom lip. His heart lurched. If only he could steal her away right now . . .

"Serena." Melanie's voice, sounding rather less impressed. "Why did you paint that?"

He followed his sister's finger to the flowers on the pillar.

Lilies.

He blinked. Peered closer. His stomach tightened. Had she meant to imply—

"Monsieur Despard suggested that corner needed something. I painted it, before I knew . . ."

"Yes, well I can imagine that Lily—and all society—now thinks Harry intends to marry her!"

He let out a silent groan at his sister's less-than-subtle volume, schooling his features to indifference as society's whispers surrounding them grew louder.

"Lord Carmichael is going to marry Lily?"

"Lillian Milsom. See the flowers?"

"I thought she was that Ashbolt fellow's mistress?"

"Well, now it is the viscount. Keep your voice down, he's standing right in front of you."

He stilled, listening to the blatant speculation, overhearing other whispered conclusions that his relationship with the artist was anything but honorable. A wave of revulsion passed through him. How could they think such things? What more must he do to live down his reputation? Would it forever follow him like the bad smell of a mangy dog? He drew in a deep breath, clenching his fists as a wave of anger rushed through his chest. Why had Serena painted in those blasted lilies? Why hadn't she at least told him? He glanced at Serena, who seemed to recoil.

"I . . . I'm so sorry," she whispered.

"You're sorry?" His voice sounded like shards of ice.

"Good lord! It's Carmichael," boomed an especially unwelcome voice.

He gritted his teeth before turning to greet London's biggest gossip. "Buffy. Fancy meeting you here."

"Yes, fancy." The dark eyes roved between Harry and Serena. "Well, look who we have here. My dear." He bowed.

She gave a stiff nod.

"So, have we discovered anything more about the mysterious artist? Everyone is abuzz." His gaze slid between them, dark, poisonous. "Surely you must recall, Carmichael, after spending all that time with him?"

Harry swallowed. The innuendo was clear. As was the agitation of the ladies he escorted. How *dare* he? "On the contrary. I have recalled—an important engagement." He jerked a nod, and offered an arm to his wilting grandmother, Melanie moving ahead, parting the crowds as a kind of siege engine.

Buffy's voice oiled behind. "You might want to be careful, Miss Winthrop. That painting suggests Carmichael has kept rather a large secret from you. Quite the character flaw, eh?"

"How dare you cast aspersions about such a *true* gentleman?" Serena said, her words like acid. "Such a poisonous presence tends to drive others away. Have you ever noticed? Quite the character flaw indeed."

Under the simmering rage Harry felt a scrap of gratitude at her defense of him. Beside him, Grandmama was drooping, leaning heavily on his arm. "Henry, I cannot understand . . ."

"No."

"An excellent rendition, but . . ."

"Yes."

He pushed aside the hurt crowding his chest, worked to ignore the humiliating stares and laughter, and concentrated on the welfare of his grandmother. He had to get out. Be gone. Leave this shame-inducing farce with all its skin-crawling personal observations and sniggers—

"Harry?"

He paused, following Melanie's frown to glance behind him.

To see Serena, white-faced, being caressed by a dark-haired Lothario.

꧁꧂

Serena's mouth dried. No. No, it couldn't be . . .

"Serena?"

She yanked her arm free, stepped back. Had to get away. Get away *now*. Danger was found in staring into those eyes for too long. He was a snake, a slimy, lecherous—

"Serena? I can't believe you do not wish to say hello." He leaned in toward her ear. "You were not always so indifferent, I remember."

She shook her head and moved to go past. Where was the viscount? He might not like her much right now, but right now she *needed* him.

Mr. Goode stepped closer, his smile wide, and reached out a restraining hand. "Not so fast, my dear. I admit to some surprise at finding you here. I just wish to speak to you. Just for a moment. Where we will not be overheard, you understand."

Before she knew what to do he was half hugging her, half pulling her through the crowds to the next room. Away from where the viscount had exited. Fear twisted within. Around her, nobody noticed, their faces fixed on the paintings, the crowd's jostling and gossip filling the room. She glanced about wildly, but the only person noticing was fat old Buffy Snorestream, watching her with his arms crossed, with a suggestive smile and raised brows.

Mr. Goode's fingers pressed deeply.

"You're hurting me."

His grip at her waist tightened and he tugged her tighter to himself, pinning her arm to her side. "And you, Miss Winthrop. Your scurrilous accusations wounded *me* deeply." His face contorted. "I went to prison because of your lies."

She struggled to break free. "Which is where you should still be!" With her free hand she beat on his chest once, twice, before his free hand grasped hers fiercely.

"If it was true what they said, those rich men, but it was not. It was lies. I never tried to ravish you, you insipid girl. You wanted my attentions. Wanted all that transpired between us."

Her efforts grew more desperate but his arm at her back held firm. There were fewer people here, and those who were seemed less interested in what might seem like a lover's tiff than the drama on the walls. She twisted her face to the side, eyed ladies, silently pleading for help, but they turned away.

"But now, an opportunity presents itself. Perhaps now we can enjoy everything you sent me to prison for. Perhaps a short carriage ride . . ."

No! Her head snapped back and she felt his hot breath full in her face.

But only for a moment. He suddenly pivoted to drag her toward a wide staircase, one different from the entry, wrenching her arm in the process. "Ow!"

"Miss?" An older man frowned. "Are you quite all right?"

"My sister," Mr. Goode lied smoothly. "She's hurt her toe, but she's been quite naughty so you shouldn't feel too sorry for her."

"No—"

"Ignore her, please, sir. She's a trickster. Such a burden I would not wish on anyone."

The man's frown remained, but he nodded, leaving her tormentor to impel her down the stairs. Toward a door that opened to the street beyond.

Oh, dear God—

"Stop."

Serena glanced over her shoulder. Lord Carmichael wore an icy look, colder even than that which he'd given her earlier. "My lord, help me!"

"Ignore her, my lord. She is my sister—"

"Release Miss Winthrop at once."

His grip relaxed fractionally. "You know her?"

"Fool." The viscount drew closer.

"Then you'll know she's nothing but a common, lying whore—"

Crack!

Mr. Goode fell backwards, dragging her down with him. Her shoulder and head crashed into the stone-tiled floor, splintering pain through her body. She groaned, shutting her eyes at the stars.

"Serena!"

The voice, textured with fear, drew her eyelids open. Lord Carmichael. Leaning close. Wrapping a strong arm around her. Drawing her up. Speaking softly.

"Tell me you are unhurt?"

Her eyes filled and she burrowed into the safety of his arms.

"Shh, my dear."

For a lovely, long moment she felt the same warm reassurance his embrace always provided, felt the fear ease, felt her heartbeat slow. She drew in a deep breath and released it.

He abruptly unhanded her, and she staggered to the wall as he glared at the man still sprawled on the marble floor, a cut above his eye trickling blood. "I will utterly destroy you if you ever go near Miss Winthrop again."

"You?"

"You wish to take the chance? Try me. I promise, I will not be so lenient next time." A ghost of a smile crossed his face. "I was one of Jackson's better students."

Lord Carmichael's face hardened again, streaking a new ripple of fear through her. Who was this man whose fist could fell a man with one blow?

Straightening her gown, she watched as he motioned to a couple of men who helped him bundle her nemesis into an empty chamber and lock the door.

"Miss Winthrop?" Without looking at her, the viscount held out a hand. She grasped it, wincing at his glacial tone, all trace of compassion gone, and he led her through the crowd whose chatter now started anew.

His grip was steady, strong, as relentless as Mr. Goode's had been, yet he did not hurry her, instead slowing his pace to match hers. She caught glimpses of people: Buffy Snorestream, Mr. Kentell, Lady Milton, an open-mouthed Caroline Hatherleigh. She ducked her head, mortification scorching her cheeks, shame filling her heart.

"Quite the show for one shilling," Buffy's voice called.

She stifled a sob, her vision blurring. How would she ever live this down? How could Lord Carmichael ever live it down? Pain writhed within. How could she ever make it up to him?

Once outside, his pace held steady as he marched her to the waiting carriage. Without a word he handed her in and she sank into the seat next to Melanie.

"My dear, you are white!"

The viscount climbed in, thumped the ceiling, then slumped beside his wan grandmother. The carriage began moving.

"Harry, what on earth—?"

"Melanie, no."

"But Serena—"

"No!"

She peeked across, then wished she hadn't. His eyes, oh, his eyes were so cold and distant. He hooded them, shifting to look out the window, as the air thickened with the unsaid.

Heart writhing with recriminations, she turned to gaze outside unseeingly. What a fool, what an idiot she had been in so many ways. Her eyes burned.

A tear traced down her cheek, but she refused to move, keeping herself still, wishing her emotions could be so easily restrained. Stillness, silence, coolness might quiet the roar in her head and heart. Move, and the façade might crack.

The carriage rounded the corner. She recognized the park, the fascia, the bricks of Berkeley Square. The carriage slowed, stopped. The viscount flung open the door, descended, assisted her to exit, then released her hand posthaste, as if dropping a hot coal.

From somewhere deep within she summoned up a smile and farewelled the two ladies, who nodded gravely, their expressions worried. Without rejoining them, the viscount ordered the carriage's return to Cavendish Square. He knocked on the door, which now opened to admit them. Still he did not speak, or even look at her. In a terse voice he enquired after Lord Winthrop's whereabouts, and informed by the footman Jon was in the study, he started across the room.

"Lord Carmichael."

He stilled; did not turn.

"Thank you."

The viscount turned, bowed the smallest bow—still not meeting her gaze—and, without waiting for her curtsy, strode unannounced into the study.

Leaving her to rush up the stairs to her room, lock the door, and huddle on her bed.

Sobbing. Desperately ashamed.

And feeling, more than ever, alone.

❧ Chapter Thirty-Three

Bevington House

Fear pulsed through his body, chased by regrets. He sat alone in the darkened study, memories of his earlier visits pumping through his head.

Carlew's surprise at Harry's interruption had turned to wrath when he learned of the release of Serena's attacker and what had happened at the exhibition. Together, they had returned to Somerset House, accompanied by a constable, who had been more than a little nonplussed at the situation, until Carlew's coin had convinced him of the need to arrest the felon.

But neither the sight of the lecher being dragged away nor Carlew's repeated thanks had managed to tame Harry's own fury, one borne more from fear and frustration. What if Melanie hadn't spied her at that moment? What if the monster had dragged her away to exact the revenge he sought? How could Carlew keep her safe?

His head slumped into his hands. *"Dear God, help me . . ."*

Prayers for himself turned to pleas for his grandmother. His visit to his grandmother's room had sparked fear; she did not look at all well. But she'd refused to acknowledge his concern, insisting he listen to her. "Never mind how I look. There's something you should know."

His grandmother had handed him Serena's sketchbook, which he'd handed her for safekeeping when he'd rushed off to find Serena. "Look inside."

"Grandmama, this is her private work."

"Just do it."

So he'd looked. Seen her artistry. Seen her early sketches of his niece and nephew, the temple, himself. He'd turned another page. Another. They were filled with sketches of him, complete with little comments: Has a dimple on the right cheek, like dough dipped by a flower stem. Eyes, green or brown? Gold in depths. Smiles wider when pretending; with eyes when real.

His heart had twisted, his throat closed, as his grandmother watched.

"She knows you."

"Too well."

"No, not too well, Henry. You know she would never have included that silly nonsense about Lily if you hadn't gone along with it."

Truth grated his soul. He nodded.

"You can see in her design she never included it. Go on, look for yourself."

He flicked through the pages, devoid of any lilies, of any flowers at all. What had she said? That Despard said the composition demanded an extra something in that corner?

"She is a good girl. She does not deserve your coldness."

"It was not her."

His grandmother raised a brow.

"Well, not much. It was more the speculation, the gossip about me, and her, and then that fool—" His hands clenched. "I've tried so hard to prove myself, only to have this scandal . . ."

"You are a good man, Henry." His eyes burned. "And she is a good girl." She tapped the sketchbook. "She obviously cares for you, and you her. So what is preventing you?" She had sighed, like a crinkling of silk. "It would make me very happy to know my favorite grandson—"

"Your only grandson."

"—had made such a choice. She loves the Lord and you. What more do you want?"

What more did he want?

Through the dim light he studied the sketchbook. From outside came a faint clatter of carriage wheels on cobblestones. Inside, the house was quiet. His parents slept—today had been a good day, Mother had said. His sister and grandmother rested also, their questions finally answered in a manner that retained truth without exposing the full legacy of Serena's horror, his promise to make amends—to somehow try to win her heart—bringing a satisfied glint to his grandmother's eyes.

But the questions in his heart refused to die.

He loved her; that much was palpable in those moments he'd seen her in another man's arms. She should be cherished, not manhandled; her kiss bestowed, not demanded.

He loved her, but she had shamed him, painting in a rival's flower. How Lily could ever be considered a rival to perfection he knew not, but women were funny creatures.

He loved her, but he'd seen how she trembled after the attack. Could she ever learn to trust a man again? To want to be held by a man? Kissed by *this* man? More? He loved her, but he wanted her, as a man wanted a woman, as a husband wanted his wife . . .

Dear God.

He closed his eyes, forehead touching the desk's cold marble.

Dear God, help me.

Words written centuries ago flickered through his mind.

Charity suffers long and is kind, charity envies not . . . is not puffed up . . . thinks no evil . . . believes all things, hopes all things, endures all things. Charity never fails.

Love never fails.

The words swam around his head, around his heart, before settling somewhere deep within. They weren't mere words, but both a promise and a challenge. A promise from God as to how He viewed Harry, and a challenge from God to so love others.

To so love Serena.

He pressed his fingers into his scalp. In some ways, loving her was like loving his father. It might not always be easy, but God's promises held fast. Love did not think badly, but chose to think of the good. Love believed, hoped, endured all things, good and bad. Love never failed.

If he claimed affection for her in his heart, then that affection should be outworked in his attitude and actions. Which meant not shutting the door, not allowing his outraged pride to take precedence over her humiliation. Not letting her get away.

He opened his eyes, lifted his head. He had to go to Berkeley Square right now.

"I'M SORRY, BUT she is asleep."

Harry handed the sketchbook to his friend. "But I must speak with her."

"I'm sure whatever it is you wish to say can be said tomorrow." Carlew passed a hand through his hair and yawned. "Forgive me. Catherine did not sleep well last night and—"

"Yes, I get the picture." He shook his head as if to clear the image. Oh, to have a wife—

"Jon, dear?" Through the open door passed Lady Harkness. "Why, Henry, dear boy!" She stretched her hands towards him. "How wonderful to see you again."

He kissed her hand. "And you, ma'am. It has been an age."

"I've been rusticating in Worthing. But one must return for the birth of one's first grandchild."

"Of course. It is good to see you again," he said politely. And it *was* good, only he longed to speak with Carlew alone—

"But I must confess, it hasn't been so long since I saw you." She gave a strange smile. "Admittedly, it was late this afternoon, on the wall at Somerset House."

"Ah. I see."

"And I gather you were not best pleased? But why ever not? The painting truly is remarkable. And painted by a Mr. S. Winthrop, I believe. I cannot recall any artist of that name, although I do recall a Miss Serena Winthrop possessing more than her fair share of talent in that department." Her brows rose. "I see my conjectures are not misplaced. Well! To think such a fine work was painted by a mere chit of a girl! Serena *is* a talent."

"Yes."

"You looked very handsome, if I may say so."

"Mother," Carlew muttered.

"Jon, you simply must see it. Our little artist is quite the talk of the town."

Harry sighed.

The redheaded woman eyed him thoughtfully. "I've never quite understood what it is about these Winthrop girls that causes a man to lose his head. Perhaps you can enlighten me, dear boy."

"Thank you, ma'am, for your great interest in my welfare, but I must refrain from answering at this time."

"A pity, but no doubt wise. Tell me, how is your father? I gather he has not been terribly well?"

"The doctors here have given some hope, but I fear he will never be what he once was."

"So you will take on his responsibilities at Welmsley?"

"Yes."

"Good." She smiled. "I do like to see young men given opportunity to thrive."

He forced a smile. Finances were still quite grim, so it was more a case of survive than thrive.

Her head tilted. "I seem to recall a conversation about mines. Is it true you own one?"

"Yes." He raised his brows at Carlew, who shrugged. "It is a fluorspar mine."

"Fluorspar." She nodded. "I once saw an urn at Chatsworth made from it. Simply divine. So how is the mine going?"

"It isn't."

"What?" She frowned at her son. "Are Jon's arms proving too short for his pockets?"

Carlew glared. Harry chuckled. "I'm sure he wouldn't see it that way."

"How much do you need?"

"Mother . . ." Carlew cast her an exasperated look, before sending Harry one suggesting to not take his mother seriously.

Harry played along and named a sum.

"Easily done." She nodded. "Shall I be invited to stay at Welmsley if I invest?"

"Mother!"

"Jonathan, as I neither need your permission nor your advice on how to spend my money, I would appreciate your staying out of this conversation I'm having with the dear viscount here."

Harry cleared his throat. Lady Harkness was an independently wealthy woman, but did she truly know what she was in for? "Perhaps if you were to call at Bevington House tomorrow, we might discuss this further."

"A sound idea." She nodded. "Well, I suppose if that baby refuses to budge I'd best toddle off to sleep. Goodnight, dear boys."

Harry bowed as Carlew kissed his mother's expectantly raised cheek.

She flashed him another smile. "Don't forget tomorrow, Henry."

"I look forward to it."

After assuaging Carlew—and subtly reminding him of his mother's words regarding her independence—he made his farewell, disappointment at missing the chance to explain to Serena mingling with the slightest pulse of hope that the future of his mines and estate might not be as dim as he'd believed.

But when he finally returned to Cavendish Square, everything was forgotten as he entered upon a brightly lit house with its inhabitants in an uproar.

"Oh, my lord." The butler helped Harry from his coat. "We're so pleased you've returned."

"What on earth has happened?"

Peters opened his mouth when a sound drew their attention to the stairs.

"Melanie?"

"Oh, Harry!" His sister stumbled down the stairs towards him, wrapper over her nightclothes, tears streaming from her eyes. "It's the most terrible thing."

Fear trickled through his chest. "What is it?"

"It's Grandmama." She gulped. "She has died."

✺ Chapter Thirty-Four

Winthrop, Gloucestershire
July

SERENA DIPPED THE brush in the gesso and applied it to the canvas. From a window far above came a baby's cry. The melancholy, so long her companion, lifted a little as she smiled. Darling Elizabeth. The sweetest baby ever born, even though her arrival came the very day after another sweet person's demise. Her spirits sank again, as the memory of the service before the dowager countess's funeral arose. Jon had described it as a splendid funeral, attended by many of society's elite—even the Duke of Clarence had appeared. But in the Sunday service prior, despite the whispers and pointed fingers, her gaze had been unable to shift from one person.

Her eyes stung at the memory. She blinked, placed the brush down. The viscount had seemed so forlorn, his grave expression far removed from the smooth flirt she'd first met so long ago. He was a man now. A burdened one, neck-deep in responsibilities administering the estate his father could no longer care for.

Her eyes blurred. So coldly handsome, his expression had appeared far too distant and aloof when she'd finally moved closer later. Perhaps he, too, had been heavily aware of society's eyes upon them both. Or perhaps it was simply reaction to how she'd offered scant sympathy compared to what she knew she ought to have offered. She ached at night to think what she could have said, should have said, but didn't.

Regret made her write a score of letters only to throw them into the fire because they could not express her heart plainly enough.

That she was sorry, desperately sorry, to have brought such pain into his life.

That she was sorry, so *desperately* sorry, to have been the cause of his grandmother's demise. Her heart twisted. If the dowager had not been so shocked, in such an overheated room, surely she would have been alive now. Serena's painting had caused pain more far-reaching than she could ever have anticipated.

The dry, chattering *krrr* of a mistle thrush rattled from a nearby treetop, stirring, teasing emotions from within. If only she could write like she could paint, she might express something of her sorrow, and also her devotion. For she loved him. Would always love him. Would always see him as the man of honor, the protector, the generous kindly uncle. Even though he despised her, and his coldness on that last day still hurt, she understood his ignoring her now as completely justifiable. She could not blame him.

She loved him.

He did not love her.

That was all.

Serena released a shuddery, hiccupping breath and wiped her cheeks, as the sound of little Elizabeth's cries intensified. Her lips lifted at the corners. Poor Catherine. She did not envy her sister the loss of sleep one bit, but if she would choose to tend to her baby rather than let the nurse do her job . . .

Picking up her brush, she returned her attention to her easel. A landscape—no more portraits for her!—of Winthrop's garden in summer, as a cooling breeze played with fallen leaves.

A crunch of gravel behind her. Probably Tilly, unnecessarily checking on her again at Mama's request. She studied the painting, tilted her head for the correct perspective.

"Good afternoon, Miss Winthrop."

She jumped. Turned. And stared.

If he hadn't seen the flash of her eyes he would've sworn she felt nothing, so calmly did she nod and return to her canvas.

"I hope I'm not disturbing you."

"I am not so easily disturbed, my lord."

His heart sank. So they had returned to formality. Very well. "Miss Winthrop, Serena"—she stiffened at his use of her name—"may I have a word?"

"You may."

Harry sighed, crossing closer. He understood she might not wish to see him; it had been too long since the service, when he'd been numbed by grief and overwhelmed by responsibilities to do or say the things he wished. He hoped today would finally permit release, but was it too late?

Serena glanced at him, brush aloft, one brow arched.

"Please? Your manner tells me my presence is unwelcome."

She placed the brush down, gave a small sigh. "Very well. What is it you wish to say?"

Now her face tilted up, and he could see her beautiful eyes, he could also see they were smudged with disillusionment. This was not the unruffled miss of his first acquaintance, rather the battle-weary artist whose notoriety had led to social ostracism. Fresh guilt twisted his insides.

"Miss Winthrop, please permit me to express my deep regret for my reaction in London. I ask for your forgiveness."

Her eyes flickered, though her face remained expressionless. "The fault is mine, sir, in not requesting your permission before attempting such a thing. I . . . I hope you will forgive me, both for"—she swallowed—"both for the painting and for the tragic aftermath."

"That despicable excuse for a man—"

"No." She dipped her head, but he caught the slightest tremble of her lips. "Your grandmother."

"Tell me you do not blame yourself for her demise."

Her eyes sheened. "I'm so very sorry."

His heart panged with a thousand memories, but blame would not bring her back. He said gently, "You were not responsible. Grandmama was old, and feeling poorly for some time, but she insisted on seeing your painting. You know what she was like."

Some of the strain seemed to ease from her features. "Still, I'm so very sorry."

"Serena, please don't condemn yourself."

She bit her lip, nodded. "She was a remarkable lady."

"Yes, she was."

The silence between them grew thick again. Somewhere a bird sang, somewhere a baby bawled. What could he say to ease this tension?

"Speaking of remarkable ladies, I still cannot conceive how you could create such a thing from memory. You are so talented."

Nothing. Not even a flicker of an eyelash.

Desperation grew. "I was most sorry to learn you have forgone your lessons with Monsieur Despard."

Now the eyes flashed.

"Jon said your mother has forbidden it."

"She has." Sadness crossed her features before they cooled again. Her chin lifted.

"It is truly a shame, for I can only imagine how extraordinary your work would be should you have kept going."

"Why do you say this? To upset me? Do you not think I've thought this, too?" Her eyes sparked. "If I were a man I could continue lessons, but because I'm female I'm not allowed. So, I must hide away here, pretending to be content with sketching and watercolors." Her lip curled as she scowled at her easel.

Harry swallowed a smile. She was so passionate, so beautiful. "There is another way."

Her gaze snapped to meet his. "There is not. Don't you think I have explored every possibility?"

He coughed. "I don't think you've explored this one. Well, I hope not."

Serena frowned, not wasting a syllable as she waited.

"You could . . . marry."

She paled then flushed from cheek to neckline. "Marry? Are you mad?" She looked away. "I cannot imagine any man wishing to be the husband of such a social wretch as me."

"You'd be surprised," he murmured.

"I know you wish not to dismay me, and truly, I'm not being miss-ish, for I'm quite aware, as are you, of what a poor bargain I am." She counted off her fingers. "No dowry, poor health, little in the way of social accomplishments, though some might accord a little artistic talent—"

"Some men might prefer a lady of your intelligence, poise, kind-ness, beauty . . ."

Her brows furrowed as at a wayward child. "No, I am resigned now. I'll never marry."

"Such an answer cannot fail but to dismay me."

"I beg your pardon?"

He sighed. "Serena, I cannot bandy words with you any longer. Despite my many failures, surely you know something of my regard?"

Her breath caught. Blue eyes found his, held, instilling courage that she might finally hear what he'd traveled miles—days—to say.

"Dearest Serena, how I wish you knew that I am yours to com-mand, that I am . . . yours."

"Mine?" She shook her head. "No. I do not know that. You went away—I have not seen you . . . you never said—" Her voice broke, her eyes sparkling with tears.

He drew nearer. "I'm so sorry, my dearest. I had much business to attend to, and Father, Grandmama . . ." Grief panged deep again.

She placed a hand on his arm, her touch infusing him with hope. "I'm so sorry."

"You are so good, so kind, so lovely. You should know that I adore you."

Tears tracked down her cheek. "You should not."

"Why? I love you. I wish to fill your days with gladness, to help you achieve your dreams." He drew closer still, thumbed away her tears, heard her intake of breath as he continued, his voice hoarse, "I know that I'm imperfect, in many ways not ideal, but God is work-ing on me and in me. I feel His love changing me, which only helps me want to love you more, dearest Serena. And though you might not love me in return, I will always protect you, and seek your best."

"But I . . ." She licked her lip, shook her head. "No, I cannot."

"Why? You do not believe me?"

"I believe you *think* you mean that, it's just . . ."

A baby's cry filled the air. He saw her face tighten, and finally understood.

"Dearest, I thought I made it clear before, when I said your illness doesn't change my feelings at all."

"But . . . but you need an heir."

"So we will make provisions to leave what is unentailed to Tom. But you cannot truly know, not until . . ." He raised a brow.

She blushed, glanced away.

"Do you hate me so much?"

"You know I do not."

So her painting had not lied. He possessed himself of her hands, lifting one then the other to his lips, smiling a little as he kissed her paint-smudged fingers. She stiffened, but did not pull away. Encouraged, he placed a long, lingering kiss on the palm of her left hand, then lifted his gaze to meet hers. "I love you, dearest Serena. Please let me love you."

Her breath caught. She stared at him a long, long moment, time suspending between and around them. Could she let him love her? Could she trust him? Could she really? *Lord?*

Something inside whispered yes.

She placed a hand on his chest, felt his heart beating strongly as she had once before. For a moment she wondered about the curve of his chest beneath his coat, beneath his shirt, imagined painting him thus. Her cheeks heated, yet she dared glance up.

He stood motionless, apart from his eyes, which remained as alert as ever, watching her, seemingly pleading with her. With one hand still on his chest she slipped her other hand free from his clasp, moving to gingerly, tenderly, touch his jaw. He closed his eyes as she savored the slight roughness of his lower cheek, his chin. His breath warmed her fingers as she touched his lips: soft, sensuous, sensitive. Then she explored the contours of his face, the high cheekbones, the forehead, the dark eyebrows, her smoothing motion seeming to cause his breath to catch. She leaned closer, reaching up to touch his hair, to feel the smooth, velvety texture, the color of cocoa.

His breath caught again. She peeked at him but his eyes remained closed, though a tiny smile tweaked the corners of his lips. Pushing to her toes, she gently tugged his head down, closer, closer, until an inch remained between their mouths.

"I love you, my lord," she whispered.

His eyelids flew open, yet he did not move, as if waiting for her permission. She gave a tiny nod, and with the slowest of movements he lifted a hand and caressed her cheek, just as she had him, before sliding his fingers through her hair.

Shivers raced along her skin, breath caught in her chest.

His other hand slowly, courteously, moved around her waist, until she was wrapped in the lightest of embraces.

Then he bent to close the final distance to place his lips on hers.

She closed her eyes, exulting at the sensations coursing through her body. He tasted of sweetness and hope, ardor and joy. She felt protected. Treasured. Respected. Cherished. Loved.

When it seemed he wished to withdraw she pressed in closer, her lips firming, one hand behind his shoulders, as she sought to prevent his escape.

This . . . this was wonderful, delighting every sense.

This . . . she had no desire whatsoever to escape *this* embrace.

Something like a low moan sounded from the back of his throat, and he drew her still closer, wrapping her more securely in his arms, kissing her more deeply, more ardently, until finally she had to pull away to breathe.

Happiness bloomed across her chest as she leaned back in his arms, studying him, sure she wore the same kind of dazed expression as he.

"I thought of you a thousand times."

He had?

"I began a dozen letters 'Dearest Serena' but never hoped, never dreamed you would let me kiss you, and that your kiss would be so sweet." He closed the distance between their lips again. "My dearest Serena."

She was his, his dearest, and he was her . . . "Dearest Henry."

His eyes lit. "I love to hear you say my name. I love everything about you. Even these paint-stained fingers." He picked up her hand and demonstrated with five quick pecks. "You enchant me."

"I suspect you are a little biased, my lord."

"Henry," his eyes crinkled.

"Henry."

"Darling girl, would you do me the greatest honor and deign to marry me?"

Breath caught in her chest, causing her to sway. He gathered her close to his chest again. His reassuringly broad, strong chest. Oh, how safe he made her feel. "I could never be a countess."

"You would not need to be at first. Only a viscountess."

She laughed. "Still, the responsibilities would be severe."

"Because I am such a trial of a human being? I *am* trying you know."

"I know," she said drily, smiling.

He laughed, kissing the top of her head. "And you're delightful." He captured her hand and pressed another kiss to the palm.

She trembled, peeking at him through her lashes. Oh, he was smooth. And deliciously handsome. And—

"I gather by that look you're at least considering my proposal? It comes with benefits, you know."

"Such as?"

"Such as stewards and servants aplenty. The freedom to paint as much and as often as you wish. A lifetime of treasure to gaze upon. A terribly handsome man waiting to adore you all your life. The opportunity to do this whenever you desire."

He moved close for another skin-tingling kiss. Oh . . . yes.

Gradually she became aware of birds chirping, sun-warmed breeze tickling her curls, a faraway crunch of gravel and a voice.

"Serena!"

He moved, but she held him fast. "Mama will be pleased to know we are betrothed."

"So you *will* marry me?" His eyes lit with hope.

"Yes."

Her happiness was echoed in the smile in his eyes and on his lips. "My dearest, darling Serena." He drew her close, kissed her forehead, her nose, her left cheek, her right. Her lips. That low sigh sounded again. "I could kiss you for eternity."

And she would quite happily let him, his kisses as sweet as nectar, each caress igniting fire in her skin. Joy unfurled within. They were now betrothed. Promised to each other forever. She laughed again as Mama drew near.

"Serena! My lord, please release my daughter."

"I find myself quite unable to do so. She has my heart, you see, and I believe I have hers, so parting might prove quite hazardous for us both."

Mama blinked as Serena stifled a giggle. "That may be, but until you are betrothed I must oppose such liberties."

"Then oppose no more, good lady, as she has finally deigned to accept my suit."

"I beg your pardon?"

Henry pressed another kiss to Serena's forehead. "You may offer us your congratulations, madam."

"Really?" Her eyes widened. "Serena will be a countess? Oh, my dear girl!"

In the midst of her voluble felicitations, Henry managed to murmur, "I think a short engagement then a swift removal north might be in order?"

Serena chuckled. "How do you feel about elopements?"

"Elopements?" Mama said. "No, no, no! Things must be done correctly. I want the world to know my *dearest* girl has managed to find herself a future earl!" Her expression filled with glee, she embraced them both, before saying, "I must go tell Catherine this marvelous news. Oh, how wonderful!"

Henry smiled at Serena, lifting her hand to his heart as Mama hurried away. "I know a little girl who will say exactly the same thing when she hears her uncle is finally to marry Miss S'ena."

"Darling Ellie."

"Darling S'ena." He kissed her cheek before his lips met hers for another long, delicious moment.

She finally pulled back, and gazed into his muddy green eyes. "Darling Henry."

And his lips on hers filled her with the promise of delight.

🙋 Epilogue

Bevington House, London
Twelve weeks later

THE FAINTEST SOUND interrupted her rest. Early light seeped through the window but she refused to move, content to feel the warmth of her husband beside her. Tiny bubbles of delight throbbed within as she consciously relaxed, encouraging her husband's seed to seed within. The physician Henry had sought had been very blunt about her condition, agreeing with Dr. Hanbury about the need to eat more fruits and vegetables, to exercise, and to avoid stressful encounters, but optimistic also, mentioning something of a stomach migraine, which should not preclude her ability to either conceive or bear children.

His diagnosis—married relations with great regularity—had been enough to make her wonder if Henry had put him up to saying such things, but her husband had denied it, laughing, his eyes telling her he spoke the truth.

Her husband.

Smiling, she reached across and rested her hand on his chest. Without opening his eyes, his hand captured hers, stroking the sapphire and diamond ring on her third finger she'd worn since their marriage seven weeks ago.

"Serena, give a man a chance to rest."

"Love not sleep lest thou come to poverty; open thine eyes and thou shalt be satisfied with bread." She traced his unshaven jaw.

His lips twitched, his long lashes lifting as he rolled to face her. "Good morning, bread."

She chuckled. "Good morning."

"If only I had known what simmered under that cool exterior—"

"You would have married me long ago."

The sound came again. Her ears strained. "Who would be knocking at the door at this hour?"

"Let them knock."

"But what if it is something important?"

"Let the servants get it."

"But apart from Cook, and her room is right at the back, we don't have any, remember? You sent them all away so we could have the house to ourselves." Her cheeks heated.

"I have enjoyed getting to know my wife so well." His sleepy eyes crinkled.

She grinned. Three weeks of banns reading in church, a wedding in London, then a trip north to Scotland for an idyllic honeymoon in an ancient castle had helped her get to know her husband as together they overcame her walls of fear that precluded intimacy. Thank God for the gift of marriage.

The noise came again.

"Whoever they are, they sound desperate." She shifted up, hair flowing around her shoulders.

"Don't go." His fingers entwined with hers.

"I'll just peek from the window."

She slipped her hand from his and shrugged into the Chinese silk wrapper Catherine had given her for her wedding trousseau. She moved to the window and carefully pulled the curtains back an inch.

Below, at the front door, stood a young woman, a beggar woman judging from the condition of her clothes. At her feet something was wrapped in a large basket. The woman wiped her face, staggering slightly, as if a profound weariness had settled within.

Serena's heart stirred. She recognized that weariness. "I'm going downstairs."

"They'll go away if we pretend not to be here."

"And that would be fine if it were my mother, but this is not. Something troubles me about her."

"Her?" He raised an eyebrow.

"Her." She raised both of hers.

He shook his head. "There are no ladies of my acquaintance who would ever knock on my door at this hour."

"I'm so pleased," she said drily, smiling to cover the ache in knowing that there'd been several ladies of Henry's acquaintance before her. But that was the past. He was a new man now. He proved it every day, in how his eyes only saw her, how he hovered near, even spending hours with her as she painted, talking, teasing, laughing. Loving.

She pulled the wrapper closer. "I'll be back in a minute."

"If you're not, I'll come in search of you."

"Hmm. That may tempt me to tarry," she murmured.

His laughter chased her down the corridor and steps.

Smiling to herself, she shrugged into a dark cloak, fiddled with the lock and catches, and opened the door.

The woman had gone. The basket remained.

Serena tugged the cloak more firmly, her bare feet cold on the marble steps as she hurried to the path, in time to see the dark-hooded woman stumble. Ignoring the street sweeper's gape, she hurried toward her, wishing she had put on shoes.

Now she drew closer she could see the woman was thin, pitifully so, the curve of her cheek carved too sharply. Her clothes, though worn and dirty, showed signs of good quality. "Miss? Can I help you?"

The woman blinked, shook her head, and her hood slipped, revealing more of her face. She could not be much older than Serena herself.

"You came to Lord Carmichael's house?"

"Yes."

"I am the viscountess." How amazing to say such words and know them true. "Please, is there some way we can help you?"

"He's married?"

"Yes." The woman didn't look the sort to have once been his *par amour*; for all her dirt and fatigue, her face possessed something of innocence. "We've been away, and only returned two days ago."

The woman nodded, allowing herself to be helped up. "I s-saw the lights last night and knew someone must be in. Nobody is in at Berkeley Square, or Portman. I don't know . . . Mama . . . John."

Serena gently led her to their door. "You left your basket—oh, it's empty."

"No!" The woman's hands flew to her mouth. "Oh, no . . ." She stepped back, head pivoting, as if searching . . .

The door opened, revealing Henry, dressed in a quilted dressing gown, holding a white bundle and a bemused expression. "There you are! Serena, can you tell me why we have a baby on our front step?"

"A baby?"

She swiveled, studying the woman, who had crept closer, her blue eyes and fair hair evoking the faintest memory. Berkeley Square. Lord Carmichael. *Whose* name had she said?

An image of someone she'd only met on two occasions years ago floated into remembrance. Heart thudding, she peered closely, before her breath caught. No . . .

"Julia?"

❧ Author's Note

GOOD HEALTH AND ready access to medical care and facilities are blessings that we can easily take for granted. Whilst I've experienced the rare migraine, I never knew about something called an abdominal migraine until more recent years. I can imagine that in Regency times this type of debilitating condition would have proven most difficult to diagnose and alleviate, and would have led to the kind of challenges Serena is presented with in this story. Dementia is another condition that poses major challenges for both patients and their families today; relationships and the paths of people's lives are significantly altered in the clutches of this disease. Imagine dealing with these conditions in an era when even less was known and understood about them.

On the lighter side, as someone who enjoys art, I thought it would be fun to write a story about a female artist, which led to research in the Regency world of artistic endeavor. In a moment of utter God provision, I was attending our local Australia Day celebrations and came across a copy of the Royal Academy Pictures catalogue from the 1800s—sufficient to give further details about what such an exhibition would have consisted of several decades earlier when attendance at the Summer Exhibition was all the rage. (Needless to say, dear reader, I bought it!) It was fascinating to learn more about the Royal Academy of artists, and to discover that in a very male-centric world—and alongside such well-known artists as Joshua Reynolds and Thomas Gainsborough—two of the founding members were ladies, a Miss Angelika Kauffman and a Miss Mary Moser. (And that after these two ladies, no more women were added as full members to the Royal Academy ranks until 1936!)

In 2015, I was fortunate to visit Chatsworth and Lyme Park in the counties of Derbyshire and Cheshire, two stately homes used in filmed versions of *Pride and Prejudice*, which provided visual inspiration for setting the scenes in *Miss Serena's Secret*. A story set among the Peak District and its amazing mineral deposits, with a character who holds private interests very different to his public persona, tickled my interest.

Welmsley is fictional, as is the valley and village, but the house I envisage is not dissimilar to the magnificent Castle Howard, which is situated farther north in Yorkshire, but which possesses the grandeur and beauty I can see the Earls of Bevington enjoying.

For photos and more information about my trip to England, and to check out the book club discussion guide and more behind-the-scenes details, please visit www.carolynmillerauthor.com.

❧ Acknowledgments

THANK YOU, GOD, for giving this gift of creativity, and the amazing opportunity to express it. Thank You for patiently loving us and offering us hope through Jesus Christ.

Thank you, Joshua, for your love and encouragement. I appreciate your willingness to read my stories, and all the support you give in so many ways. I love you!

Thank you, Caitlin, Jackson, Asher, and Tim. I love you, I'm proud of you, and I'm so grateful you understand why I spend so much time in imaginary worlds.

To my family, church family, and friends—whose support, encouragement, and prayers I value and have needed—thank you. Big thanks to Roslyn and Jacqueline for being patient in reading through so many of my manuscripts and for offering suggestions to make my stories sing.

Thank you, Tamela Hancock Murray, my agent, for helping this little Australian negotiate the big American market.

Thank you to the authors and bloggers who have endorsed, and encouraged, and opened doors along the way: you are a blessing!

Thanks to my Aussie writer friends from Australasian Christian Writers, Christian Writers Downunder, and Omega Writers: I appreciate you.

To the Ladies of Influence, your support and encouragement are gold!

To the fabulous team at Kregel, thank you for believing in me and for making *Miss Serena's Secret* shine.

Finally, thank you to my readers. Thank you for buying my books and for spreading the love for these Regency romances. I treasure your kind messages of support and lovely reviews.

I hope you enjoyed Serena's story.

God bless you.

REGENCY BRIDES

A PROMISE *of* HOPE

BOOK 3

THE MAKING OF

MRS. HALE

COMING

NOVEMBER 2018

❦ Chapter One

Cavendish Square, London
October 1818

JULIA HALE LIFTED a weary hand and rapped on the yellow painted door. *Please let him be in. Please!* To whom she begged she did not know. The last person to pay her any heed had only wanted payment, and when she could not offer what he wanted, he'd sought payment of a vastly different kind. Which was why she now stood here. Hoping, begging, desperate for a miracle.

To no avail.

As the door remained closed, the now familiar ball of hopelessness swelled within, pushing against her chest, pushing against her thin veneer of self-control. She should have known it was too much to ask for help from a God she scarcely believed in, who would turn His back on her now even if her faith were as deep as Jon's. Stifling fears, she tugged at the blankets and peered at her tiny bundle. She *had* to do something. Perhaps God would respond to the innocent, even if He turned His back on the guilty. And this was her last hope, every other avenue had closed. All that remained were the paupers' homes, and she'd heard what those places were like. Nothing on this earth would induce her to leave a child in such a place.

Arms aching, feeling heavier than lead, she rapped again. *Please answer. Please!* She had seen the lights last night. Someone *was* home, even if it were just the servants kept to mind the house while the Earl of Bevington attended his estates in Derbyshire. Why wouldn't they answer?

Another fit of coughing wracked her body, sending fire through her lungs and up her throat. She placed a hand on the iron balustrade as lightheadedness swept through her again. But she'd had no opportunity to rest, and no money for medicine even if she could. When the spots cleared from her vision, she peeked at the face asleep in the blankets. Thank God the babe had not caught her illness. Not yet.

She bent down to place the bundle back in the willow basket, tucked the blankets around to protect from the dank morning air. "I'm sorry," she whispered, her voice scratchy and raw. "I cannot help you anymore."

Blissful ignorance was the only response, one she was growing more accustomed to as the days dragged on. How long had it been since she'd been deemed worthy of anything more than a scrap of attention? Three months? Six months? More?

She bent to press a kiss on the downy head before rapping a final time on the wooden door. Still no answer.

With a final desperate glance at the basket she stumbled down the marble steps, grasping the balustrade for balance. God forgive her, but she had no choice.

Guilt pressed heavily on her heart. She tugged the dark hood closer, hiding the dirty, stringy locks of fair hair of which she had once been so vain. Not that anyone would recognize her now. That girl had existed in another world, one that now often seemed more fairy story than real.

She stumbled over a broken cobblestone, refusing to look behind. That way lay regret. But she *had* tried, had hoped to somehow see this wasted life redeemed, at least in part, through her actions today. Though what lay ahead of her now she could scarcely imagine. Was she now considered a fallen woman? Or had she been regarded as such since her flight from Bath all those months ago? A blur of tears filled her vision. Foolish, *foolish* girl . . .

A street sweeper glanced at her, his lip curled in derision. She did not blame him. She looked exactly what she was: pitiful.

Somehow, she stumbled on. God help her—what *would* she do now? Where could she go? Who could save—?

"Miss? Can I help you?"

A well-bred voice, a youthful voice. Julia peered over her shoulder, blinked. Shook her head as if she could clear the blurriness. The lady—if lady she was, dressed in a most odd ensemble—seemed to own a poise Julia had never known, yet appeared younger even than her.

"You came to Lord Carmichael's house?"

The lady knew Lord Carmichael? Was she a maid? Julia swallowed. "Yes."

"I am the viscountess."

Julia blinked again. No.

"Please, is there some way we can help you?"

She moistened her lips, before managing to rasp, "He's married?"

"Yes." The lady smiled, glowing with internal satisfaction, tinged with something almost like surprise, as if she couldn't believe her good fortune.

Envy tugged within. Oh, how well Julia remembered those days.

"We've been away," Lady Carmichael continued, "and only returned two days ago."

Julia nodded, surprise filling her as the viscountess drew closer and offered a hand, helping her to her feet. What an unusual bride Henry had chosen.

Conscious she was being watched closely, she stuttered, "I s-saw the lights last night and knew someone must be in. Nobody is in at Berkeley Square, or Portman. I don't know . . . Mama . . . Jon."

Where *were* they? Mama almost never left town, and Jon's business interests made his staying in London something of a necessity. Surely he hadn't been serious about retiring to that dreary corner of Gloucestershire?

Her arm was gently clasped, and she was led back to Bevington House, away from the prying eyes of the street sweeper. Now she noticed her benefactress had bare feet, her undressed hair. What an odd woman! Was she serious about being Henry's bride? Oh, if only she could remember—

"You left your basket—oh, it's empty."

Julia gasped. "No! Oh, no!" What could she do? She had failed! Who could have taken—? Guilt misted her senses, and she stepped back, desperately searching for the culprit. But she had passed no one! Oh, where could he be?

"There you are!"

She swiveled back to the now opened door, stifled another gasp. Lord Henry Carmichael, dressed in a quilted dressing gown, held a white bundle and a bemused expression. His white teeth flashed as he smiled at the lady dressed equally *dishabille*. "Serena, can you tell me why we have a baby on our front step?"

"A baby?"

Serena? A memory flashed. A black-clad, cool-eyed schoolgirl. Henry—her Henry—had married *her*? The lady drew closer, her expression now even more alive with interest, alert with piercing intent.

She swallowed, heart thudding, as the viscountess's breath caught, her expression clearing into comprehension.

"Julia?"

Spain

Major Thomas Hale shifted, the perpetual ache from the hatch of welts on his back easing a mite as the pressure released. He drew in a breath and opened his eyes. The nightmare remained.

A dark, dank cell with barred window. A sloshing sound. A screech of laughter. Babble in a foreign tongue. He glanced at the other occupants. Grimy and unkempt as he, no doubt wishing they had never agreed to be ensnared by fortune's fickle fancy, and thus be caught in this dire situation for—how many months now? He peered at the wall, counted the strokes denoting the days as if he didn't already know, as if—by some miracle—he might have miscalculated, and this episode not be near as severe as he knew it to be. Five months. Five months!

Pain rippled through his chest. He'd been absent for almost half a year. A mission that should have taken a quarter of that time had been thwarted by lies and loose lips. A rumble of indignation churned within. How could the Crown abandon them, leaving them to rot? He peered across at young Desmond, whose right foot held all the signs of gangrene, the black decay creeping a little further each day up his leg. How much longer did the lad have? Weeks? Days?

A creeping sound, like the slither of rats, slid through the room. He swallowed the bile. Muttered a curse. Wished for a boot to throw at the perpetrator. Settled for a barked utterance, not dissimilar to those he used to bark at men a lifetime ago when his Majority meant something.

The creature scuttled away. The room lapsed into silence. Desmond's half-crazed moanings had ceased. Benson wouldn't speak. Smith and Harrow, the two men with whom he'd communicated the most, had retreated into despondency. Fairley had been taken away two days ago. Thomas shivered. He dared not think on his fate.

How could a simple desire for gold have led them to utter misery? It was not as though they had engaged in anything illegal. The Crown itself had endorsed such activity. And it wasn't as if he'd been motivated by greed. He swallowed regrets, focused on the truth that he'd *had* to do something; his prize money was near all spent trying to establish themselves respectably enough so she did not feel a whit of deprivation. His fingers clenched. If only he'd planned things better, if he had not listened, had not succumbed—

"Señor."

Thomas blinked, refocusing, his gaze cutting through the dimness to the creature at the door.

She smiled. "I *weesh* you would not reject me." She tipped forward, her soiled garments doing little to constrain her buxom figure. "Just a *leetle* talk, eh?"

He swallowed. Magdalena might be just another ploy used by the guard to get them to admit to their supposed crimes, but she was certainly the least unattractive one.

"You were not so cold last time, señor," she continued provocatively, in that lilting, wheedling voice.

Guilt speared him. He closed his eyes. *Forgive me*, he cried within, turning away from temptation. God forgive him, but he'd stupidly thought he could learn something, possibly even learn a means of escape.

He'd learned something, all right. Learned that even the comeliest wench in Spain could be responsible for guilt every bit as lethal as that inflicted by thoughts of his wife.

His wife. *Oh God*, his wife. As the instrument of torture sauntered away with a lewd comment and a ribald laugh, his thoughts clattered. What was she doing now? How could she have borne so much time apart? Had she given up on him? Wretchedness echoed within. Probably. Still, she at least had options. She could always return to her family, even if he would stake his life that they'd take care never to receive him, should he ever return to the land of the living. He hoped, regardless of what happened, that his Jewel would not forsake him completely.

"H-Hale?"

A whimpering sound drew his attention to the prone figure nearby. "Desmond?"

The boy gasped before emitting a series of piercing shrieks. "Get it off! Get it off! It's eating me!"

Thomas stumbled from the pallet, hurrying to the boy's side. A large rodent was indeed nibbling at the boy's foot. He grasped the furry pelt and slammed it at the wall where it spattered with a sickening, satisfying thud.

The boy's eyes turned to him, his teeth chattering. "I c-cannot do this anymore. Please, *please* make this stop."

His heart wrenched at the hopelessness he saw in the boy's eyes, hopelessness reflected in his heart. "I wish I could. But we have told them all we know."

A tremor ran up the boy's frame. "They will never believe us." He groaned, the low sound soon changing to an ear-splitting shriek.

"Desmond, calm yourself." If the lad weren't injured he'd slap him.

"I want to die! I want to die! I want to—"

"You there!" A heavily accented voice growled from the door. "Shut up!"

"I want to die! I want to die! I want to die!"

Thomas shook him fiercely. "Desmond, you must be quiet, else they will—"

A heavy boot knocked his feet from under him, and he crashed to the floor, his jaw cracking on the refuse-smeared stones. He tried to push to his feet, but a musket butt smashed against his temple, felling him once more.

Panic reared within as the guards dragged Desmond to the door. "Leave him! He's just a boy! He knows nothing—"

The business end of the musket poked at his face. "*Cállate!*"

He pushed to his knees, begging them in English, in Spanish, in French, but Desmond—his high-pitched cries continuing—was dragged from view.

Head throbbing, Thomas staggered to his feet, the taste of blood trickling into his mouth. He stood at the bars and shouted for mercy, but he could barely hear his own voice over Desmond's shrieks.

There was a shot.

Desmond's cries ceased.

And the now familiar soul-numbing despair crashed over him as he sank to his knees.